OUTSIDE THE BADGE

OUTSIDE THE BADGE

Mitchell Grobeson

VANTAGE PRESS
New York

With the exception of historical background used to provide a setting, all of the characters and characterizations contained in this book are completely fictitious. Although the inner workings of the Los Angeles Police Department are described, these descriptions are often fictitious. However, many incidents of harassment and discrimination similar to those described in this book have actually been experienced by gay and lesbian LAPD officers.

"Boulevard," by Jackson Browne, © 1980 Swallow Turn Music, Warner Bros. Publications U.S. Inc., Miami, FL 33014. All rights reserved. Used by permission.

Cover Photo: Steve Savage   Model: Mitchell Grobeson

FIRST EDITION

Published by Vantage Press, Inc.
516 West 34th Street, New York, New York 10001

Manufactured in the United States of America
ISBN: 0-533-11559-0

Library of Congress Catalog Card No.: 95-90394

0 9 8 7 6 5 4 3 2

To the eleven special teenage Americans who commit suicide each day and to Virginia Uribe (Project 10) and Dr. Lois Lee (Children of the Night), who have tried to do something about it.

Also to David Zamarripa, whose work for the Make-A-Wish Foundation enabled several children to experience their dying wish. His work couldn't make his own last wish come true; he died from cancer on December 13, 1985, at the age of twenty.

To my cousin, Joe, for his guidance and support.
And especially to my brother, Jay.

I'm not a writer, I'm a storyteller.
Cops are great storytellers.

BOULEVARD

Down on the Boulevard, they take it hard.
They look at life with such disregard.

They say it can't be won, the way the game is run.
But if you choose to stay, you wind up playin' anyway.
 (It's okay.)

You know, the kid's in shock, up and down the block.
The folks are home, playin' *Beat the Clock*.

Down at the Golden Cup, they set the young ones up.
Under the neon light, sellin' day for night.
 (It's alright.)

Nobody rides for free. (Nobody, nobody.)
Nobody gets it like they want it to be. (Nobody, nobody.)
Nobody hands you any guarantee. (Nobody, nobody.)
Nobody, baby. No. Nobody, baby.

The hearts are hard, and the times are tough.
Down on the Boulevard, the night's enough.

And time passes slow,
Between the store front shadows and the streetlights' glow.
Everybody walks right by, like they're safe or something.
 (They don't know.)

Nobody knows you. (Nobody, nobody.)
Nobody owes you nothin'! (Nobody, nobody.)
Nobody shows you what they're thinkin'. (Nobody, nobody.)
Nobody.

Hey, baby, you got to watch the street, and keep your feet
And be on guard.
 (Make you pay, baby.)

It's only time on the Boulevard.
It's like this; I mean that's the way it is.
 (On the Boulevard.)
It's only time on the Boulevard.

—Jackson Browne

Contents

OUTSIDE THE BADGE

I

Section A

Steve first noticed him out of the corner of his eye. The man was a brunette, with a brown beard and dark eyes. He was over six feet tall and outweighed Steve by at least thirty pounds.

Both Steve and the other man were inside the men's clothing department of J C Penney. About twenty-five feet to Steve's left was the men's rest room. Between Steve and the men's room door stood the other man. Surrounding Steve and the stranger were racks of clothing. Behind Steve and to his left was the cash register desk.

When Steve looked up from the clothing rack a second time, his blue eyes met the dark brown eyes of the other man. Steve then knew that the stranger had come to J C Penney to do more than shop. Steve was shifting through a rack of Brittanias, pretending to look for a pair of jeans that were his size. The stranger was bolder, just standing there and leaning against a clothing rack. And looking at Steve.

On his third look at the stranger, Steve held the man's gaze a second or two longer than before. The stranger was young and, Steve thought, quite handsome despite the beard. He was the type of man that Steve's old girlfriend would have fallen for in a second.

Steve moved to a different rack of clothing, the stranger's eyes following his every movement. Steve turned toward the register desk to see what the store employee was doing. *Surely the employee must be wondering what's going on between these two guys*, Steve thought. (*And don't call me Shirley*, was the next thought that passed through Steve's mind.) Looking over his shoulder, Steve saw that there was no employee in the department. As far as he could tell, he and the young bearded man were the only people in that area of the store.

When Steve moved farther down, closer to the men's room, he could sense, more than see, his young friend starting to move. Steve's heart hit an extra beat as a spurt of cold adrenaline shot through his body.

What the hell are you doing here? The thought pushed its way into Steve's head before his defense mechanisms had a chance to check it.

1

He allowed himself the same answer that always came back as a reply: *I don't really have a choice.*

It was a large department store, three levels high. The store was in a shopping mall and could be entered on the first or second level. The first level, selling housewares, had a bathroom in the corner of the furniture area. The third level of the store offered stationery supplies and had a rest room between the coffee shop and the stationery displays.

Steve was standing in front of the second-level rest room in the center section of the men's clothing area. This was the rest room that Steve went to the most often.

Here he comes, Steve thought, as the young man lightly brushed against him before stepping up to the door. As the young man pushed the rest room door to enter, he turned to meet Steve's gaze. Steve couldn't hold the man's stare and quickly looked into the rack of clothing before him.

Steve knew what the young man wanted. And Steve knew that the man could tell by the look in Steve's eyes that Steve was also interested.

A couple of moments of waiting, and then Steve, too, headed for the men's room. As he walked inside, Steve looked back around the department. There was only one other person in the area, a bald man who was looking at sport shirts.

Immediately upon entering the rest room, Steve saw that there was no one else inside the john except his bearded companion. The toilet stalls had no doors; store security had removed them several months prior because of customer complaints.

The bearded man was standing at the urinal. He turned in Steve's direction. The man appeared to be urinating, but Steve could hear neither the sound of water against porcelain nor the gurgling of a drain.

He's waiting for me, Steve thought.

Steve approached the row of sinks that lined the wall across from the urinals and toilet stalls. Steve washed his hands, watching the young man's reflection in the mirror above the commode. The man was standing perfectly straight, staring at the algae green–colored tiles before him. Had Steve not known what to look for, he might not have seen the telltale movement of the young man's right arm slowly pulsating back and forth.

It suddenly dawned on Steve who the young man reminded him of. The man actually looked a little like a tall version of Robert Redford in the movie *Jeremiah Johnson*. And now Redford was standing here. And he was masturbating.

Steve let Redford continue to masturbate for some moments, silently wishing the young man would turn in his direction and they could end this game. Steve washed his hands, dried them, combed his hair, and watched his young friend in the mirror. Steve realized that Redford was waiting for him to make the first move.

Steve walked slowly over to the urinal beside the young man. When Steve looked to his right, he could see the young man's erection.

Standing at the urinal, Steve unzipped his pants but went no further. Several moments passed, in which, Steve guessed, they were both lost in their silent reveries and, possibly, self-condemnations. But it took Steve only a second to snap awake when he noticed that his friend was now slowly edging his way in Steve's direction.

Steve felt like running out of there, yelling at himself, *What are you doing, you crazy faggot?!* But Steve stayed. And the young man moved closer.

Redford suddenly stopped moving. In slow motion, like in a movie, Steve saw Redford's left hand move away from his own crotch and toward Steve's.

Steve shivered as a second shot of energy moved through him, and he mentally ordered his body to be still. He hoped that the brunette didn't notice his shake. Redford obviously didn't, because his hand was now in front of Steve's groin, swaying like some drunk helicopter pilot unsure of landing.

Then the pilot made a decision, and Steve felt Redford's hand grab his groin. That was enough. Redford had violated Section 647(a) of the California Penal Code: lewd conduct in a public place.

Steve called to his bald partner, who would be waiting outside the rest room door, then took the wallet containing his badge from his pants pocket and identified himself to the young bearded man.

3

B.J.

At twenty years old, Robert Joseph Antonio stood at six foot three and weighed 175 pounds. No one on the street knew his real name, and B.J., like most of the hustlers, preferred it that way. One of the rules on the street is that you never give out any information about yourself. The less they knew, the less they had to burn you with. If they could get something out of it, hustlers would sell their brothers. In fact, on the streets of Los Angeles, some of them did.

B.J. had dark skin, straight black hair, and dark eyes. He told everyone that he was 50 percent Comanche Indian. No one on the street believed him, of course, since everyone knows that bullshit makes the world go round. The hustler who got away with the biggest lies or who was able to fool the cops with an alias was looked up to by the street kids. B.J. prided himself that his "brother" often said that B.J. could "bullshit a saddle off a horse." But nobody ever cared enough to challenge B.J. about his ancestry. On the street, no one cared much about anything, except making money and getting high. The only thing more important than bullshit was money. Every hustler knew at least two axioms: "Money talks and bullshit walks" and "Payback is a son of a bitch." Street kids lied out of fear of the latter. They only looked out for themselves because of the former.

B.J. claimed to have been molested three times during his youth. First, an older married man who was a friend of the family had cornered B.J. alone in his room and had masturbated the two of them. Of course, B.J. had trouble understanding what was going on, let alone getting excited by it. After all, B.J. was only three at the time. The second time was when B.J. was thirteen. This time it was by a Roman Catholic priest.

The last time was when B.J. was seventeen. He'd never had any homosexual fantasies that he knew of (or would admit to himself), but he'd gone into a "leather bar" in his hometown of Chicago. Gay men were standing around dressed in leather outfits and leather motorcycle gear: jackets, chaps, boots, cockrings. In some leather bars, men just like to dress up. In a few, some of the participants get very heavily into the sadomasochism, slave/master fantasies. (More than one person has died because a man he met in a bar didn't take him seriously when he yelled, "Stop that! You're killing me!") B.J. had chosen a bar that was of the latter variety. There, he'd been sexually assaulted by three men. That he'd gone into the bar of his own volition is not something that B.J. was willing to admit to himself—or others.

Despite living in the counterculture world of street hustlers, B.J. bought into most of the beliefs of larger society. He had no conception of himself as having homosexual desires, despite having sex with men every night. B.J. blamed those three childhood instances for his being a street hustler now.

B.J. had been in Los Angeles for over a year. He'd started hustling the second he stepped foot off the Greyhound bus. He also had hustled all the way from Chicago to L.A. B.J. realized right away that every state has an area for hustling.

B.J. liked the money. He usually made about forty dollars a trick. His rates would vary, depending on how late it was, if the trick was clean and good-looking, and if there were narcotics involved. If the man had some good shit, he could do whatever he wanted to B.J.'s body for as long as he could keep B.J. blazing.

B.J. had managed to keep his record clean in L.A. Not that he hadn't been arrested. He had. But he always used an assumed name. Sometimes he used his brother's name. His attitude was simple; if a warrant went out in his brother's name and his brother didn't like it, fuck him.

Tonight B.J. needed to get high. He had used crystal all night the night before, and he was getting paranoid about coming down from his high. Crystal meth had the tendency to do that. But for right now, B.J. could afford to be choosy about who he went with.

Standing out on Santa Monica Boulevard, B.J. saw a middle-aged fat man, who probably had a wife at home, circle the block in his car. He nodded to B.J. When the man pulled over to the curb, B.J. got in. He made the fat man drop him off on the next block. As much as he needed the money, he wasn't about to suck that fat man off and swallow his sperm. He'd wait for the next trick. Maybe if the fat man would have been willing to pay him a lot more money. After all, one of the other rules of the street was: "Money makes the rules."

B.J. used to spend a lot of his time at Arthur J's coffee shop before he got into a fight with the new security guard. Now B.J. hung out at Oki Dogs or along the Boulevard.

He usually wore a bandanna, either in his pocket or around his leg. He often wore a red one and sometimes a blue or black one. To the discriminating driver, these handkerchiefs had special significance. They would tell the driver what the hustler was into. Black meant S & M, yellow meant "golden showers," red meant fistfucking, and blue just meant that B.J. was for rent. Usually B.J. worked in the evening, when the married men came home from work, and after 2:00 A.M., when all the gay bars closed.

B.J., unlike many of the other street hustlers, had graduated from high school. He'd actually enrolled in Ohio University, but after six weeks he'd dropped out. He then began a more mobile career.

He soon learned the first rule of street hustling: take enough money to the next city to rent a room. The room could be used for tricks, thereby generating more money. B.J. often shared sleazy hotel rooms with other hustlers, staying with as many as five at a time. They would take turns with their tricks. And if a hustler couldn't turn a trick, he could still stay with the other hustlers.

Throughout his stay in L.A., B.J. had moved in with several gay men. The men would let B.J. live there in exchange for sexual gratuities. One of the men he stayed with was a chickenhawk and had B.J. bring young boys who were new to the street to his home. The man could afford to give the boys a place to stay and some money. In exchange, the boys had to have sex with the older man. The boys never stayed for long.

B.J. never had sex with men unless he was getting something out of it, though he did feel that one of the men he was living with was his "lover." B.J. felt that he only had sex with men for money. It was his job. For enjoyment, B.J. dated women. His girlfriend lived in Virginia, but he met many girls in the discos and had sex with many of the street girls who stayed with him when they needed a place to stay or wanted him to buy them drugs. In fact, all of B.J.'s sexual fantasies were of women. While growing up, B.J. was no different than any of his peers in his beliefs: homosexuals are sick people and prostitutes are "dirty."

B.J. always got high before hitting the streets, or he got his tricks to buy him booze or drugs. This made it easier for him to have sex with people he didn't care for. Almost all of B.J.'s money went for drugs. When he scored big, either with a rich trick or with a number of clients, he bought enough crystal to stay awake and blazing for several days before finally crashing and sleeping for three days straight.

After he got his first trick, he always bought himself cigarettes, a Coke, and a quick meal from a fast-food stand on the Boulevard. If he could, he tried to get the trick to buy the cigarettes and soda for him by stopping at a liquor store on the way to the hotel. If they were really hot for him, he knew they would buy these items. And B.J. could tell when some old man was really hot for him.

B.J. drank beer and cheap wine daily. He also smoked some grass a couple of times a day. The grass made his high more mellow so he didn't have any bad trips when he used LSD or other hallucinogens. He preferred Quaaludes or barbiturates for the nighttime.

B.J.'s drug of choice, like most of the hustlers and girls working the Boulevard, was "speed," a methamphetamine solution. He usually melted it down with water in a bottle cap held over a match. Holding one end of the tie in his mouth, he would tie off his arm to make the veins pop out. Once the pill had melted, he put the cotton from a cigarette filter into the solution to take out impurities. B.J. would then get a used syringe from one of the girls and pull the liquid from the bottle cap through the cotton filter. Then he would shoot it directly into his vein. The head rush was almost immediate.

He used to let others shoot him up, but because they liked to get high first, they were usually too messed up and would keep jabbing through his vein, causing blood tattoos.

B.J. smoked at least two packs of cigarettes a day. When he woke up in the morning, instead of brushing his teeth, he would drink a Coke and have a cigarette. Lately, it took him a few hours after waking up to stop coughing. B.J. knew that he was lucky he was well built and his muscles were well defined. His health habits would have made him look bad otherwise, and his income would have been less. To get some additional bucks, B.J. had had one of his hairdresser tricks put some blond highlights into his hair, which made him look even younger.

B.J., like the other hustlers, planned on leaving the street within a year. He was just doing this for a short time to get himself some money. B.J. didn't want to admit to himself that he never saved any money and that it was immediately blown on drugs. And he had no job skills. The only jobs he had ever worked were for a few weeks at a time. And these jobs were always given to him by his "friend-customers," who always wanted sex in addition to paying B.J.'s salary.

B.J. was able to have sex with the ugly guys ("trolls") because he believed that he had been given a gift from God and that he could bring happiness into some lonely men's lives by having sex with them.

B.J. did have one remarkable talent: his ability to draw. Whenever he got a rich trick, he had the trick buy him art supplies. Whenever he had spare time, which was usually when he was high, B.J. made charcoal drawings. But B.J. wanted to be a model, and he had the goal of one day working with dysfunctional or runaway children. B.J. wanted to pursue these other things soon. He feared staying on the street for too long. He was fond of saying, "Some of these hustlers have been on the street for so long that they begin to look like the street."

Having no real family, B.J. had adopted some of the hustlers and given them special significance in his life. His "brother" was a thin blond hustler he had traveled with to several cities.

B.J. told everyone that Dan was his "brother," explaining the difference in appearance by telling them that they had different mothers.

7

In this way, B.J., like other street hustlers, maintained some semblance of family ties. When they were together, Dan and he told everyone that they would do anything for each other. And having a "brother" on the street was important. It was someone to back you up if you got into a fight and someone to watch your back for you. But in truth, B.J. knew that if something better came along, he or Dan would dump the other in a flash.

It was already 7:00 P.M. when B.J. woke up. After a three-day rush of staying awake from speed, B.J. had slept for twenty-four hours straight. When he awoke, B.J. was starving. He had no money left from the tricks of the day before, so B.J. rummaged through the apartment of the man he was staying with. Finding no money, B.J. took one of the man's old watches and sold it on the street for four dollars. He then bought some cigarettes, a Coke, and a McDonald's cheeseburger.

By eight, B.J. was at Santa Monica and La Brea, working. The L.A. County Sheriff's Department, which contracted with the city of West Hollywood, patrolled the streets on the west side of La Brea. News traveled fast in the street community, and B.J. knew that the sheriffs were having a "sweep," clearing all the hustlers off the street. So B.J. stayed on the LAPD side of La Brea, where the police cars just drove by and the officers ignored him.

B.J. just wanted to turn a couple of quick tricks so that he could get enough speed to last him the night and some to sell to his friends, at a profit of course.

He stared into the cars that drove by, watching the drivers. Occasionally he stroked his penis through his pants, to keep it stimulated so that he looked bigger through his tight jeans. B.J. was good at his business, and he knew that a lot of the gay men were "size queens," only interested in a big dick.

A brown van drove by slowly, and the driver checked B.J. out. B.J. could tell that the driver was interested by the way he looked back and slowed as he made a right turn and drove around the corner. A few minutes later, the brown van again passed by B.J. (B.J. was glad that the guy inside looked young; he hoped the guy wasn't too bizarre.) The driver had long brown hair and looked a little bit weird. B.J. had had one man pick him up the prior week, who'd paid B.J. to stay with him and not bathe for three days, wearing the same dirty underwear. The man loved dirty underwear. Finally, B.J. felt so dirty that while the man was gone, he showered. When the man got back and saw that B.J. had showered, he threw a raging tantrum. B.J. had had to grab his things and the money he'd been given and run from the house.

8

But B.J. didn't feel cheated. The man was such a jerk that B.J. had also taken a gold cross that was given to the man by his mother before she passed away. B.J. pawned it later that night for ten dollars. B.J. also remembered another weird trick. The man had been a comedian from the television show *Hollywood Squares*. He'd picked up B.J. on the Boulevard and taken him to his home in Beverly Hills. He'd even flown B.J. up with him to Las Vegas, where they filmed the show. B.J. had gotten to have lunch with Joan Rivers, who was also a guest on the show. Anyway, the man had been really nice, and he'd loved sucking on B.J.'s dick, which was okay with B.J. because B.J. had just closed his eyes and pretended that he was with a woman. But the man had also liked to have B.J. take a shit on him. This *really* turned the man on.

B.J. had thought that was really gross. It was even worse than what that other famous comedian had made B.J. do. The other comedian, a really fat guy, had a wife and kids. But B.J. had thought that everyone must have known that the guy was a faggot. And that guy had liked to be "fisted." B.J. couldn't understand how anyone could enjoy having a whole hand and wrist put up his asshole. But that comedian had paid well!

B.J. walked to the corner as the van slowly pulled to the curb after circling a third time. The young guy with the long brown hair was the only person B.J. could see inside the van. The curtains between the front and the back were closed.

B.J. nodded to the guy, who nodded back. B.J. walked over and opened the unlocked passenger door and sat inside, closing the door as the van pulled away from the curb.

B.J. hoped he could con this guy into buying him a pack of cigarettes.

Intensity

People become police officers for a wide variety of very different reasons. Some become cops because they want to help people. Others become cops because they can't stand office work and don't want to be tied to a desk. Being a patrol officer, you never do the same thing twice. And without a boss standing over your shoulder, there is a freedom in police work that can only be found in a few other jobs.

Many people become cops because it is a step up the mobility ladder. Without a college education, there are few jobs that offer similar benefits and none that offer as excellent a pay scale. And all you have to do is be willing to be shot! Still others choose the job because of the high degree of respect that they believe society places on the police officer. The uniform provides them with a degree of respectability that they could never have had by just being themselves.

Many Vietnam War veterans became police officers because they could not stop fighting the war. Becoming a police officer on the streets of Los Angeles allowed them to simply switch venues. They still had their guns, their tactics, their troops, their violence, and, most of all, an environment that accepted their thoughts and behavior as normal. The streets of L.A., with no shortage of gangs, drugs, and murder, were not that much different from Cambodia or Laos.

The Los Angeles Police Department was so accepting of these veterans that they even did away with their psychological screening for a two-year period while the vets were coming home to the States and applying for jobs. The Minnesota Multiphasic Personality Inventory, developed in the 1940s, was adopted by the Los Angeles Police Department to weed out homosexuals, who were viewed as psychologically ill when the test was developed. Unfortunately for the Vietnam vets, the exam also tested for neuroses, psychoses, and a host of other mental "abnormalities." Virtually all of the vets failed to pass the test once they had been through the mental trauma of Vietnam. Commiserating with society's treatment of the vets and feeling excommunicated themselves, the LAPD management discarded the test so that the vets could be hired. It didn't hurt that most of the police management were war veterans themselves.

Some officers had joined the Department for all the wrong reasons. They had been bullies all their lives, and the only way they could legitimatize their behavior was to join the ranks of the LAPD. And what a perfect job this was for them. Not only were they given the authority to continue bullying and beating on people, but now they were being paid to do what they had done all their lives for free!

Stephen Cainen joined the police department for one reason: to quit and become a reserve officer in Santa Monica. Steve's best friend from high school had become a Santa Monica officer, and Steve wanted to work with him on the weekends while going to law school. Steve *stayed* a police officer for a totally different reason: the money he was being paid allowed him to move out of his mother's house and into an apartment of his own. Which meant he could have sex for the first time in his life.

At five foot ten, Steve was very well built for his height. Years of karate training and later weight training had turned the 135-pound weakling into a 165-pound young man. But the thing that most people who met Steve noted about him was his eyes. It wasn't that they were blue, which was startling because of his brown hair, but because of their intensity. It was this intensity that had made Steve a great detective. Even the hardest criminals had squirmed under Steve's intense gaze.

Steve had reason to be intense. He was the older of two boys. His brother had been a hemophiliac during Steve's developing years and had gotten all the attention of the family. When Steve was eight, his mother had separated from Steve's father. By the time Steve was twelve, his mother had divorced his father and remarried a rich Beverly Hills attorney. Steve's mother was the attorney's fifth wife. The man had abused Steve's mother, and she'd divorced him by the time Steve was thirteen. His mother's powerlessness over the men in her life and her inability to protect herself from the men she married had caused her a great deal of anger and anguish. And because Steve reminded her of her first husband, she'd taken her frustrations out on him. Between the ages of eight and twelve, Steve had been physically abused by his mother. When she wasn't hitting or kicking him black and blue, she'd psychologically abused him, telling him that he was no good and that he would never amount to anything.

When Steve was twelve, after not seeing his father for two years, the man suddenly reappeared. With him, he had a new wife. Financially strapped, Steve's mother had taken his father to court for more child support. When he'd refused to pay, the court had ordered that he spend a weekend in jail. After two days in that hellhole, Steve's father, who had been a boozer and a gambler but was a law-abiding man nonetheless, had agreed to the child-support payments. But rather than have any equity, he sold the catering truck, which had been his business for twenty-five years, and took a job that did not give him the pride and independence he needed to enjoy his life.

11

As a last-ditch effort to get back at Steve's mother, his father and his new wife contacted Steve and told him that if he truly loved his father, which Steve did, he would leave his mother and come and live with them. They'd told him that if he stayed with his mother, that meant that he didn't love his father. In retribution, Steve's mother had responded by telling her twelve-year-old son that he had to make a choice between her and his father. If he loved his mother, he would not speak to his father again.

Steve was intelligent for his twelve years of life. And even at that age, he'd realized it was wrong and incredibly irresponsible of his parents to use a twelve-year-old as a pawn in their psychological war. In Steve's mind, it was unforgivable that his parents were insisting that he, a twelve-year-old child, must choose between his parents, and no matter which he chose, that would mean he did not love the other.

Steve did make a choice, and he stuck by his choice the remainder of his life. He chose neither parent. He felt that neither parent deserved his love because of the game they had chosen to play with his emotions. And though Steve had lived under his mother's roof until he graduated from the police academy at age twenty-three, he'd never felt any attachment to his mother or father since that decision when he was twelve.

So Steve had reason to be intense.

* * *

Steve had always been told that he was a slightly better-than-average student by his mother. As a self-fulfilling prophecy, Steve always brought home Bs on his report cards. Being a ninety-eight-pound weakling with thick glasses, Steve tended to mind his own business and was often picked on by the other children.

In the eleventh grade of high school, Steve decided to completely break his parental bonds and become his own person. From that moment on, he'd received straight As in his classes, and he ran for and obtained a position in student government.

Though he had never learned to play any sports and was deathly frightened of baseball and football, Steve found that wrestling was an individual sport, rather than a team sport, which he could relate to. After he'd lost every match he'd competed in, Steve's best friend, Cal Thompson, the wrestling team captain, had taught him how to get mad and to focus that anger. It was a lesson Steve would value the rest of his life.

To the astonishment of his teammates, Steve took the league finals without a loss, defeating his opponents and becoming the league champion within his weight class. And before he graduated from high school, Steve had broken virtually every student record, becoming student body president and editor of the school paper, obtaining a student seat on the city council and board of education. He graduated with more honors than any other person in the history of the school.

Before he'd developed this independence in the eleventh grade, Steve's mother had retained control of his life. And before he'd dropped his last obligatory psychological attachments to his mother, she had taken him to a meeting of the Santa Monica Police Explorer program, which was developed in order to begin preparing future police officers while they were still in high school.

Since the finalization of her last divorce, Steve's mother had determined that Steve needed a male role model. Subsequently, she'd dragged him away from the television set that he had become inseparable from. Steve, choosing the fantasy of TV over the misery of his own life, spent every hour outside of homework watching the boob tube—primarily *Gilligan's Island*, *The Bob Newhart Show*, *The Mary Tyler Moore Show* (Steve thought Ted was great), *Get Smart*, and, of course, *Kung Fu*.

The Explorer program was Steve's first introduction to law enforcement. It was also his first experience with a disciplined life since he had dropped out of his Kung Fu classes when he was thirteen. Though he'd hated it at first, Steve could relate to the maturity of the law enforcement community. Steve had spent much of his life as an introvert, constantly thinking to himself. Because of this, Steve was more mature than most of his peers.

More than anything, though, law enforcement gave Steve his first taste of respect. The respect he had never gotten at home Steve now found in his ability to carry out a task.

Steve had always believed his mother. When she told him he was bad (not that what he *did* was bad, but that *he* was bad), he'd believed her. And when she told him that he was just like his father and that he would never amount to anything, Steve had started on the path of that self-fulfilling prophecy.

With Steve's first taste of independence, he began living a life of his own. Befriending the student body vice-president in high school, Steve became involved in student government. At the same time, he started using his writing skills on the student newspaper. The high school staff and faculty, as well as his peers, praised him for his constant work. Steve learned that there were really only two barriers to his abilities: innate and artificial.

Steve learned that when he set his mind to it, he could do better than virtually anyone and he could accomplish almost anything.

Steve had changed himself from a B student in high school to a straight A student. To keep this pattern, Steve knew that he would have to choose a college major that did not involve math or science. Though he was extremely bright, he had learned that these two areas were his weaknesses. Also, Steve found that anything outside the real world was incredibly boring. Life-and-death decisions were much more interesting. So Steve chose to major in the one area in which he had experienced a desire to learn more—police work.

Unfortunately, Steve was so involved in developing a student grievance procedure and running the school paper that he forgot to apply for college before most of the deadlines. Luckily, he was accepted on a scholarship to a college near his home.

A few months before graduation, Steve also got a call from a college in Ventura County, California. When Steve picked up the phone, the caller told him that they wanted an excellent student like him and were willing to pay the full tuition costs for the first semester. Thinking of his high school math and science classes, Steve advised the recruiter that he must have the wrong number. Steve went so far as to provide the recruiter with the name and telephone number of the class valedictorian. But the recruiter was obstinate; he wanted someone as involved in his school as Steve was.

Before Steve could make a decision about which college to attend, his mother recommended that it would be best for the family (meaning her, not Steve's brother) if he went away to school.

By the time Steve graduated from college, he held summa cum laude honors, honors for criminal justice research, honors for his perfect grade point average in his chosen field, and he had received an award that had not been given in ten years: Criminal Justice Student of the Year.

Within three weeks, Steve was in the Los Angeles Police Academy. Elected class president by his academy classmates, Steve also graduated as the honor cadet, with the highest overall scores in driving, academics, physical fitness, and self-defense. With only two years on the job, Steve took and passed the Field Training Officer (FTO) exam. With less than four years on the job, he took and passed the prestigious detective examination. By the time he had five years on the Department, Steve had received more commendations and saved more lives than any other LAPD officer. Steve's ability to excel had carried on into his career with the Los Angeles Police Department.

Until they found out that Steve was homosexual.

14

Lancaster

Lancaster is the largest city in the Antelope Valley, at the northern tip of Los Angeles County. Though the city houses such large corporations as Hughes Aircraft, Boeing Airplane Company, Lockheed Aircraft, NASA, Northrop, and Rockwell International, it was originally a Piute Indian campsite.

To many of the Los Angelenos who take weekend excursions into the neighboring areas of their suburban homes, Lancaster is best known for the Tropico Gold Mine. Almost every Angeleno family has taken their children to see a real mine from the gold rush and to pan for gold at Tropico.

The residents of Lancaster love their city for its sunshine and clear skies. At 2,350 feet above sea level, Lancaster is a high desert region that is far different from the smog-congested L.A. basin. Unlike the City of the Angels, in Lancaster the residents can actually tell the changing of the seasons. Most people transplanted from the Midwest and East Coast complain about the inability to tell the difference between the seasons in L.A. Those born and raised in L.A. like wearing tank tops, shorts, and sandals all year round and often suggest that these transplants try living back in their home states for one winter before they complain.

Every few years, Lancaster is blessed with a light snowfall during the winter.

The senior residents of Lancaster bide their time away sitting in the sunshine among the cherry orchards. They often debate how Lancaster was named. Some of the seniors claim that it was named in 1882, when a Scotsman named Wicks moved from Lancaster, Pennsylvania, and tried to start a Scottish colony in the region. Others maintain that it was one of the staff of the expanding Southern Pacific Railroad that gave Lancaster its name. Most of the younger people choose the former rhetoric. Younger people have a tendency to prefer rational thought, and no one knows just exactly why Mr. Purnell, of the Southern Pacific staff, would have chosen the name Lancaster.

Borax was discovered about the same time that gold was found in the area. But silver was the leading metal mined, and produced $26 million from 1881 to 1924. The ore found in the Tropico Mine was so pure that it was appraised as high as $100,000 per ton.

When the First World War broke out, the farming industry in the region became the most prosperous business. The money acquired in agriculture helped build Lancaster into a sizable town.

Finally, in 1921, two paved streets were added to the Mint Canyon Highway, which curved its way through the town. This opened the doors of Lancaster to the outside motoring world. Shortly thereafter, Edwards Air Force Base was built near the dry lakes of the area. The air base gained worldwide attention on October 14, 1947, when Air Force Captain Charles Yeager broke the sound barrier for the first time. And again on December 12, 1953, the same man, now a lieutenant colonel, flew his Bell X-1A at 1,650 mph, more than twice the speed of sound.

Today Edwards Air Force Base plays host to America's latest achievement, the space shuttle program. Hundreds of thousands of people gather yearly to watch the landings of the shuttle at the base.

In 1977, Lancaster was officially incorporated as a city. Just prior, the Antelope Valley Freeway was completed, linking Los Angeles to the area.

It was on this freeway that, in the middle of the night, a brown van was driving at exactly 55 mph. The van continued on past the homes, patios, and backyards, past the Highway Patrol offices on I Avenue, and to the northernmost tip of the county.

At the north end of the county is an area that has long been abandoned. Signs posted throughout the area warn travelers to avoid entering any of the mines. In addition to the mines dug into the sides of hills, hundreds of seemingly bottomless mine shafts quilt the area as if a giant gopher were in search of food.

The mine shafts, long since abandoned for more economical ways of mining gold and silver, have never been filled. Though every dozen years or so some politician will help his campaign by having the mines covered to protect the children of the area, most of the coverings have been broken by would-be miners or juvenile pranksters.

It was to this area that the van drove. At night, nowhere is darker than the desert. To any person watching, it would seem unusual for a car to drive in this hazardous area without lights. But there were no eyes to see this van, and no person to challenge the van's occupants when the van stopped.

Had there been an insomniac to witness the events that occurred once the van stopped, you could be sure that the person would have had even more to keep him awake at night.

As the driver exited the van, long brown hair showed in the dim compartment light. At the opposite side of the van, the driver opened the side door. With the assistance of a second, thinner figure, he hoisted a shadowy form through the door, half-dragging and half-carrying the figure, as a sound like an animal's whimper could be heard.

The form was hauled quite a distance to an abandoned mine shaft. By the time the three figures reached the shaft, the driver and his companion were breathing hard, testimony to the heaviness of their burden.

Unceremoniously dropping the form onto the ground, the thinner of the two walked back to the van and retrieved what could have been a baseball bat, a thick pipe, or a shotgun. The thinner figure returned to the mine shaft and handed the thing to the driver. When the leaner of the two propped the prostrate figure into a square, it almost looked like a human figure kneeling in prayer.

The driver then bent down beside the kneeling form, but the desert wind carried away whatever whisper was said. Without a second pause, the driver stepped back and put the stick to the head of the figure. A large boom, shattering the desert stillness and violating the almost religious serenity of the desert, demonstrated that it was no stick.

Before the figure completed its forward fall, the driver was kicking the form into the adjacent mine shaft. The figure disappeared down the shaft without a resounding thud, as if it fell straight to hell.

Holding the shotgun over his shoulder, as if returning from a hunt, the driver led the remaining figure back to the van, where another, feminine figure stood beside the open side door, watching.

When the driver started to whistle a carefree tune, also swept away by the desert wind, the thinner figure shivered, though the breeze was quite warm.

LAPD

Members of the Los Angeles Police Department have a saying: "You cannot break the law if you are the law." So, when the Los Angeles City Council passed an ordinance forbidding discrimination based upon sexual orientation in 1979, the police department management conveniently exempted their department.

Until 1987, the Department asked every applicant for police officer if he had ever had a homosexual experience. Any applicant that answered in the affirmative was disqualified based upon his "moral character" being unsuitable for police work.

In 1987, with pressure from the gay community and various city politicians who wanted the donations from the gay Municipal Elections Committee, the Department removed that question from their background investigation interview. Much to the chagrin of the gay organizers who lobbied for that omission, the Department still continued to disqualify all gay applicants.

Instead of openly asking whether an applicant was homosexual, the police department background investigators now instructed every applicant that he or she must be able to provide the name, address, and phone number of a member of the opposite sex that he or she had dated. Any male applicant who could not provide this data was then placed on a polygraph, for "suspected drug use," and asked if he had ever had sex in a public place, such as a "beach, park, or car." Not surprisingly, every applicant that took the polygraph was subsequently disqualified, due to "moral turpitude."

The police department management argued that these questions were not discriminatory, because they didn't ask for anyone's sexual orientation, and they were asked of all applicants, hetero or homo.

The gay community couldn't understand why only gay applicants had ever had sex in a car or on the beach.

In 1975, the deputy chief of the Los Angeles Police Department had issued an offical memo to every one of his police officers. The memo decried the possibility of ever allowing gays to become Los Angeles Police officers. In the memo, the deputy chief accused homosexual activists of attempting to bypass and override the laws of the country by claiming discrimination protections in employment as a minority group. The deputy chief wrote:

> There is no area sacred from the homosexual when it comes to furthering their insurgent ideals . . . Homosexuals are preoccupied with illegal sexual relations. Sexual contact is very easily had and other things become

18

clouded and the real value of things is lost because they spend so much time seeking self-gratification. Homosexuals have great difficulty establishing relationships. It is difficult to give of themselves with another person . . .

Homosexuals tend to associate with disreputable persons, and otherwise lead disorganized lives . . . they are continually on the prowl looking for new sexual partners . . .

Homosexuals have a corrosive influence on their fellow employees because they attempt to entice normal individuals to engage in perverted sex practices . . .

Any person who willingly engages repeatedly in homosexual activity is an emotionally sick person and definitely constitutes an unacceptable risk when qualifying as a police officer . . .

Moreover, any person who deliberately adopts a way of life repugnant and abhorrent to the great majority of society, and who openly scoffs at the norms and laws of society, has questionable personal values making suspect the character factors most needed in a police officer: reliability, trustworthiness, judgment and integrity.

As individuals we can say we don't want a homosexual as a policeman, which is our own personal position, based upon a strong moral upbringing. The point is that somewhere along the line of law and reason, the collective wants of society must rule. The hiring of homosexuals as police officers is repulsive to nearly all persons . . .

Habitual or repeated participation in homosexual acts constitutes behavior and activities which: (1) are evidence of such immaturity and character . . . as to indicate that the participant is not reliable or trustworthy; and (2) are reckless, irresponsible, and wanton in nature and indicate such poor judgment and instability as to suggest that the person involved might make a deliberate or inadvertent disclosure of sensitive information to known criminals or look the other way while crimes take place.

Since homosexuality in many cases is an underlying symptom to a much more serious mental disorder, the medical examining staff, working within long established and proven medical and psychological practices, has disqualified those individuals who exhibit characteristics incompatible with the norms of this society and its police. To retain the current trust of the community and the high level of efficiency enjoyed by the Los Angeles Police Department the disqualification of police applicants based on substantiated homosexual conduct must be continued.*

When the LAPD chief of police left to hold an elected post in the state government, the new chief of police promoted the deputy chief who authored the memo. The memo has never been rescinded.

---

*The actual Report of the Commission on Personal Privacy, December 1982.

At the time that the memo was written, the chief of police was outspokenly antigay. The chief was an extremely quick-minded man and, as the chief of the most influential department in the nation and elected president of the International Peace Officers Association, the LAPD chief urged police chiefs and officers throughout the nation to fight against allowing homosexuals to become police officers. He also urged that there be strict enforcement of victimless crimes as they pertained to homosexuals and that law enforcement personnel should speak out strongly about their religious faith and "moral values."

In the Los Angeles Police Department in 1975, the chief of police was an Episcopalian, actively involved in his church. The deputy chief was a lay minister, who preached from his fundamentalist church's dais and made religious cassette tapes that were later distributed throughout the United States.

One of the most extraordinary examples of the LAPD chief's outspoken antigay sentiment was in response to an invitation sent him by the gay pride organization that sponsored the Gay Pride Parade in Los Angeles. In responding to the president of that organization, the chief wrote:

> As you no doubt expected, I am declining your invitation to participate in the celebration of "GAY PRIDE WEEK." While I support your organization's constitutional right to express your feelings on the subject of homosexuality, I am obviously not in sympathy with your views on the subject. I would much rather celebrate "GAY CONVERSION WEEK" which I will gladly sponsor when the medical practitioners in this country find a way to convert gays to heterosexuals.
>
> Very truly yours,
>
> Chief of Police
> Los Angeles Police Department**

(It is interesting to note that once the LAPD chief left to hold an elected state office, he had a sudden "change of heart" when communicating with his electorate. In a 1984 letter to one of his constituents about an assembly bill outlawing discrimination, the former chief wrote: "My vote for this bill was based on my belief that it is wrong to discriminate based on an individual's status or orientation . . . I appreciate your support and will continue to approach such important issues with an open mind."†)

**McCadden Place/Morris Kight Exhibit, Hollywood, California, 1990.
†Morris Kight Exhibit, Hollywood, California, 1990.

The new chief of police continued the "morals" campaign that his predecessor had started. But the new chief lacked the charisma and intelligence that had allowed the prior chief to become a mini-celebrity for his conservativeness.

(The new chief pointed out to *every* academy graduating class that the late great former chief William Parker had single-handedly cleaned out all corruption from the LAPD. What he *didn't* tell each graduating class was that Parker had also gone on television during the 1965 Watts riots to warn Los Angeles residents, "It is estimated that by 1970, 45 percent of the metropolitan area of Los Angeles will be Negro; if you want any protection for your home and family . . . you're going to have to get in and support a strong police department. If you don't do that, come 1970, God help you.")

Despite the overwhelming increase in crime in Los Angeles, making L.A. the drug and murder capital of the West Coast, the chief removed over 250 officers from the streets. He assigned these officers to enforce "morals offenses," victimless crimes that primarily targeted male homosexuals and the places they congregated. Until the 1960s, it was illegal to serve alcohol to a known homosexual in California. The chief, a police officer brought up in this era, continued bar raids into the eighties and the nineties. He explained to the gays who questioned him that these raids were conducted due to "overcrowding." Yet, more than once, gays were beaten during these raids. And at the same time that one black youth a night was being killed in South-Central Los Angeles, the gang capital of the United States, the chief had young male police officers dress in tight pants and act as decoys, arresting gays who solicited the officers. And throughout the 1980s and into the '90s, citizens who called the Los Angeles Police Department's emergency 911 phone number received a recording asking them to stay on the line and wait if they had a real emergency. Yet over 250 officers handled crimes between consenting adults.

Like their predecessors (Gates and Vernon), the current chief and the assistant chief explained that they felt it was their primary duty to re-establish morals in the city of Los Angeles. At the same time, the chief informed his command staff that "gays are the scourge of the modern era." And despite the constantly worsening relations between the Department and the gay community, the chief adamantly refused to establish a liaison. Every other community ethnic group had an officially designated representative from the Department except gays and lesbians. Liaisons with the other community groups had only been established after those groups involved the judicial system. The LAPD management had mistreated other community groups for a long period of time as well.

When the Los Angeles Police Department first established their recruitment guidelines, applicants had only three requirements: they had to be over six feet tall, male, and white. This policy stayed intact until after the Vietnam War.

The management of the Department had allowed women "matron" officers to join the Department. These officers were required to wear shin-length skirts and were not allowed to work in patrol. Even the chief had gone on television explaining that women could not perform the job of a police officer, as they lacked the upper body strength necessary to perform the job.

Unfortunately for the chief, one of his captains, the only officer in the Department with a Harvard degree, chose to do his thesis on women in law enforcement. Using purely empirical data, the captain demonstrated that not only could women perform the job, but they outperformed their male counterparts. Without the macho head-trip, women had nothing to prove by provoking fights. Subsequently, women officers had the tendency to act more rationally, using intelligence to talk a criminal into jail, rather than resorting to brute force.

The LAPD management also refused to recruit from the black community, despite the obvious problems that resulted in the Watts riots. Black leaders constantly decried the mistreatment of blacks by LAPD officers. The LAPD "choke hold" was made famous in the black communities of L.A. LAPD officers would have contests with black arrestees to see which officer could choke the suspect unconscious the fastest. The management expounded that the reason blacks could not be recruited is that the whites in the other areas of the city would not accept a black officer and would not allow them into their homes, thereby hindering the efficiency of the Department.

Despite over 50 percent of the L.A. population having a Spanish surname, LAPD also refused to recruit from the Hispanic community. Ensuring that the Department would not be reflective of the community it served, the LAPD spokesman explained to television viewers that Hispanics were too short. An Hispanic officer would have to expose too much of his upper body if he had to shoot over the top of his police car during a gunfight. Therefore, the spokesman rationalized, it would not be cost-effective, and would be deleterious, for LAPD to recruit Hispanics.

It wasn't until 1980 that the courts ordered LAPD to integrate their male, white department. In establishing a consent decree, the

LAPD management begrudgingly gave the false impression that the Department would integrate in compliance with the court mandate.

But even as late as 1988, every specialized division in the Department, with the exception of the Narcotics Division, which utilized officers of color to buy drugs undercover, was still between 95 to 98 percent white males.

And the beatings and mistreatment of minority group members by LAPD officers increased. Amazingly, between 1984 and 1988, the taxpayers' money was spent paying out a record $13 million in civil police misconduct cases against the LAPD ($35 million between 1973 and 1990).

Despite the court-ordered settlements and proscriptions, some LAPD managers tried to ensure that only officers of their choosing would be accepted in the Department. Despite civil service testing procedures by the city, the chief ensured that only white males would be promoted within the ranks and that only those applicants who fit the "LAPD mold/mind frame" would be allowed into the Department.

How the chief of LAPD is selected established the first precedent for LAPD "purity." When the former chief left to take a political office, the top contender for the vacancy was the chief of a small police agency. With the possibility of an outsider being selected as chief, the city immediately "bonused" any incumbent LAPD contenders. To no one's surprise, the new chief of police for Los Angeles became a male, white, religious LAPD commander.

In promotional examinations in the LAPD, it is only high-ranking LAPD staff and command officers who make up the promotional boards. Objective written examinations account for only a small percentage of the score. It is the scores given during the oral interview with the LAPD staff officers that determine who will be promoted. Therefore, it only takes one phone call from the chief or one of his staff to the officers giving the orals to let them know who is "liked" or "disliked" by the chief. Those officers that are liked by LAPD management will be given choice special assignments prior to the promotional oral, so that the boards will know whether the officer who is before them is in the chief's favor or not. Few members of the oral boards are willing to disappoint the chief. Anyone hoping for a successful career in the Department knows that the chief oversees all assignments and promotions.

Even during the recruitment phase, LAPD supervisors sit on the oral boards given to entry-level applicants. Only those applicants that fit the LAPD mold are given high-enough scores to be selected as officers. In attempting to ensure impartiality, the city civil service department assigns a civilian along with the supervisor to sit in on the orals

23

and also provide a score. It has long been rumored that, unknown to the civil service representatives, LAPD supervisors are given strict instructions by LAPD management: never provide your score until after hearing the score being given by the civilian personnel department interviewer. In that manner, the LAPD interviewers are told to raise or lower their ratings to counter the civilian's scores.

That way, anyone who won't "fit in" with the rest of the LAPD officers will be rejected.

This is how the chief ensures that his beliefs are perpetuated among the Department, despite any court order.

One of the most extreme examples of this nepotism occurred in 1982. In 1979, the city gave in to the pressure of gay activists and enacted a municipal ordinance forbidding discrimination based on sexual orientation. In 1982, when rumors circulated that gays might be allowed into the LAPD, officers began a campaign against permitting them to join the Department. Several of the officers went on the front pages of the largest-circulation community paper in the city. The officers stated that they would never tolerate a gay in their Department and that any who joined would be openly harassed. The officers, in print, stated that all gays are "immoral," "mentally sick," and "potential child molesters."

The entire antigay campaign in LAPD was led by one officer. Within a year of the publication of the article, the officer was promoted to a supervisor. Now the officer could impose his and the chief's discriminatory views upon the rest of the Department.

The first sentence of the 1979 municipal ordinance that forbids homosexual discrimination reads: "Discrimination based on sexual orientation exists in the City of Los Angeles."

II

Danny

Danny wasn't sure what had happened to his "brother," B.J., but as happens in living on the street, life goes on and missing people aren't noticed too much. But it *was* unusual. Danny had gotten used to having B.J. around. Not that he really trusted B.J., who would sell him out in a second for a better offer, but B.J. had been the one who always got the hotel room first. B.J. was just a good talker. He could get gays to fall in love with him and then use them to buy all kinds of things. Boy, what a sweet-talker B.J. was.

Danny and B.J. told everybody they were brothers. It was nice to kind of have a family. Their own families didn't want them. They were just another mouth to feed. So for the last three cities or so, B.J. took Danny along. And Danny and B.J. had watched each other's backs.

Dan was nineteen years old, with blond hair and green eyes. He dyed his hair even blonder than it really was. He was thin but muscular, at just over six feet tall and weighing 145 pounds. Dan had tattoos on both arms. He had gotten them recently and still had little scabs covering some portions of the tattooed skin.

Dan was hitchhiking one day when he was solicited by the driver. After that, Dan started "hitchhiking" for money. He had known B.J. for several months before he found out that B.J. was "hitchhiking" too. Unlike B.J. and most of the other hustlers, Dan thought of himself as gay. He even had a lover in Texas. His lover, an older "sugar daddy," was a probation officer. The lover once came out to Los Angeles to try to get Danny to come back with him. But Danny wouldn't go. His lover had only rented a car for the weekend, but it took him two weeks of pleading to finally convince Dan to leave the streets and come back. In the meantime, the rental car agency reported the car as stolen. Dan's lover was soon arrested while driving the car, which made it easier for Dan to go on working Santa Monica Boulevard.

Because Dan was nineteen and blond, he frequently made up to two hundred dollars a day for five hours' work on the streets. Sometimes he made above three hundred dollars. Danny knew that blonds could make more money. He had also appeared in some pornographic pictures to subsidize his income, and often proudly showed his "Porno Actor's Guild" card.

Usually Dan got a "small high" before going out and working. As soon as he turned his first trick, he blew his money on fast food and "scoring a high for the night." Because he was always buzzing, he ate constantly (when he had money), but he never gained any weight.

Dan left high school after two years and joined the navy for a six-year stint. Dan claimed to have begun his training in the SEAL program, a highly developed unit in the navy that trains for counterterrorist or insurgent operations. Dan got fed up with the training and told them he was gay, earning himself an immediate discharge. He then met his lover in Texas, who insisted that he attend college. He quit after nine months. While attending college, Dan became a heroin addict, which left long track marks on his arms and large cysts where the needle holes became infected. At one point, his arms became so infected that he had to be hospitalized for two months. His immune system never fully recovered from the addiction, and Dan was constantly besieged by colds and flus.

Danny built up a list of sugar daddies, being able to ask any one of them for a job in their respective field. Danny's last sugar daddy, a dentist, put a $4,000 capping job on his teeth for free. His current sugar daddy owned an underground porno store and mail service. Dan's goal was to get one of his sugar daddies to buy him "wheels."

When he was younger, Dan and his friends used to beat up homosexuals and take their money.

Soon after arriving in L.A., Danny met a young boy in one of the gay bars in West Hollywood. Dan then turned a number of tricks and saved the money, paying for a weekend in Palm Springs for the young boy and himself. The boy's parents had bought the boy a car, and the boy and Danny drove to Palm Springs together. The boy was also a tall, thin, blond. After arriving back in L.A. the following weekend, the boy wanted to get back to El Monte, where he lived with his mother. Danny convinced him to drive down the Boulevard and wait while Dan made some money. Danny then took the boy out onto the Boulevard and made a deal with the potential customer. He then persuaded the boy to go with the man.

Most of the hustlers are introduced to the street by someone they know.

Danny wasn't afraid that his young friend would get arrested by LAPD Vice, for the first thing he taught the boy was the "vice test." As soon as Danny got into the car of a potential customer, Danny told the older man, "Put your hand where it feels most comfortable." If the man didn't grab Dan's crotch, Dan would say that he was only hitchhiking and ask to be let off at the next stop.

Danny used to read from a card given to him by the Gay Community Center in Hollywood. He would read the question to the customer: "Are you now or have you ever been associated with a law-enforcement agency?" But one time the customer said, "Sure I am. Are you?" and then proceeded to arrest Dan. Another time, the undercover officer said, "No," and then arrested Dan when he offered sex for money. Dan threw the card out, realizing that undercover officers probably weren't bound to tell the truth.

Standing on the street corner, Dan never thought about all the tourist attractions in Los Angeles that he had never seen. He had never been to Disneyland, Universal Studios, or even the Farmer's Market, which was only five blocks away from his corner. Unlike the vast majority of out-of-towners who came to Los Angeles, Dan did not come to see the sights. He came to hustle.

Dan had been sitting on the bus bench in his brown cowboy hat for two hours, so he was thankful when his first customer circled the block twice and then stopped farther down on the Boulevard. Dan had made eye contact with the long-haired driver. Dan got up and slowly walked to the brown van. He looked inside. When the driver again made eye contact, Dan opened the unlocked door and easily swung himself inside, saying, "Howdy," to the driver.

Without answering, the driver looked into his sideview mirror and pulled away from the curb and into traffic. Dan heard a noise coming from behind the closed curtain that was to the rear of his seat. As Dan turned to look behind him, something crashed into the back of his head. As blood immediately poured out from the fresh cut on the back of his head, the force from the blow sent Dan's upper body forward. Dan didn't feel any pain as his face smashed into the dashboard, breaking his nose and making two of his front teeth cut through his upper lip. The force from the blow to the back of his head had mercifully rendered him unconscious. Later, Dan would wish he could have stayed that way.

My Friend Charlie

Charlie Corcoran had been a rotten child. At his nicest, he was uncontrollable and incorrigible. Having no father in the home didn't help, and Charlie's mother, who bore him when she was sixteen, soon gave him to his grandmother to raise.

Though Charlie's grandmother tried dearly to give him the love she thought every child should have, Charlie reminded her too much of his father, who had been the town bully and had eventually gotten himself thrown in jail after beating one girlfriend too severely. And Grandma couldn't understand Charlie's mean streak. Even as a baby, Charlie used to love pulling on cats' tails and hurting the little chickens and ducks all the kids got for Easter.

By the time Charlie had entered his tenth year of life, he got his thrills from setting off firecrackers in the mouths of lizards and frogs. He would light the explosive, then stand back and watch as the squirming animal was blown to pieces.

It was no surprise to the neighbors that when Charlie was fifteen he beat his dear old grandma because she wouldn't give him money for the movies. And by the time Charlie was sixteen and had been kicked out of every school his grandma had put him into, he had already spent a year in juvenile hall, if you added up all the twenty-five separate occasions he had been sent there.

But Charlie did have some good qualities. And one of them was his leadership ability. Despite what some sociologists argue is a learned trait, Charlie was a born leader. And the only qualification that his followers needed was to be less intelligent than he was. And while Charlie wasn't educated (he couldn't even read at a third-grade level), he was street-smart. And despite his reading disability, he always carried a copy of *Helter Skelter* with him wherever he went. For one thing Charlie did have was a hero: Charlie Manson. His namesake.

* * *

Charlie had been on the street since the time he beat his grandma. Charlie spent ten years on the streets in his home state of Ohio. Most of the time, Charlie dealt in drugs or stolen property. He was known to all the police departments as a small-time thief who occasionally led high school kids in daytime residential burglaries.

Prior to coming to California (or, more correctly, fleeing to California), Charlie had begun a legitimate job in construction work. It didn't require much brainpower, and he could use his well-developed muscles to get the job done that the boss pointed out to him. Soon after, Charlie began freelancing, placing an ad in the local paper and doing small household repairs. Without a boss looking over his shoulder, Charlie digressed back to his nature, smoking pot and stealing from the houses he worked in.

Charlie's first big-time crime was when an older lady hired him to put up some shelving in her bedroom. Charlie couldn't stand the way she kept nagging him. And, to make it worse, she reminded him of his grandma. The only time she left him alone was for the brief period she went to the store.

Unfortunately for her, she returned too quickly and too quietly, and caught Charlie going through her dresser drawers and helping himself to some of her jewelry. Charlie didn't plan on going to jail and he didn't want to leave an eyewitness around, so he beat the older lady with his hammer. The claw side.

Seeing the old lady struggling, with blood pouring from her head as her struggles lessened, Charlie felt kind of stimulated. It also made him feel powerful, in control. It was even *godlike*, because he could decide whether this woman lived or died. And his choice was obvious.

Once the old lady was dead, Charlie helped himself to the rest of her jewelry, which he would pawn on his way, and also went through her purse. While looking for her car keys, he came across a small .25-caliber automatic. *The old bitch never had a chance to use it*, he thought.

Charlie then took the old woman's car and headed for California. For the first time, he was armed.

Soon after arriving in Los Angeles, he headed toward the downtown bus terminal.

All the would-be criminals in every major city hang around the bus terminals. Young black men stand around the terminal trying to convince the young girls who arrive that they could make money being prostitutes for them. Young white boys stand around waiting for the opportunity to find the luggage of an unwary traveler (preferably Japanese, since they carried large amounts of cash and new cameras) before it was lost. Men of all ages and colors surround the terminal selling a wide variety of drugs, apparently immune to police intervention.

This was where Charlie met Lisa, who had run away from her parents in Nebraska. Charlie dumped the stolen car and, together with Lisa, rode to the terminal in Hollywood, where Charlie planned to pimp Lisa so that he could get enough money to get a hotel room. Charlie never wiped his prints off the stolen car. Though LAPD doesn't

29

bother taking prints from the over one thousand stolen cars they re-cover each month, this one had been involved in a homicide, and prints were taken. The prints matched up with those taken during Charlie's teenage prison stint and his earlier escapades, and a "want" was en-tered into the system, stating that Charlie was wanted for murder, was probably armed, should be considered dangerous, and was believed to be in the L.A. area. Charlie didn't know or care though, since he never carried any identification and didn't plan on using his real name again.

Most of the time, Charlie found, police officers just took down the name you gave them and checked it in their system and then let you go. They never even realized that it was a fake name, except some of the older cops, who always wanted to take you in for prints.

After hooking Lisa and making enough to get a room and get high, Charlie made friends with some of the guys down at Oki Dogs in West Hollywood, on the Boulevard. The guys knew where to score pot and speed. And even some black beauties for when he wanted to sleep.

Charlie began hanging around a Puerto Rican street hustler named JoJo. JoJo was as slimy as they came, doing anything for money. Unlike many of the hustlers, who view themselves as "straight" because they only sleep with men for money and only accept the "top" position (the "enterer" in anal intercourse), JoJo didn't care, as long as he got paid for it. And when he was desperate to get his speed "rush," he would do it for five dollars. More than once, in fact, JoJo had gotten himself out of an arrest by giving the Los Angeles County deputies some good information and selling out a friend. *Hey, whatever it takes to stay alive on the streets. The fastest cat wins, you know.* And JoJo wasn't about to go to jail, where he couldn't get his speed.

Charlie eventually worked out a plan where JoJo took a desk job at one of the Sunset Boulevard whore hotels. These hotels, abundant in Hollywood, charged by the hour instead of the night. Most were owned by Koreans, many of whom let the whores use the rooms in return for a part of the take. And if their wives weren't around, they'd let the black whores have the rooms for free in return for a blow job. There were no black women in Korea, after all.

Charlie's half brother, Cameron, from his mother's remarriage, came out to Los Angeles to stay with Charlie. As per the plan, one night when JoJo was working the desk, Charlie came in with Cameron, who had taken the bus out the week before, and "robbed" JoJo of all the money in the desk. When the police arrived, JoJo explained that he couldn't describe the robbers, because they had been wearing ski masks.

Since their plan was so successful, two weeks later they repeated the procedure. But the LAPD detectives assigned the case weren't as believing of JoJo's story as they had been the first time. With JoJo's record, they figured that he was part of the crime.

JoJo, of course, solved his worries by getting high. While he was wasted, he complained to Charlie about his fear that the detectives were onto him. Charlie knew JoJo couldn't last through the pressure and that he would probably talk.

Charlie figured that they had found out about his murdering the old lady in Ohio a long time ago. So if JoJo pointed the finger at him for the robbery, he would probably have to go to Ohio to stand trial for murder. And Charlie wasn't about to let that happen.

Unfortunately, the LAPD detectives were persistent, and picked JoJo up one night and took him to the Hollywood station. JoJo was later released and came back to Charlie's motel, getting high and telling Charlie that he had had no choice but to tell the truth: that he had been forced to go along with the robbery by Charlie and Cameron.

Charlie became furious and immediately abandoned his motel room with Cameron and Lisa. They left minutes before the police arrived to pick them up.

"That two-timin', mother-fuckin', no-good faggot!" screamed Charlie, as he drove to another fleabag motel in a Chevy van that he had stolen and changed the license plates on. Charlie had taken the new license plates from another Chevy van that was in a junkyard.

On the way downtown, Charlie stopped and bought some maps at a gas station. One of the maps was of Lancaster. The next night, Charlie parked outside the motel where JoJo was working. As JoJo left the motel, Charlie walked up to him and said, "No hard feelin's, huh?" Charlie offered to pay for JoJo's speed fix. JoJo wasn't one to turn down this token of generosity.

As they drove to Lancaster, JoJo got high in the back with Cameron and Lisa. It took Charlie into early the next morning until he located the area of the abandoned mines. Making sure the shotgun was still in front of the passenger seat, Charlie parked and got into the back of the van.

Lisa had passed out. Cameron and JoJo were still blazing on their high from the speed, talking a mile a minute and eating Twinkies, Ding-Dongs, and Hostess cupcakes that they had bought from an all-night AM/PM Minimart.

Charlie, his eyes blazing with fury but his voice controlled, sat down beside JoJo and put his arm around him. Even through his haze, JoJo detected some of the menace in Charlie's eyes.

"Hey, man, you're not mad at me about talking to the detectives or anything, are you?" asked JoJo nervously.

"No, man. It's cool. Hey, they didn't get us, did they?" answered Charlie. But his eyes never changed expression.

Charlie pulled his arm a little tighter around JoJo's neck. "I'm just always horny in the morning, you know. And I figure since you give blowjobs to guys, you know . . ." Charlie left the sentence unfinished.

JoJo didn't want to anger his friend, who he knew was a psycho. He squirmed slightly. "Hey, I only do that for money, man. You know how it is. I don't like it, you know. Hey, we can wake up Lisa. Man, I'm sure she wants to get laid and all."

Charlie tightened his grip even more. Cameron sat across from the both of them on the opposite tire hub, trying to figure out what was going on. He had popped a black beauty about an hour before and everything was hazy and slowing down like a 45 rpm record on 33.

Charlie undid his zipper with his free right hand. "Why don't you just show me what you do for all those guys on the Boulevard?"

JoJo knew that Charlie never hustled. So he knew that Charlie was straight. During the nights JoJo had stayed with the group, Charlie always screwed Lisa. "Hey, man. You know I'd do anything for you. But you wouldn't want me to do that."

"You think I'm dirty or something?" asked Charlie, looking at JoJo accusingly. "Just get down and suck me off."

JoJo was really scared. "OK, no problem, man." JoJo got down on his knees and leaned forward as Charlie pulled his limp penis out from his pants. JoJo put the penis in his mouth and began sucking back and forth.

Charlie leaned his head back against the van wall and closed his eyes. "Yeah, man, that's it. Oh, yeah. You know how to give head. Suck it off." Charlie felt himself starting to get hard. He smiled to himself as he began to urinate.

"What the fuck!" JoJo jumped back, spitting repeatedly onto the floor of the van. "Man, you peed in my mouth." He spit over and over onto the van floor.

Charlie looked evilly at JoJo. "Man, finish sucking me off."

JoJo looked at Charlie. "No way. Man, you just peed in my mouth. That was disgusting! I can't believe—"

Before JoJo could finish his sentence, Charlie grabbed him around the neck with both hands. Charlie pulled him down onto his knees and leaned close to his face.

"Suck me, you motherfucking faggot," whispered Charlie.

JoJo began shaking with fear as he leaned forward and again began orally copulating the big man. Charlie stood almost six feet tall, and his body had developed powerfully due to his life on the street and his construction work. Though he had a slight beer belly, he was still powerful and outweighed the thin speed freak by at least fifty pounds.

Charlie stood in the back of the van as JoJo, on his knees, continued to suck him off. After a few minutes, Charlie moaned. JoJo took his mouth off Charlie's penis and leaned his head to the side, continuing to stroke Charlie with his right hand as Charlie shot his wad.

"Oh, yeah. That was hot, man." Charlie smiled as he buttoned up his pants. "Now let me do it to you."

"What do you mean? No, that's OK, Charlie. Man, it was just a favor. No sweat. Listen, what are we doing here, anyway?" asked JoJo. He was beginning to get nervous because of Charlie's behavior.

Charlie ignored his question. "Pull down your pants. I want to see your dick."

"Hey, that's OK."

Charlie suddenly reached forward with his powerful hands and grabbed JoJo by the neck. Cameron slid so that he was seated behind the driver's seat.

"Hey, no sweat," JoJo gasped, as he undid his pants.

"Take them all the way down," ordered Charlie.

JoJo lowered them all the way to his knees. His small penis was hidden among a bush of dark black pubic hair. "See, man, that's OK; you don't need to do it," pleaded JoJo.

Charlie glared at him. "But I *want* to do it." Charlie slowly lowered himself onto his knees. With his left hand, he grasped JoJo's penis and gently pulled it forward. His right hand, hidden by his green army jacket, went into his rear pants pocket.

No way, thought Cameron. *Charlie wouldn't give no guy a blowjob. I can't believe this. What's Charlie up to?*

Cameron's question was soon answered. As Charlie leaned his face forward toward JoJo, gently pulling the Puerto Rican's penis taut, he suddenly pulled his right hand out of his pants pocket and brought the straight razor up, slicing the penis in half. As Charlie fell back to avoid the spurting blood, JoJo looked down in disbelief. He quietly moaned, "No. Oh no. No." He then fell to his knees, screaming at the top of his lungs as spurts of blood pumped out of his sliced penis.

Cameron's eyes were wide in horror as Charlie attempted to slice JoJo's throat with the razor. But JoJo was thrashing around, screaming, and Charlie just wound up cutting JoJo on the face and head. This only enraged Charlie more, since blood was getting on his army coat.

"You fucking back-stabbing piece-of-shit snitch," Charlie yelled as he stood up and began stomping JoJo's head with his army boots. Within seconds, JoJo was silent, lying on the floor twitching, with blood seeping from his ears and what was left of his manhood.

Charlie wiped off his straight razor on JoJo's pullover sweater and put it back in his pants pocket. He looked around the van. Lisa was still sleeping soundly. He yelled to Cameron as he pulled JoJo's pants completely off.

"Hey, come on and help me get this heap of shit out of the van. And we got to use this motherfucker's clothes to wipe up all this blood."

Cameron, in shocked silence, helped Charlie strip JoJo's body and then carry it out the rear doors of the van. Charlie looked about and ensured that there was no one around. They then carried the body to a nearby mine shaft and threw it inside.

After wiping up the blood from the van with pieces of JoJo's clothing and tossing them down the shaft, Charlie made Cameron wait outside while he fucked Lisa. Then they drove back to West Hollywood. Across the street and down from Oki Dogs was a self-scrub car wash. Lisa waited outside while Cameron and Charlie washed out the last of JoJo's blood. And a piece of his penis.

Charlie was still furious at the street hustler for turning him in. And after two days of fuming, he decided to get even with the faggot and do the world a favor at the same time. He was going to rid Santa Monica Boulevard of the vermin that infested it. He was going to personally do what the LAPD and sheriff's vice squads couldn't do. He was going to eliminate every fag hustler working the street.

Hollywood

The punch came speeding toward Steve's face. A fraction before it connected, Steve ducked and deflected the punch with his left hand. Simultaneously Steve threw a powerful sidekick to his attacker's mid-section. The opponent stepped back, bringing both his hands down on top of Steve's right foot, crossing his arms at the wrist. But before the opponent could grab ahold of his foot, Steve quickly pulled his foot back. At the same instant, Steve jumped in the air and landed a round-house kick lightly to the side of his opponent's head. His opponent stepped back, dizzy from the blow, as the black belt instructor maneuvered between the combatants yelling, *"Barro!"* Steve walked backward away from the center, still keeping his eyes on the other brown belt he was fighting.

In karate, those with brown belts had to be watched closely. Unlike white belts, who were dangerous because they hadn't learned how to control their power, brown belts were dangerous because they had learned the skill. But because they were still one step below black belt, brown belts felt that they had something to prove. So they fought harder.

The other students sat around the mat, watching as Steve and Yesar, the other brown belt, fought. The Hapkido studio, located in Santa Monica, was small but provided enough room for the entire class to be trained.

Steve had sought out a style to take after graduating from college, where he had trained in Kung Fu San Soo. Los Angeles was famous for its hundreds of studios. Many were run by well-known masters; even more were fly-by-night operations that changed locations every year.

Steve had visited twenty-five studios before choosing the Hapkido studio in Santa Monica. This studio was supervised by Master Hyl Yon Kim, a ninth-degree black belt who had trained in Korea. Master Kim had trained under the grandmaster in Hapkido and had then gone to train with the Korean monks in the mountains before coming to America.

One of the legends that passed down among the students concerned Master Lee, another of the Hapkido practitioners who had studied with Master Kim in Korea. Master Lee, who had trained for less time than Master Kim, had come to America first. At that time, America was in the midst of its martial arts boom, with Bruce Lee being the favorite star and David Carradine having his own "Kung Fu" series on television.

Wanting to impress and gain students, Master Lee painted the front glass window of his studio with large black letters advertising himself as a ninth-degree black belt, though he actually held a sixth-degree rank.

Soon after, Master Kim, the senior master, came over from Korea. He was only a seventh-degree black belt at the time. When he saw that Master Lee had promoted himself as a ninth-degree black belt, he entered the studio and told Master Lee that it *would* be changed by the following day. It was.

Shortly after opening his first studio, Master Kim was invited to put on an exhibition. Present in the audience was an actor, Bill Conklin. Conklin was so impressed that he trained with Master Kim for six months and worked with him on a movie. In the movie, Master Kim did all of the kicking scenes. Their movie was a tremendous success, and Conklin wrote a part for Kim in the sequel.

Steve had found that most of the other studios in Los Angeles were run by American teachers, and the students were not very disciplined. With the formality associated with the martial arts in foreign countries, it was only those studios with true masters that conducted classes in a serious manner.

Hapkido means "the way of coordinated power." Though each teacher of Hapkido has been taught differently, under those who trained with the grandmaster, Hapkido is a fighting art and has no forms, or katas. Only in Hapkido does every kick start from the same movement, so that there is no telegraphing of the *karateka*'s attack.

Hapkido is perfectly balanced between hands and feet. The hands operate in a soft style, redirecting an opponent's force against him. The hand techniques are identical with those of Aikido, using joint locks and throws. The kicks are similar to Tae Kwon Do, but are more polished. In Tae Kwon Do everything is done to develop force and power. In Hapkido, the two principles are stretching and technique.

Also unlike Tae Kwon Do, all the kicks in Hapkido are aimed at the head. It is believed that if you can strike the highest point of your opponent, anything lower is easy. The reverse is not true.

Because Master Kim oversaw every class, Steve found that the rules of the studio were obeyed and the class was run very respectfully and formally. There was none of the horseplay that had been prevalent in the classes at the other studios Steve had visited.

Steve was also impressed by the first rule posted inside the Hapkido studio: "You are never to ridicule another martial art." Prior to Hapkido, Steve had taken classes and received his lower belts in Kung

Fu, Shotokan karate, Shorin (an Okinawan style), and judo. He appreciated the respect shown these other arts.

After two years of rigorous training, Steve had received his brown belt. Every day before going to the gym to lift weights, Steve went to Hapkido class. Whenever he could, Steve attended the afternoon class, to train with a black belt who had prior training in Jujitsu and was an excellent teacher in hand techniques, particularly with joint locks and pressure points. At night, Steve would attend class to develop his kicks.

It took approximately three months of hard work to promote to the next highest belt. The order was: white, yellow, green, blue, brown, and then black. In between each color were two tests, allowing the successful tester to add a stripe to his or her belt. Steve was currently testing for his first brown belt stripe. Having already completed the techniques, he had to spar someone at his same belt level to demonstrate that he could use his new techniques in a fighting situation.

To prepare for the match, both Steve and his opponent donned protective gear: a cup covered the groin, a protector was in the mouth, and there was padding on the hands and feet. The punches and kicks would be pulled on impact, but the power would still be felt.

As Mr. Hisky, the black belt, walked between the two, he raised his right hand. He brought it down quickly yelling, "*Anjo!*" Steve and his opponent were to spar some more.

Master Kim and two other black belts, Mr. Veluz and Mr. Plumber, watched from behind a wooden table placed on the matted floor. Veluz and Plumber periodically wrote notes on the testing papers regarding the style and techniques of the two contestants.

As the two opponents neared each other, Steve quickly somersaulted toward his opponent, throwing a sidekick from the ground. His opponent backed off and then charged toward Steve as Steve quickly jumped up. Steve spun, only partially deflecting the roundhouse kick that struck his unprotected rib cage. Steve knew he would be sore there tomorrow.

Without thinking, and with his body reacting, Steve continued his spin, keeping his body low to the ground. Since his opponent had kicked him, that meant only one leg could be used for support. Steve swept out the opponent's foot, quickly rolling away as his opponent slapped the ground with both of his arms to absorb some of the impact of his fall.

Steve jumped up, as did his adversary. They appeared equally matched, which meant that the one with the most brains would win. Or the one who used deception.

Steve had studied his opponent, and though there were some openings, the opponent was very fast to cover them.

Steve had studied the bible of the martial arts, Musashi's *Book of Five Rings*. "Sankai No Kawari To Iu Koto" was the "mountain and sea change." This referred to it being bad to repeat the same tactic. To do so more than twice was unforgivable. Yet this was exactly what Steve planned to do.

As he and his opponent circled, Steve did a double roundhouse kick at lightning speed, first feinting to the knee, then aiming at the head. The opponent quickly moved out of range. Steve followed quickly with a ridgehand toward his opponent's head and then a left-handed punch to the midsection.

Steve did this same combination a second time.

As expected, when Steve started this same combination a third time, his adversary quickly entered within close range, blocking Steve's roundhouse kick and aiming toward Steve's head with a backfist. Seeming to melt around his opponent, as is the "water principle" of Hapkido, Steve quickly changed his ridgehand into a backfist, coming in the opposite direction toward the unprotected right side of his opponent's head. Steve's right arm blocked the backfist that had been aimed for his head and struck his opponent a blow, sending him staggering backward.

As the other brown belt staggered backward, Steve leapt quickly into the air, landing a powerful jumping sidekick into his opponent's unprotected midsection.

The students sitting around the edge of the mat jumped up to catch the falling brown belt.

Mr. Hisky quickly stepped between the two fighters, yelling, "*Barro!*" and instructing them to prepare to bow toward each other. The instructors had seen enough. Out of the corner of his eye, Steve saw Master Kim nod his approval. Both Steve and Yesar turned and adjusted their karate *gi* and belts, and then turned to face each other, with Mr. Hisky standing in the center.

"*Chirriup!*" They stood at attention. "*Kunyee.*" They bowed to each other. They then turned to face Mr. Hisky, as he said, "*Chirriup! Kunyee.*" They then bowed to him. Both Yesar and Steve turned toward the black belts at the table and repeated the procedure.

They would not find out the results of their promotional test for at least one week. In the meantime, Steve had to hurry and change to get in his two hours of weightlifting at the Holiday Health Spa in West Los Angeles.

Steve had studied Arnold Schwarzenegger's book on weightlifting and followed Arnold's principles. Steve did three sets of between eight and twelve repetitions, at the highest weight he could lift. He did this on each machine he used. And Steve used four machines for each body part he worked on. In keeping with his martial arts training, Steve developed a design of "balanced isolation."

Steve had quickly decided that circuit training wasn't for him.

He did no exercise that worked more than one body part. He isolated that muscle and exhausted it before going on to the next muscle. And he worked the top, bottom, and middle of each muscle, so that the muscle was toned and equally developed. He periodically changed his workout to surprise his muscles, thereby stimulating muscle development. And his "balanced isolation" had him work both sides of each muscle group.

Steve worked calves, thighs, chest, lats (back), biceps, and triceps. At the gym, Steve soon discovered that many of the enormous black bodybuilders that he worked out with never worked on their lower bodies. Between their naturally limited body fat and their steroid treatments, these blacks would have enormously large arms and upper bodies. But as soon as they took off their three pairs of sweatpants, they would have thin legs. Steve found it hard to believe that they could support their amazingly large upper bodies on those thin little legs.

Most cops only worked on their chest and biceps and neglected their other body parts. Periodically Steve would lift weights at the police academy gymnasium. True to form, in keeping with the macho tradition, Steve would invariably see young cops assigned to Metro, the LAPD tactical unit, standing around competing to see who could bench-press the most weight.

What bullshit. From his readings, Steve had learned that the triceps muscle, at the back of the arm, covered two-thirds of the upper arm. Yet all those cops spent their time trying to enlarge their arms by working on their biceps, which was only one-third of the upper arm.

During the first semester at college, Steve had begun to realize that his sexual attractions might be more than a phase he was going through. If this were true, Steve conjectured, then he had better start lifting weights so his body wouldn't match the conception that most people had of "fairies."

When Steve returned home and was living with his mother, he set up the garage as a gym and bought equipment so he could lift weights and practice karate. His mother had heatedly objected to his working out, insisting that it was bad for him. Steve had tried to get his overweight younger brother to eat less of the pastries his mother bought and join him in working out. While his mother had had to put up with one son staying healthy, she had set her foot down when it came to her baby boy. If Steve continued to pester his brother to exercise, he would have to move out. Steve stopped his coaxing, and his brother gained weight.

Much to his mother's chagrin, when the younger son moved out of her home after graduating from law school, he became a marathon runner. To add insult to injury, Steve convinced his brother to drop out of the enterprising and wealthy field of business law and become a low-paid district attorney in Los Angeles.

After his workout, Steve would go hurriedly home to his one-bedroom Santa Monica apartment to shower and change for his 11:00 P.M. to 8:00 A.M. shift at Hollywood Station.

Steve had overheard West Los Angeles Vice officers joking about the sexual activity in the showers and steam rooms at the spa. And Steve was aware that West L.A. Vice used young undercover officers wearing bathing suits under their towels so as to appear as if they were naked.

The young officers would loiter in the sauna and steam room at the spa, appearing to play with themselves. They would then arrest anyone who assumed the semblance of engaging in the same behavior.

Steve had heard these officers joke that more than one wife was shocked to get a call from Vice. The officers would ask the stunned wife to come bail her husband out, because he had been beating off in the steam room with another man.

* * *

Los Angeles Police officers had two theories on the design of their stations. The first theory was that the Army Corps of Engineers built the stations modeling them after an army bunker. The second theory was that the police department management told the designers to be functional and ignore any human factor, since the buildings were only for police officers, who weren't that human anyway. Regardless of which theory was correct, the majority of the eighteen geographical police stations in the city were identical. And the best thing that could be said about them was that they were functional.

Most of the remaining stations were built in the 1970s. Central Station, nicknamed The Fort, epitomized the lack of any aesthetic value. But because most of the stations were virtually identical, when officers transferred they had no problem locating any of the offices. Hollywood Station was no exception.

Cainen parked his car in the side parking lot. The only security for the officers' personal cars was the constant presence of returning black-and-white police cars. In fact, many officers had had their cars burglarized while they were out protecting the streets of Los Angeles. Because of this, Cainen set his car alarm. He then used his police "999" key to open the rear door of the station.

Cainen was dressed in his "Metro tuxedo." This was the nickname given to the blue jeans and clean white T-shirts that officers wore before and after work. The Metropolitan Division was the supposedly elite unit of the LAPD that handled serious crime problems throughout the city by taking over that area as if martial law existed. The officers of Metro, who spent their off-duty time lifting weights or getting laid, could be seen from miles around getting off or going to work. It looked as if it were a manufacturer's test for Fruit of the Loom. The only other additions to the police wardrobe were cowboy boots or a dark blue windbreaker to hide a gun.

Cainen walked down the hallway and up the stairs to the locker room. He still had fifteen minutes to change before roll call for morning watch. His loan to Vice had only been for two weeks this time. Now that it was over, Cainen had to get back into the swing of patrol. As he walked down the aisle toward his row, he saw Billy Kidd putting on his Sam Browne belt with the breakfront holster. Cainen nodded hello, but Billy just snickered and looked away.

Cainen checked the extra-large key ring for his locker key. Watching his feet to make sure he didn't step on any officer's boots set under the bench, Steve walked to his locker. When Cainen looked up, he realized why Billy had been snickering. There, glued to the front of his locker, was a picture of Rock Hudson. And it wasn't a picture from *Pillow Talk*. The picture showed a decrepit Rock, suffering from AIDS. One of the officers had written on it: "Hope the same happens to you!"

Cainen heard footsteps. He looked to the end of the row. John Canus from night watch and Tommy Champion from mornings were at the end of the row looking for his reaction. Cainen wondered whether they had placed the picture or if they had heard about it and would report back to the artist who had glued it on. Not that Cainen really cared. He had learned long ago to keep his mouth shut about the harassment, or it would get worse.

John and Tommy walked away, scoffing.

Cainen remembered talking with Dave Jinkens, a sergeant friend of his. Back last year, when the harassment first started, Jinkens had told him, "Steve, just ignore it and it'll go away. If policemen know they're getting to you, they'll just keep digging. Ignore it and they'll start up on someone else who steps on his meat."

At the time, it had sounded like sage advice. Unfortunately, the officers had never given up nor found anyone more deserving of their attentions.

Cainen unlocked his locker and dressed in his uniform. He had two stripes on his arm, which designated him as an FTO. He had tested for the position directly off probation and had been the youngest officer to be promoted.

Cainen had spent one year in the 77th Street Division, the biggest gang, coke, and homicide area of the city, before transferring to Hollywood. It had been fun to train probationary police officers in the safety tactics needed for that type of environment. But then the rumors had started and Cainen figured it was time to move.

Cainen walked to the mirror and adjusted his gig line so that his belt, pants, and shirt openings all lined up. He looked at the clock above the mirror. Two minutes to eleven. Cainen walked to the roll call room.

The joking immediately ceased when he walked into the room. Not the talking, just the joking. Cainen noticed the officers whispering to their partners for the night and to the new officers on the watch. The new officers and the others turned to look at him before whispering back. Cainen walked halfway down the center of the room, between the rows of tables. He went to a seat at the far end of a row, turning the chair so that his back was angled toward the wall.

No matter which division you went to, the officers all sat in the same pecking order. The probationary officers were in the first row. The new police officers just off probation sat after them. New training officers or officers with less than five years on the department sat next. Smart-asses who wanted to heckle the watch commanders sat on the inside ends of the rows. In the back, the old-timers sat, even if the most seasoned officers on the watch only had seven years on. Tenured police officer-2s, who had no stripes on their arm because they didn't or couldn't promote, sat wherever they wanted. These P-2s generally sat between the middle and last rows.

Within one minute of the clock showing 11:00, Lieutenant Wilder, Sergeant Cochran, and Sergeant Newman walked in. The sergeants carried the folders with the kickbacked reports and tickets that the officers had made some mistake on the previous day. The lieutenant carried the "Rotator," the blue notebook that had all the most current material to be read to the officers in roll call.

42

The lieutenant took his seat on the raised platform and pulled his assignment log out of the notebook. "Champion and Willespie, A3. Thompson and Childers, A49. Gillulie and Kidd, A63. Marshall and Phillips, you're the hill car. Sanchez, you're the report car again." The officers said, "Here," after their names were called.

The lieutenant had finished his assignments without calling Cainen's name.

"Sir," Cainen said.

The lieutenant squinted at Cainen as the sergeants continued to pass out the kickbacks.

"Oh, Cainen. You're working alone. L57. Welcome back to A.M.'s."

Champion and Kidd guffawed, obviously thinking of the warm reception their picture had made for Cainen. It was obvious from the lieutenant's less than receptive welcome that he didn't like the idea of having a faggot on The Job either.

When roll call ended, the probationers rushed down to get the equipment for their cars, including radios, shotguns, and Tasers, LAPD's stun gun with fifteen-foot-long wired darts. The other officers slowly sauntered down.

Marshall, who had seventeen years on The Job, with ten of them at Hollywood, grabbed a radio from one of the probationers.

"A.M.'s are down. Come on home," Marshall announced to the ending watch. Within seconds, patrol cars were squealing into the lot. The P.M. officers hastily logged their ending mileage on their Daily Field Activity Reports and turned over their cars to the A.M. watch officers. The probationers quickly checked under the rear seats of the turned-in cars to make sure no suspects had stuffed guns or narcotics between the cushions.

Cainen walked out looking for the car with his assigned shop number on the side, 88-029. After waiting for some moments, Cainen picked up the police radio and waited for the frequency to clear before he asked the RTO dispatcher the status of the P.M. unit assigned the car.

"L57. What's the status of Adam 45 P.M.'s?"

After a pause the dispatcher answered back, "L57 mornings, Adam 45 shows out to the station."

"L57, roger. Thank you," Cainen responded. Carrying his equipment, he walked back to the rear door of Hollywood Station and went to the report writing room. The officers who were booking suspects or completing reports would be either there or at one of the desks back in the detective division. The detectives worked business hours, and patrol officers often used their desks at night to write reports. Or to eat on.

When the detectives came into work in the morning, they would invariably go to the on-duty watch commander and rant and rave about the mess left on their desks. They often brought papers with ketchup and coffee stains up to the watch commander. Being detectives, they thought that physical evidence would make the best case.

The end result would be a note in the "Rotator" telling the officers that they were welcome to use the detective unit for reports, but not to eat on the desks. The officers would still eat there, as they wrote their reports, but for two weeks they would get paper towels from the bathroom to put under the food. Those officers that had been on prior loans to detectives would even go so far as to clean up their spills.

But by the end of two weeks, the officers would go back to eating on the desks without paper towels, and the process would begin again.

Cainen located the officers from A45 P.M.'s sitting in the detectives' office, with the probationer writing an arrest report while his FTO sat with his feet on the desk. Cainen noticed that the FTO was leaning back and eating a bag of chips from the machine in the snack room upstairs. It looked to Cainen as if most of the chips had wound up on the FTO's open shirt and hanging tie.

"Do you guys still need the car?" Cainen asked Berranca, the FTO.

Berranca stared at Cainen for a moment without answering. Even Millendez, the probationer, looked up from his attempts at writing the report to see why his training officer wasn't answering.

Berranca finished chewing his chips. "You need the car?"

Shop 029 was a 1988 Chevy, which drove a hell of a lot better than the powerless LTD Crown Victorias. "Yeah. If you guys don't need it, I'd like to take it out." If it had been a Ford, Cainen wouldn't have bothered but just gone to the kit room and checked out a different car.

Berranca turned to his probationer. "Eddie. Go clean our stuff out of the car and give the keys to Cainen. Don't forget to write down the ending mileage."

Millendez finished making his umpteenth erasure on the report, then stood up and took his car keys off the desk. "Yes, sir." He then walked out of Detectives, toward the rear lot where the car was parked. Cainen followed him.

As they exited the room, Berranca tossed the empty bag of chips at the nearest green metal wastebasket, missing it by less than an inch. He watched Cainen reach the end of the hall and turn toward the rear door. Berranca spoke softly, but with vehemence: "Fucking faggot."

The first and primary procedure taken as soon as an officer comes on duty is to take a coffee break. That way, if the night turned to shit or the officer got stuck on a homicide scene, at least he'd have had one break that night.

The only unfortunate aspect of this practice was that those officers from the prior watch would "submarine" for the last hour, staying on their last call until the end of watch to avoid having to work overtime. If the officers from the prior watch didn't get a call, they would show themselves "out to the station" to write reports and hide in a far corner of the parking lot so that a sergeant couldn't find them and assign them one of the many calls that had backed up in the last hour of the watch.

Between those officers "submarining" from the prior watch and the new watch officers taking a coffee break before clearing, the city went unprotected for one hour every night, with no officers available to respond to citizens' requests for service.

Cainen believed in the chief's motto of "A full day's work for a full day's pay," feeling that if the citizens were paying his salary, they expected him to be available to assist them.

Cainen didn't take a coffee break so he could handle the backed-up calls, five at a time. Besides, he didn't like the taste of coffee.

Tonight the entire Hollywood A.M. watch of officers, except for Cainen, had a pre-set meeting at Donut Time on Santa Monica and Vine. While Cainen handled calls as an L-car, the other officers' status showed that they were still preparing their cars for patrol. The officers took their free cups of coffee and stood around, leaning against their cars, sipping the burned brew. None of the officers ate "stomach bombs." Most cops never ate doughnuts, except in movies or in letters to the editors criticizing them. But because they had to stay up until the sun reappeared, they constantly made trips through the divisional doughnut shops between their calls to get their free cups of coffee.

The owners of the doughnut shops offered the free brew for exactly that reason: financially it made sense. The free coffee was a minimal cost compared to the amount they lost due to the nightly robberies when the patrol cars weren't around. And the cop cars always came around for the free coffee. Cops would willingly drive to the opposite side of the city for a free cup, rather than have to pay the seventy-five cents at the 7-Eleven down the block from the station.

As soon as Cainen cleared, he was assigned five "415" calls, of "390 groups" of men drinking and making enough noise to disturb their neighbors. The calls were two hours old, and the groups had undoubtedly left. But it was the policy of the department to respond to all citizen calls, regardless of how long they had been holding.

While Cainen quickly drove by each location and cleared the calls, Tommy Champion addressed the A.M. officers at Donut Time.

"I don't think we should have to work with this faggot," Tommy griped. "I mean, what's the Department coming to, hiring fruits and all?"

Gillulie, a five-year female officer who had been at Hollywood since getting off probation, chimed in. "It's the new breed." The other officers laughed. They had laughed at the same remark five years before, when females were first working Hollywood A.M.'s.

"I think we should do something to get rid of the guy," Champion proposed to the facsimile jury of officers.

"Like what?" asked Childers, who wasn't looking forward to an entire night with a dumb-ass like Thompson for a partner.

Billy Kidd put his thumbs into his gun belt. His coffee rested on the hood. "In Vietnam, we used to frag assholes like Cainen. But since we don't have any grenades, I suggest we do the next best thing."

Gillulie snorted derisively. "Like what, shoot him in the back of the head during a 459?" A 459 was a burglary call. Despite the danger, if an alarm was activated and an open door was discovered, the officers would have to search the building for suspects even in total darkness.

"I think it's a good idea," retorted Kidd. He didn't like Jayne Wayne, as Gillulie was referred to behind her back, making fun of him in front of the other guys. Kidd didn't know that he was called John Wayne behind *his* back, because of his gunslinger attitude.

Marshall cleared his throat. Being the senior officer, he was the informal opinion leader of the tightly knit A.M. watch.

"If you try to set someone up, you'll probably only get yourself nailed," Marshall said, referring to Internal Affairs or the divisional complaint investigator initiating a complaint against an officer for misconduct.

"But," Marshall paused for effect, "if we were all tied up with calls, priority calls, nobody could hold us responsible if we couldn't back Cainen up. He just might get himself into a dangerous situation, and we wouldn't be able to help him out."

The other officers nodded their heads in approval at the well thought out scheme.

"Then it's agreed?" asked Kidd.

Before anyone else could respond, Sergeant Newman pulled into the lot in his new Chevy patrol car. He pulled alongside the group and leaned out his rolled-down window.

"I hate to break up the party, boys and girls, but outside divisions are being called in. How about clearing and buying some calls?"

"We were just doing that," answered Marshall.

The officers exchanged looks and everyone except Willespie lifted the lids on their cups and poured out half the coffee before resealing the lid. They then tore a piece out of the lid, so they could drink. This way, none of it would spill if they had to respond somewhere quickly.

When Willespie, a probationary officer, first arrived in Hollywood from the academy, Champion forgot to tell him about this practice. Willespie set his cup on the dashboard while he filled out the daily log. A3 was assigned a hotshot, ADW in progress, a man stabbing a woman with a knife, and Champion quickly whipped a U-turn to respond to the call, which was in the opposite direction. As he did so, Willespie's cup flew off the dash. Because Willespie had removed the lid to drink, the entire steaming contents of his cup landed in his training officer's lap. The thick wool protected Champion from any serious burns, but not before he had let out a yell that was several octaves higher than his usual baritone voice.

Since then, Willespie always threw out his coffee before getting back into the car.

* * *

While the other officers cleared and handled the backlogged calls, Cainen thought to himself. First of all, assigned to an L-car, Cainen didn't have to handle any of the more serious calls. Instead, he handled the most amount of calls, which were calls of disturbing the peace. Cainen was only too happy to handle these calls. He could remain in the security of his car, with his gun hidden behind the door with his finger on the trigger, if he needed to talk with a group of drinkers in order to disperse them.

He was also glad because the majority of the other calls in Hollywood that were supposedly of a serious nature wound up being psychotics. In Central, along skid row, no matter what the call was assigned as, from a lost purse to a kidnapping, it always wound up being a wino that was the real cause of the problem. In 77th, "the ghetto," many of the calls wound up being family disputes. But in Hollywood, regardless of how serious the call started out, it inevitably ended with some psycho talking to himself or explaining something about the relationship of the Earth to neon lights and bells.

Cainen remembered the first time he had been loaned to Hollywood patrol, when they had had their divisional Christmas party. Officers from all the neighboring divisions were loaned to Hollywood and spent most of the night looking at their reporting district maps trying to find the address of the calls (and asking any of the other patrol cars they passed on the way). Cainen had finally given up on his pride and pulled into an ARCO station for directions to Beechwood. En route to the assigned prowler call, Cainen saw the suspect exiting from between two darkened homes. The suspect, a black male carrying an old suitcase, smelled as if he hadn't bathed in months.

Because the man matched the description and was exiting from between two darkened homes in the middle of the night carrying a suitcase that undoubtedly contained stolen property from one of the homes, Cainen called in his location as best he could pinpoint it and proned the suspect out at gunpoint. When a backup unit arrived, Cainen handcuffed the suspect.

Due to recent case law requiring the necessity of a search warrant for containers, Cainen attempted to obtain the suspect's consent to look in the suitcase.

"What's in the suitcase?" Cainen asked the suspect.

"It's just my shit," was the suspect's not too friendly reply.

Cainen always believed in treating people to the highest degree of respect they will allow themselves to be treated with. But this suspect was failing the personality test *fast*.

Cainen tried again. "What's in the suitcase you were carrying?"

"Man, it's just my shit!" The suspect was becoming more hostile.

Cainen considered which approach would most likely get the desired response and chose to play the hard cop.

"Now we can play this easy or hard. I'm going to ask you one more time. You can tell me what I want to know and probably walk free, or I can book you for probable-cause burglary at the station and get a search warrant for the suitcase. Now what's in the suitcase?"

The suspect just looked at Cainen with hard eyes. "Hey, I told you, man, it's just my shit."

The backup officers had searched the two homes and found no signs of forced entry. There was no answer at the one house, but the person who had notified the police lived next door and stated that she had been up watching TV when she heard noises. She looked out her window and saw the suspect come out from behind the house and walk between the two homes.

Until the owner of the second home could be contacted, there was no way to determine if a burglary had taken place.

Cainen had the backup unit transport the suspect and evidence to the station and put him into a holding cell. Cainen continued to search the area, looking for footprints that led to any doors or windows. He didn't have any luck.

At the station, Cainen saw his suspect seated on the bench of the Plexiglas-windowed holding cell. The suspect stared into space. The backup officers had signed the cell sign-in board with a "John Doe." Cainen opened the door of the cell, keeping his gun side away from the suspect.

"What's your name?" Cainen asked.

The suspect replied with his sullen stare. Cainen noticed that the suitcase was against the wall outside the cell.

Cainen tried one more time. "What's inside your suitcase?"

"It's just my shit," the disheveled black man replied.

Cainen stared at the man for a moment. "Can I have your permission to open the suitcase?"

"Man, it's just my shit!" the suspect yelled.

Cainen closed and locked the door of the cell. The suspect stood and leaned forward against the Plexiglas window.

Cainen debated for only a second. He could search the suitcase and take the chance of losing the case for a violation of search and seizure. But if he didn't find any property, he really didn't have enough probable cause to book the suspect into jail.

Cainen lifted up the suitcase and placed it on the stainless-steel writing table, staring at it. The suspect started screaming in his cell, "Man, that's my shit, man!" That helped Cainen decide.

The two officers who had been writing reports in the room had turned to watch him.

"Fuck it," Cainen said to himself. He undid the latch. As the two officers watched, Cainen unzipped the case and lifted up the lid.

Cainen's face slowly turned a bright shade of red. The two officers got up to look. They were the two who had started the legend. The story was still being told to every new officer who came to Hollywood. Undoubtedly, one day this incident would appear in one of Wambaugh's books.

Inside the open suitcase were 100 plastic sandwich bags, neatly closed and folded. In each of the bags was a piece of fecal matter.

The suspect's shit.

Behind Cainen, the suspect continued to yell, "It's just my shit!"

That's why the police officers who worked there had coined the phrase "Hollyweird."

* * *

49

Cainen had only been that embarrassed once before on The Job. Directly following his graduation from the police academy, Cainen had to report to Central Division, where he would spend his probationary year of training.

As soon as he was assigned to Moltz, his eighteen-year-veteran training officer, Moltz handed Cainen a small jar. The jar was the same type used for taking urine samples from DUI drivers and those arrested for being under the influence of drugs.

"With the new mandatory drug testing for probationers, you have to take a sample your first day and turn it in to the watch commander." With that said, Moltz had walked away.

As dutifully as he had been taught to obey orders in the academy, Cainen went into the men's rest room (it was easy to find, since every station was designed the same) and peed into the jar. Cainen then walked into the office of Lieutenant Lopez, the watch commander, and put the small container on his desk. "Here's my urine sample, sir."

Lopez, who had fifteen years on the job and planned on making captain on the next list, turned bright red in anger and glared at Cainen. How dare this punk probationer defile the desk he ate his meals on twice a day!

Neither Cainen nor the lieutenant saw Moltz or the other three A.M. watch officers laughing hysterically in the report writing room across from the windows of the watch commander's office.

Moltz and the others hated promotables like Lopez, and they weren't too fond of *any* Mexican, anyway.

And there was no mandatory urine testing at LAPD.

*   *   *

With Dan in the back unconscious, Charlie drove the brown van north toward Lancaster. Cameron sat in the back with Lisa. Charlie liked to talk with Cameron as he drove. Charlie never bothered talking with Lisa, who was so buzzed from the dope they constantly smoked that she couldn't form an answer anyway. Neither of them needed to watch over Dan. As soon as he came up with his plan, Charlie had gone down to "Thieves Alley" behind the LAPD Central Police Station. There, anything can be bought for a cheap price, even guns. Charlie had bought a stolen drill and some large screws, rings, and bolts. With Cameron's help and Charlie's carpentry experience, they had drilled four holes in the van's floor and installed large bolts with rings attached. Each one of the bolts was in a corner of the back of the van. The three had then gone scrounging behind carpet stores and had found some large scrap pieces to cover the floor.

50

Dan was lying on the carpet, face down, with each arm and leg tied to one of the bolts in each of the four corners.

"You want to know why we'll never get caught," boasted Charlie to Cameron. "Because the cops don't care. They're only too happy to have someone else do the dirty work for them."

Cameron was too frightened to disagree.

"Cops hate these fuckin' faggot hustlers runnin' around Santa Monica Boulevard," explained Charlie. "They're happy to have someone clean up the streets for them."

"I-I-I'm sure you're r-right," Cameron agreed. He would have agreed if Charlie had said that the world was flat.

By the time they reached Lancaster and had pulled into the area of the mines with their lights out, both Charlie and Cameron had smoked out along with Lisa.

Charlie climbed into the back and stood over Dan. Before tying Dan to the four rings, spreadeagle, they had taken his clothes off.

Charlie waited for Cameron to slowly make his way into the back of the van. Lisa watched, though she was so wasted that nothing really registered.

"You know what these hustlers like, don'tcha?" Charlie asked Cameron.

Cameron just shook his head. Dan tried to look back over his shoulder, but his hair was in his eyes.

"They love to take it up their ass," Charlie said. "Don't you, faggot?"

Dan laid his head down on the carpeting that was under him. "Hey, what do you want, man? You can have my money." Dan hadn't begun to plead. Yet.

Charlie kicked Dan brutally in the thigh. "What we want is for you to keep your faggot ass off the street."

Dan had yelled as the kick changed into a charley horse. He didn't like the situation that was developing but wasn't clever enough to talk this psycho asshole into letting him go. He just kept his mouth shut.

"You'd really like to take it up the ass, wouldn't you?" It was the psycho asking. The other wimpy guy wasn't saying anything. He was just rocking from foot to foot.

Charlie turned to Cameron. "Why don't you fuck him?"

Cameron cringed inside. "Uh, naw, that's OK. I'm, uh, not horny or anything."

Charlie glared at Cameron. "You're not a faggot if you fuck this guy. It's only the faggot that *likes* to get fucked. Go on and fuck him."

51

"I-I-I don't want his germs on my dick," Cameron said lamely. He hated how he sometimes stuttered when he got nervous.

Charlie undid his pants and pulled out his penis. He started moving his foreskin back and forth.

"Man, this faggot loves to get fucked. But this faggot has never had a real man. Have you, asshole?" Charlie kicked Dan again.

Dan tried to turn his head around to see what the psycho with the long hair was doing, but he was tied too tightly. "Hey, if you let me go, it ain't no big deal. I can't go to the police or nuthin'. I'll just pretend that it didn't happen."

Charlie laughed evilly as he spit into his hand, rubbing the saliva over his erection. He slowly lay down on top of Dan, pulling apart Dan's cheeks and putting his penis against Dan's rectum.

Though Dan had been hustling for a long time, he had only been fucked twice. Once he had been paid $500 to spend a weekend in Chicago with two businessmen. And once he got $100 to get fucked in a movie. But Dan realized right away that he didn't like anal intercourse performed on him. Air rushed out of his lungs as Charlie's only slightly lubricated member was forced into him.

"Ouch! Ouch! Ouch!" Dan cried as Charlie went back and forth.

Charlie used his hand to smash Dan's face onto the piece of carpet on the van floor. It broke Dan's nose. "Shut the fuck up, you fucking faggot. You can't even act like a man when you're getting fucked!"

Dan bit his lip to keep from yelling. Tears were coming from his eyes faster than the blood pouring from his nose.

Charlie had lowered his voice. "Yeah, you like that. Don't you, you little faggot. You like that, don't you. You like feeling a real man. Come on, faggot, take it all the way. Yeah!"

Dan yelled when Charlie slammed into him hard, obviously ejaculating. Then he felt the weight being lifted off his back.

"You better not have got shit on my dipstick!" the psycho yelled as he stood up. Dan turned to look as the psycho came around into his line of vision. The psycho was buttoning up his pants.

"What are you looking at, you fucking faggot!" Charlie yelled.

Dan never got a chance to answer. Charlie smashed his foot into Dan's face, sending him back into unconsciousness. The last thing Dan heard was the Black Sabbath tape playing loudly from the large boom box behind the driver's seat, beside the girl.

When Dan came to, he was face up. As he slowly gained consciousness, he dreamed that he was on a surfboard. But his nipples were getting sore from rubbing against the surfboard all day. His consciousness flowed in and out with the tide. Dan tried to stand up on the surfboard, but passed out again.

When Dan fully awoke, he realized that he was screaming in pain. His head jerked up, making him feel nauseous. Blood still seeped from his nose and from the side of his head. Dan coughed to open the air passage in his mouth. He couldn't get any air in through his nose.

A face was right above his. The psycho. He was still in the van. A feeling of defeat permeated his mind. Utter hopelessness. And a question: why hadn't he left the streets like his lover had wanted him to?

The psycho was sitting on Dan's stomach, straddling him. He held a needle-nose pliers in his right hand.

"You like having your tits played with, don't you?" asked the psycho.

"He likes it." It was the skinny guy talking.

Where was the girl? Dan tried to look above him. There she was. *Just sitting there, vegging. I wonder what she took*, he thought.

Psycho was putting the pliers on Dan's left nipple again, and squeezing. Hard. Dan screamed in agony again, his body lifting up off the floor, despite the weight of the heavier man on him. The rope burns around his wrists and ankles were bleeding now.

Dan realized that the pliers were closed completely on his nipple. He stopped screaming for the moment and felt faint. Then the psycho smiled an evil grin and pulled. Dan's skin tore as the nipple pulled away from him in the grip of the pliers. Dan fainted and didn't feel anything as Charlie ripped off his right nipple.

Dan had fallen off his surfboard. He was drowning. Why couldn't he climb back on and get above the water so he could get some air?

He woke up.

Psycho had unwound a metal clothes hanger and put it around his neck. He was turning it slowly, tightening it, with the needle-nose pliers. Dan could only whisper, "Please. Pleasssse. I beg you. Don't. Donnnnnn't."

*   *   *

Lisa stirred. Even in her stupor, she realized that there was something evil going on. Something bad. Something she wanted to lose from her mind.

Sometimes when Lisa started to come down from her high, she'd think about things. About her life. About herself. She'd see or hear what was going on around her. And she'd remember her stepfather, who had molested her, and how her mom had blamed her and accused her of seducing her stepfather, though she was only thirteen. And she'd remember all the strange men who had pawed her body. And her black pimp. She had dumped Charlie for a while in Hollywood to be with him. He was the only person who had ever loved her. He had proved it by beating her with a hanger on her legs when she was bad, or burning her inner thighs with a cigarette. But nowhere that would show. You couldn't sell damaged merchandise. And he was so nice when she was good and made him money. And he wanted her to be his woman and have his baby. He only hurt her when she misbehaved or tried to run away. She knew she deserved it.

So Charlie wasn't so bad. Charlie was nice to her. *After all*, she'd think when she started to come down, *I'm only a street whore.* And then she'd realize that she was *only* a street whore. So what if Charlie hurt other people? They probably deserved it.

And then Lisa would quickly get high. Before she started remembering. And feeling.

In the back of the van, Lisa took another Quaalude.

* * *

Charlie smiled as he turned the needle-nose pliers around, making the wire tighter around the hustler's neck.

"Pleasss . . . Don. . . . Plee . . ."

The fucking faggot was begging. It figured.

Dan peed over himself. With a lack of oxygen, his body was convulsing. His mind seemed to be separate from his body. He was raising up. No, not him, but his eyesight. He could look down and see that there was someone sitting on his body. And there was the girl behind the driver's seat, staring into space. And the little guy, looking like he was going to throw up.

Dan felt himself sinking. He could see the surfboard above him. Just a black shadow in the green water. *I wonder why I'm not swimming to the top anymore*, Dan thought. He was just sinking. Under the water.

Where did the music go? Where was the tape player with the Black Sabbath tape?

Dan looked across his shoulder at the tape recorder.

The last thought Dan had before he suffocated was how weird it was that the psycho was recording the murder.

* * *

54

Cameron had to stop twice to throw up as he dragged the body toward a mine shaft. He had to do it alone, because Charlie was fucking Lisa in the back of the van.

Cameron didn't mind. He liked being away from Charlie. He knew that Charlie was crazy, just like he knew that Charlie would kill him if he ever questioned anything Charlie did.

No, it was safer to just go along. You didn't argue with people like Charlie. You probably didn't argue with people like Charlie's idol, either. People like Charlie Manson.

I wonder why Charlie likes that Manson guy so much, Cameron thought when he had finished throwing up the second time. *Maybe this Manson guy can control Charlie? Naw, probably not.* Charlie was beyond control. He had really lost it. Of course, Cameron was smart enough to know not to say these things to Charlie. If not smart enough, then streetwise enough.

Cameron rolled the body into the mine shaft. He stood up to catch his breath. He looked at the van. It was rocking while Charlie pounded it to Lisa.

I wonder if anyone can stop Charlie, Cameron thought to himself.

III

Without Backup

It was toward the end of the shift, when businesses were opening up, that the call came out. Though the location was in Cainen's area, it was a high-priority call and therefore needed to be assigned to a two-officer unit. The call was a "211 silent," an armed robbery alarm from 3105 Sunset Boulevard, Khazian Jewelers.

In California, the second most frequent call at which an officer is killed or seriously injured is a call with possibly armed suspects. A robbery of a jewelry store virtually guaranteed that not only would the suspect be armed, but there would be more than one suspect.

Cainen was driving down Sunset Boulevard in the opposite direction of the call. He had "bought" a "390 group" call and was looking for the drunks when the higher-priority call came out. When no one bought the 211 call, Cainen picked up the microphone. That was his first mistake.

"Six-L-57, I'm in the 2200 block of Sunset now," Cainen advised the dispatcher. "I can respond, but I'm a one-man unit."

The metallic voice of the dispatcher answered, "Six-L-57, roger. Six-L-57 and any unit to back, 211 silent, 3105 Sunset Boulevard, Khazian Jewelers."

"Six-L-57, roger. En route," Cainen said as he waited for a break in traffic and whipped a U-turn in the tight-steering Chevy.

There is a written policy of the LAPD that states that only a two-officer unit, or two L-units, can be assigned a 211 call, due to the danger of the call and the likelihood of coming into contact with armed and dangerous suspects. There is an unwritten rule that at least one additional two-officer unit will back up the assigned unit.

In fact, whenever a 211 alarm call is assigned, one unit advises over the air that they're backing, but the entire division of cars backs up the first unit, driving to the location as fast as possible. The only units that don't respond are those handling equally high-priority calls.

Down in Communications Division, a basement sublevel under the east side of City Hall, the dispatcher looked at her console. The computer screen, like the other twenty-one in the room, showed what each unit in the division was doing and their location.

There were consoles for the eighteen geographical divisions, though the consoles and the radio frequencies were combined, and two divisions were handled by one RTO dispatcher. There was a matching screen beside the RTOs for the assistant ATO, who handled the requests by officers for notifications to be made or victims called. And there were four larger screens at the end of the four two-sided tables, where the senior RTOs oversaw the entire bureau and had the ability to take over in a major incident.

Until 1983, before Communications was automated, the outdated card/conveyor belt system was used by the LAPD. The senior RTO was known as the "Link" and was the only police officer RTO. The Link would monitor all the divisions, and break in whenever a pink card came his way showing an emergency call. He would also break in and take over any pursuits that occurred. But the deep-voiced pursuit broadcaster went the way of *Adam 12,* and now every RTO broadcast his/her own pursuits.

The LAPD Communications Division also became the Emergency Operations Center communications link for the entire city in the event of a major earthquake or other disaster. Underneath twelve feet of solid steel and layers of concrete, the EOC could survive a bomb dropped directly on top of it.

A bullet-proof module in the main entrance is constantly monitored by armed city guards. The door to the level is actually a vault made of solid metal weighing a thousand pounds, with the same locking mechanism that would be found in a bank. A hand grenade would not faze the door or locking system.

Directly outside Communications Division's locked door is the EOC. The conference table and attached offices are for the police chief, the mayor, and the heads of each city department. Any natural disaster could be coordinated from there, with the LAPD's Communications linking the city services. That is, of course, if any of the officers on the outside survived.

Since Los Angeles' big 1974 earthquake, a practice drill has been run each year. The Los Angeles County Sheriff's Department runs their own drill from the bombproof center where their communications division is housed.

Unfortunately for those unlucky enough to be working in the L.A. City Hall at the time of any major earthquake, the freeway system would trap them downtown, forcing them to be self-sufficient and without outside services. All of downtown is surrounded, in four directions, by large freeways: the Hollywood, to the north; the Harbor, to the west; the Santa Monica, to the south; and the Santa Ana, Pomona, and San Bernardino, to the east. The LAPD and the City's General Services Department discovered long ago, and kept it secret, that if the overcrowded, highly populated area of downtown was hit with a major quake during business hours, they would be "shit out of luck" (as the LAPD Research Division put it, when they advised the Central Division officers during a training day). The gigantic broken blocks of concrete would crash down, crushing cars and people, and leave no way for additional fire department units to enter the downtown area to pick up after the damaged (collapsed?) skyscrapers of downtown. So much the worse if a fire or looting broke out.

The existing, and limited, hospitals, police, and fire services already trapped downtown would have to handle it.

None of this went through the RTO's mind as she looked for a clear unit to respond with 6-L-57. To her surprise, though there had been three clear units, now all units showed busy. Even more surprising, they all showed on felony calls, so they couldn't be reassigned. The RTO checked A63, but Gillulie and Kidd had apparently stopped a felony suspect. Of the other two units, one showed on a self-initiated 459 burglary call. The other unit, A3, showed that Champion had just put "felony" in the "DESCRIPTION" line.

Elise was a good RTO. She had three years' experience, and the job had been an upgrade from the secretarial work she had resigned herself to, before being told about the LAPD position. It was more exciting, and she was pretty enough, or had a pretty-enough voice, to get asked out by cops all the time. Her mother had also been very bright, but growing up black at the time she did left her with few options. She had been a maid. She was proud of Elise, working for the city and all. Elise was even considering becoming an officer.

"Any unit to back," Elise tried again, broadcasting the call. Surely one of the units would clear. "Six-L-57 is responding to a 211 alarm at 3105 Sunset."

No one responded. *What the hell's going on here?* Elise wondered. She looked up and looked around to see if any of the other girls (and Bill, but he was gay and they considered him one of the girls) had heard what was going on. But the senior RTO was away from her desk. It figured. That fat bitch was probably down in the snack room raiding the candy machine again.

Usually cars came out of the woodwork to back up one another. Weird. Elise tried another approach. "Six-L-50, 6-L-50, can you back 6-L-57 on a 211 alarm at Khazian Jewelers, 3105 Sunset?"

Elise said the name of the business before the address. At a jewelry store, it was more likely that the call was good and that it was actually being robbed. Same as a bank.

After one minute, 6-L-50, Sergeant Newman, still hadn't responded. This was really weird. What was going on here? Sergeant Newman showed in the field. And he only screwed that other policeman's wife on Wednesday nights. So what was going on?

Elise began broadcasting to units all the way in Northeast area. Maybe one of them could drive over to back up Cainen. But if it was a good call, Cainen would be all alone. "Eleven-A-33, can you back a Hollywood unit?"

* * *

For his short time in the field and limited experience, Cainen had excellent tactics. As he watched addresses, he made sure that he didn't drive directly up to the location. That would be suicide. As he neared 3105 Sunset, he drove slower, checking cars on both sides of the street for passengers.

If the 211 alarm was an actual robbery, there would probably be a get-away driver. If the robbers were pros, then the driver would also serve as a layoff man, with the duty of shooting any cops in the back if they arrived while the robbers were still inside the location.

As he was driving, Cainen used one hand to unlock the shotgun at his feet. He flipped open the lock and checked to make sure that the gun would slide out easily. He set the gun back down.

Before going on patrol, Cainen had checked the shotgun's barrel for obstructions, the ejector and extractor grips, and the firing pin. He had test-chambered a round. Cainen was confident that the gun, his only protection against multiple suspects, would work smoothly. The gun would also serve to shoot through any car doors or wooden surfaces that the robbers might decide to hide behind while they were shooting at him.

Cainen's classmate, Peterson, had been killed a month earlier when he accidentally walked into a jewelry store in Chinatown. Accidentally because he was going in just to say hello and the 211 alarm hadn't been pushed yet. Also accidentally because it was Peterson's last call. The Chinese gang members robbing the store put two holes in Peterson before he could clear his gun from the holster. Peterson's partner was able to take out one of the robbers before he went down with a bullet in his stomach.

Peterson had been one of the nicest people in Cainen's academy class. Just like Cainen's old FTOs Zyrna and Merkle, who had also been shot. *Why is it that only the nice ones get killed,* Cainen wondered, *while assholes like Kidd and Champion seemed to live forever?*

Cainen concentrated on 3105 Sunset. Thinking about a dead classmate killed at a jewelry store wasn't going to help out his psyche.

Cainen lowered his window so that he would be able to hang the microphone outside. It would reach farther than the radio on his belt. He heard the dispatcher trying in vain to get another unit to back him up. Why weren't they responding?

The dispatcher was calling him. "Six-L-57, 6-L-57. Eleven-A-33 will be responding from Northeast to back you. They advise long delay due to distance."

Northeast. A long way away. On the other side of the hill, in the Valley. They'd have to drive down Glendale Boulevard and then try to figure out which way to turn on Sunset from the RD maps.

The entire city of Los Angeles was divided into Reporting Districts (RDs) by the police department. The Planning and Research Division of the Department put out notebook-page-size maps listing as many of the RDs as they could fit into the space. But the names of the streets were so small that it took a magnifying glass just to locate the street you were looking for. And forget about trying to find street numbers.

Yep. It was going to take Northeast a while to get here.

He could be killed by the time a unit got there.

Where are my Hollywood units?!

Cainen picked up the microphone. He was near 3105. "Six-L-57, roger. Show me Code Six on the 211 alarm."

"L57, roger," the dispatcher responded. "Any unit to back, 6-L-57 is Code Six on a 211 alarm, 3105 Sunset!"

Cainen gave the RTO credit. She was trying her damnedest to get him backup. Where were they? Usually half the division would have been here by now.

Cainen checked the cars parked on both sides of the street. No occupants. And no police cars backing him. Cainen stopped in the center of the street, just west of Khazian Jewelers. He didn't want to drive in front of the location. Not only would the suspects know that the cavalry had arrived and possibly take hostages, but they might just as likely decide to shoot their way out, and Cainen would be their target.

Cainen exited his car, flipping the microphone out the open window. The shotgun was in his hand, but he hadn't chambered a round, yet. *No use risking an accidental discharge.* Cainen took up a position of advantage, keeping the solid engine block of the Chevy between him and the jewelry store.

Cainen took a quick look above the hood. The store was definitely open. No sign of anyone, though. He looked behind him. Nope, no layoff men.

Why aren't they backing me up? There must be some logical explanation, even though I can't think of it, he wondered.

Cainen found it impossible to believe, and even more impossible to accept, that the officers wouldn't back up a brother officer in danger just because of his sexual orientation. No way.

You could travel around the world, and in any country, all you had to do was show a police officer your badge and he treated you like a brother. They put you up, took you to dinner, first-class treatment. It was one gigantic brotherhood. Nobody understands cops except other cops. And assholes are assholes the world over. The "they versus we" attitude permeates law enforcement in every continent.

But here his fellow LAPD officers weren't backing him up on the second most frequent call on which officers got killed or seriously injured. Cainen couldn't accept it. Not police officers. He had been with cops all of his adult life, and their moral fiber was unquestionable. No, it was unthinkable. Preposterous. No way.

But where were they?

Cainen could not conceptualize that all police officers were not of the same high ethical character that he was. Cainen, on-duty and off-duty, had backed up officers from many different agencies. He would back up an officer that he hated. That was what being a police officer was all about. When it came to The Job, you always ensured the safety of your brother officer. Could they not be backing him up just because of his sexual orientation? Could it be that vile of a threat to them? He could get killed. . . .

Cainen pictured cops as the defenders of the underdogs. That was why he became a cop. The criminals broke all the rules and the police none, yet the police always won. Because they were the good guys.

A thought quickly flashed through Cainen's mind: Of his first time in patrol after graduating from the academy.

It was A.M. watch in Central Division, Skid Row. As he and his training officer responded to back up officers on a business burglary in the garment district, they quickly rounded a corner to pull in behind the big warehouse. There were two A.M. officers, holding a thin Cuban "Marielito." While one officer held the man with his arms pinned behind his back, the other officer, wearing one black glove on his right hand, punched the man in the testicles, yelling, "How many more are there inside?!"

It was apparent that regardless of how the man answered, he was going to get punched in the nuts. The officer was really enjoying himself.

That was the third time Cainen almost resigned.

The first time was in the academy. The recruits had been ordered to get haircuts every weekend. And not from any "faggot stylists." They were ordered to get their hair cut at a barbershop. And the shop had to have a red, white, and blue cylinder outside, just like in the old days.

It took the recruits most of their first Saturday to locate a barbershop that still had one of those old poles. The sixty-five-year-old barber watched forty young men line up outside his store in Pasadena with a look of amazement on his face.

Unfortunately for one recruit, Green, he had his sister cut his hair. To save money. The recruits had to march for two hours on the damp, muddy track, in their newly polished shoes, chanting, "Green! No good!!" The class would have had to march longer, but Green turned in his hat and books and resigned.

During the middle of the chanting and marching, the LAPD drill instructor, DI Brodie, ordered the class to goose-step while chanting. Cainen was already sick because of the psychological treatment being administered to Green. And because he hated the way most of the recruits fell for it so easily, hating Green instead of the instructors for ruining their shines. It wasn't a game to the recruits, and many of them were pushing, punching, or tripping poor Green as they marched. Being Jewish and seeing how the psyche of the class could be twisted and molded so easily . . . to hate . . . Cainen was reminded of the words: "I was just following orders." When the DI ordered them to, "Goose-step! Raise those knees!" Cainen slowed to a walk. He had refused to chant from the beginning, despite the glares from his classmates. Luckily for Cainen, being only five-foot-ten and his name starting with a *C*, he was in the center of the columns and went unnoticed by the academy staff.

Being ordered to goose-step, like the Nazis who ran the concentration camps that killed so many of his relatives, was the first time Cainen almost quit.

Crouched behind his car in the middle of Sunset Boulevard, Cainen had no way to stop traffic from driving through his line of fire. Still without any backup, Cainen slid into his car and flipped on his rotating light bar. Only his rear flashing yellows had been on. Within moments, the owners of the stores on either side of Khazian Jewelers came out and looked at the police car. (*Where is my backup?*)

Cainen crouched to the rear of his police car. Keeping his eye on the entrance of the jewelry store, Cainen yelled to the older man who had just exited the adjacent tailor shop.

"Go inside and call the jewelry store and ask them to come out," Cainen yelled. He couldn't ask the RTO to do that, because LAPD had recently enacted a strict policy against calling back 211 locations and having someone exit—since the exiting person could possibly be the robber, who could turn on the unexpecting officers.

The old man waved and entered his store. Within moments, a bespectacled man with dark hair and two days' growth of a beard exited Khazian Jewelers. With a heavy Armenian accent, he yelled to Cainen as he started to walk off the curb toward the police car.

Cainen was more concerned with the man's safety due to the traffic than any fear that he was a suspect. Nonetheless, Cainen kept his hands on the shotgun and yelled for the man to stay on the curb.

In a heavy accent the man admitted that he had activated the robbery alarm because two people were fighting on the sidewalk. But they were gone now.

Getting mad was no use. Cainen would write a note to the Police Commission licensers to provide some training to the proprietor.

By now, half the businesses in the neighborhood had people exiting to see what was going on. Even the cars were stopping, which, in Los Angeles, is nothing short of a miracle. (Except on freeways, where everyone stops to look at anything and traffic is equally snarled on one side by lookie-loos as on the other with an accident. On streets, people won't even stop for a body in the road. *Everyone's* in a hurry.)

Cainen just smiled and waved at, undoubtedly, Mr. Khazian. Cainen checked his chamber to ensure it was empty and put the gun back in its rack.

The RTO was still trying to get a unit to back him up when Cainen picked up the microphone.

"Six-L-57. Code four," Cainen broadcast, "no 211, 415 group only, suspects GOA. Repeat, no 211. Code four on Sunset."

"Six-L-57, roger," intoned the RTO, repeating his advisement. "No 211, 3105 Sunset. Four-fifteen group only, suspects GOA. Code four."

After a moment, the RTO stated, "Eleven-A-33, cancel your response. Code four, no 211, 3105 Sunset."

A beleaguered voice sighed out on the Hollywood/Northeast frequency. The voice was bored with this stupid action, since a Hollywood unit should have "bought" their response long ago as they slowly crawled to a division that was not their responsibility.

"Eleven-A-33, roger. Show us en route back to Northeast."

"Eleven-A-33, roger," answered the RTO.

* * *

When the call to back up Cainen came out, 6-A-3, Champion and Willespie, were clear. Champion, who was driving, looked over at his partner. Willespie returned his look and quickly typed on the Mobile Digital Terminal in his car. Willespie then pushed the SEND button on the MDT.

The message that was immediately transposed on the RTO's screen showed that A3 was handling a felony on Fountain and Western. Because it was a felony, they could not be reassigned another call.

Champion drove to the end of the block. They were only five blocks from Cainen's call on Sunset, and Champion didn't want to get within view. *Hey, there was only so much misconduct one could expect to get away with.*

Champion pulled into the Winchell's Donut shop and drove to the rear of the building, out of sight from the street. Willespie got out of the car and went inside to get them two large black coffees. It was free. And they could stay back here and wait out Cainen's call.

* * *

Gillulie quickly typed that they had stopped a felony suspect. She sent the MDT message.

"Let *her* try to figure out what kind of felony suspect it is," Gillulie said to her partner in her smart-ass voice.

"What location did you show us at?" asked Kidd.

"The opposite end of the division," answered Gillulie, proud of herself, "far away from that faggot's call."

"Well," harrumphed Kidd, who had decided that he disliked Jayne Wayne only slightly less than Cainen, "we better do something to CYA." Kidd quickly drove to the southern end of the division, using side streets, in case some goody-good sergeant was driving around who might see them going in the opposite direction of the backup call.

Kidd was an expert at "CYA." Most of the citizens of Los Angeles thought that the motto of LAPD was: "To Protect and to Serve." But the patrol officers knew better, particularly the ones who had experienced the Department's disciplinary system . . . the ones who had gotten "burned." These cops knew that the motto of the street officers was "CYA." Cover Your Ass.

Marshall slowly drove the old Ford LTD up the hills below Mulholland Drive. He turned to his black partner when Cainen's backup call came out.

Phillips knew the ropes. He had come up the hard way. He had joined the Department before blacks were recruited. And he had stayed a patrolman for ten years. If the officers wanted to burn someone, that was just fine with him, as long as he didn't have to do extra work.

Phillips had made an art out of avoiding work, which was why he got along so well with Marshall, who thought that he hated blacks, but guessed he really didn't, since he liked Phillips. He would never invite Phillips to his home for dinner, of course, but he was still a partner.

They had an understanding.

So when the call came out, Marshall, who knew his area better than anyone in the division and was on a first-name basis with many of the residents, drove up to the area where they were having a nighttime burglary problem.

"That house looks like one that will be 459'd pretty soon, whadya think?" he asked his partner.

"Yep," answered Phillips, "no alarm, no dog, no bars."

Marshall slowly drove to the curb. (Marshall did everything slowly, except drink.) "I guess we better check it out. Better put us out on a possible 459."

Phillips, who hated the new computer that took up his leg space in the car, was tempted to use the microphone but thought better of it. Using his two index fingers, it took Phillips three tries to get the message sent to Communications. Which was fine with Marshall. It meant he could sit longer.

Eventually, they both decided to get out of the car and act like they were looking around the house. In case someone was watching. And in case anyone from the Department later interviewed the neighbors.

CYA.

* * *

Sergeant Newman was the field supervisor that night. He liked being the field supervisor because then he didn't have to be in the station, where all the brass were. "Out of sight, out of mind," he was fond of saying when asked why he avoided all the higher-ranking members of the division.

Being in the field meant Newman avoided being assigned all the projects. He hated staff work. He was a sergeant, a field supervisor. So why did they keep giving him projects and reports to write? He was one goshdamn overpaid secretary.

When the RTO tried to raise him, asking 6-L-50 to come in, he cursed himself for not having put himself Code Six on something. Oh well, there was more than one way to skin a cat, as he liked to say.

Newman never checked out a shotgun, a Taser, or more than one radio. Willie, the kit room officer, always asked him if he wanted the stuff, though. Willie was a light-duty old-timer who had pensioned off and then was brought back and forced to work at the station. Doing everything except police work.

Boy, when I retire, thought Newman, *ain't nothing gonna bring me back to this shithole. Let them mail me my pension check to Idaho or Montana. And when I'm dead, ten years after I retire, let my ex-wives fight over the checks. Or give them to the chief, who can use them as toilet paper for all I'll care when I'm six feet under.*

The only one who ever beat the system was Marlin O'Callahan, thought Newman. *That fucker lived to be a hundred and six. Pensioned off when he was fifty-five, after putting thirty-five years in. Screwed the system real good.*

Too bad about all the other coppers, though. Boy, as soon as they retired, five years at the most and they were dead. Nothin' to do, since they had made The Job their whole life.

But not me, thought Newman. *Nope, I'm gonna take up sport-fishin' and then start giving fishing tours. Offer 'em to cops at discount rates. Hell, these young cops got all the money. And a cop will buy anything at a discount. Hell, jack up the price 50 percent and then give them a cop discount of 20 percent and they'll be standing in line.*

And I'll even be able to catch up on a little shoptalk, not that I'll care anything about police work after I quit, but . . .

With only one radio, Newman would have a reason for not hearing a call that came out if he was outside of his vehicle.

Driving down Vermont, Newman passed all the restaurants. *Wouldn't want to give a ticket there, since they go half-price for cops.* Newman drove down to the bowling alley and stopped his black-and-white near the side of the street where the street cleaning was done. Yep, sure enough, about six cars in the "No Parking, 6 A.M. to 8 A.M., for Street Cleaning" zone. Not that they ever cleaned streets in L.A.

In L.A., you're lucky if they clean the streets once a year, thought Newman. A long time ago, when he had to go to court when someone contested a parking ticket, he heard the judge tell a man from Beverly Hills that he still had to pay the fine. Even though the man had seen the street cleaner pass. In Beverly Hills, the judge had told him, they clean the streets *twice* each morning. *Damn!*

Newman checked the cluttered trunk for his cracked black leather ticket holder. It had to be in here somewhere. Yep. There it was, under the used coffee cups, candy wrappers, and recruitment packets. *I hope it's still good,* thought Newman.

As the third call came from the RTO asking him to respond to back up Cainen on the robbery alarm on Sunset, Newman completed the first parking ticket he had written in over fifteen years.

* * *

When the Koreans first started pouring into Los Angeles, they stayed in Koreatown in Wilshire Area. They opened restaurants and retail and wholesale stores.

When Koreatown was all bought out and the Koreans were still looking for somewhere to invest their money, they began buying liquor stores. They started with the liquor stores in the south end of Los Angeles, in the black part of town. But they slowly spread throughout all the poorer retail areas. And when they finished with the liquor stores, they started buying cheap motels. And the cheapest and most flea-ridden were in Hollywood.

The motel rooms were rented by the night and by the hour. The Koreans owned and managed the motels. Hookers and hustlers rented the rooms, trying to sneak four or five people into one room.

Some of the motels were strictly for transvestites, while others were used for vices and criminals of all types. In every one of the motels, at least one room held the motel drug dealer, who would take cash, stolen goods, or sex in exchange for his wares.

The Vagabond Motel was not on Hollywood Boulevard with the rest of the motels. The Vagabond was on Ivar, just above Fountain Avenue. The motel had no sign on the outside, just a large metal gate. All the smaller signs on the inside had had the *V* scratched out and an *F* scratched in, so that they read: "Fagabond."

One of the motel rooms had a metal security door. This was the dealer's room. At first, the owners had tried to clean up the motel and make it a respectable business, something they could be proud of. But with the vandalism that occurred on a nightly basis, and the neighborhood, they could only turn a profit by renting to the street people.

Once, the owner/manager had even tried to evict the drug dealer. After all, he had children of his own. The next morning, a fire had broken out in the manager's office. The fire department investigator said it was arson. Later that same day, the owner/manager received a death threat against his family.

Since then, Mr. Huk had allowed in anyone who could afford the rent. Anyone.

When Charlie Corcoran moved in, under the alias of Willie Nelson (since he figured that Koreans didn't listen to country music), he paid for one week in cash. After that, he paid each night he stayed there. Sometimes Charlie would stay in his van in the motel parking lot. Mr. Huk was wise enough to stay clear of Charlie.

Lisa, on the other hand, had made friends with Mr. Huk's children and was very pleasant when she wasn't high. She had even helped Mrs. Huk sew some clothes for the little ones. Why she hung around with the likes of Willie Nelson, Mr. Huk would never understand.

Tonight, Willie Nelson, AKA Charlie Corcoran, was on the warpath.

"Open the motherfuckin' door!" Charlie screamed as he pounded on the security gate. He hated being straight and wanted to get loaded. "Dammit, Luther, open the damn door or I'm gonna drive my van through your fucking wall."

And Charlie is just crazy enough to do it, too, thought Luther, as he opened up the room door but stayed behind the security gate.

The small, wiry junkie and pimp stared at the wide eyes of the taller white man. In a second, he could see the man was going through withdrawals. He was needin', but he had nothin' worth takin'.

"Say what you want, man?"

Charlie lowered his voice down to a yell. "Man, I need some more speed. I'm comin' down and it's makin' me nervous and shit."

"You want to play, you got to pay." Luther thought that Muhammad Ali would be proud of his rhymes. *Maybe when I score it big, I'll become a rapper like C. R. Cool.*

Charlie was talkin'.

"Man, I gave you $200 in the last two days."

"Yeah," replied Luther, "and you used up all your shit. Unless you got the dough, you gotta blow." *Yeah, I'll be a rapper.*

"Hey, Luther, man, I'm broke for a coupla days, can't—"

Luther cut him off short. "I don't loan to no one, dig. It just ain't where it's at. See, I'm a businessman, jack, and it ain't no business if you ain't makin' bucks. Right?"

Charlie pounded a thick fist against the gate. Luther stood back. He looked to his right at the .357 sitting on the cracked simulated-wood drawers.

Charlie put both hands against the metal and put his nose up against it. "C'mon, Luther. What you want? I'll give you my van?"

Luther smirked. "I don't want no beat-up old van. I got a nice, new '76 Caddy. With a burgundy interior."

"I got a .25-caliber automatic." Charlie reached into his back pocket. Before he got it all the way out, he was staring through the door at a Colt Python .357 Magnum.

"Hey, relax." Charlie eased the mini-auto back into his pocket. "I was just trying to make a deal."

Luther glared. "Then keep your motherfuckin' white hands where I can see 'em, jack." Luther looked around through the metal door, keeping the revolver on Charlie. "Where's your woman?"

Charlie immediately caught on to something. He lowered his voice conspiratorily. "Hey, Luther. I think Lisa likes you, you know. What would it be worth if I could set something up?"

Luther unconsciously reached down to his groin with his free hand, moving around his family jewels. Yeah, he could use some new pussy. He'd had nothing but his usual working girls in over a week. Yeah, some white pussy would be nice. And she had big tits, too.

Luther looked at Charlie and saw Charlie starin' down at Luther's hand, where he was playing with himself through his pants.

"What the fuck you lookin' at?"

Charlie looked up immediately, his hands back on the door beside his face.

Luther thought of Richard Pryor's line about how white people were always wondering why black men always played with their thing all the time. "You white folk done *took* everything else!" Pryor had said.

Yeah, I could use some white pussy. He looked at Charlie. "Man, let me fuck your woman, and I'll give you both some speed that will knock your fuckin' shit into next year."

Charlie was gone in a second.

Charlie quickly ran to the manager's office. Lisa was always fucking around with the little Nip rugrats. Sure enough, she was inside watching TV with the little shits.

Charlie pulled open the screen door and went quickly over to Lisa. "Lisa, you gotta come with me."

Lisa looked at him. He was hurting; she could tell. She had smoked a joint and was mellow and didn't miss the Ludes or crystal at all.

"The cartoon's almost over, and—"

Lisa was yanked by the arm to her feet. Mr. Huk came out of his office but said nothing.

Charlie put his face against Lisa's. "I said now!"

Lisa put her hand on Charlie's. "You're hurting me. OK, now. But let go, OK, Charlie?"

Lisa grabbed her sunglasses and followed Charlie out the door, sneaking a little smile and wave to the Huk children. They didn't smile back but stared at the departing pair.

Lisa followed Charlie as he stomped back to their room. Cameron had gone off down Hollywood Boulevard. Charlie opened the door and walked in. Lisa followed. She stopped inside the door.

"Why did you have to walk in like that in front of the kids?"

Charlie answered with a vicious backhand across her face. The blow sent Lisa down to the carpet. Charlie crouched down. Lisa put her hand to the right side of her face. Her long brown hair hung down, covering the moistness in her eyes.

"Now you listen to me. I'll only ask you once. I was the one who pulled you out of the gutter, didn't I?"

It was true. Charlie had beaten the shit out of Lisa's pimp on Hollywood Boulevard one night. Took the knife that he pulled, too. None of the pimps tried to get her back. They were too frightened of Charlie. So was she.

"You got any money?"

"No," answered Lisa, taking a deep breath. "You took it yesterday." Charlie had gone ripping through her purse and her pockets, desperately afraid of coming down from his high.

"You like Luther?"

This question caught Lisa off-guard. She knew it had a double meaning, but her years of getting wasted had ruined her ability to apply cognitive reasoning to any great extent. Like adding two and two. Being nice to kids was a different matter.

"No. I think he smells like *High Karate* aftershave."

"Well, learn to like him," growled Charlie, " 'cause he likes you, and you're gonna fuck him. He's gonna get you high for free if you let him."

Lisa cringed inside herself but didn't move. She hated being a whore again. Not that she had ever really thought that she had left. She knew what was coming, remembered it from her pimps. But she spoke anyway. At least she could pretend that she had some dignity. Some control over her body.

"But I don't want to fuck Luther. I'm your girl."

Charlie slapped her once, on the hair, mostly. "That's right. And you'll do what I tell you. Come on."

Charlie grabbed her by the arm. He was tired of playing around. He pulled her out the door and headed toward Luther's room. He only had to pound once before the metal security door opened. Luther had greased his jeri-curled hair and put on some more *High Karate* cologne.

"Here's my end of the bargain," stated Charlie, pushing Lisa farther into the room.

Luther never took his eyes off Lisa. (The .357 was between the box spring and mattress.) He reached out and took her by the arm. "On the counter," he told Charlie.

Charlie picked up the two wrapped-up tissues of white powder. He walked out, closing the metal door behind him without a second look.

Charlie went back to their room, opening the cupboard under the bathroom sink. Among the rat feces was a metal spoon with brown rust stains in it and black burn marks under it. Charlie grabbed a belt and tied his arm tight, pulling it tighter in his teeth. He had gotten the lighter from Lisa's purse and held it under the spoon.

Charlie had ripped open a pillow in the room and removed a piece of foam. He tore off a corner. Putting tap water and powder from one of the packets into the spoon, Charlie held the lighter flame under it, watching the powder melt and become liquid with the water. It was just like miniature waves underwater. Using a syringe he had taken from his sock, he put the tip of the needle into the flame to sterilize it. Disregarding the carbon that would tattoo his arm, Charlie put the torn piece of foam in the spoon and stuck the needle in the foam. That would keep out any large impurities.

Once the needle was full, Charlie pulled the belt in his teeth until his veins popped out. He preferred Lisa to stick him, but he could do it. Hell, in prison, all the prisoners had to get themselves high after they bought the shit from one of the prison guards or had their girlfriend bring it in in her vagina. (Then they'd pretend to cough and swallow it and wait for the balloon to come out in their shit.)

As the liquid entered his vein, Charlie immediately felt more relaxed. He would start speedin' after the knot in his stomach went away. This was better than sex.

When he shot heroin, it was just like an orgasm, only longer, and internal.

It took Charlie less than a second to decide that Lisa would have to get her own shit. He then hid the other tissue and the piece of foam. When you were chippin', using a little bit of shit with some water,

71

under the same scab as before, just to get a head rush, you could just put the foam in the spoon and still get high.

Hell, Charlie knew hypes that had shot peanut butter, just to get that sensation of something entering their bloodstream. The body's memory would bring back that pleasant feeling.

Charlie lay down on the bed. He wasn't about to go to sleep. He was starting to feel the buzz. He would go for at least twenty-four hours now without sleeping. As soon as Luther finished with Lisa and Cameron came back from lookin' at cement footprints or whatever, they could go out hunting. The Boulevard—Santa Monica Boulevard—had plenty of game.

And when Charlie was the hunter, any day was open season.

*　*　*

In 1959, the California state legislature established the Commission on Peace Officer Standards and Training, known as POST. It is POST's responsibility to develop and implement programs to increase the effectiveness of law enforcement through education and training. POST worked with every police department in the state, as well as with colleges and universities, establishing these training classes. Every state has since developed a similar governing body to oversee their police departments, establishing training guidelines.

In the mid-1970s, the federal government completed a study that determined that the average educational attainment of police chiefs in the United States was less than that of a high school graduate.

In 1977, the legislature expanded the powers of POST, in order to ensure that California remained in the forefront of professionalism in law enforcement.

For the purpose of "raising the level of competence" of local law-enforcement officers, POST was empowered to establish statewide minimum hiring and recruitment standards. The standards related to "physical, mental and moral fitness."

The Los Angeles Police Department, which had been a model police agency, at the forefront of training and professionalism, did not meet the minimum standards of POST. The LAPD *refused* to change or alter its academy to meet the POST guidelines established in 1985.

Using the power of its reputation, the LAPD held onto its organizational standard. Similar to the individual officer's concept of "we cannot break the law, because we are the law," so the LAPD felt that "no one can tell us how to train; we *invented* police training."

POST disagreed. And before all state funding was pulled, particularly the hundreds of thousands of dollars given to the LAPD as reimbursement for their academy training, the LAPD management suddenly decided to "reorganize" their training. Coincidentally, this reorganization happened to exactly match the new POST guidelines.

And LAPD never admitted they were wrong.

Despite the standards governing police departments, after several years of police work, patrol officers inevitably "burned out."

Some cops decided to make their fortunes doing something other than police work while still having the guarantee of a police income.

Other cops were just too intelligent and couldn't put up with the idiots who were promoted faster than they were and became their incompetent bosses.

Many cops had received "discipline" from the Department, which, by LAPD definition, was a positive action taken to ensure no repetition of an unacceptable behavior. Translated, this meant five days' suspension without pay.

In any case, these disciples of discipline usually continued to, as police officers stated it, "fuck up." But most cops didn't mind being punished for being caught doing something wrong. Cops have a deep-seated belief in justice. Their rule was that you don't play if you can't take the stakes. But they believed that the LAPD disciplinary philosophy was "No good deed shall go unpunished."

While these cops didn't mind being disciplined for everything from farting to hiring contract killers, they often felt that the Department was penalizing them too heavily. And the Department often did. One officer, who had used eight white envelopes belonging to the Department, was charged with eight counts of theft. Not one count for all eight envelopes; eight counts—one for each envelope.

The Department believed that the cop was using the envelopes to conduct business for his off-duty job, a job that he hadn't requested a permit for. So when the Internal Affairs investigators couldn't prove that he had an off-duty job, they went for the next best thing. Criminal charges for stealing envelopes.

The disciplinary system wasn't fair. LAPD called it progressive discipline: each time the officer fucked up (or got caught at it), the penalty increased. Five days' suspension, fifteen days' suspension, six months' suspension, termination.

But it all depended on your rank and whether the Department management liked you or not. A deputy chief that used confidential records and department computers for personal business was admonished; told not to do it again. Yet the officer with the envelopes received a five-day suspension.

73

And officers who worked as adjutants to the command staff just bought eight envelopes and returned them to the Department. Internal Affairs never even saw a complaint.

Gregory Whalen had worked Rampart Division. Having twelve years on The Job, he had seen it all. And he couldn't stand all the dumb-shits he got stuck working with. He would tell his probationers, who usually didn't understand anyway, "Petty jobs, petty personalities, petty jealousies, petty minds." Whalen couldn't stand the dumb-shits on The Job.

The police mentality amazed him. Of course, like "military intelligence," there was no such thing as "police mentality."

Whalen was intelligent. He had come up with at least a dozen get-rich-quick scams since joining the force. His last two had actually paid off.

Whalen ran an office cleaning business, making an equal income to that from his police job, and he only had to organize a work schedule for the cleaners.

He had joined up with a partner for his last scam. He had come up with it since he worked in Rampart.

Rampart Area had more car thefts than forty-nine of the fifty states in the United States. One division. And most of those cars were never recovered.

Some of the cars went to "chop shops," where they were disassembled within minutes and on their way to other states to be marketed.

Other stolen cars, like the mini-pickups, were taken down to Mexico, on their way to South America, to be used as army transport vehicles in the escalating wars in Nicaragua and El Salvador.

Since the largest immigrant population in Rampart was Mexican nationals, many of the stolen cars were driven south for a weekend visit home. The theft trail could be followed all the way south. The LAPD stolen Datsun would be recovered in Orange County, where an Orange County Datsun would be stolen. The Orange County Datsun would be recovered in San Diego, where a San Diego Datsun was stolen. That Datsun would be found at the Tijuana border, if it was found at all.

It was a lot easier to steal another Datsun than to fill up the tank with gas. And a lot faster.

There were only a limited number of different keys for the ignitions of Datsuns in the United States. And a "shiv" key, with the sides filed down, fit all the current models.

In 1985, the FBI went to a rural city in Mexico, and copied down all the license numbers of the vehicles parked in the streets. Back in the United States, they ran all the plates through their computers. It turned out that 75 percent of the cars had been stolen from the United States.

Of course, in the interest of international relations (and the fact that Mexico had recently found large oil deposits), nothing was done.

Without a close examination, police officers could only judge a stolen car if the license plate had been reported. So the thieves often stole a front license plate off a different car and put it on the rear of a stolen car. The owner of the plate wouldn't notice it until after the thieves were safely in Mexico.

The only other way to tell that a car was stolen, if a fresh ignition had been put in, was to check the Vehicle Identification Number. The VIN was located on the dashboard in the front window and also in two places on the engine. One of the two places was concealed.

When the LAPD put computers into its patrol cars, the officers began checking license plates at random and increasing their arrests by thousands. The car thieves quickly began VIN switch operations. They would buy the junked body of Datsuns and Toyotas from scrapyards. The scrapyards received all the cars that had been totaled in accidents. The thieves would then remove the VIN plates, and use them to switch with recently stolen Datsuns and Toyotas.

All it took was a ratchet gun to secure the thin metal plate, and a "hot" car became cool transportation to Jalisco.

Whalen had developed a system using a glass etching process in labeling every window of a car with the original VIN.

Not only that, but Whalen had worked with several major insurance companies to allow discounts for new vehicle buyers who had this treatment done.

Whalen was only waiting the eight more years until he could retire from LAPD with his pension and then work full-time in his business.

The LAPD was a nice job, but there was work to be done.

Whalen's motto, which his probationers cared even less about than they did his opinion of the Department, was: "Never let service to your constituency stand in the way of personal convenience."

Most of the probationers couldn't figure out what a constituency was, anyway.

Because of Whalen's intelligence, he felt like an outsider at Rampart. Because of his years on The Job and at Rampart, and because he had never squealed about all the beatings and misconduct he had witnessed by the other officers at Rampart, Whalen was considered one of the boys. He hated that consideration almost as much as he hated police work.

But Whalen's intelligence, and existentialist viewpoint of life, had given him an extremely bizarre sense of humor. Some would call it sick.

For example, Whalen laughed when he talked about the starving people of Biafra, India, or Ethiopia.

And he loved jokes that made other people nauseous. And it took a lot to make a cop nauseous.

Though he wasn't considered an outsider by his peers, Whalen was viewed as an oddball.

When Whalen transferred to Hollywood, his reputation had preceded him. In LAPD, whenever an officer transferred, one officer and one sergeant always called down to the old division to get any scoop on the incoming. And everyone in roll call was asked if they knew the new officer's "rap."

So even before his transfer to Hollywood, Whalen was accepted, but viewed as being on the periphery. An oddball.

As if anyone in Hollywood could be considered "normal."

It was because of his feelings of being outside the peer group that Whalen had tried to assist Cainen. Whalen had tried to offer Cainen advice on how to be accepted and how to fit into the system.

He had even offered to work with Cainen when the other officers refused.

He had been drinking with the boys on many occasions. He had even been one of the officers who had diddled one of the fifteen-year-old female probationers at Hollywood the year before. But she had kept her mouth shut during the investigation.

So Whalen wasn't worried that the other officers would think he was a fruit for associating with Cainen.

Just an oddball.

Besides, he never talked with Cainen when there were other officers present.

So when he came to work five minutes before the day watch roll call, as he always did, he heard the scuttlebutt about Cainen's call on Sunset.

He heard all the A.M. watch officers bragging.

And since he always walked in late to roll call, he was alone in the locker room, changing, when Cainen came in to get out of his uniform.

"Hey, Jew-boy." He liked to call Cainen that, since he, Cainen and Hamish were the only Jews working in the division. At least the only ones who admitted being Jewish. Or the only ones who had been found out.

He was also proud that he and Hamish were always sought out to help put on the division Christmas party. It had nothing to do with their religion; it was just that they were the only ones who knew how to get things wholesale, or to talk local store owners into giving them large "police" discounts.

Or, as the asshole officers put it, "You two really know how to Jew those prices down."

"What's up, Greg?"

Whalen liked it that Cainen treated him decently. Cainen was also the only one who called him by his first name. Since officers only wear their last name on their uniform nameplates, there is a tendency to call everyone except your friends by their last names.

Greg didn't have any cop friends.

"When you coming to day watch?" Whalen asked Cainen.

"Whenever they switch me." Officers were rotated every several months to a different watch, working different hours. They were usually rotated just about the time their bodies started getting used to the hours they *were* working.

"So when you going to quit and go to law school?" This was Whalen's standing line to Cainen.

Cainen had confided to Whalen one night when they were both working A.M.'s that his aunt had offered to pay the full cost of law school if Cainen would get away from the dangers of law enforcement.

"About the same time you retire. Or get a stress pension," Cainen joked back, but his eyes showed no humor.

Cainen had changed out of his uniform into jeans and was putting his gun into his gym bag and tying his tennis shoes. Cainen looked tired.

Whalen looked around them. No one. They were between two rows of lockers. You could never tell who was on the other side, though there wasn't any sound.

He walked closer to Cainen and lowered his voice. Cainen had his foot on the bench, looking down while tying his shoes.

"I heard what happened out there," said Whalen.

Cainen looked up at him, uncomprehending.

"You didn't get any backup out there."

Cainen couldn't tell if it was a question or a statement. And Cainen was always guarded. Even with someone who was possibly a friend, if there was such a thing in police work.

Whalen was looking at Cainen as he put on his gun belt. "Did you?" So it was a question.

Cainen answered with one word. "No."

"They're trying to teach you a lesson."

Cainen felt the blood draining from his face. Or was it from his whole body? He couldn't feel his body. Like when you were a little boy in the principal's office, about to be yelled at, and the principal seemed to be moving farther away. Like you were shrinking. Like you were outside your body. Like it wasn't really you. And the principal's voice was from far away. Hard to hear.

Cainen realized he was sweating.

So it was true. It hadn't been an accident nor a coincidence that no one showed up at his call for backup.

It had been planned. Purposely. They deliberately hadn't backed up a brother cop. They had broken the most solemn vow of police work, that you always back up your brother officer. No matter what.

Unless that cop was gay.

After all the harassment he had taken. All the lockers glued shut, the banners calling him a faggot, the handwritten messages from all the officers calling him names, the new officers being told that he's a pervert, the repeated interrogations by his supervisors, the sergeants and lieutenants assigned to force him to resign . . .

But this.

This was almost too much to bear.

I can't take it. Cops are good *people, not bad.*

WHY? No more. Please . . .

I'm losing it, said a voice from somewhere deep in Cainen's mind.

Cainen desperately tried to stay normal in front of Whalen. He had to show control. Karate had taught him control.

He couldn't control his paleness or his sweating. But he would control his actions.

But, God, he felt like running out of there screaming!

He went back to tying his shoes, hoping his legs would hold up.

Whalen was still looking at him.

Probably out of courtesy, Whalen moved past him toward the door, to go to roll call. But he stopped at the end of the bench.

Cainen finished tying his shoe. He stood on both feet.

I think I'm going to throw up. No, I won't.

Cainen closed and locked his locker and picked up his gym bag. Sweat was rolling into his eyes. Cainen blinked it away and looked at Whalen.

Whalen was giving a final adjustment to his gun belt.

They looked at each other. Only Whalen spoke.

"Steve," Whalen said in a soft voice, "get out of here before they kill you."

IV

Dino

Dino was twenty-one years old. Thin, with wiry muscles, he stood at five foot nine and weighed 155 pounds. His naturally blond hair contrasted well with his azure eyes; it also helped him make money.

Dino was a hustler.

Dino had been born in Texas, in a town with just over two hundred people. After building up a long juvenile criminal record, Dino was kicked out of town by the local sheriff. As Dino explained it, "Calling me a juvenile delinquent is calm compared to what I was."

By seventh grade, Dino was an accomplished daytime burglar. He had also assaulted his seventh-grade teacher.

Dino started hustling when he was eleven years old. Dino, like all his friends, knew of one "gay guy" back in their hometown. Whenever Dino or his friends were hard up for money, this guy would pay them five dollars to let him give them a blowjob.

This man told Dino, "If ever you want to get out of this dump, this is how you can make enough money to survive."

So Dino hustled his way to California.

Dino didn't leave much behind. When asked about his father, Dino would reply, "I've never seen the man." Dino had one brother and one sister from his parents' marriage. Dino's sister had also worked the streets at times. She'd also been married before.

Dino's older brother, who was twenty-eight, still lived in Texas, doing manual labor.

After Dino's parents divorced, his mother remarried twice. Dino had four brothers and sisters from his mother's third marriage.

Dino's mother taught him to iron and sew. She also told him, "One of these times you're going to run away and I'm going to tell you not to come back."

Dino wasn't sure if it took guts or stupidity for a child to leave home and explore the world on his own.

When Dino was thirteen, he joined a motorcycle gang called Satan's Angels, based out of Texas. He met his "brother" there, and they traveled together for more than a year.

It was during that time that Dino got one of his two tattoos. He had an "S.A." tattooed on his right middle finger.

When Dino was sixteen, he went to join the marines. The marine recruiter forged Dino's mother's signature, his FBI record clearance, his Sheriff's Department clearance, and his Texas general education degree. This allowed Dino to join.

Soon after joining, Dino refused to do his assigned "Extra-Punishment Duty" (EPD) of cleaning the latrines. He refused by punching a ranking officer. Dino then went AWOL to Hollywood for seven months. In those seven months, Dino was arrested three times.

Before Dino could be thrown in the brig and dishonorably discharged, he pointed out his enlistment at sixteen and the Marine Corps–forged documents. Rather than risk public embarrassment and legislative scrutiny, the marines gave Dino an honorable discharge.

Dino had been in Hollywood for the five years since his discharge.

Dino thought of prostitution as a logical employment alternative for youths. When trouble starts at home, a child often chooses to leave rather than work out the problems. The job market will not allow them to work due to their age. Even if they can find work, the type of work available is so unenjoyable or unbearable that the children often want better.

These children would rather sell their bodies than take a free meal from a soup kitchen or live in a flea-infested mission.

"Contrary to popular belief," Dino would say, "twelve-year-olds do have opinions and tastes."

Additionally, he'd add, no job could match the ninety-dollar-a-day spending money he made when working the street. And he got to pick his own hours and be his own boss.

Dino would concede that in his time working the streets, he had been beat up, shot, and stabbed with an ice pick once when a trick "freaked" and wanted more sex when Dino was done and ready to leave.

Dino had two arrests on his Los Angeles rap sheet. One of the arrests had occurred about a year ago, on a day when Dino hadn't been hustling. A handsome young white man drove up beside Dino as he was exiting a fast-food store on the Boulevard. The man signaled for Dino to come over. When Dino approached the car, the man asked Dino if he wanted to smoke a joint. Dino said, "Sure," and got in the car.

The man then drove around the block and into a parking lot. The man then ordered Dino to get out of the car and put his hands on the roof. Two other plainclothes officers grabbed Dino and pulled him into a chain-link fence and handcuffed him to the fence. The young white guy told the other officers that Dino had solicited him.

Dino was about to argue when he noticed two other plainclothes officers beating another youth cuffed to the fence. Dino chose to keep his mouth shut and avoid the bruise-bath.

And all on a day he wasn't hustling!

Dino had also been arrested for possession of nunchakus, an Asian martial arts weapon with two pieces of wood connected by a short length of rope. This happened shortly after Dino left the military.

Dino was picked up by a friend, and as they were driving down the Boulevard, an LAPD unit pulled them over. Dino still had his Marine Corps pistol in his belt. The nunchakus were in his boot.

The officer arrested him for the nunchakus. Though the gun was taken from him by the officer, he wasn't charged for it. And he never knew what happened to the gun.

Dino had several girlfriends. He had almost married one of them in San Francisco.

She was from a wealthy family, and he met her while he was hustling up in the bay area. But he dumped her when he found out he got venereal disease from her.

He wasn't too upset about it. "Anyone who has ever had sex has had a disease," Dino liked to say. Dino knew that twenty out of every fifty hustlers were carrying a sexually transmitted disease. "I know six guys right now that have AIDS, five that have gonorrhea, and one who's had syphilis for four years . . . you think he doesn't know he has it?"

Dino knew that hustlers didn't stop prostituting when they got a sexually transmitted disease. "Those guys don't care about anything except gettin' money in their pockets."

When a hustler got a disease, Dino explained, "You just don't go with your regular clients. And you cover up with the other customers. You wipe yourself if you're dripping."

Dino once left the street to work in a hardware business. He made good money and was allowed to live in the Hollywood Hills with the eighty-year-old owner.

But Dino had an affair with the owner's thirty-year-old wife and had to return to his life on the street when the owner found out.

Dino had grown up in the subculture of the street and felt uncomfortable outside it. These were his "people."

Dino, preferring to diversify his income, also ran an illicit drug business. He ran a small stable of dealers, and also personally dealt himself.

Dino ran a pharmacy from the back of his old 1965 Chevy Malibu. Dino also directed a legitimate cleaning business with another man. After cleaning pharmacies, Dino would plan out a burglary, knowing where all the valuable street drugs were located. Keeping the alarm off for a night, Dino would break into the business, without using any keys, making it seem as if the alarm had been left off accidentally.

Dino then sold the drugs through his street salesman and out of the trunk of his car, which he kept parked by the Spotlight bar in Hollywood. With all the LAPD cars driving up and down Gower, Dino felt that his car was safe from burglars.

Dino, like other hustlers, was proud to boast about the number of friends he had. He would often boast that he had twenty friends who would back him up in a fight. Yet Dino believed that no hustler was trustworthy, since they were so self-centered. Dino, like B.J. and Danny, made friends with all the other hustlers for self-preservation. "How many people you know on the street means how much you have to watch your back."

Police officers never sit with their backs to a door in a restaurant, in the event a robbery takes place. Just like police officers, Dino never sat with his back to a door, so he could see who was coming in, in the event he had to get out fast. Dino always tried to sit with his back to a wall when he was in a coffee shop.

Dino wore a chain that attached his wallet to his pants belt loop. Dino had had his wallet stolen once by one of his tricks and twice by whores that he had bought with the money from his tricking.

Dino was always on his guard. He once intervened to protect one of the female prostitutes who had come down to work on Santa Monica. Many of the Sunset Boulevard girls have tried to work on Santa Monica Boulevard, to avoid being forced to work for a pimp. They become friends with the hustlers and receive some protection from them.

Once, when one of the pimps from Sunset came down and harassed a girl by the Shakey's Pizza Hut on Santa Monica, Dino had intervened. He had punched the pimp and taken a knife away from one of the pimp's poo-butt assistants. Though the girl had been saved for the moment, the pimp had vowed to get Dino. And Dino had believed the pimp.

Dino had been inside Denny's coffee shop on Sunset Boulevard on the night it was blasted with machine-gun fire. The gunfire had been in retaliation for Denny's telling the pimps they couldn't loiter inside the restaurant.

The pimps were now allowed to loiter there. And they got free refills on coffee.

So Dino believed the pimp. And he always watched his back. But he knew that he'd do the same thing again, if the situation arose. Though Dino didn't know the word *chivalry*, Dino lived by a code of honor.

It was the same code that forbade him to take "slops" in pool. Regardless of the stakes, and Dino always gambled, and regardless of how much the other player cheated, Dino never waivered from his code of conduct.

In pool, Dino always tried for the harder shot, so as to improve himself. There was no challenge in an easy shot, he thought, even if it meant winning (Unless, of course, the stakes were real high. . . . Dino might be a gentleman, but he wasn't *stupid*.) And Dino never accepted shots where his ball went in the pocket if it wasn't the one he had aimed for. He played "gentleman's pool."

Dino liked to think of himself as a modern-day old-fashioned southern gentleman. After all, he figured, Texas *was* in the South.

When Dino wasn't hustling and his drug supply was low, he lived by pool-sharking. He would often lose two or three games, and several dollars, before betting a bundle and clearing the table without giving his unwary opponent a single shot.

Dino constantly smoked marijuana. He also smoked almost two packs a day of cigarettes. Recreationally, Dino preferred Quaaludes and Percodan.

In his less philosophical moments, Dino felt that hustlers were merely kids who were "partying." The reason that many hustlers had been on the streets so long is because "they're still partying."

Every so often Dino got a certain tired look in his eyes that showed he had seen too much for his twenty-one years, that he had seen almost all and that most of it had been bad. It was during these periods that Dino admitted to himself that one of three things would happen to every hustler: he'd find a place he was happy with and settle down; he'd "burn out," usually by an overdose; or he'd get killed.

Alone

When he was in high school, Steve wrote a poem for himself and posted it in his closet. It was hidden from everyone but himself, just like most of his true feelings were. The poem was titled "Alone":

No one knows my innermost fears.
Neither friend, nor lover, nor father, nor mother.
I know these fears aren't rightful,
But they are nonetheless genuine to me.

For they are feelings.

I am not even sure that they can be shared.
For they have never been spoken.
But these are the feelings that make me alone,
even when I am not.
For these fears make me lonely.

Or perhaps they *are* loneliness.

How can someone else understand my fears—
When I cannot?
They are a closer companion to me than any being
or possession.
For they have been with me
for as long as I can remember.
And are my constant companion when I am alone.

Many gays choose the career of acting. It isn't that they want to be the center of attention; it is just that this is a career that they can relate to. They have been acting most of their teenage lives, pretending to be someone they are not for fear of being rejected: rejected by their family, their friends, and even complete strangers.

There is no loneliness like the loneliness of a gay youth. That is why more than ten gay and lesbian teenagers commit suicide every day in the United States.

There are no role models for a child who is experiencing feelings that attract him or her to members of the same sex.

Many boys dream of becoming firemen or policemen or joining the military. The military in the United States doesn't accept gays. It refuses to enlist them and discharges them if they are found out after they have joined.

84

There are virtually no gay police or fire fighter role models for these children. Most police departments refuse to hire gays and lesbians. And none of the thousands of police or fire fighter television shows have a gay protagonist. Usually it is just the opposite, showing the cop off-duty with his wife or the fireman being pursued by a bevy of beautiful "Charlie's Angels."

In fact, there are very few gay or lesbian role models on television.

While growing up, the worst insult a preteen boy can call his peer is a "sissy," "pansy," or "faggot." So the child learns early on that this is the least acceptable lifeform. And yet he has to reconcile this societal teaching with the ever-growing feelings inside himself.

Usually the child learns to despise himself. And the more fundamentalist the religious upbringing of the family, the more the child loses his self-esteem.

The worst part of the loneliness is due to the fact that all children, following their experimentation with the same sex around age nine, hide their feelings. Consequently, the gay or lesbian child feels that no one else in the world has the same feelings. They are the only ones who can't "control" their emotions. And they believe they are the only ones who have these attractions.

Even worse, if there is a gay or lesbian in their environment, that person has often been ostracized by the community. Except in some areas of New York and San Francisco, where the lifestyle is so prevalent that tolerance becomes imbued in the upbringing of some youths, there are only "dykes" and "queers." These individuals are pointed out to children as oddities. Most often they are referred to as mentally sick or child molesters. Unfortunately, these are the only apparent members of the gay community that can be easily identified. So it is believed that all or most of the other gays and lesbians are similar.

Most people still believe that gays and lesbians that have relationships have to establish roles in which one plays the husband and one the wife.

So the boy cannot relate to the man with the lisp, wearing women's clothing. And the girl cannot relate to the woman dressed in men's jeans, wearing a man's flannel shirt with no bra, and having a man's haircut.

So they have no one.

These youths feel totally isolated. And it is all within themselves, within their own minds.

There is no smaller prison cell than the one a person can build in his own mind.

And there is no loneliness greater than that of the youth attracted to members of his or her own sex. They feel they are alone in the entire world. And the sad part about it is that there are many positive role models available to them in the community; businessmen, city council members, and priests. Even sadder, there is often a gay community in a nearby town. But because the parents don't want to contaminate their youths, they rarely educate them in this area. And the parents forbid the schools to provide this education.

Steve was no different.

After Steve got off work, he would drive to the high school and layout the student newspaper until two in the morning. Then, desperately lonely, he would drive past all his friends' homes. They lived in an almost circular pattern on the perimeter of the small city, and Steve could pass each of their homes before returning to his house. Then he would stare at the ceiling, thinking about how lonely he was and wishing he could change himself, finally falling asleep.

Everyone else in high school had girlfriends or was dating. All the guys, except the major nerds, were holding hands with girls, hugging or kissing. This only highlighted Steve's loneliness.

Steve never thought in terms of sex. He didn't desire to have sex with another guy. He just wanted to touch. And be touched. Mostly, he wanted to be held.

Though this was a faggy feeling, Steve knew this was what he most wanted. Steve was very masculine, being on the wrestling team and all. And he couldn't really picture himself being held by a guy. No way. Not really. It just wasn't in the mental image he had of himself.

And yet, this was what he desired. Even when one of his friends from the football team would grab him in a bear hug. It just felt good.

Weird.

Or at least weird to a youth who had never been told that there was such a thing as gay people.

When his loneliness became unbearable, Steve would sneak over to his friend John's house. John was a stud from the basketball team. He had done tons of girls and had even fucked one girl up her ass. He did it with another teammate. With two of the cheerleaders.

When the teammates weren't trying to gross each other out by picking gum or dogshit off the sidewalk and chewing it, then one would be pissing while another drank it to prove he was the grossest.

Yeah, John was superstraight. But Steve would sometimes go over to his house at 2:00 A.M. and climb in the backyard window into John's room. Steve would lie down on one side of the bed, making sure he didn't touch John.

John was cool and didn't mind. Steve was an oddball, but he was a nice guy. He had even bought John a genuine leather basketball for his birthday. No one else had one of those.

Maybe John understood that Steve just needed the companionship. Anyway, after an hour, when Steve would start to doze off, he would sneak back out and drive home. When he got home, he would fall asleep right away, not feeling lonely.

Steve loved the night. He loved knowing that every one of his friends was at home. And he loved feeling that only he knew what was going on in their community at that hour. Just he and the cops, who worked twenty-four hours.

And Steve loved the night because he could share his loneliness with the world. With the stars and the moon. And with the knowledge that *everyone* was alone then, because high school kids slept at home.

At 2:00 A.M., Steve felt much more and much less alone.

Unfortunately, Steve's sneaking into John's room ended abruptly one night when John's mom came into the room holding a Saturday night special that her husband had left when they divorced. Aiming the gun at Steve, she explained that she had thought he was a burglar. And that it was better if he stopped coming by. She'd hate to accidentally shoot him, mistakenly thinking that he was breaking in one night.

Looking down the barrel of the gun, Steve agreed.

Steve had been busy working in the student government, on the school paper, and at a job he had each day after school. Consequently, he didn't have time to apply to many universities. Because he graduated with many honors, however, several colleges did offer scholarships. To get his mother back for making him live away from home, Steve chose one of the colleges that had offered him a full scholarship for the first semester. A Christian college.

Steve's Jewish mother didn't like that. (She liked it even less when Steve's younger brother chose Pepperdine.) But at least Steve was out of the house.

As soon as Steve moved away, his mother began court proceedings for increased child support from the boys' father. Remembering the psychological scars that he still carried from the way his parents had used him as a pawn in their previous court proceedings, Steve left the college after one semester. He felt that he had to return home to protect his younger brother from being used as a pawn in the tormenting game his parents were playing.

Steve completed his Associate of Arts degree at a community college while living at home. He was able to spare his brother most of the brunt of his parents' hostility, but only by taking it on himself.

87

While Steve was completing the work on his A.A., he continued hanging around his friends from high school. One of the group had become a local police officer, another was the son of an LAPD captain, and a third was a girl. She was one of the guys.

The girl, Tina, came from a wealthy family and was dating one of the frat-boy golfers from USC. While *USC* stood for the University of Southern California, Steve and the other guys referred to it as the "University of Spoiled Children." In fact, the son of the captain was working on his bachelor's in political science at USC, at a cost of $20,000 a semester. A lot of money to pay for an education for someone who was going to become a cop.

Tina loved to dance. Unfortunately, Tina's current boyfriend would only take her to the chic nightclubs and not the ones that were the most fun. Tina liked a place called the Odyssey.

The Odyssey served no alcohol. Kids eighteen and up hung out there every night of the week. Half the kids were gay, and another group hung out in the pool room. These pool players were hustlers. And they didn't just hustle at billiards.

But the club was the fav. Exotic light shows, with sirens and moving stalactites, covered the ceiling. And they only played the best dance music that could be imported from New York. But because the crowd was primarily gay, Tina's boyfriend wouldn't go there. Jocks who played macho games, like golf, couldn't be seen in places like that. Even with Tina.

One day, Tina asked Steve if he would go dancing with her. She explained that the place was kind of weird, but she left out any information about young gay men being there.

Steve always had a great time with Tina, who was intelligent and free-spirited. So he consented. This turned out to be his first contact with any gay people.

While dancing, Steve saw a couple making out in the corner of the dance floor. No big deal, until they turned around and Steve saw that they were both guys.

Steve left the dance floor and got his jacket. This place was too weird for him. It took all of Tina's coaxing to get Steve to stay.

Steve had never seen gays before. He had never known that they existed, let alone that they congregated together. Steve was shocked. But his shock soon passed.

The next night, Steve returned to the Odyssey. This time, he didn't take Tina.

Steve couldn't relate to the effeminate guys on the dance floor, and Steve was frightened because those people watching the dance floor were often asked to dance by other guys. So Steve stayed in the poolroom, watching the pool games and enjoying the music. The guys in the poolroom, being hustlers, were masculine. Steve could relate to them better.

It felt right to be with his own kind for the first time in his life.

The thing that had most disturbed him about high school and about the Police Explorers wasn't there. He had something in common with these people. Even if he came from a different background, at least he had the thing in common with these people at Odyssey that he had lacked with the others. And at least he didn't have to worry about being ridiculed for his feelings. Even if he didn't understand those feelings yet. And it was going to be a long road until he could ever accept those feelings.

Steve stayed to himself and didn't talk with the others. Until one night when one of the guys playing pool set his pool stick down on Steve's knee, saying in a deep voice, "What are you doing here?"

Shocked, Steve looked up to see the face that was attached to the cue stick. It was Dave, one of the guys from the boxing club at the Christian college.

Could Dave be gay?

For the next month, Dave showed Steve the city of West Hollywood. The "gay city." Dave couldn't believe Steve's naiveté.

And Steve couldn't believe that all the young men standing on Santa Monica Boulevard were male prostitutes. Steve had always assumed that they were high school kids loitering around looking for trouble, just like they did on Van Nuys Boulevard in the Valley. The kids looked the same.

But Steve's opinion changed when Dave, who always brought a thin, effeminate, blond English boy named Laramy along, stopped and gave a lift to one of the boys.

While he drove the boy to the Odyssey, he discussed how business was that night. Watching Steve out of the corner of his eye, Dave wheeled the conversation around, aptly revealing that the boy, who was seventeen but had fake ID, had been waiting for a trick.

Shortly thereafter, the court proceedings between Steve's parents ended, with Steve's mother sending her ex to jail on the weekends. Steve then returned to college, twenty-one years old and a virgin.

While completing his bachelor's degree, Steve began a program for departmental honors in criminal justice. As part of his honors, Steve had to write a thesis. Dr. Minken, Steve's advisor, provided six topics that Steve could choose from. One of the choices was "Male Prostitution." Steve chose this topic.

The thesis required extensive fieldwork. So Steve interviewed Hollywood Vice officers, patrol officers, counselors, and religious workers trying to save the youth of the night. And Steve dressed up for the part and walked with the hustlers, talking with them on the street corners as they plied their trade, selling their young bodies.

Though Steve never had sex until after he graduated from the police academy years later, he never forgot those young street hustlers.

Steve had learned about his own sexuality from these prostitutes.

The Hunt

As soon as Cameron got back, Charlie grabbed Lisa out of Luther's room. Charlie was blazing on speed, and he wanted some action right away. He had to do his good deed to clean up society. And speed made Charlie feel godlike. He also felt that it increased his sex drive, though he found it difficult to keep his hard-on because his concentration kept slipping.

"Where we goin'?" Cameron asked nervously.

Charlie had wrapped the shotgun in a blanket and was leading them to the van.

"We're going huntin'," sneered Charlie. He was carrying Lisa with his other arm. Luther had given her some good shit, and she was out there in never-never land, loaded out of her mind. She was more down than downers, Charlie thought, watching Lisa on the nod.

Lisa could answer questions, though she appeared to be asleep. Her eyelids were almost closed. Periodically she would scratch her face as if she was moving in slow motion.

"Let's go see who's out pollutin' the Boulevard," said Charlie as he opened the side door of the van and pushed Lisa in.

Cameron saw the .25-caliber revolver in Charlie's waistband and quickly decided against arguing with him.

Mr. Huk watched the three get into the van. It was just starting to turn dark outside. He could tell that they had a rifle under his blanket. But Mr. Huk had learned not to get involved. It was a lesson that most Los Angelenos learned from their parents at an early age. If it doesn't concern you, stay out of it. Or you might get hurt.

Besides, Mr. Huk always felt relieved after Charlie left the hotel.

With Lisa lying behind the driver's seat and Cameron in the rear, Charlie closed the curtain behind the seat and drove down to Santa Monica Boulevard. It only took him two passes down the Boulevard to spot his target.

A wiry blond about five-nine was standing on the corner one block west of Highland.

"You fucking ready?" Charlie asked toward the back of the van.

"Y-yes," answered Cameron. He held the heavy pipe in his hands. Maybe he could kill this one with a smash to the head. That way the guy wouldn't have to suffer. But it would probably piss Charlie off. *Not only would he take it out on me*, thought Cameron, *but he'd probably make us go after another hustler. What's the use?*

"Stay in the fucking back until I start moving. Then clobber him," Charlie ordered the curtain.

Charlie made eye contact as he slowed the van and passed the young blond, then pulled the van around the corner and stopped just after the Versateller machine. This area was all commercial, with residences to the north. Now that it was dark, the area was closed up. Because of the nature of the area, with hustlers looking for a fix, everything of value was either behind heavy metal bars or had already been stolen.

Charlie leaned over and rolled down the passenger window. He was used to the routine.

The blond came up to the window and leaned on top of the door frame. He didn't open the door as he checked out the interior of the van. His eyes stayed on the curtain for a moment before focusing on Charlie.

Charlie's right hand was squeezing his crotch as he locked eyes with the hustler.

"What's your name?" asked the prostitute.

"Mike," lied Charlie. "What's yours?"

"Dino."

"Want a ride?" asked Charlie.

"I'm not really hitchhiking. I'm working," responded Dino, using the SHL, the Standard Hustler's Line.

"Maybe I can help you make some money."

Charlie didn't have to ask Dino twice. Dino opened the door and sat down in the van, closing the door after him.

"Where you all from?" Dino queried, looking at Charlie.

Charlie started up the van without answering, driving slowly down the street into the darkness of the commercial area.

Dino was still watching Charlie. He noticed that the man's demeanor had somehow changed. "You have a place we can go? Or are we gonna use the back of the van?"

Charlie glared at the faggot. "Yeah, right, we'll use the back of the van all right."

Dino saw a movement to his left rear and started to turn when something hard and heavy struck him in the back of the head. Dino's vision was swimming as the force smashed the side of his face into the glove box area.

But Dino had grown up on the streets. In addition to fighting all of his stepfathers, Dino had fought in the motorcycle gang and was always getting into fights on the street. He was as tough or tougher than the company he was in. Before Cameron could hit him again, Dino was kicking toward Cameron and reaching for the door handle.

A kick caught Cameron in the midsection, sending him backward. Charlie grabbed Dino's blond hair and yanked, pulling him toward the center of the van.

Lisa had risen unsteadily to see what was going on.

"Take the fuckin' wheel, Lisa!" yelled Charlie as he grappled with Dino with his free hand. As Lisa took the wheel of the slowly moving van, Charlie grabbed Dino and picked him up, throwing him between the seats into the rear of the van.

Though she was only going 10 mph, it seemed to Lisa that she must be speeding at over 50 mph. She tried to slow down as Charlie and Cameron were fighting in the back.

Dino fought like a cat. With a broken jaw and blood rushing down from the gash in the side of his head, he clawed, kicked, and used every dirty trick he knew to get away from the big guy and the guy with the pipe.

The pipe came down twice more, and Dino lost sight in one eye and felt his forearm break. He continued fighting. He knew he was fighting for his life.

Cursing out fags and hustlers, Charlie made sure that Dino couldn't get to the rear or side doors of the van. His body blocked the driver area.

As Lisa turned right on Lexington, the first street north of the Boulevard, Dino threw himself between Charlie's feet. Climbing into the front seat, Dino grabbed the handle of the passenger door. His broken jaw prevented him from screaming, even if there had been someone around to hear his yells.

Charlie grabbed Dino around the front of his face and by the back of his shirt. Dino almost passed out from the pain as he forced his jaw to move, biting down on Charlie's hand.

When Charlie released his hold, Dino lunged forward. His shirt ripped, and Dino fell to the ground, outside the van.

Dino pushed himself up to run. Looking around with his one good eye, he saw that Highland was directly in front of him, less than thirty feet away.

Seeing that the van was moving slowly toward Highland, Dino started to run in the opposite direction. Simultaneously, the rear door of the van opened. Dino turned to look. If he could have opened his mouth in fear, he would have.

Charlie stood between the open back doors of the van, aiming a shotgun at him from less than ten feet away.

Before the blast hit him, Dino wondered if the local sheriff back home would tell his mother, "I told you that boy would turn out no good."

The blast practically cut Dino in half. He died instantly in the street between two buildings. One of the buildings was a wholesale photo finishing plant, primarily working for the Hollywood movie studios. Ironically, the other building housed the Gay and Lesbian Community Center.

Dino never considered himself gay and therefore, like most of the hustlers, had refused to enter the community center. Dying in the street ten yards from the center doors was the closest Dino ever got to asking them for assistance.

The brown van was long gone. Charlie had quickly shut the doors and pushed Lisa out of the driver's seat, speeding off onto Highland.

Dino's body lay in the street. His upper torso pointed toward Highland, and his lower torso was at an extreme angle lying vertically, blood and intestines pouring into the street. It wouldn't take a necrophiliac to know that Dino was dead.

But in Hollywood, it was more likely that a pervert would discover the body than would the overworked and understaffed local gendarme.

In fact, it was two hours until the Hollywood Division of the LAPD received a call. And it was almost three hours before a police unit finally made it to the scene. (The caller had been transferred three times before getting an officer who would take the information.)

Six hours from the minute that Dino was killed, the first LAPD homicide detective arrived and stepped under the yellow POLICE LINE—DO NOT CROSS crime scene tape to examine the body.

The paramedics had left three hours before, but the coroner and the crime scene technicians wouldn't be there for at least another two hours. They were tied up on two homicides in the south end of the city.

That would give the arriving uniform officers plenty of time to trample any evidence (though there originally had been no available units to respond, once the officers heard about the grotesque remains, the units poured in from three divisions) and the homicide detective on the scene sufficient time to discover that there were no witnesses.

NHI

The Los Angeles Police Department has a report form for everything: crime report, employee's report, overtime report, personnel report, evaluation report, sick report, administrative report, etc. The primary purpose of these reports is not to capture data. The purpose of all the reports is for the exception; so that if something goes wrong, the Department management will be able to find a scapegoat to point the finger at.

The reports are a paper trail of blame. Administrative CYA.

The Police Administration Building, referred to as PAB or Parker Center, is located across from City Hall East in not-so-beautiful downtown Los Angeles.

The eight-story building is fronted by a reminder of the hazards of police work—a fountain memorial with the name of every LAPD officer that has died in the line of duty. The list encircles the fountain many times.

Parking is nearly impossible in downtown L.A. Parker Center houses many specialized police divisions, including Juvenile Narcotics and the Robbery-Homicide Team that investigates Officer-Involved Shootings (OIS). Because of this, only those ranked lieutenant and above have parking in the police lot. All the other employees assigned to Parker Center are required to locate and pay for their own parking.

If these employees can make it through the gridlocked traffic, locate a parking lot, protect their car against theft, and make it to PAB without being mugged or pissing off (or getting pissed on by) the thousands of winos, they still have to wait in the lobby in excess of fifteen minutes for the infamous PAB elevators. There are only four, and three don't work.

Rumor has it that the elevators were specially designed when the building was built. Because of this, there are no replacement parts. The city electricians have devised and rigged, and spent thousands of dollars, to keep the elevators running. By definition, city efficiency means that it is cheaper to spend $100,000 in repairs over many years than to spend $25,000 one time to replace the damn thing.

So Department employees wait for the one working elevator—which stops on every floor whether it needs to or not. The OPEN DOOR and CLOSE DOOR buttons are equally effective—they're for display only. But at least it gives officers something to vent their anger on.

Some employees sneak and use the freight elevator in the side hallway. The chief can usually be seen with his driver/bodyguard waiting for this elevator, which is only slightly faster than the other four.

95

The relative importance of each administrative office, as viewed by the chief, can be determined by the closeness to his office. The sixth floor of Parker Center houses all the "brass," so named because of all the decorations on their uniform collars.

The chief has the northeast corner. If a person could get past the chief's secretary, Nancy, he would see a nicely appointed mahogany office with the walls covered with awards and photos. But it is easier to carry a suitcase of cocaine past Lizard, the Department's urine-soaked narcotics dog, than it is to get past Nancy. In fact, it would be easier to sneak an SPCA truck past the entire K-9 division than try to sneak by Nancy to talk with the chief.

Beside the chief's office is the director of the Office of Operations, which oversees all of patrol; Operations Headquarters Bureau, which oversees detectives and SWAT; and the Office of Administrative Services, which oversees the Department's automated services. Closest to the chief is his only personal friend on The Job, the commander in charge of press relations. The commander reviews anything that is to be released to the media and tidies up any matter that might make the chief look bad.

Officers working the sixth floor think the primary duty of the press relations commander is to use all of his contacts and influence to ensure that the chief gets elected to a political office.

The only other office near the chief's, except for the chief's conference room in the center, which is used for news conferences, is the office of the chief of staff. The chief of staff conducts all the business for the chief. This position is filled by the most competent commander in the Department.

These same sixth-floor officers agree that the primary duty of the chief of staff is to protect the chief from himself. It was realized long ago that the chief was inept and such a poor manager that someone more intelligent was needed to protect him.

This was realized even before the chief told the national media that "Blacks aren't beaten any more than anyone else by LAPD officers. Blacks just bleed more."

If the chief of staff is successful and there are no major media or departmental faux-pas (at least none that reach the attention of the public), he is rewarded by being given the first place on the next promotional list for deputy chief.

The most powerful position beside the chief is the assistant chief in charge of the Office of Operations (OO). This position oversees the 3,000 patrol officers that work in the eighteen geographical areas. Though there are more than 8,000 LAPD officers, only about 3,000 of them work in patrol cars answering the community's requests for service.

Because this is the second most powerful position in the Department, the assistant chief's office is located directly beside the chief's.

Every position from the rank of captain up to assistant chief is assigned an aide. This prestigious position, known as an "adjutant," is considered to be a promotional assignment given only to those expected to promote up through the ranks.

Until the 1980s, the positions were only filled with male Caucasian officers. La Ley, the Hispanic LAPD officers' organization, had to file a lawsuit to force LAPD to allow Latins into this assignment.

La Ley, which is Spanish for "the law," was only partially successful. On the sixth floor, the adjutant positions are primarily filled by white, male, born-again Christians.

Even the city council was unsuccessful in opening up these positions (as they usually are any time they challenge the Department).

Due to the drastic increase in street crime, blatant narcotics sales, and gang-related criminal activities, it was determined that more officers were needed on the street. No one on the city council was willing to increase the taxes to pay for more officers, because it was close to an election year.

The city council attempted to civilianize many Department positions, replacing those officers doing paperwork jobs with civilians so that those officers could return to the streets. The brass of the Department didn't mind, until their own assistants were included in that redeployment.

Immediately, the brass went to work. Since every manager of the LAPD was promoted up through the ranks, they share the universal belief of sworn police officers: that you can't trust anyone who doesn't carry a gun and badge.

If it just affected the street officers, the brass could live with any change. But this was blasphemy! The city council was taking their own private assistants out of their offices!

Immediately these adjutants were reassigned, through OO, to geographical divisions. Before the paperwork for their reassignments had even gone through, the officers had been placed on an "indefinite loan" back to the bureaus.

According to the reports developed by the Automated Services Division (the bureau commander's adjutant personally approved the report) and forwarded to the city council, the number of patrol officers responding to calls had been increased. In actuality, these adjutants had never even cleaned out their desks.

On top of that, all the new civilians assigned to the Department managers were placed overseeing paperwork jobs, freeing more officers to assist the brass.

The LAPD brass considered this a major coup. After all, the only ones who suffered were those citizens being robbed, burglarized, or murdered in the streets. And they never seemed to care before.

Every captain has a sergeant who works as his adjutant. Every commander has a sergeant-2 (a slightly higher rank). Each deputy and assistant chief gets a lieutenant to preview his paperwork. And to pick up his lunch or his dry-cleaned clothes.

In fact, most of the captains, deputy chiefs, and assistant chiefs also have several police officer assistants to handle special projects for them. Such projects include the completion of a commander's thesis for his master's degree.

This is not to say that the brass of LAPD have a cushy job. Only the street officers think that the management works nine to five, with Fridays and weekends off.

In fact, there are so many projects that come from the chief and from each of the city council committees and offices, as well as from the geographical areas and specialized divisions, that most of the brass work late into the evening. After they finish at the office, they pack a briefcase and take the rest of the paperwork home to review during dinner. They take two briefcases home for the weekend.

Of course, their weekend *does* start at noon on Friday.

Just like his predecessor, the new assistant chief of OO is a white, male, born-again Christian. When he isn't on The Job, he can be found conducting a sermon at his community church in Orange County.

He also conducts Christian police retreats once a year, which are attended by hundreds of LAPD officers. As a side business, he makes videotapes on various religious topics, including, "Jesus, Heterosexuals, and Law Enforcement."

These tapes are retailed by a born-again Orange County sheriff's deputy, who runs a small "Christians with Guns" business, when he's not putting bad guys in jail.

Of course, the assistant chief's adjutant is also a born-again.

The assistant chief's blond, blue-eyed adjutant sat at his desk reviewing the twenty-seven-page homicide report and the attached memo from the captain of Hollywood Area.

Attached to the memo was the LAPD routing slip. The routing slip has a box for the initials of all the appropriate command staff who are supposed to read the attached document. Of course, the adjutants read and summarize the document for their bosses. Oftentimes they even sign their bosses' initials to the slip.

The slip also has a list of actions to be taken. This list is only for the head honcho. He checks one or more of the lines, requiring anything from an extensive amount of additional work to "no additional action."

Because there was a chance of major publicity and this becoming a high-profile incident, the adjutant decided to hand-carry the document in to the assistant chief.

The adjutant rapped twice, lightly, before walking in without waiting for a reply. Due to budget constraints, the assistant chief's office was decorated in old, functional office furniture. (The chief of police had his office decorated from a donation for that purpose from a large corporation in the city.)

The assistant chief sat behind his scarred wooden desk, leaning back in his chair, reading the Bible. The New Testament, of course.

This was a common sight to the adjutant. Before making any major decisions, the assistant chief often read a verse or two. Or three. Or a dozen.

The adjutant didn't really believe in any of the crap he listened to every Sunday and on Wednesday nights upstairs on the eighth floor in the Bible study group. The only thing he cared about "saving" was his career.

He had bought clothes, including shoes, that matched the assistant chief's. He started attending the retreats and the assistant chief's community church. And now he was making more money due to his promotion and was an adjutant, which allowed him access to study groups and materials so that he could be guaranteed a spot on the next captain's list. Praise the Lord!

The adjutant waited respectfully.

The assistant chief, who was the only manager who continued to wear his uniform, raised his gray head. His uniform was immaculate; he had learned to keep it that way from his years in the Marine Corps.

" 'For Christ is the end of the law; for righteousness to everyone that believeth.' "

The assistant chief took the Bible off his knees and set it on the desk, closing it. His eyes were glazed over.

"Do you know which book that's from?"

"Romans 10."

The assistant chief beamed. "That's right! Verse 4."

The adjutant reflected on how lucky it was that his wife, who really was a devout Christian, had put that quote on their refrigerator. But he said, "Sir, I think you should review this."

The assistant chief waved his right hand dismissively, as his eyes cleared. "That's what I hired you for."

The adjutant smiled. "It's a homicide that occurred in Hollywood over the weekend."

"So what? I had six of them over the weekend in South Bureau. Including one drive-by triple homicide."

"Yes, sir. But this investigation had the Prostitution Enforcement Detail doing some of the follow-up. It seems that the victim was a bunboy on Santa Monica Boulevard. Other bunboys told the PED team officers that there have been several such homicides in the past couple weeks."

"Have they found the bodies?"

The adjutant was hoping that he wasn't going to look like a fool. He had reviewed the report completely and even called the assigned homicide investigator to review any angles not included in the report.

"No, they haven't found any other male prostitutes murdered. Only overdoses. But the PED officers were told—"

The assistant chief interrupted. "If there are no other bodies, then no amount of conjecture will illuminate any more evidence. It sounds like a closed matter."

The adjutant tried one last angle. "From a media perspective, being as how things are between the Department and the gay community right now, I thought—"

"I don't give a damn about the concerns of a community of sinners. If a homosexual prostitute was killed, it was probably by another homosexual. The degree of violence perpetrated by homosexuals is astounding."

"Yes, sir. I just thought you might wish to generate some type of investigation into the matter or a report, in the event the chief wants a briefing."

The adjutant held out the document toward his boss.

"I appreciate your concern, but it seems misplaced in the present case. Homosexual suspect. Homosexual victim, and a prostitute at that. Their community approves of that kind of thing."

"Yes, sir. Did you want to check the routing slip?"

The assistant chief took the document. He hastily scribbled his initials in the appropriate box and checked the line: "No Additional Action." He handed the report back to his adjutant.

The adjutant turned to leave.

"Homosexual suspect and homosexual victim. NHI."

The adjutant exited the assistant chief's office and closed the door behind him.

NHI. He hadn't heard that since being a sergeant in patrol. It was a patrol term.

Though the assistant chief actually only worked two years on the street, working administrative assignments ever since then, he still considered himself a "policeman's policeman," which was why he probably wore the uniform.

NHI was a term originally used by officers working the south end of the city. It originally referred to a crime where both the victim and the suspect were black.

With the increasing criminal street gangs, the term was used to refer to the killings that occurred between rival gangs.

Later, younger street officers adopted the term for any crime in which a member of a minority group was the victim. That was how the "new breed" of officer was.

The strata of police discrimination were similar to those of the larger society; the further away in skin color the group was from being white, the more stigmatized they were.

So police seldom discriminated against Asians, except for constantly saying, "Wha-happen?" when they had traffic accidents.

And most of the officers didn't particularly dislike Hispanics, as long as they spoke English, "since they're in America now!"

But most police officers disliked blacks, except some of their partners. In fact, many times it was the black officers who were more discriminatory toward black civilians and suspects.

Of course, since many LAPD officers were in the military or the active reserve, none of them cared for Arabs or Iranians, either.

And no matter what their skin color or ethnic background, the group that was at the absolute bottom of the police scale was homosexuals.

Lesbians were OK. In fact, the only complaint made against lesbians was, "That's one woman that I can't get into bed. And if she's got a lover, she's taking *two* women away from me."

Additionally, lesbians were viewed as a challenge to get into bed. LAPD officers loved to raid lesbian bars for overcrowding for this reason.

But homosexual males were considered less than human by many LAPD officers. That's why they used the term *NHI* whenever a homosexual was killed. The attitude was: why bother to investigate it?

There's "No Humans Involved." NHI.

* * *

The rumors of Cainen's homosexuality began during his background investigation. As part of the routine investigation, Cainen's name was run through ANI, the countywide Automated Name Index, to see if he had made any police reports. Cainen had. One of these reports had been filed with Hollywood Division in 1978.

Cainen's car had been burglarized and his wallet taken. The car had been parked in the lot at 3460 Beverly Boulevard. The reporting LAPD officer had duly noted that this was the parking lot of the Odyssey, a teenage homosexual discotheque.

The background investigator, following the LAPD policy of disqualifying all homosexual applicants, recommended that Cainen be removed from the academy waiting list. Luckily for Cainen, by 1982, when he had applied to the LAPD, the Odyssey had been taken over by heterosexual owners, and changed into a chic nightclub.

The lieutenant in charge of the background unit was one of the Department "golden boys," expected to move up through the ranks. But he wasn't a born-again Christian. The lieutenant overruled the investigator's recommendation, keeping Cainen on the list for the next academy class.

After all, the club couldn't be for homos, since he took his wife dancing there every Saturday night.

Nonetheless, the background investigator felt it was his duty to make an informal call to the academy training staff to let them know about Cainen. (Once again proving another LAPD maxim: "telephone, telegraph, tell a cop.")

Following up on the suspicion, the physical training staff used Cainen as the "suspect" in training maneuvers, injuring him. Cainen refused to be "recycled" (leaving the academy to return in a later class), despite his injuries. He continued on with the physical training, causing permanent injury to his already-damaged knee.

Cainen graduated from the academy with top honors in everything except shooting. His martial arts training allowed him to excel in self-defense, and his college had well prepared him to ace the academic portion of the academy. As for shooting, Cainen did remarkably well considering he had never held a gun before the academy.

Despite his high status, the academy staff dutifully notified his first division of assignment, passing on the rumor that Cainen was a faggot.

Cainen blended in well, though, and his prior experience as an Explorer allowed him to handle the people with whom he came in contact. This earned him the respect of all but the staunchest fag-haters in the division.

The rumors began circulating even more virulently after Cainen was sent into the telephone booth in the Shortstop bar in Rampart. The Shortstop was a cop "watering hole" on Sunset Boulevard. The entire A.M. watch of Rampart and officers from several other divisions and the California Highway Patrol would meet at the bar at 8:00 A.M., after their shift.

Usually these officers would drink till 4:00 P.M., then go home to sleep until 10:00 P.M., when they had to get up to get back to work at Rampart. This allowed them six hours of sleep a day, plus what they could catch while on the taxpayers' time clock.

They'd be back at Shortstop by eight the next morning.

It was believed that most A.M. watch officers were pale because they had to sleep during the hours of daylight due to their work schedule. A.M. watch officers are usually referred to as "the vampires."

In reality, many of them were still hungover from the same morning. Only *menudo* from the Mexican restaurant on Sunday or a quick shot from a bottle in a call box would get rid of the hangover.

Many divorces resulted over the Shortstop. Even more great war stories, which made up the verbal heritage of the LAPD, were developed, embellished, and agreed upon inside that one little bar.

Many personnel investigations completed by Internal Affairs originated out of the Shortstop. Joseph Wambaugh, the internationally acclaimed police writer, used several of the incidents in his books.

In one incident, the entire male contingent of the Rampart A.M. watch had had sex on the pool table in the bar with a female records clerk.

Two stupid Cuban Marielitos once decided to rob the SS. They obviously were too new to the neighborhood, and to the United States, to know that it was a cop watering hole.

Old Danny Innes, the baby-faced, army-jacketed, gung-ho twelve-year policeman from Central, was in the bar that night. Danny spent his days off at the range and owned a personal gun collection that rivaled the entire arsenal of the LAPD SWAT team. While some people admired the arsenal Danny kept at home, many just admired Danny, who *was* a walking arsenal.

Danny had been in more shootings than he, or his commanding officer, wanted to count. In many of them, the supposed gun or knife used by the suspect was never recovered. Danny usually testified that the weapon had been taken from the scene by one of the other fleeing suspects.

No one ever refuted Danny's stories. No one had ever lived to refute his statements.

Both the Marielitos wound up shot in the back ten feet from the door of the SS, as they had been leaving with their loot. They had been shot with a pistol-grip shotgun.

Both the suspects were killed, which pleased most of the cops inside. They simply stated, "Good. No wits." And went on drinking their hard liquor. They continued drinking until the OIS team from Robbery-Homicide arrived, led by the impervious Lt. Lance Larson.

Even the OIS team, who would question even the shooting of a fleeing felon, if the shots were in the back, didn't bother with this one. They figured that anyone who would hold up the SS was too stupid to live, anyway.

The gun policy at the LAPD is among the strictest in the nation. Not a single pistol, on- or off-duty, carried by LAPD patrol officers or detectives can cock. It is LAPD policy that all guns carried by officers must be "neutered" by the LAPD armory, to prevent accidental discharges (as well as to prevent the ability to cock the gun and threaten suspects).

The most practiced LAPD officers can still cock their weapons by pulling back on the trigger until just before it fires. More than one locker has been shot to death by officers practicing this while changing out of their uniforms.

Until 1988, when the LAPD began switching to the Baretta 9mm automatic, officers could only carry a Smith & Wesson .38-caliber four- or six-inch.

Most police agencies are lax in their restrictions about which guns their officers may carry off-duty. Many allow the officers to carry any legal handgun of their choice, as long as the weapon is registered with their agency. The LAPD is so restrictive that officers are only allowed to carry their duty weapon, a two-inch version of the Smith & Wesson .38-caliber revolver, or specific semi-automatics.

Even the ammunition used by officers must be approved by the Department. Until 1986, LAPD officers were only allowed to use ball-point lead rounds in their revolvers. The Police Commission, in their wisdom, determined that LAPD officers were more likely to accidentally shoot themselves than to purposely shoot suspects. To lessen the costs for officer-involved injuries, it was determined that ball lead would go right through a body, causing minimum injury. Hollow-point bullets caused serious internal injuries. Some police commissioners felt it was cheaper to allow suspects to run away or still be standing so they could shoot back than to pay out to officers who were injured as a result of accidental shootings.

Besides, it was getting expensive to keep replacing lockers.

Most police agencies had long before switched to hollow-point rounds, for their superior stopping power. (Even after the LAPD changed in 1986, the officers still had to carry flat-nosed, semijacketed rounds.)

The upper torso of a person is referred to as the "ten ring" by LAPD officers. This is because the officers must qualify on the range by earning ten points for every round that hits the center mass of the silhouette target.

The LAPD has one of the strictest shooting practice requirements in California, requiring officers to shoot their guns every other month. They must qualify twice a year with the shotgun.

Because of the low power load in the bullets used by LAPD officers, on more than one occasion officers have unloaded their entire revolver into the ten ring of a suspect without knocking the suspect down.

Six rounds, and the suspect, particularly one high on PCP, still faces or runs from the officer.

In one shooting, the PCP suspect was found face down two blocks from where he had been shot six times in the ten ring. The coroner determined that the suspect had died from loss of blood.

As the officers referred to it, the suspect had died from "lead poisoning."

In Danny's shooting, because it was the Shortstop, even the Internal Affairs captain didn't question the use of the shotgun.

Of course Danny had stated that he had retrieved the gun from his car, which was only in there since he had just bought the weapon from the LAPD Revolver & Athletic Club, which is the police academy store. The club sells weapons at manufacturers' discount rates to LAPD officers.

No one in the entire chain of command questioned how Danny had time to exit the bar, go to his car, load his new weapon, and still shoot the suspects only ten feet from the door.

Of course, twelve A.M. watch officers from two LAPD divisions, one CHP sergeant, and six civilian female groupies all provided declarations that were indistinguishable from Danny's statement.

However, the Rampart patrol captain did issue a verbal directive that no Rampart officers were to drink at the Shortstop anymore. And none of them did. They obeyed the order for almost three entire days.

Part of the mystique of the Shortstop was the old-fashioned telephone booth with the painted sides that sat in the back of the poolroom. Every probationer to Rampart and Central A.M. watch was required to make a call from that booth. As such, Cainen was taken down in his fourth month in the field, when he changed watches.

Cainen, who was twenty-three and still a virgin, came out of the bar and walked directly to his training officer, a fifteen-year veteran who was still seated in the patrol car. Cainen had been given twenty cents and told to go inside and use the phone booth to call the station.

Cainen came out with his face as white as a ghost.

"What's wrong?" asked the FTO nonchalantly.

Cainen fumbled for words for several moments before answering his training officer.

"Do you know what she wants to do to me?" Cainen finally blurted out.

"Yeah. And go back in there and do it."

This was Cainen's first test on A.M. watch, which was the watch with all the old-time LAPD officers.

Cainen failed the test. He refused to go back inside the SS and into the telephone booth.

In the booth was a woman known as "Iron Lips." And she wasn't given the moniker because of her choice of lipstick color.

* * *

Instantly the LAPD rumor mill developed a proprietary interest in Cainen's private life. The information passed on by the background investigator resurfaced immediately.

Cainen was discriminately transferred off the older officers' A.M. watch in the middle of the deployment period. No one was ever transferred mid-DP.

Cainen was also forced to work the desk or the report phone for four months, evidently because no one would work with Cainen as a probationer.

The harassment included constant obscene photos glued to his locker and messages written on the blackboard in roll call. The officers also started taping BEWARE: AIDS CONTAMINATION! dymo-labels onto all of Cainen's personal belongings whenever they were out of his eyesight.

They even managed to tape a sign reading FAG PATROL to the passenger side of his patrol car. He rode around with it for almost the entire shift while he was assigned to work a U-car taking reports, until an older woman pulled up beside his patrol car to point it out.

Cainen finished his probation and transferred to 77th Street Area. Things were so hectic with all the homicides and gang-related narcotics activity that no one appeared to have time to harass Cainen.

Then, in 1984, Cainen was spotted by a West Hollywood Los Angeles County sheriff's sergeant who had just transferred up from the Firestone Station.

The Firestone district is an unincorporated area of the county. Like the contract city of West Hollywood, police services are provided by the LASD. Firestone is adjacent to the LAPD's 77th Street Area. The sheriff's sergeant had backed up Cainen on several hot calls within 77th.

The LASD sergeant hated West Hollywood, which had no real crime, but which had plenty of sicko faggots running around holding each other's booties. He couldn't wait until his year was up so that he could transfer back to Firestone or even to that pit of a substation in Lynwood. *Hell*, he thought, *anywhere is better than working with all these lisping ALs*. (LASD deputies refer to gays as "Alternate Lifestylers.")

As the sergeant drove his patrol car up Robertson toward Santa Monica Boulevard, he had to look twice. In fact, he looked in his rearview mirror to be sure, but the man who had just come out of that fag disco Studio One was the same guy who was an LAPD officer that he had backed up in 77th Street Area on a couple drive-bys and street 211s.

Though he couldn't remember the guy's name, he found it out when he called the LAPD 77th Street Area captain's secretary the next day. He had dated her a couple times and knew her well enough to be sure that once he told her that there was a fruit in her division, she would tell every officer who was willing to listen.

V

Roy

Roy was eighteen. At five foot nine and 170 pounds, he was stocky, with blond hair and clear blue eyes. Roy made sure his eyes were clear by using Visine after he smoked out.

Though Roy was well built, he habitually sucked in his minimal beer belly whenever he was in public. It wasn't that Roy, who was very masculine and usually had at least one girlfriend on the sidelines, was vain; it was just good for business.

Roy had been a professional prostitute for over four years. He worked in both New York and Los Angeles, living in either an apartment financed by one of his rich, married clients or with a gay friend, who was usually in the movie or recording industry.

Roy started working the Boulevard as soon as he arrived in Los Angeles. After working the Boulevard for one week, Roy set up his own private clientele list.

Several of Roy's clients were very wealthy. Two of his New York businessmen clients flew out to L.A. twice a year, putting Roy up in his own room in the Beverly Hills Hotel, all expenses paid, with all the room service he could use. Roy only wished that they served drugs!

Roy's parents were divorced. His mother lived in Southern California, and his father lived in the upper half of the state.

Roy always made plans to visit his parents, but he usually forgot to tell his parents. Which was OK, since he never seemed to actually make the trip.

Roy's client list was a handful of index cards and pieces of papers with names, phone numbers, and prices. On a corner of each card was written: "$15," "$25," or "$100." This way, Roy knew whom to call depending on the amount of money he needed. The prices were based on what act was expected of him and to what degree Roy was friends with the "client."

Roy, like many male hustlers, gave discounts if the client was young or attractive. He met new clients in gay discos or bars and at parties. Many of his current clients had referred some of their friends to him.

Like most hustlers, Roy sometimes had sex with his "client-friends" for free. In return, if Roy was hard up for money, he called on these client-friends for quick trick money. He also periodically called his client-friends when he needed a place to stay. When Roy got kicked out by a client-friend he was staying with, Roy counted on these others to give him an emergency place to stay.

Prior to his hustling career, Roy's only homosexual experience was with another boy on his high school football team. Roy and the boy jerked off together. But, of course, they didn't touch each other. As Roy described the boy, "he was the biggest black stud in school."

In Roy's opinion, it is "sick" to believe that a man could fall in love with another man. In fact, Roy was in love with one of his two current girlfriends.

Prior to his two girlfriends, Roy was "going steady" with a transvestite.

Before his most recent move to California, Roy lived in New York with two queens. He referred to the two effeminate guys in the female gender; one of the "girls" was a recording star.

Before that, Roy had stayed in an apartment financed by a married millionaire.

One of Roy's best clients was a very wealthy Roman Catholic priest. The fifty-two-year-old priest was only interested in young boys. Often Roy got out of having sex with the priest by bringing some sixteen-year-old, new to the street, and introducing him to the priest. The priest explained to Roy that it was okay for a man of the cloth to have sex with boys.

"My oath of celibacy only holds for women."

The priest often promised that he would take Roy to his second home, which he maintained in Rome, since he was one of the advisors to the pope.

Sometimes, like many of his peers, Roy did odd jobs for his clients to make extra money. He really didn't do much work, but it provided him with a sense of self-esteem and gave the clients quick and easy access to him for sex. If asked, though, Roy stated that he was a "construction worker."

Because of his constant movement, Roy carried few possessions on him. One of his few personal possessions was a string necklace that held a safe-deposit key. Inside his safe-deposit box, Roy kept his valuables, including his birth certificate.

From experience, Roy knew that many of the hustlers got robbed of their possessions. Those that didn't get robbed usually lost the items while they were high.

Roy also kept some emergency money inside the box. He had never touched these funds, even the one time that he was in constant pain from an infected tooth and desperately needed a dentist. Instead, he later found one who did the work for free; the dentist had picked Roy up in his Mercedes on the Boulevard.

Roy had done some reading on sexuality. As a result, he regarded bisexuality as an inherently beneficial lifestyle. Roy felt that bisexuals were "more intelligent and not as close-minded as straights or gays."

Roy had had a variety of sexually transmitted diseases but had always seen a doctor for treatment as soon as he became aware of the problem. He didn't do this out of concern for personal hygiene. Rather, Roy believed that "business is business, and you gotta take care of the investment."

Like many hustlers, Roy blamed his current career choice on a single incident.

"Right after I got out of high school, I met my dream girl. I got a job to support the two of us. I worked real hard so that I could afford a car for her. She always wanted a Cougar. Anyway, right after I got her this car, you see, I found out she was dating this other guy. So I confronted her. And the bitch told me that she had never really loved me and that she had only been using me the whole time. That really crushed me. And then she moved out. And she took the car with her. So I vowed never to be used by a woman again."

Roy felt that he had only been taken in because he was "pussy-whipped." He vowed to master his sexual desires and make them work for him.

So he became a bisexual homosexual prostitute.

Roy's story was probably bullshit, but on the street, such a story was held in high regard by the other hustlers.

Roy was currently living with a songwriter who had written a number of disco hits. Roy spent his free time hustling pool at the Odyssey disco.

Around town, Roy had the reputation of having a "horse dick." Because of this, he was constantly sought out by all the "size queens," who liked to be fucked by a man with a large penis.

Roy used to have the reputation of being exclusively a "top," the inserter in anal intercourse. Recently, however, Roy had costarred in the porno video *Billy Does Hawaii*. In it, Roy got fucked for the first time. And, according to Roy, for the last time.

For the past week Roy's clientele had all been out of town or too busy. Despite his many calls, no one had been interested in getting together. And it seemed that the only ones with money at the Odyssey had been the other hustlers.

Roy found that it was even hard to deal drugs for profit. Either everybody had them or nobody could get some.

So tonight Roy decided to do something he hadn't done in a long time. For the first time in almost two years, Roy decided to hit the Boulevard.

And it was also going to be his last time.

Helter-Skelter

Charlie Corcoran claimed to have read *Helter-Skelter*, written by the district attorney who had prosecuted Charles Manson. In fact, Charlie claimed to have read the book over a dozen times.

But anyone who knew Charlie was aware that he couldn't read past the third-grade level. Not that anyone would ever question Charlie. It was more likely that Charlie had somehow obtained the newspaper articles that had come out about the trial following the 1969 killing of Sharon Tate and the LaBiancas. Or that Charlie made his half brother, Cameron, read the book to him.

In any case, despite his lack of education, Charlie's intelligence allowed him to understand aspects of the murders, and of Manson, that even the DA seemed to have missed. The only ones who wouldn't have missed these aspects were the court psychologists who examined those related to the case.

Charlie's street-smarts, and his unfailing leadership abilities, allowed him some insights into the way that Manson had engaged in mind control. And Charlie's ego caused him to view himself as a modern-day Manson, with the same capabilities and accomplices.

Manson's lieutenant was Tex Watson. Manson had changed Watson from a drifter to a murderer within one year. He did it by providing Watson with as many women as he desired, and the constant presence of mind-altering drugs.

Charlie viewed Cameron as his own Tex Watson. Starting the third week after Cameron took the bus out to visit Charlie in California, Charlie kept him inundated with drugs. Unlike Manson, though, Charlie used fear instead of mind control to force Cameron to do what Charlie wanted.

Also, unlike Manson, Charlie took just as much drugs as he gave to Cameron. Manson, to maintain control, used drugs less than his followers.

Charlie viewed Lisa as his Leslie Van Houten. Though Lisa, like Van Houten, had a well-adjusted exterior, drug use had freed her enough to leave her family in Nebraska. Charlie then introduced Lisa, as well as Cameron, to LSD. Though Manson had used a more powerful hallucinogen, belladonna root, LSD had much the same effect.

Amazingly, there were similarities between Lisa and Van Houten. Lisa had been a very good student until her final year of high school, when her new boyfriend introduced her to marijuana and other drugs. Also, Lisa, like Leslie, had gotten pregnant from a boyfriend and had an abortion when she was sixteen.

With the mind-altering effects of the drug, Charlie guided his two cohorts through their first trips. The effects were mind-blowing to both Lisa and Cameron. And the only source of calm and control was Charlie. They grew to trust and fear him.

Like Manson, Charlie used the drugs as part of a program to desensitize his accomplices. Charlie told them that there was really no such thing as wrong, or good and bad, that these were just subjective values placed by the greater society to control its people. Under the effects of the drugs, this made sense to Lisa and Cameron.

While they were on their LSD trips, Charlie, who much preferred speed or heroin, had Lisa and Cameron visualize killing people who had harmed them in their childhoods: people upon whom they wished revenge and death. Charlie guided them through killing these people. And he told them how "right" it was. And then he took them further in their misguided imagery.

Charlie kept them high on all kinds of drugs. He kept them high twenty-four hours a day, even when they were sleeping.

During this indoctrination period following the killing of JoJo, Charlie never let Cameron or Lisa out of his sight. He kept them constantly high for more than a week. By the end of the tenth day, though both were experiencing flashbacks, Cameron and Lisa had developed a belief that LSD made them more alert. It allowed them to think more clearly and to see the goings-on in their own minds. It allowed them to see things for what they really were, unclouded by the values of society.

Borrowing liberally from Manson, Charlie further desensitized Cameron and Lisa to killing. To do this, Charlie took them out in the van and picked up stray cats and dogs. He explained to Lisa that they would be hit by cars and die a painful death if they were not put out of their misery.

At first, Charlie killed the animals. Sometimes he used his .25-caliber. More often, he used a mallet that he kept in the back of the van. One smash on the head killed the animals. At least it worked until Lisa tried it. Without upper body strength, it often took her three or four strokes until the squirming animal was put out of its misery.

In any case, Charlie accomplished his goal of teaching his assistants to kill on command, or at least to watch a killing without feeling.

Charlie explained that this ability was necessary for them to accomplish their goal. Again borrowing liberally from his idol, Charlie explained that he was preparing them for a God-given mission to save society.

Acquired Immune Deficiency Syndrome, AIDS, was a plague sent to test the Earth. If the Earth failed, the disease would destroy all mankind. In order to save the world, Charlie told his cohorts, they had to personally take risks to end the spread of AIDS.

As Charlie explained it, fags were the plague of society. Manson had explained that Helter Skelter was to be a bloody race war between blacks and whites. Charlie Corcoran explained that the way to stop the spread of AIDS was to kill off all the homosexuals before they spread the disease to "normal" people.

And they would start by killing off the most conspicuous of the plague carriers: the street hustlers.

Charlie was proud of the fact that the hustlers they killed, like Manson's victims, were chosen at random, just by driving around.

Charlie and his associates were actually a part of the street world. Despite their actions, they were part of the same counterculture as their victims.

Though the world was approaching the millenium, the street society was stuck in the era of the 1960s. Their hair, dress, and drug use matched the "hippies" of that bygone era. The Grateful Dead was still the favorite musical group.

Even the rebellion against the "establishment" remained within the counterculture of the street. The only exception, and it was a major one, was that the "hippies" believed in letting go of their possessions. Hustlers, in their screwed-up version of what the sixties meant, actually held the highest regard for material goods. Whereas the hippies of the sixties pointed to money as the evil at the center of the world's problems, the street hustlers saw wealth as their most sought-after goal.

The hustlers bought into the societal goal that their forebearers had fought vehemently against, the idea that self-worth was determined by material possessions, that he who dies with the most toys wins.

Just as any subculture defines what behavior it will accept, so Charlie taught Lisa and Cameron that the removal of the hustlers, by any means, was an acceptable goal. And with each recurring murder, both Cameron and Lisa found that the only solace they could find was with the same man who was becoming increasingly more brutal—Charlie.

And Charlie kept reassuring Lisa and Cameron that the killing of the hustlers was serving to save the world and that soon many others, such as gay-bashers and skinheads, would join in until it was acceptable to all of society.

What Charlie didn't tell his accomplices was that he was psychopathic. That was because even Charlie wasn't aware of it.

While still a child, Charlie was constantly abused by his mother. The abuse was mental as well as physical.

When Charlie's mother hit him, she struck him in the face or in the genitals. Sometimes she used objects, like shoes or hangers, to beat him. While she beat him, she yelled at him, calling him a "faggot" and telling him that he would never be a real man.

Although he had superior intelligence, Charlie Corcoran was a borderline psychopath. True to form, he had blamed every one of his crimes on circumstances that were not his fault.

Even his murder of the older lady who had hired him for carpentry work was entirely her fault. She was the one who came home early and discovered him taking her jewelry.

Charlie felt that he had been mistreated, misunderstood, and falsely accused throughout his entire life. Mostly, he felt that he had never been given any opportunity to demonstrate his abilities to succeed in the legitimate world.

For most of his adult life, Charlie had tried to evade responsibility for all of his dangerous actions by blaming them on others. His actions, he told those closest and most afraid of him, were in response to the wrongful deeds of others: others were to blame; others should accept the consequences of his wrath.

Charlie was a sociopathic psychopath—a redundant term that meant he could not get along in society. He could never learn from mistakes or understand or follow any of the rules of society that guide the behavior of others. His sociopathic behavior followed a path of growing intolerance and acting out.

During his pubescent years, Charlie began experiencing excruciatingly painful headaches. These headaches lasted until Charlie's attention was focused on his outward behavior. He started by stealing candy bars. He progressed to stealing bikes, and then strong-arming the other children in the neighborhood for their allowances. He graduated quickly to daytime burglaries.

By the time the headaches disappeared in his teens, Charlie was already using massive amounts of drugs and stabbing his robbery victims for the fun of it.

Prisons are referred to as "colleges for criminals." This is because the American criminal justice system is so overcrowded that they have very little ability to separate the hardened criminal from those who have committed violent acts for the first time.

115

Once Charlie entered the criminal justice system for his petty crimes, he met and was taught by experts in the commission of criminal acts. Intelligent as he was, Charlie sought out those who had committed the crimes that interested him.

Though these felons were hesitant at first, he used his manipulative personality to befriend them. Though he was far smarter than these criminals with below-average intelligence, they recognized the commonality. A fellow sociopath. Someone else who had no regard for the rules of society. Someone else who turned the societal value system around, so that the most prestigious act was the killing of a cop. Taking a life earned respect, not saving a life.

And Charlie memorized every detail they told him about how to commit crimes and how to avoid capture.

After all, these criminals told him, it wasn't their fault that they were criminals. It was society's fault that they had been mistreated. And now they were merely giving society back what it deserved. Right?

Of course, a little factor like the killing of an eighty-year-old woman would not be a serious transgression when viewed from this perspective . . . at least not to the sick minds of people like the alumni of "Folsom College."

Charlie became an extremely dangerous man. He had no internal controls or conscience. He acted on his every impulse, using his cunning to manipulate others or allow him to escape punishment.

When Charlie killed, he did it without hesitation. Or remorse.

Charlie Corcoran was not insane, according to the legal definition. Legally insane people cannot distinguish the difference between right and wrong. Charlie knew the difference; he just didn't care.

Charlie not only didn't care about the rights or feelings of others; these things were nonexistent in his world. Being a sociopath, he treated people as objects. Objects that he could control, avoid, or destroy.

Though Charlie explained that his goal was the elimination of those that could spread AIDS, the actual act of murder was his only real goal.

While most mental disorders affect the mind, with sociopaths it is the conscience that is affected. For this reason, psychiatrists have never been successful with sociopaths.

In court or prison or in the presence of police officers, where there will be the clear result of immediate punishment, sociopaths can control their behavior. More than that, they can be model citizens or prisoners. Once out of this environment, though, they cannot control the acting out of their impulses. Without constant external controls, they have no inner controls, or conscience, to prevent harming others.

At the same time that Charlie finally reached his potential of killing, society was increasingly adapting itself to accept and reward many sociopaths who exhibited the same behavioral traits but in socially acceptable channels.

Many occupations are particularly encouraging of sociopathic behavior. And many sociopaths get along successfully in society in these jobs. Careers geared toward sales or business, which encourage manipulation and lying, are perfect for the sociopath. While these traits can be learned within the executive structure, the true sociopath can excel without formal training.

Charlie sat in the motel room watching the television they had stolen from a prior motel. Lisa, who had passed out on the bed, had already checked the newspapers.

There was nothing on the TV and only a small article in the "Westside" section of the *L.A. Times* had reported Dino's killing. The papers had described it as the result of a drug dispute between male street prostitutes. Narcotics had been found on Dino, and the coroner had found amphetamine in his blood.

An easy explanation. The cops liked that. It meant that the case would be shelved with no further investigation.

There was nothing about their brown van.

Charlie got up and turned off the television. He had considered throwing his boot at it and smashing the screen to turn it off but decided to wait in case there was some publicity about the decrease in hustlers working the streets.

Someone on the street was suspecting something, because a lot of the hustlers were staying off the Boulevard and working the bars like Numbers on Sunset. Maybe they just couldn't explain where their friends had disappeared to.

But there was such a high turnover on the Boulevard, with everyone being *from* somewhere, that it wouldn't be noticed for too long. And you never knew when vice had picked someone up or a vice task force was working.

Maybe that was it, thought Charlie. *Maybe the faggots are worried that a vice task force is out there taking away the hustlers.*

No. That couldn't be it, because the hustlers were always back on the street within forty-eight hours of an arrest.

And it couldn't be the one killing. Murders were as common to the hustlers as they obviously were to the media.

One fucking little article on the third page in the middle of the paper. Fuck!

But Charlie smiled to himself. Though he loved to see publicity for his crimes, he had chosen to dump the bodies in Lancaster because he didn't want them discovered. Not only would this allow him more victims, but Charlie didn't want any clues for the police to follow up on.

Charlie didn't want to get caught. *That bullshit you see in TV movies where the murderer writes notes to help the police like "Please Stop Me" or other crap with the victim's lipstick on the bathroom mirror is bullshit*, thought Charlie.

You'd have to be three kinds of a fucking moron to leave the police clues. And you'd have to be insane to want to be caught and deep-fried in the micro-chair.

And Charlie wasn't insane.

"Wake up, bitch." Charlie shook Lisa. "Come on. We're going out to do some work. Get the fuck up."

Luther, that spade pimp, had given Lisa some free Quaaludes. They had really put the bitch out.

Charlie reached inside Lisa's blouse and pinched her right nipple hard.

Lisa yelled. "Whadya do that for?" she asked, sitting up and rubbing her breast through the blouse, with her eyes still half-closed.

"We have work to do," answered Charlie, getting aroused at Lisa's pain.

Charlie pushed Lisa back on to the bed. Roughly. He began unzipping his pants.

"Hey, no." Lisa turned to sit up. She was fully awake now.

"Lie back down," Charlie said harshly. He had unzipped his pants and taken his hardening penis out.

"Come on, Charlie. I can't do it now."

Lisa was frightened of Charlie's reaction. But she was still hurting because of Luther.

Charlie pushed her by the shoulders and climbed on top of her. He reached down and started undoing her pants zipper.

"I'm having my period."

Charlie paused for a moment. He then stood up and put his flaccid member back into his jeans.

"Where's Cameron?"

Lisa looked out of the corner of her eyes to be sure Charlie wasn't going to hit her, and then she sat up and fixed her blouse. Her nipple smarted.

"He said he was going onto Hollywood Boulevard."

Charlie turned toward the door. "Let's go find him. And bring the broom from the closet."

Charlie reached under the bed and picked up the baseball bat he kept there. He opened the door and walked toward the parking area where the van was. He left the door open.

Lisa stood up and walked to the closet. *I shouldn't go. I should just go to the Hollywood Greyhound station and grab a bus back to Nebraska*, thought Lisa.

Then Lisa thought of what was back in Nebraska for her.

She took the ragged broom with the blue wooden handle out of the closet. She had no idea what Charlie wanted the broom for. And she wasn't sure she wanted to find out.

She locked and closed the door behind her.

Community Watch

To the Hollywood Division patrol officers, Hollywood is the beat where "the men are men and the sheep are scared." Handling calls between the Hollywood Hills and Wilshire Boulevard, the officers contact every kind and form of human life: the punk rockers, the street hustlers, the pimps, the prostitutes, the drug dealers, and occasionally a good citizen. For the most part, the cops aren't even sure if it really is human life they're contacting. There's been more than one joke in the Hollywood roll call about the takeover of Hollywood by aliens from another planet.

The patrol officers spend most of their eight-hour watch responding to calls from citizens requesting police service. They take report after report of crimes that occurred between fifteen minutes and fifteen hours prior. Periodically they respond to a call where the suspect has been stupid enough to hang around, providing the officers with a misdemeanor or felony arrest.

Hollywood Area is 18.7 square miles of insanity. There are 314 street miles in this small area and over 10,000 people per square mile. Not including commuters, who quadruple the population, Hollywood has over 169,000 residents living within its borders. And that doesn't even include the tourists that hit Hollywood Boulevard by the thousands on a daily basis.

On Friday and Saturday nights, the cruisers come out, with their cars, trucks, and motorcycles polished and shining. They block up Hollywood Boulevard until it is bumper to bumper, while the Latin girls fix their fifties hairdos, glancing at the Chicano boys and black boys riding by.

When the police close down Hollywood Boulevard, the cruisers move to Sunset. When the police change to Sunset, the cruisers move back up to Hollywood. (It took five years for the police to realize that they should shut down both streets to vehicular traffic.)

The cops, wearing their hats as is required of foot-beat officers, don't even drive in their police cars. The traffic is too heavy. With ticket book in hand, the cops stand in the middle of the streets and yell at the cars to pull over. They write their ticket and then turn around and wave over another car before they can even make it back to the center of the street.

While the cop writes the ticket, the occupants of the car use their feet to push their guns even farther under the seat.

Every type of culture is represented in Hollywood. During the daytime, the buses are loaded with Armenian students going to and from school. Mexicans and Mexican-Americans stand drinking beer on the sidewalks or in the apartment building yards, while others use the street as their personal car repair shop or urinal.

Black and white female prostitutes still walk on Sunset Boulevard. On Santa Monica Boulevard, male homosexual hustlers stand on the corners between La Brea and Highland. Transvestites and transsexual Latins stand on La Brea Avenue.

Young homosexual men cruise and try to find parking by the Tower disco at Santa Monica and Poinsettia on Wednesday, Saturday, and Sunday nights. Black gang members and young black girls take over the club on the remaining days. The club, a converted factory, is the site of repeated stabbings and shootings.

Other homosexual clubs can be found between Melrose and Santa Monica Boulevard on La Brea or Highland. Carloads of black and Hispanic youths periodically patrol the area with baseball bats in their hands, waiting for the unwary fag to bash.

More gays can be found above Sunset Boulevard at the Coral Sands Hotel. The occupants leave their room doors open at night, waiting for a good-looking man to step inside and shut the door. As the night gets later, their standards lower.

And between 11:00 P.M. and 3:00 A.M., the black pimps take over the Pioneer Chicken stand on Sunset Boulevard. They wait while their girls are working. The poo-butts, pimps in training, stand across from their property, guarding the girls against kidnapping or other pimps moving in on the territory. Any girl without a poo-butt is considered open property. The poo-butts attempt to entice and recruit these independents while they are out there. If that doesn't work, they threaten the girls.

There are very few independents working.

The corners are reserved. If a new girl shows up, the others yell at her until she leaves. No one accepts competition, particularly if she is younger or prettier.

The free economy only works until the younger girl gets stabbed or her face messed up.

The pimps also use the Denny's coffee shop on Sunset.

A few of the officers assigned to Hollywood work patrol, answering the thousands of citizen calls for service. Occasionally the police have some free time and get to go onto Hollywood Boulevard and make some arrests.

When they're not answering calls, the cops are grabbing free pizza from the shop by Mann's Chinese Theater, where all the movie stars' footprints are.

Most of the cops have never seen the footprints, not even the ones who have worked in Hollywood for over a decade.

"We're here to make a living, not do a tourist trip," the older cops tell their new probationers. "Who'd want to ruin a perfectly good pair of shoes by putting them into cement anyway? Besides, all those movie stars are coke-snortin' dykes and fairies."

It is the same thing the prostitutes say.

The majority of the cops spend their time doing enforcement of victimless crimes, such as arresting prostitutes. According to the chief, this work is a priority assignment of the Department.

While the police are making arrests for prostitution and possession of drugs for personal use, the crime rate is soaring in Hollywood and victims are literally lying in the streets. Within the first six months of the year, there were 14 people killed, 47 raped, 736 robbed, 732 assaulted, 1,031 residences burglarized, 2,208 cars broken into, and almost 2,000 cars stolen.

And the police walk up and down the aisles of porno bookstores, watching to see if someone is playing with himself.

That's why Cainen laughed when he heard tourists refer to L.A. as "the City of the Angels." *Hell, the angels gave up on this city years ago. There aren't any angels in Los Angeles . . . unless maybe they were caught in traffic.*

When Cainen first transferred to Hollywood Division, he was assigned to work a P.M. watch A-car, a two-man unit that worked from 3:00 P.M. until midnight. Being a new training officer, Cainen was partnered with Paul Simonett, a thirteen-year veteran who was one of the senior training officers.

Because of Simonett's seniority, Cainen had to go along with Simonett's manner of handling police work. Simonett liked to work, which was good. But he also liked to take the easiest way out. While Simonett didn't break any rules, like virtually all of his peers, he tended to bend them until they resembled a pretzel.

Simonett's area was the hill car, A75. This area was north of Hollywood Boulevard, and included a score of seedy old hotels. In times past, famous movie stars lived in these hotels. Now, for cheap monthly rates, they were inhabited by working-class singles and drug dealers.

The hill area also covered the beautiful homes in the Hollywood Hills. Though the area was much poorer than Beverly Hills, the homes still ranged in the $200,000 to $2 million range. The soaring crime and burglary rates had long ago caused many of the younger or richer residents to move to Brentwood or Bel Air.

During his first week in the area, Cainen accompanied Simonett to a Neighborhood Watch community meeting conducted in one of the homes in this residential area. Because the meeting was higher up on the hill, most of the attendees were older white couples and a few younger white couples who had bought their first homes. Many of the Neighborhood Watch group were senior citizens, including Irene Levy, the chairperson in whose home the meeting was held.

"In our first meeting, I discussed how the Neighborhood Watch program works," droned Simonett, standing in front of the seated members. "It's necessary for all of you to watch out for your neighbors' homes. Any time you see someone who doesn't belong in the area, you're supposed to call the police department and let us check them out."

Simonett was immediately interrupted by an older gentleman: "But any time we call you, it's just a recording."

There was a murmur of agreement from the group. The old man felt encouraged to go on.

"Last week I saw two Mexican kids breaking into a car and dialed 911. All I got was a recording telling me to stay on the line if I had an emergency!"

Simonett had obviously heard it all before. He was imperturbable.

"I know it seems bad. But understand, we only have about 8,000 police officers for over 4 million people living in the city. We need more officers. There's nothing we can do until the city council approves more positions. I encourage you to contact your city councilperson."

It was the canned speech endorsed by the Department.

"But what are we supposed to do if we have a *real* emergency?" asked a white-haired older woman with sharp blue eyes.

"Last meeting I gave all of you the direct number to the station. If it's between three and eleven, you can ask for me. I'll recognize your name if you're in this group."

"Sometimes it takes the police almost two hours to get here when we call them." It was a husband from one of the younger couples.

"I know. But we have to handle the calls based on a priority system. And we have to handle those emergency calls where a life is in danger or a suspect is at the scene first. So you have to be patient."

The man's wife leaned forward. "I've had my car broken into three times since we moved here. And we've only lived here two months!"

Simonett remained cool. "That's why we're forming this Neighborhood Watch group. The police can't be everywhere; there's not enough of us. So you will be our eyes and ears for your neighborhood."

Simonett looked around the room. "Did all of you get the Neighborhood Watch stickers for your windows?"

Several of the people shook their heads no.

"If you check with Irene, she has the stickers. The more we get up, the less burglaries and thefts you'll have. We've interviewed actual burglars, and they really look for those stickers. They'd rather burglarize a neighborhood that doesn't have them."

"How do we get the Neighborhood Watch street sign?"

"Once the group gets going, I'll tell you how much those signs cost," answered Simonett. "But for now, let's first get the group going. Tonight, I'd like to talk about home security."

Simonett had rebounded each of the sincere questions back onto the group, never really addressing their concerns.

He went on to talk about arranging home security tours with the Hollywood detectives. He talked about alarms, dogs, lighting, leaving radios on, and making sure the mail was picked up when they left town. He discussed which windows were safe to put bars on in the event of fire, whether it was wise to keep a gun in the house and what happened if they shot a burglar, and how to secure louver windows and sliding glass doors with a piece of wood.

When Simonett was finished, the crowd seemed pleased with the information. Yet if any of them were to call the emergency line of the LAPD, they would still get a recording, not a person, asking them to remain on the line if they had a real emergency. And they would still have to wait for at least two hours if they needed to make a report because their house had been broken into.

But the crowd appeared more appeased than Cainen was.

When he and Simonett left Irene's house, they went back to the police car. Simonett bitched about how annoying the meetings were and that the Community Relations Office (CRO) should handle them instead of the area police car.

Simonett then spent the night doing the same police work that he had done every night, never once doing extra patrol of the area where the Neighborhood Watch group lived. In fact, he did nothing different. It was as if the meeting had never been held.

This was how officers were told to conduct their community watch meetings. Though LAPD espoused the principles of the "basic car plan," "community policing," and "community involvement," this was only lip service.

LAPD pioneered community-based policing, where the same officers worked in a given area, allowing them to become familiar with the goings-on and the citizens to become acquainted with the officers.

Yet, soon after they began the program, the Department management abandoned the philosophy and doomed it to failure. Other modern police departments, particularly Kansas City, copied the LAPD model and carried it to an extremely successful conclusion.

Simonett had given the community watch talk that was approved by the Department management. The officer was supposed to be congenial and apologetic, leaving the citizens with the appearance that they had been served.

Actually, the talk with the group was political, meant to cause the citizens to contact their councilperson to engender votes for more resources for the LAPD.

The community watch program was little more than a dismal failure, nothing more than a public relations project for the LAPD.

Virtually all of the community programs out of the Department were the same. The management has held the same view for three decades and three police chiefs: citizens were to be given the proverbial handjob.

The LAPD management decided long ago that only they should determine how police resources are deployed. *They* knew what was best for the citizens. *They* knew how the public was best served.

The citizens of the city of Los Angeles were treated as children, not intelligent enough to know what was best for them. Even worse, the citizens accepted this treatment.

The LAPD has denied the public any input into the decision-making processes of law enforcement in the community. Regardless of what the priority for enforcement was in the minds of the public, the officers themselves decided how and when to do enforcement.

For the taxpayers, the LAPD was a $300 million a year rip-off. If the LAPD were a private corporation, it would have shut down years ago, due to mismanagement.

* * *

Months later, Cainen drove to a Neighborhood Watch meeting alone. He and Simonett had worked together for almost two months. When the rumors about Cainen became too intense, Cainen was separated from Simonett. No one else was willing to work with him.

It was too hard for the LAPD to explain why Cainen was the only officer working without a partner in the entire Department of eighteen field divisions. At night, everyone worked with a partner.

So Cainen had been transferred without an explanation. But the reason was obvious: on day watch, Cainen worked alone.

Cainen was already fifteen minutes late for the meeting when he left the station. He had tried to find out what was supposed to be talked about at the first Neighborhood Watch meeting.

Incorrectly, Cainen had assumed that the groups would be coordinated by the CRO. That way, the running of the groups would be systematic. Any officer could take over the meetings and still know what was supposed to be discussed and what had already been presented. Since officers transferred in and out of divisions so often, this would have been the logical approach. As Cainen was learning, LAPD was not logical.

Since no one knew what should be talked about at the first meeting, Cainen reviewed all the crime statistics for the area of the meeting and determined any trends or repetitive crime problems. And there were many.

Cainen drove at his usual patrol car speed of ten miles over the posted speed limit. He figured that the way to make up for the time lost at red lights was to speed between them.

Some officers even blew red lights. After all, who was going to give them a ticket? But some officers also got killed. So Cainen just sped.

As he raced down Santa Monica Boulevard toward the meeting on Gardner, a brown van pulled out from the curb in front of him.

Stupid! If you were going to pull out in front of someone unsafely, Cainen thought, at least you shouldn't do it in front of a cop.

Obviously the driver of the van had just picked up one of the hustlers. Probably some old, respectable businessman on his way home to his wife and kids, wanting to get his rocks off with some young hustler first.

Cainen was debating whether he should pull the van over and give the driver a ticket. If not a ticket, at least a warning. Probably getting stopped by an officer while he had his hand in some young boy's lap would be enough to scare off the old man for a month or two. He'd most likely do penitence at church if he got out of this one. He might even vow to be faithful to his wife, at least until the urge became too powerful again.

But Cainen knew that if he was any later to his meeting, it would give the watch commander enough excuse to write up something negative about him.

Being gay and a cop (as well as being the only suspected gay who hadn't resigned), you had to be near perfect. Everyone was watching, hoping you'd screw up. Even the gays would probably say, "Yep, shoulda expected it."

126

The van suddenly turned off the Boulevard down a side street. Another violation: turning without signaling. Probably going for a quick handjob in the back of the van.

That made the decision easier for Cainen. He put his foot down harder and sped toward his meeting.

He didn't see the long-haired driver look in his rearview mirror to see if the police car was still behind him. The young man then said, "Gone." Cameron, sitting in the back with the shotgun pointing toward the rear door, relaxed. A little.

* * *

As Cainen passed Fountain, driving up Gardner, he looked at the recreation building in the park. Sitting on the steps outside the complex were six Hispanic gang members. With baggy pants worn low, Pendletons outside the pants buttoned at the neck, and thermal underwear tops underneath, they were dressed down. Several of them wore black baseball caps with the brims turned up exposing gang writing.

Seated on the top step with a 7-Eleven Big Gulp soda in his hand was a light-complected twenty-five year old with close-cropped hair. Though he was wearing khaki pants, he was not dressed down.

"Probably not on a school field trip," Cainen muttered to himself as he hurriedly drove past to his meeting.

Cainen had slowed down just enough to stare the gang members down.

A second after Cainen drove by, a gang member on the center step flipped him off. The fifteen-year-old on the bottom step adjusted the Saturday night special in his waistband, making sure it was concealed by the Pendleton hanging outside his pants.

An older home, which must have been old-fashioned even back in the 1940s when it was built, was where the meeting was being held.

Cainen drove farther up the street until he found a red zone near the corner.

"Reserved parking," Cainen said, as he pulled the black-and-white into the space. He exited the car, pulling on the handle to make sure it was locked.

While it only took a few seconds to break into a car, at least locking it offered a deterrent for whatever punks there were in the neighborhood who would like to get their hands on a police radio.

Many police officers forgot to lock their cars. The officers had to replace the stolen radios, costing them $1,500. It also cost them an additional $300 in lost pay for the days they were suspended for failure to maintain control of city property.

Cainen also locked his car to stop other officers from getting in. Of course it didn't always work. An extra set of keys to each unit was in the watch commander's office. And since the sergeants supported the harassment, the keys to Cainen's vehicle were easily accessible.

More than once, Cainen had finished handling a call and unlocked his door to sit down on a car seat soaked by some officer's hot coffee.

In the dark, the wet seat didn't show.

But Cainen had to work the rest of the night in damp pants, not to mention the awkwardness of constantly keeping his back toward a wall so that suspects and citizens wouldn't see it and think he had wet his pants.

Cainen, in his uniform with two stripes on the sleeve signifying him as a training officer, walked back down to the house. All north–south streets in Hollywood were at a slight uphill slope, leading into the Hollywood hills, which housed the famous HOLLYWOOD sign.

Cainen didn't need to carry in the stats of crimes in the area. He had an outstanding short-term memory and had memorized the crime problems and statistics on the drive up.

Cainen also had a great memory for faces and could even recognize people he had attended kindergarten with. But his memory for names sucked. Cainen couldn't remember a person's name by the time he had finished shaking the person's hand. Many of Cainen's acquaintances thought he was rude for failing to introduce them to others. In fact, Cainen never introduced anyone, because he was too embarrassed for not remembering either of the people's names.

Thinking about it, Cainen quickly opened up the small white officer's notebook that all LAPD officers carried with them. Cainen carried his in his left rear pants pocket, just like they taught in the academy.

He opened to the page with the paper clip, which was marked by today's date with the crime information given out in roll call.

"Miranda." Cainen had written down the last name of the Neighborhood Watch captain who was hosting the party.

Cainen shook his head. He couldn't believe that he couldn't remember a name like Miranda . . . when the suspect's rights advisement, known as the Miranda admonishment, was printed on each notebook cover: "You have the right to remain silent . . ."

Cainen put the notebook back in his pants pocket.

After meeting Mr. Miranda and remembering his name, Cainen stood in front of the community watch group. There were thirty people gathered in the living room of Miranda's house.

The group was representative of Hollywood home owners, home renters, and apartment dwellers. They were young and old, black, Hispanic, Korean, and white. One young white couple had just bought their first home. An Hispanic family lived in the apartment building south of Fountain. Their neighbors were the Armenian couple and the black man who was seated on the floor since there were no more seats.

There were even two hippies and a Jesus freak.

And there were three gay men.

A microcosm of Hollywood.

Cainen reviewed the crime problems and statistics for the area in which the group members lived. There were, of course, a lot of car thefts, and a lot of daytime burglaries while the occupants were away at work. Most of the couples had both members working. Several of the senior citizens spent their days in the park gossiping with the other seniors.

Cainen explained that having a Neighborhood Watch group would assist in lowering the daytime burglary rate. They would know who lived where and who belonged in the area, and they could tell each other when they were going to be away. Essentially, Neighborhood Watch was just being a good, and sometimes nosy, neighbor.

Cainen also provided them with his business card and told the members that they could contact him at the police station if they had a problem, and he would get back to them right away, as long as they said they were from the Neighborhood Watch group.

He also took the time to explain the difference between robbery and burglary. This was a common error of nonpolice, one of the many misconceptions caused by the inaccuracies of TV.

"A house can't get robbed. Only a person can," Cainen explained. "You can't aim a gun at a house and say, 'Give me all your valuables.' But burglars can break into your house. So a house gets burglarized; people get robbed. You need to be accurate when you call 911. It helps us, the responding officers, know what to be ready for."

For most of the meeting, Cainen had to defend his Department. Despite their harassment, Cainen remained loyal to his childhood belief in the goodness of the police and the police department.

"But the gangs are overrunning the whole city!" said the black man who lived in the apartment building down the street. "How can *you* expect to do anything about it when your whole Department can't?"

Cainen spoke calmly, reassuring these citizens, who obviously had been given the runaround by previous officers.

"As long as you tell me what you want done, I'll take care of the problem. I don't care if it's gang members that are bothering you or professional criminals; I'll take care of it. I know it's hard to believe, but one person, when that person's a cop, can do a lot."

It was Miranda who responded. "You have to understand our disbelief. All the other officers that have talked to us in the past gave us excuses about why they couldn't handle the gangs in this area. They say it's a citywide problem, so they can't just focus on it here. Meanwhile, we're being robbed on our own streets, and our homes are being spray-painted with graffiti."

"It's true that the gangs are running rampant in the entire city. In Los Angeles alone, we have over six hundred gangs, with over seventy thousand gang members."

Someone in the room let out an astonished whistle.

"Last year," Cainen continued, "there were almost four hundred gang-related homicides in Los Angeles. But that doesn't mean that something can't be done about them. It just takes an officer who works in the same area and is willing to get to know who the players are."

"But Officer Janus, who used to be the senior officer for this area, told us that nothing could be done. It was because the LAPD didn't have enough officers." It was one of the three gay men.

Cainen was angry. That was the typical excuse used by many of the lazy officers. And it was encouraged by the LAPD brass. They felt it would get the citizens to put pressure on the city council members to vote for increased officers. The chief's little kingdom—all at the expense of the citizens' safety.

Cainen kept his cool. "It's true that we are understaffed. We only have seven thousand officers to handle between three and six million residents in Los Angeles."

Cainen gave a reassuring look around the room. His eyes were hard as obsidian.

"I work in this area now. You have my name and number. If you have any problems, you can call *me*. I will take care of the gang problem in this area. I guarantee that you will see a significant improvement within one month."

The hard look in Cainen's eyes left little room for doubt.

The Caucasian husband, who was now a home owner, spoke up after a pause.

"But what about the graffiti these jerks keep putting on our walls? Not only is it ugly, but the news reports say that it encourages gang violence."

"Not to mention that it ruins our property values," said Miranda.

The others in the room nodded their heads in assent.

Cainen looked around the room. Once again, the Department was out of touch and didn't care about what the citizens wanted. Even Cainen had believed the Department line that citizens wanted arrests. And here he was, face to face with the citizens, and the reality was that they could care less about who or how many went to jail. The graffiti was of greater concern to them. And the chief was still demanding more and larger task forces to hit the streets and make arrests. Cainen, and all the Department brass, knew that the task forces, which cost thousands of dollars, had no permanent effect on crime. What Cainen hadn't realized was that the chief just wanted the headlines that the task forces inevitably bring. The publicity helped the chief in his campaign for public office.

In fact, though it hadn't been public knowledge, during the task force in the south end the prior month, with more than two hundred officers blanketing the 77th Street and Southeast Areas, there had been five drive-by killings. At the same time as the task force.

Task forces had not stopped the shootings, nor had they ever helped protect any of the residents who had to go on living in the area after the officers left.

Graffiti.

Cainen had an idea. If it worked, it would restore some confidence in the police department from these citizens.

"Does anyone have any extra paint and brushes?"

The watch group just looked around at each other.

Not wanting to let the momentum of the idea die, Cainen spoke again. "That's OK. I'll get some donated. I'll get the *gang members* to paint over their graffiti."

"You'll do what?!" It was the Jesus freak. He wasn't sure he had heard correctly.

He had.

"I'll encourage the gang members to paint over the walls," repeated Cainen. "I'm a very persuasive guy once you get to know me."

* * *

Hollywood had never been dirtier. The flyers handed out the night before blew around the street as if an invisible tornado were blowing.

It was evening, and Charlie was still driving around Hollywood Boulevard with Lisa in the back of the van.

Charlie was in a foul mood, if it could be said that he was ever in any other kind.

Lisa had suggested that they try Doggies. On Saturday nights, Doggies operated as a "rice bar" for Asian homosexuals and those who were attracted to Asian boys.

On Sundays the bar had its usual collection of Hollywood lowlifes. And at midnight, there was a Latino strip show, where the old men got to put a dollar into the jockstrap of some hot young Mexican. They usually got a quick grope for their dollar, too.

Doggies was located across the street from the Clown Bar, which offered underage girls as part of its attraction for clientele. Ever since Hollywood Vice had cracked down on street prostitution, particularly girls under eighteen, the youths had taken their business either to the Valley or into local bars and massage parlors.

As the additional attraction of Doggies, it was also a place for street hustlers and drug deals. And that was where Charlie found Cameron.

"Let's get the fuck out of here," commanded Charlie, as he stood over Cameron and some other lowlife sitting in a booth.

"Uh, I was just gonna come back to the motel."

"We got work to do."

Charlie turned around and started toward the door. Cameron knew better than to piss him off further.

Cameron made a hasty good-bye, giving a hustler's five-part handshake to the young man he had been making a dope deal with. He said, "Catch you later," and headed out to the van.

Inside the van, Charlie handed the bat to Cameron. "I'm going to get the fag to sit in the front. When I say your name, I want you to smash him in the back of the head. So listen for your name."

Cameron was tired of the killing, and more frightened since the problems with Dino's kidnapping. "Uh, I mean, can't we j-just offer the guy to get high, and then take him into the mountains where you can b-blow him away?"

Charlie turned to face Cameron with fury etched into his face. "You gotta fucking problem?! If you gotta problem in helping me out, Bro', then just say so. I can let you go back into that faggot bar, and you can find yourself some wienie to suck. And maybe the next one we pick up off the Boulevard will be you!"

Cameron backpedaled as fast as he could.

"No, it's OK, Charlie. Hey, you're the boss. However you want to work it."

Charlie didn't say a word. He turned and started the illegally parked van. He pulled out into traffic and headed west. On Wilcox, Charlie made a left turn and drove past the Hollywood police station.

132

On Santa Monica Boulevard, he made a right turn and slowed to look for a blond hustler.

Charlie drove the van through to West Hollywood, on the other side of La Brea. The hustlers were scarce on the LAPD side.

At Genesee Avenue, Charlie turned into a large parking lot beside the Pleasure Chest.

"I need to get something," he told the others and disappeared inside the doors of the brick building.

The Pleasure Chest was a sexual erotica store, the largest in the Los Angeles area. A large variety of dildos was displayed within glass cases throughout the store. A red button below each dildo provided potential customers with a view of the motorized movements of the fraudulent penis.

Another section of the store displayed gag gifts and a wide variety of sexual joke greeting cards. A third section displayed an enormous amount of leather and bondage paraphernalia. It was to this area that Charlie headed.

For less than thirty-five dollars Charlie bought two sets of metal handcuffs without so much as a second look from the salesperson. Handcuffs were a popular dress appendage, particularly with punk rockers.

Charlie got back into the van and put the bag between the seats. Without a word, Charlie backed the van out and drove through the alley, back onto the Boulevard.

Five blocks east, Charlie spotted Roy walking slowly down the street, looking into the windshields of passing cars.

After circling the block twice, Charlie pulled off the Boulevard onto a side street and pulled the van to the curb. A minute later, Roy nonchalantly walked to the passenger side door of the van.

"Don't forget," Charlie whispered. "When I say your name."

Cameron was sitting behind the passenger seat. Lisa was across from him. The closed curtain hid their presence. Both were silent.

Charlie, knowing the routine, reached across and tugged upward on the already-open lock. Roy opened the van door and slid easily into the seat. Roy knew the routine even better.

"My name's Bill," Roy lied, extending his hand.

Charlie didn't take the extended hand. With fraudulent congeniality, Charlie smiled. "How's it going? How's business?" Charlie's hand slid down to his own crotch, and he unenthusiastically squeezed his groin.

Roy repeated the same motion on himself. "Not too bad. Just trying to make some money to score some crystal, you know."

"Hey, I can relate. You wanna take a ride to a darker area?"

"Sure. But I don't get fucked and I don't suck for under twenty-five."

At first, Charlie wasn't sure whether Roy meant years or dollars. Not that it mattered.

"That's cool," Charlie said. He started the van and drove down the dark street. Charlie then circled back down to Vista and pulled into the far end of the darkened parking lot of Plummer Park.

When the van stopped, Cameron quietly stood up and positioned the bat. The silhouette of the hustler's head was clear through the van curtain because of the streetlights.

"I'll have to introduce you to my friend," Charlie said. His voice was calm but exuded evil. "His name is Cameron."

Aztlan

The fact that gang members overran the streets of Los Angeles and could openly deal drugs on the streets never ceased to amaze Cainen. After all, they even committed *murder* on the streets and got away with it.

It wasn't that the police could catch every drug dealer. The entire Department would have to be in plainclothes and working twenty-four-hour shifts to do that. What absolutely astounded Cainen was that the patrol officers never did any preventive gang enforcement.

By definition, gang members were stupid. Who else would want to join a gang? Sure, some were forced to because of the neighborhood they lived in, for a sense of personal safety. But how safe were they really, when joining the gang made them a thousand times more likely to get shot during a drive-by?

What especially perplexed Cainen was that despite there being seventy thousand–plus gang members in the city of L.A., every one of the hardcore members could be identified easily. Once you knew who the gang members were, why not watch them until they screwed up and then put them in jail?

But the police just waited until a citizen called them to the scene of a crime.

It was easy to identify gang members. Whenever they did graffiti, all the gang members' *placas*, or gang monikers, were signed after the questionable artwork. The artist usually signed his name last, in the lower right corner. So by copying down the names, an officer could easily tell how many members were in the gang.

And this was exactly what Cainen did.

Using his skills as an interrogator, Cainen then set out to identify the members of the Aztlan gang. The gang had inhabited the area of Hollywood covered by the Neighborhood Watch group Cainen had just met with.

Two days after being transferred to work alone, Cainen began enforcing the law to protect the residents of the area. By late morning, Cainen made his first stop.

The sixteen-year-old Hispanic was dressed down. His pants were so low in the back that his entire butt, covered by a pair of shorts underneath, was sticking out.

After patting the youth down, Cainen took out a blank Field Interview (FI) card.

"So why aren't you in school today?"

"You talkin' to me?" the youth responded in an exaggerated Hispanic accent.

135

"No, actually I was talking to the man across the street. I just thought that I'd search *you* while I talked to him."

Cainen's sarcasm wasn't lost on the streetwise kid.

"Hey, you know," the boy looked at Cainen's nameplate, "Cannon, you be a funny guy."

"I'm glad you appreciate a sense of humor. So do I. We can laugh all the way to juvenile hall."

The gang member's eyes stopped laughing.

"Hey, I didn't do nothin' wrong."

"Then why aren't you in school."

"Hey, I had a stomach ache, all right?"

"You have some identification?"

The youth didn't even check his pockets. He continued looking Cainen right in the eyes.

"No. It all got stolen. I was robbed. You know there's never a policeman around when you need one."

Cainen smiled, not too unpleasantly, at the young one's joke. "Then you won't mind if I search your pockets for some kind of ID."

"Hey, knock yourself out."

Cainen reached into the youth's front right pants pocket and took out the two large markers he had felt when he did the pat-down for weapons.

"Let me guess. You're taking up art after you graduate?"

The gang member was a little surprised. He felt guilty, because he had done quite a bit of graffiti with the markers. But Cainen couldn't know it was him. The police couldn't match up the ink with the marker.

Could they?

Being street-smart, the gang-banger felt something coming. But as he was a dumb gang member, his powers of abstract reasoning were limited. He knew Cainen was going to drop a bomb, but he couldn't tell the megatons.

"Hey, no, I just found those on the sidewalk. I don't know who they belong to."

Putting the markers in his own pants pocket, Cainen reached forward and turned the little shit around by the shoulders. Cainen removed a folded piece of paper from the kid's rear pocket.

Cainen had suspected what it would be and wasn't disappointed.

As the banger turned back to face him, Cainen unfolded the paper to reveal a hand-drawn artistic portrayal of a *cholo*. The lowrider had his hands in his pockets, a cigarette in his mouth, sunglasses, and was covered with tattoos. On his head was a gangster hat.

Cainen murmured, more to himself than to the youth. "You know, if you weren't so caught up in all this gang crap, you have enough talent to do really well."

The youth didn't respond. Cainen hadn't expected him to.

Karma. The youth had his path in life, and Cainen was stuck with his own. In that truth, the gang-banger and Cainen were very much alike.

But only in that respect.

Cainen had noted that above the *cholo* was the word *Aztlan*.

Cainen folded the paper and put it with the markers.

"Hey, that's mine."

"No," Cainen replied, "all evidence is the property of the police."

"Whatchumean, evidence?"

Cainen ignored him. "What's your *placa?*"

"Hey, I don't run with no gang."

The kid felt the megatons increasing.

"I'll ask you one more time. What's your gang-name?"

"I ain't in no gang. A friend of mine gave me that paper."

Without a word, Cainen took out his handcuffs.

The tough gang affectation was dissipating.

"Hey, what do you need those for?"

Always the martial artist, Cainen turned his body so that his gun was away from the youth and his crotch was not a target. Cainen's free hand could block anything else.

Cainen leaned into the gang-banger's face. "First, you don't have ID. Second, I asked you what your gang-name was and you said you weren't in a gang. Lying to a police officer is against the law. Section 148 of the California Penal Code. Lastly, I think you're probably on probation right now, and one of the conditions of your probation is that you not associate with gang members. The piece of paper that I got from your pocket will give me enough evidence to violate your probation." Cainen straightened up to let his pretend ranting sink in with the juvenile.

While working in the south end, Cainen had come across several black youths so hardcore that killing was a leisure activity to them. Those gang members were unbreakable and should have been locked up for the remainder of their lives. Unfortunately, they were not, and they became career criminals, creating thousands of victims before they, themselves, became a statistic.

But in the Hispanic community, particularly among the Mexican-American youths, the tough talk was more an aspect of machismo, a self-image perpetuated by an outer toughness. Unlike the outer hardness of many black youths, which was enacted to protect their own lives and was based upon witnessing or taking part in dozens of killings, most Chicano youth merely enact a facade.

Cainen, knowing the inner psyche from so many years of his own inner turmoil, knew how to tear down this facade.

The youth wasn't so tough anymore. His accent diminished noticeably.

"Hey, no, man. Listen, man, I'll tell you whatever you want to know."

"First of all, I'm not 'man.' I'm Officer, or sir, or Officer Cainen. Second of all, you already had your chance. I asked you your *placa*, and you lied to me. Turn around and put your hands behind your back."

The youth started whining as his exterior melted beneath his feet. "I'm Riddler. From Aztlan."

Cainen pulled out the officer's notebook issued to every LAPD officer and required to be carried at all times. In it, Cainen had copied the name of each member of Aztlan from the graffiti. At the bottom of the list, in the righthand corner, was Riddler's name.

"You're the artist."

It was a statement, not a question. Riddler didn't respond, confirming Cainen's information.

"I want you to give me the real names and addresses of each of the Aztlan gang members. Payaso, Pachuko, Joker, all of them. And describe them to me."

"Hey, I can't do that. If I told you—"

Cainen didn't let Riddler finish. If Riddler got control of the conversation, he would get his confidence back. He would also start lying. Cainen's voice was harsh.

"Now you listen to me! I'm going to take you to Hollywood Station. Then I'm going to call your mom. I'm going to tell her about your probation violation, and your hooky, and that you're going back in. I don't think she can afford the bill again."

Riddler was looking at his feet.

The county charged those parents who could afford it for the upkeep of their incarcerated youths. It was expensive.

Cainen also knew that Chicano families were tightly knit. As merciless as they were with other gang members, the pukes were equally respectful and loving of their mothers.

It stemmed from the genesis of the Chicano gangs. The gangs were originally developed as protection for the community. The police wouldn't venture into the barrio, so the neighborhood set up their own policing. Similar to how the police force started in all of America, the barrio's forces became gangs.

The gangs soon started competing for turf. When the action was boring, or to prove themselves or initiate new members, the gangs would drive into other turfs to fight.

Originally, guns were never allowed. Hand-to-hand soon became knife fights. Most gang members had several scars from stab wounds.

While many of the gang members' fathers were also gang members, the mothers were always treated with the highest respect. The beating of wives was often accepted due to cultural mores, but no one was disrespectful to his mother.

This was also true in the black community. The best way to ensure a fight from a suspect en route to jail was insulting the suspect's mother in some way. All new officers to any south end division received the same admonition: "Call the bastard whatever you want, and beat him as often as you like. That'll teach them respect. But don't ever call them a son of a bitch, and don't you ever insult their mother, aunt, or grandma. If you do, it'll take the whole damn division to get that fucker into jail."

Cainen played on Riddler's desire to avoid causing his mother emotional upset.

"OK, man. Just don't tell my homeboys."

Cainen finished the list of names and descriptions. "I have one more favor you need to do."

"Now what?! I've given you all the information you wanted."

Cainen smiled. It wasn't a pleasant smile.

"Riddler, come with me. I'm going to give you your first public art exhibition."

*　*　*

When Roy regained consciousness, he was lying face down in the back of Charlie's van. His hands were handcuffed to the bolts in the van floor, pulling his arms out to his sides. His legs were tied at the ankles, also to the bolts.

When Roy moved his head to look down the length of his body, shock waves of pain caressed his head, blurring his vision. Even in the darkness, Roy could see that his legs were tied to bolts in the floor of the van. His legs were spread-eagled. His jeans were down to his ankles but were still on one leg, as if he had been tied in haste. Roy wore no underwear. The T-shirt he had worn before the blow to the back of his head was still on his body. He could feel his naked lower body rubbing against a piece of carpet set on the cold van floor.

Roy set his chin down and looked in front of him. He could make out two figures. A young man was against the back of the passenger's seat. It appeared that the figure sitting on something behind the driver's seat was that of a woman.

"What's going on here?" Roy tried to make his voice demanding, but it came out as a harsh, hoarse whisper.

The two ignored him. The bumping of his chin against the floor made Roy feel dizzy and nauseous. He laid his head down.

He had been involved in a lot of weird scenes before, but none as brutal. Many of Roy's regular clients were into bizarre sex. That was why they felt they needed the services of a prostitute. Several of his regulars were into S & M, demanding to be tied up or spanked.

But Roy knew that this scene was far more serious. So he began screaming.

The young man behind the seat moved fast, shoving a cloth into Roy's open mouth. He leaned forward to whisper in Roy's ear. "Shut up or you're gonna get hurt. Hurt bad."

Roy shut up. Not because he was intimidated, but because of the guy's voice. It wasn't threatening. It was more fearful. The guy was frightened.

And why did he have to whisper the warning?

Roy's subconscious was working at full speed. A picture of the long-haired guy that had given him the ride flashed into his mind.

Then he remembered the rumors.

Street hustling was a transient profession. Or at least the hustlers themselves were transient by nature. Though some worked the same vicinity for years, you had to move to the same type of area in different cities to continue making good money.

But word on the street traveled quickly. The famous tradition of oral communication had survived TV, newspapers, and radio.

And as soon as Roy hit the Boulevard, he heard the rumors. Hustlers had been disappearing.

It was common for a hustler to disappear for a day or two, sometimes even a couple weeks. If you got a rich trick, he would keep you up until he got tired of you. Or until you ripped him off.

But these hustlers had disappeared and were never heard from again. Some of the street people were saying that they had been killed by some Jesus freak who was having sex with them and then killing the hustlers in guilt afterward. And there were other rumors.

Because the police kept no ties or informants in the homosexual community or its subcultures, they were far behind in the clues that the street people had gathered on their own.

Roy had heard that only blonds had been disappearing. One black hustler had told Roy that he wouldn't take rides from tricks in vans. The word was that some of the missing guys had last been seen getting into a van.

Roy's eyes grew wide and he strained at his bonds, in vain.

Roy's screams died in his throat behind the cloth. The guy moved to hold the cloth in place, and Roy couldn't shake his head enough to get out of the guy's grasp.

The road got bumpier, throwing Roy up and down. Roy's head hurt so much that he stopped yelling and lay as still as he could.

That was when the van stopped.

In terror, Roy raised his head. And someone kicked him in the nose. Hard. Roy felt the blood running from his broken nose as a bulky frame came into Roy's swimming view.

The bulky figure crouched above Roy's head. Roy put his head straight down to avoid a second blow to the face.

"How's it going, faggot? My name's Charlie, just like Charlie Manson."

Roy's neck was tired, and his nose was too sore to touch the floor. He set his head down on his left ear.

"And that's my bro', Cameron." Charlie nodded toward the other guy to Roy's right.

"And don't you worry none about the little lady."

So it *was* a girl.

As soon as Roy finished the thought, his eyes focused on what Charlie was holding directly above his eye-level. It looked like a broom or mop handle.

A quick glance up confirmed Roy's conjecture that it was a broom. If it was possible, Roy's eyes grew even wider.

Charlie followed Roy's gaze. "Yep. This is for you. A little present for you to remember my little family by."

Charlie took a piece of rope out of his back pocket and handed it to Cameron saying, "Tie that around the fag's mouth. We can still hear him even with the rag in his mouth."

Roy tried to shake his head to stop Cameron from tying the rope, but the pull of his extremities prevented him from fully moving his torso.

The rope tied, digging into the corners of Roy's mouth.

"Get a tape out of the glove box."

Cameron followed Charlie's orders and moved into the front area. Roy followed him with his gaze.

Cameron came back and put a tape into a boom box that he pulled out from behind the passenger seat.

Roy lowered his head and waited for the satanic music to begin. When no sound came out, he again looked at the tape machine.

Charlie had moved to Roy's feet. Roy turned to see that Charlie was standing above his thighs.

"You like getting butt-fucked, faggot?"

Roy's mind flashed to that Linda Blair movie, where she got raped inside a women's prison. He shuddered and tried rolling his thumb into the center of his hand. He had heard that that was how Houdini had done it.

But Roy couldn't get his hands small enough to fit inside the cuff. He felt the cuff bite into his wrists when he pulled. Though Roy thought it was a lot of pain, it was nothing compared to what he felt next.

Looking over his right shoulder in terror, Roy saw Charlie spit into the palm of his hand. Charlie then rubbed it onto the end of the broom handle. Placing the broom against the van floor, Charlie lifted his right boot and brought it down on the broom. The straw end broke off. Charlie kicked it into the corner.

Turning the stick so that the rounded end was aimed down, Charlie placed it between Roy's exposed buttocks cheeks.

Roy yelled for Charlie to stop, but his yells were muffled by the rag. The rope burned into the corners of Roy's mouth, and blood dripped from his mouth and his broken nose. Roy tried to crawl away from the intrusion, but his bonds held him in place.

An unbearable pressure was building above Roy's opening, since Charlie was aiming too high. Bearing down on the broom handle with both his hands, Charlie felt it slide farther down between Roy's cheeks. When Roy tried to move away, Charlie knew that he was on target.

Charlie felt his penis swelling. It felt harder than he had ever felt it.

Charlie spit down onto Roy's cheeks.

"You love this, don't you, dude. Love it, faggot, don't you? This is what you get paid for, right? So now you're going to give one for free."

Pushing hard, the handle entered Roy. Simultaneously, a muffled scream shook the van.

From his standing position, Charlie pushed the stick slowly up Roy's ass.

"You should make the faggot suck you off," Charlie told Cameron.

"But he might bite my dick off."

"No, hold the .25 to the faggot's head and tell him you'll blow his head open if you feel a fuckin' tooth!"

"No, Charlie, I don't trust no fag with my family jewels, you know." Charlie ignored Cameron as he pushed the stick farther down. Roy's screams grew more intense but hoarser.

Good shit for the tape. I musta jacked off to the last tape about a dozen times, Charlie reminisced.

Roy tried tightening his sphincter against the rape. When the pain was unbearable, he tried relaxing. But the pain remained the same.

Even had Roy not been the inserter in his sexual contacts, Charlie's roughness still would have made this entry as intolerable. Roy screamed and squirmed, attempting not to vomit so that he wouldn't choke himself.

Charlie felt no more movement in the broom handle. He tried pushing it down with both hands, but it would go no farther.

Charlie remembered that "Ripley's Believe It or Not" had said that if a human's intestines were laid out straight, they would stretch for miles. Charlie intended to find out how many miles.

Getting to his knees between Roy's legs, Charlie pushed apart Roy's ass cheeks with his left hand. Altering the angle of the broom handle so that it was level with Roy's body, Charlie eased it farther up Roy's anus.

Roy's screams instantly increased to a feverish pitch. Roy slammed his body up and down against the van floor, like a fly trapped in a spider's web.

Roy pulled inward on his arms and legs, thrashing the skin where the bonds held. His insides were on fire. As the handle pushed up farther, he could feel his internal organs ripping and tearing. He lost total control of his bowels as he felt like a gigantic piece of fecal matter was trapped inside him. Nothing came out, no release, because of the protrusion.

Roy didn't wish to die. But he begged for unconsciousness. His anguished pleas went unanswered as the stick went deeper into him. Roy strained with all his might, blood pouring from his wrists, ankles, nose, lips, and rectum.

The broom felt the size of a telephone pole as it tore into Roy's stomach. Roy thought of the Playskool game where youngsters tried to fit square pegs into round holes.

Like trying to fit a power drill into the eye of a needle. Roy's whole world was pain. Nothing existed except agony.

As his hand got closer to the hustler's shithole, Charlie began laughing. Momentarily his raging hard-on was forgotten.

Cameron stared at Charlie as if Charlie had truly blown his last gasket. Maybe he had finally gone over the deep end.

But from his position to the right of the hustler's head, Cameron couldn't see what Charlie was looking at. Charlie laughed again.

The hustler's butt hole was blue! The paint from the broom handle was rubbing off around the hustler's anus as Charlie brutally pushed the handle against the protesting skin.

Feeling his erection subsiding, Charlie stopped pushing on the handle, leaving it halfway inside and halfway outside the hustler.

"Gimme that hanger," Charlie again ordered Cameron.

Not wanting to appear reluctant to obey Charlie while he was in the middle of one of his raging moods, Cameron hastily went over to Lisa. Leaning beside her, he lifted up the wire clothes hanger and the needle-nosed pliers. He walked over and held them out to Charlie.

Charlie quickly took the hanger, hurrying and not wanting his erection to subside. He swiftly undid the neck of the hanger, making it straight. He then brought the two ends together, skipping the rounded top on one side. Charlie twisted the ends together and held it out to Cameron.

Cameron hesitated.

"Take it!"

Cameron knew better than to question.

"Put it around his neck and do it."

Cameron bent over Roy and brought the wire around his neck. He twisted the two ends together until they were tight on both sides of Roy's neck.

"Take the shit out of his mouth."

Cameron untied the rope and let the rag fall out. The hustler gulped at the air, his face a portrait of agony.

"Oh, God, Oh please. Oh God. Please, oh please, oh please . . . ," Roy rambled on incoherently.

"Tighten it, damn it."

Using the needle-nosed pliers, Cameron kept his eyes on Charlie to avoid missing an order but turned the wire tighter.

The hustler began to move his mouth like a fish.

"I . . . can't . . . breathe," Roy gasped.

"Fuck you, faggot," was Charlie's only reply.

Cameron continued to turn the pliers.

His willpower sapped, too beaten to cry out and too exhausted to fight, Roy remained silent until he passed out.

"Undo the hanger."

"What?" Charlie had never taken the wire off after they killed the other hustlers.

"Take the fuckin' hanger off!"

Again using the pliers, Cameron loosened the noose.

"Leave it there."

Cameron obeyed, leaving the wire noose around Roy's neck. He leaned back, sitting behind the passenger seat.

After several moments, the hustler's head began to rock violently back and forth. His eyes opened and shut repeatedly, finally fluttering open. Terrible half-human sounds came out of his mouth. When he was fully conscious, he screamed.

Stepping over Roy's leg, Charlie grabbed the rag that had been in Roy's mouth, visually checking the recorder to make sure it was still turning. Then Charlie stepped back behind Roy.

Putting his booted foot against Roy's behind, like King Arthur pulling the sword in the stone, Charlie ripped the broom handle out of Roy.

Roy screamed again, louder. And he didn't stop screaming as Charlie turned the stick around and began entering Roy with the splintered end.

When Roy had finished screaming, Charlie tightened and untightened the hanger three more times. Each time, Roy was transported back from the pleasure of blackness to the agony of reality. Each time, Roy begged to die. He had no will, no want, no desire to live.

There could be no greater torture. The relief of unconsciousness was a heavenly experience. The grotesque agony of reawakening was an unbearable hell.

The expectation of having to constantly awake to the pain from his torn insides was worse than the physical pain. And the knowledge that the relief could only be attained through such a brutal and excruciating means as being choked to death provided an unbearable indecision that caused Roy to plead. Roy didn't plea for mercy, for this was not possible from an evil such as Charlie.

Roy only pleaded for death.

And Roy's pleas were what brought Charlie relief. Charlie's ejaculation came as he turned the hanger a third time, cutting off the blood to the brain from Roy's carotid arteries.

As if it were some kind of perverse favor, Charlie repaid the relief with an emancipation of his own. Removing the hanger from Roy's neck, Charlie turned off the tape recorder.

Together, Charlie and Cameron untied the hustler and dragged the unconscious body out the side door of the van. Laying the hustler down beside the open mine shaft, Charlie had Cameron rip the shirt off the hustler's back. Propping the body on its knees in front of the shaft, Charlie retrieved the shotgun from the van and handed it to Cameron.

Following Charlie's orders, Cameron placed it against the back of the hustler's head and pulled the trigger.

What was left of Roy's body fell down the open shaft.

Even if the body fell straight down to hell, the deliverance from the Earth Roy had just left would have made it seem like heaven.

* * *

Officer Cainen stood watching the work that the two Aztlan gang members were doing. Complaining angrily between themselves, they dipped the brushes into the brown paint and wiped them back and forth across the wall.

When the gang members' shared anger gave them enough courage, they stole an embittered glance at Cainen. Cainen's icy stare was enough to wilt their ill-found bravado, and they quickly resumed their work.

It had taken the better part of a month for Cainen to identify every member of the gang. He had separated his list into members and associates. The associates were delinquent types who merely loitered with the gang. Outside of drinking in public, they didn't caper when the gang members committed their thefts, burglaries, or narco deals. Neither were the associates present when the middle-of-the-night escapades were conducted to graffiti the neighborhood.

The reason it had taken Cainen so long to identify the members was because several of them had lied and misidentified themselves or others. Cainen had had to give seven of the thirteen members a weekend vacation in jail before the others were willing to tell him the truth.

And never in front of any other member.

Cainen had still not been able to locate the leader of the gang. If he was among the ones already identified, then the members were frightened enough of him to protect him.

Once Cainen had identified the members and associates, he had stopped several of the members individually for minor offenses. Rather than arrest them for jaywalking when they had no identification or for a marijuana pipe, which was illegal paraphernalia, Cainen offered them the alternative of "beautifying the neighborhood."

"The mayor has assigned me as a member of his Beautify Los Angeles Committee," Cainen would tell the delinquents. "By the authority vested in me, I can allow you an alternative sentence of assisting in the mission of the committee."

With a bewildered look in their eyes, the homeboys invariably asked what that meant in terms of physical action.

"Well, you can do what I tell you for the rest of this afternoon," and then Cainen would stop smiling. As a perceptible glacial veneer suffused his eyes, he would conclude, "Or you can spend the rest of your life in jail, a day at a time."

Most of the gang members were convinced to assist with the beautification project.

As Cainen had done this afternoon, he would drive to a neighborhood paint store and explain that these former gang members had turned over a new leaf and would like to paint over their graffiti. Did the paint store have any leftover or returned paint they could donate? Any color was OK as long as it was dark.

Cainen bought the paintbrushes.

Locating the largest wall of graffiti on public property or getting the permission from a private home owner, Cainen set the boys to work. Cainen then handled calls in his area, periodically checking on the boys' progress.

The homeboys knew better than to leave.

"Hey, Officer Cainen," Riddler, the Aztlan artist, called from in front of the wall.

Dismissing his reverie, Cainen noticed the smirk on Riddler's face. Oso, the large, overweight homey beside Riddler, had also stopped painting.

"Hey, we have to stop. We ain't got no more paint left."

Cainen smiled back. Without a word, he walked down the slight incline of the barrier between the traffic lanes in which the wall was located. Reaching the bottom, Cainen took the keys out of his belt Velcro and opened the trunk of his police car.

"You're in luck! I was able to stop and pick up some more."

With the trunk lid open, Oso and Riddler could see the one-gallon cans of paint. There were eight of them.

The gang members slumped down beside the wall. Their smiles had vanished. Cainen, not wanting to demoralize them, walked two more cans up to them.

"Hey, we gotta go to dinner," tried Riddler. "You know, our mothers be expecting us."

"Just finish the wall and you can go."

"Hey, we already been here for two hours."

Cainen didn't like being challenged. "OK, then you can stop now and I'll just take you to jail for the marijuana pipe."

Riddler was silent.

"Your mom wasn't waiting for you when you painted this in the middle of the night last week, so she won't be too worried now. Just finish up."

The gang members continued painting the wall. As Cainen watched, two *mujados* from the labor pool turned the corner at Sunset and began walking down Gardner toward him. When they saw the police uniform, they quickly looked down to the open beer bottles in their hands and hid them under the flannel shirts over their arms.

As they reached the sidewalk across the roadway from the wall, they paused to watch the graffiti being painted over. Speaking in Spanish between themselves, one of them set down his shirt and beer and crossed the street.

He stopped in the roadway below Cainen. "We very happy for you painting here. We have the children here, and it no good for them to see the words of the *ganga*. Maybe we can help?"

Cainen walked down to where the young Latin man stood.

"Help . . . by painting?"

"*Si*. This is our neighborhood, no? We would like to help, hokay?"

Cainen was pleasantly flustered. None of the Caucasian residents who lived in the neighborhood had come forward to assist. But these men, after finishing a day of hard labor, had volunteered to make the community better for their children.

"You have paintbrushes, *si*?"

"Uh, sure. My name's Steve Cainen." Cainen held out his hand.

Now it was the Latin man's turn to be surprised. He had never been treated respectfully or courteously by the LAPD. His only contact had been some minor harassment while he stood on the corners of Sunset, waiting for work in the labor pool. All of the previous officers had acted like the workers were diseased and they didn't want to get near them.

The man took Cainen's hand and shook it. With a big smile on his face due to the respect shown him, he waved over his friend.

"My name is Pedro Gonzalez. This *mi amigo*, Junofre Acosta. *Usted habla Espanol?*"

Unlike the other Hollywood officers, Cainen tried to speak Spanish to the Mexican nationals. He neither refused them service nor chided them for using their native language. *At least they try to learn English*, Cainen thought. *Most Americans barely speak their own language well, let alone bothering to try to learn a second one.*

"*Si, perro un poquito. Por favor, es mejor nosotros hablamos en Englis.*"

"*No problemo*," responded Pedro, after Cainen had shook his friend's hand. "*Usted tiene otro* paintbrush?"

Cainen noted Pedro's use of the honorific *usted*, instead of *tu*. Cainen opened the trunk of his police car again and removed two new brushes. Oso was already using the only pan and roller.

"*Muchas gracias por su ayuda*," Cainen thanked the men as they scrambled up the hill to begin painting.

The two gang members glared at each other as the illegal aliens began painting over the previous week's gang work. It was one thing for them to paint over the gang writing, but it hurt to have others cover over the remaining *Az* of *Aztlan*.

Cainen watched.

By the end of the first month of his graffiti paint-over project, many of the walls had been covered over and were one neat shade. Though there were periodic strikes and regraffitied walls in the afternoon when Cainen returned on his shift, other residents had joined in the effort and were supplying paint and brushes. Under Cainen's watchful eye, every regraffitied wall was painted over by the gang members as soon as possible. And if his investigation uncovered the artist, Cainen waited until the weekend to throw that homeboy in jail for drinking in public or a drug offense. (Many of the Aztlan members were dealing PCP.)

When the homeboy was secured behind bars or in juvenile hall, Cainen was sure to tell him the real reason for the arrest, and that he would be arrested again if any walls were painted over after his release.

Amid the protests of: "I can't stop all my homeboys from painting!" Cainen repeated his words as a promise and a threat.

Slowly, the graffiti in Cainen's area began to disappear from the walls.

Miranda's Neighborhood Watch group was so ecstatic at the progress of Cainen's program that calls and letters poured into Councilman Chang's office. The city councilman had at first assumed that the work was part of some formal LAPD program. But when he spoke to the police department liaison at a city council meeting one night, he discovered that the LAPD had no gang-enforcement activities inside of patrol within the Hollywood area.

Chang had a small proclamation drawn up and presented it to Cainen at a large Neighborhood Watch meeting attended by the local press.

When the assistant chief heard that a gay officer was receiving positive publicity, he immediately sent the order down. Before the third month of Cainen's project, he was called into the office of his patrol captain. The captain informed Cainen that gang enforcement and graffiti were citywide problems and were not to be the burden of one division. Cainen's graffiti paint-over program took away from his other duties as a patrol officer.

Cainen countered, politely, that he was still handling more citizen requests for service and making more arrests for serious offenses than any other officer in Hollywood patrol. The captain laid it on the line: "Either cease your 'program' or be disciplined and suspended for neglect of duty."

The Captain also informed Cainen that due to divisional needs, he was being moved back to morning watch, and he would be in the opposite end of the division, away from A75's area. And away from the Neighborhood Watch group that had grown to become the largest and most influential in the city of Los Angeles, the one led by Mr. Miranda.

Within one week of Cainen's reassignment, most of the graffiti in the area of Fountain and Gardner had returned.

At the next Neighborhood Watch meeting chaired by Mr. Miranda, the LAPD officer present explained that there was nothing they could do about the gang and graffiti problem due to the shortage of police officers.

Two months from the day that Cainen was ordered into the Hollywood Area patrol captain's office, the Los Angeles city attorney held a special press conference. Since it was election year, the conference helped to generate enough votes to support his reelection.

In front of the media, the city attorney announced that he had developed a brand-new pilot program. His new program would assist law enforcement in waging war against the widespread gang problem that was plaguing the residents of Los Angeles.

On every television news broadcast that night, the city attorney explained the program that he had devised. The program targeted gang members convicted of crimes in the city of Los Angeles, putting an additional clause on the conditions of their probation.

The clause, the city attorney announced, beaming with self-effusive pride as he commended his new program, required gang members to paint over graffiti on city property.

VI

Jeff

At seventeen years old, Jeff was five–six and a half and weighed a scant 125 pounds. With rosy cheeks and a shaggy blond haircut parted down the center, he looked like a thin fifteen-year-old.

It was Jeff's looks that made it possible for him to boast, "I'm the most sought after by the chickenhawks." The other reason he could make this brag was that he didn't hustle. Jeff came from a wealthy family and lived in the San Fernando Valley, near Northridge.

Jeff liked to hitchhike to Hollywood on the weekends when his parents thought that he was out with his fellow Granada High School students.

The people on the Boulevard didn't know that Jeff had a nice split-level home to return to each night. While on the street, Jeff assumed a very different identity, bragging about all the things he wished he had done in his short life, and stating them as if he had already done them. Unlike his fellow Valley-ites, the street people respected Jeff's embellishments and didn't question his motivation. As they say on the Boulevard, "The truth is only as good as you can make it."

Jeff had only been to the Boulevard on four prior occasions. Nonetheless, his boyish good looks had allowed him to befriend several of the chickenhawks.

Jeff preferred to hang out with one particular sugar daddy who was willing to pay for Jeff's food and even for a pretty female prostitute the last time Jeff was out to the other side of the hill.

Jeff had also gone dancing at Rumors, the most popular hangout for young hustlers. The main reason Jeff went there was for the plentiful drug supply. Jeff also went there because there was no age limit at Rumors, since no alcoholic beverages were served. Appropriately, Rumors only served fruit drinks.

Jeff's sugar daddy also gave him quarters to play the pinball games at the disco.

Usually Jeff was able to get his sugar daddy or Eugene, the other chickenhawk he was friends with, to give him a ride home.

151

Jeff lived with his mother and his stepfather. Jeff's stepfather was a vice president of a prominent company. Jeff's real dad was a thirty-seven-year-old truck driver. But Jeff's mom had remarried four years prior and they had to leave Orange County and move to the more fashionable Valley.

Jeff hated the move, and he resented his stepfather for it. And for trying to act like he was his father.

Jeff tried to make it home before midnight on Fridays to avoid any hassles from his mom. His stepdad had given up questioning Jeff about his late-night activities. The last time his stepfather had tried to question him, Jeff had told him to go fuck himself, since he wasn't his real dad anyway.

Tonight none of the chickenhawks was willing to leave Arthur J's early enough to give Jeff a ride home. Jeff's good looks were one thing, but they had gotten the scam that Jeff wasn't putting out. They hadn't minded paying for his meals, because then Jeff would sit at their table, which caused the other old men to look on in envy. After Jeff went home, the nightly host would hint to his peers that Jeff was putting out for him. No one believed it, but it was enough to have them jealous when the cute boy sat at the table.

So the hawks remained behind at AJ's, unwilling to leave until a better offer than Jeff came their way.

Jeff left AJ's and headed north on Highland Boulevard, his left thumb out into the street, hoping that some Good Samaritan would give him a ride home.

Periodically Jeff lowered his hand to look at the Casio sports watch on his wrist. His mother had given him his first expensive piece of jewelry for his seventeenth birthday, explaining that now he was old enough to be responsible for maintaining it.

Jeff really did love his mom, almost as much as he hated his stepfather.

So Jeff hurried up the street, hoping to get home before midnight so that his mom wouldn't have to stay up worrying.

* * *

The famous Hollywood Boulevard appears to jettison out of the mountain of homes on the west side of Hollywood. Before entering the commercialism of the tourist area, there is a six-block length of residences. Most of the residences are older apartment buildings.

As would be expected, the westward expanse of inclined homes is located in a region known as the Hollywood Hills. These once-exclusive single-family residences are all that is left of the movie moguls who once ruled the hills. Even the movie stars of yesteryear have long since left the downtrodden area for Beverly Hills and Bel Air.

The homes are still spacious and well kept but are owned by the middle-class success stories of the forties and fifties.

Just before the upgrade in the roadway lies a beautifully hidden Japanese park that is known only to those who have grown up in the area. The park appears reserved for couples during the daytime. Most of the couples come to walk their dogs while admiring the artistry of the Oriental landscaper (before their prized pets defecate on it).

At night, the peacefulness of the park is eroded. The posted signs and closed gates are ignored by nocturnal venturers. Younger couples enthrone the park with their orgasms, and groups of youths from Hollywood High can prove their manhood by guzzling enormous quantities of beer out of sight of the local constabulary.

The bushes that cover the upper terraces of the grassland leave naturally hidden caverns beneath their branches. These foliage caves provide the perfect place for getting high with your friends or making out with an underage girlfriend. They also serve as a hastily obtained meeting place for less-than-legal transactions.

Charlie sat under a particularly large bush, dragging on his joint and watching Cameron.

The killing of Roy had been particularly hard on Cameron, and Charlie watched him with renewed suspicion.

Surprisingly, even Lisa seemed restless as she sat on the dirt floor waiting for her turn on the hand-rolled marijuana cigarette.

"What's on your mind, Cameron?" gulped Charlie, trying to hold the smoke down in his lungs as he spoke.

Cameron started, not expecting to have been addressed. "What do you mean, Charlie?"

"I mean that you look like you got a piece of dung in your underpants and you forgot to bring a change of shorts."

Lisa giggled and put her hand in front of her mouth. Charlie reached over and stroked the back of her long brown hair.

"I don't know what you're talking about." Cameron tried to talk tough, hoping that Charlie couldn't see the redness rising from his collar.

"Something's bothering you, boy. Let's hear it." To Cameron's surprise, Charlie didn't sound mean, but more like a father who was encouraging his son to admit a wrongdoing so they could talk it out. Psychopaths are often able to read others' feelings very well, even though they are completely out of touch with their own.

"I was, uh, just thinking about the last guy we did." Cameron avoided saying "killed" or "murdered."

"What's eating you up about it? He was a hustler, right?"

"Yeah."

"And we all agreed that somebody had to do something to stop faggots from fucking up our needles so that anyone who gets high won't get AIDS, right?"

"Yeah, but that's not—"

"We're doin' everyone a favor by offin' these faggots, right? So what's the problem?"

"I, uh, I just don't, you know, like torturin' the motherfuckers."

Charlie laughed. "You don't mind killin' the faggots, but you don't want to torture them, huh?" Charlie laughed again. Cameron looked to his right, suddenly finding interest in the branches of the bush they were under.

"You're a card, Cameron. I'm glad you're my bro' and not some creep off the street." Charlie's eyes almost glowed with concealed hostility. He innately sensed that this was what had been bothering Lisa, too. "I'll tell you what, Cam. The next punk we waste, no torture at all. We won't even fuck 'im. Just pick him up and kill off the disease. How's that?"

"That'd be better, Charlie. That's much better."

Charlie saw Lisa relax her shoulders. "But next time you gotta waste the homo all by yourself. OK?"

Cameron knew he was caught. Charlie had tricked him, and there was no backing out. But at least he wouldn't have to watch any torture.

"OK."

Charlie wasn't finished. "And this time *you* drive the van and pick out the homo faggot."

There was a long pause.

"OK," replied Cameron.

Charlie was worried by what he saw in Cameron's face. They had already had to waste one spic informant. But if Cameron did all the dirty work this time, Charlie knew that he wouldn't have to worry about Cam running to the cops. His own fate would be sealed with the next hustler they wasted. And the sooner Cam wasted one, the sooner Charlie would be able to be less wary of him. And then Charlie could stop watching Cameron all the time. And that might mean that he wouldn't have to dust Cameron, like he had been thinking of doing. Charlie smiled. It was not a pretty sight.

"When was the last time you got laid, Cam?"

Cameron coughed, choking on the Mich he had been guzzling. "What?"

"I asked you when was the last time you had a woman?"

"I dunno. Not too long ago."

"How long ago?"

"A little while ago, back at the Viking motel. With that prostitute."

"You mean Vicki. That was almost two months ago!"

"Yeah, so?" Cameron answered defensively.

Instead of replying, Charlie reached over and took Lisa's chin in his meaty hand. He turned her face gently in his direction, to Lisa's left. Charlie leaned over and kissed her on the mouth. Then he whispered to her, "Why don't you show Cameron a good time? I got some thinking I gotta do."

Though she understood perfectly, Lisa fell back upon her usual ploy of acting dumb. "What do you mean, Charlie?"

"Lisa, fuck him," Charlie whispered. "And I do mean fuck him. I want him nice and relaxed before our next ride. And if I come back and it don't smell like you had sex, I'll help you two do it."

Lisa involuntarily shuddered. A single tear rolled down her right cheek.

Charlie got off the ground and crouched as he exited from the natural cave.

Lisa turned to her right to look at Cameron. She really didn't see him in the darkness, only the red tip of the cigarette he had lit up. Not that it would have mattered. Lisa's eyes had glassed over. Lisa focused on an emptiness inside her as she undid the top button of her blouse.

* * *

Capt. Theodore Carter was not very good at anything. He was able to maintain a decent relationship with his wife but had messed up his relationship with his son. He had not been a very good patrol officer and had been promoted to supervisor quickly. His paperwork as a supervisor hadn't been very good, but he had used his vacation time studying for promotional exams instead of participating in family outings with his son.

Carter wouldn't have promoted higher than lieutenant-2, except that he was an avid churchgoer and he attended the *right* church. Though he had messed up his written exam, two of the three members of his captain's oral exam board were also members of his church.

At the time of Carter's promotion, Hollywood was considered the primary promotion-minded place to be. The Department managers had just overhauled the entire area, in the wake of the LAPD-Hollywood burglary scandal. Any of the officers that were indicted or disciplined had been transferred to other areas.

Luckily for the soon-to-be Captain Carter, the area captain was Brad Wilson. Each area had two captains, one that oversaw the entire station, including detectives and specialized units, and one that had the responsibility of managing the patrol division. Not surprisingly, Carter was chosen to take over the vacant patrol captain's spot.

Not surprisingly, since Captain Wilson also wore a "fish" ring on his finger. Carter thought of it as a fish sign, instead of as the infinity symbol, representing Jesus, because he was a relative newcomer. He had only been born again two years prior to his promotion. Before that, Theodore, or Ted (as only his wife was allowed to call him), had only seen the figure on the backs of cars. Because every one of the drivers who had the sign had failed to signal before a turn or a lane change, or had just straddled both lanes, Theodore had thought that the fish sign meant that a student driver was at the wheel. He referred to it as the "beware of driver" emblem.

That was before he saw the error of his ways.

Theodore Carter lacked common sense. But he was not dumb. Nor was he one to pass up an opportunity. As his policeman father was fond of saying, "If opportunity knocks on your door, make sure it has a search warrant."

So when Carter saw that most of the brass being promoted were all part of the same Bible study group at Parker Center, he investigated and found religion. It was easier (and much faster) than the other way around.

The church had saved more than his soul. It had saved his career.

Things had been running smoothly at Hollywood for the past year. Carter had been able to take every weekend off, only giving up Sunday mornings for church and an occasional Friday evening when the assistant chief spoke at the altar. That left every Saturday for Carter's favorite pastime: golf. Carter had decided long ago that there was no more devout practice than that of lowering one's par.

And then the Cainen bull had started up. *What was it with these gays? They always wanted more, demanding equality and demonstrating and such.* Carter had even heard that some gays were demanding that same-sex marriages be recognized by the church.

Thank God the Department had forced the Gay Pride Parade out of Hollywood and into West Hollywood. Let it be the sheriff's problem. *They should have pushed it back to San Francisco where it belonged!*

And now there was a gay on the LAPD. The Department had found out about him during his background investigation, and still he hadn't been disqualified. What was the Department coming to? *First the government forced us to put women officers on the streets, instead of in the home where they belong*, thought Carter. *And then they required us to make sure that 12 percent of every academy class was black. And as soon as they let the blacks in, Internal Affairs had to create an entire unit just to investigate cops dealing drugs. Everyone knew that would happen if blacks were let in!* (Carter ignored the Department's biannual statistical report, which showed that of the police officers fired for drug-related incidents, the overwhelming majority were Caucasian.)

Carter knew the chief's and assistant chief's position on allowing homosexual officers to be on the Department. Carter also knew that if he was going to make commander any time prior to his mandatory retirement age, he would have to gain the attention of the assistant chief. Wilson couldn't carry him that far, but the good-ole Bible-thumpin' assistant chief could.

And the best way to impress him, figured Carter, was to do it with the only homosexual officer who had ever refused to resign from the Department. Accolades would pour upon him, as well as the prestigious commander rank, which was more awarded than tested for, if he could force that officer out.

And that officer was Cainen.

All Carter had to do was think of a way to discredit Cainen, while getting the credit himself and, of course, isolating himself from any negative fallout.

Even at the captain rank, the LAPD motto was still the same. And it wasn't "To Protect and to Serve."

It was "Cover Your Ass."

* * *

The three loaded up the van and moved out. Charlie brought a large rock, closer to a small boulder, which he set in the back of the van.

While Cameron and Lisa were skipping foreplay in their haste to finish before Charlie returned, Charlie was out formulating a plan.

The idea was simply a variation of their existing modus operandi. But Charlie thought he should test the new technique anyway.

Choosing his rock, Charlie found an ideal vantage point on one of the paths in the park. After spotting and lying in wait for a lone jogger, Charlie smashed the rock down on his head. Yep, it worked.

Charlie helped himself to the man's wallet, which he emptied, wiped off, and dumped in a bush, as well as the man's watch and ring.

Charlie didn't check to see if the man was still breathing.

Heading back to their bush, Charlie prodded his two sidekicks along, putting Cameron behind the wheel of the van.

Sitting across from Lisa, Charlie felt his erection rise as he anticipated his role of smashing the rock down on the hustler that Cameron chose.

Thinking aloud to himself in eager anticipation of the next smash hit, Charlie said, "It's your lucky day. Will it be door number one, door number two, or rock number three?"

Charlie's talking only made Cameron more nervous as he headed south toward the Boulevard.

Cameron had realized that if they were nailed by the cops, his only way out would be because Charlie had done all the tortures and murders. Well, all except the last shotgun blast, which Charlie had forced him to do (and he would deny doing anyway).

Even though Charlie was his half-brother, hey!, self-preservation was self-preservation. Right, man?

If he had to, to save his skin Cameron would sell Charlie out like a big dog.

But Cameron had seen a movie where the police got fingerprints off a dead body. Whoa! Now if the police ever found the bodies in the mines, they would all be Charlie's prints. But if he had to kill this next guy and if someone saw him driving the van, even if he turned snitch, the cops were bound to put him in prison for a long time anyway.

So as Cameron drove back and forth along the Boulevard pretending to look at the street hustlers for a victim, he wondered whether he was more afraid of the cops and prison or Charlie.

The matter was decided for him. As Cameron made a left on Highland heading northbound, so that he could make a U-turn and go back down Santa Monica Boulevard, Charlie pulled the curtain aside and stuck his head into the driver compartment.

"What the fuck you doing? Don't fuck with me, Cam."

"I-I-I just couldn't see anyone who looked right," stammered Cameron. "And there was too m-m-many other c-cars around, you know."

The glare from Charlie only emphasized the inherent evil in his harsh stage whisper: "Do it *now*, or you can be the next fucker tied back here."

Cameron saw a body with his hand out in the international hitchhiker sign. Skipping over two lanes, Cameron pulled to the curb.

The boy who pulled open the door couldn't have been more than fifteen years old. He jumped into the front passenger seat of the van.

"Hey, thanks a lot for picking me up. Man, I didn't think anyone was going to give me a ride tonight." The youth stuck out his right hand for Cameron to shake. "My name's Jeff."

* * *

Following his change in shift, Cainen went through a period of massive depression. Not only was he being constantly harassed by the Department, but now the Department was making the citizens suffer. Just because of the Department's prejudice.

Cainen felt that he had accomplished so much. Just when he had finally achieved a level where everything was going right and the residents had their faith back in the police, *boom!*, everything downhill.

Cainen wondered why he should be surprised. He should have learned from all the other incidents. But he couldn't help being an optimist. And besides, hadn't his friend in the Department, Sergeant Jinkens, told him to just bear it out and it would go away. That the officers would find something and someone else to pick on. Shit!

On the second morning after his shift of working from 11:00 P.M., Cainen headed back to the station to turn in the car. He had taken reports all night, being assigned as the report car so that no one had to work with "the faggot."

Cainen had gotten hung up writing a report of an auto burglary discovered by the owner as she left her house to go to work. It wasn't until 8:00 A.M. that Cainen finally pulled into the rear of the station. He was dead-tired.

Sergeant Fritsch of the day watch was standing in the back lot with his clipboard. He walked toward Cainen's car as Cainen opened the trunk to take his supply bag out.

"Don't bother unloading."

Cainen turned to look at the sergeant, thinking, *Now what?* Cainen knew that Fritsch was a personal friend of Captain Carter.

"You've been assigned a school talk at Walker Elementary. It starts at 0830."

Cainen noted the unpleasant grin on the sergeant's face. "Can't a day watch unit handle it?"

"No. It's been assigned to A.M.'s. You should've been told last night. Since you're the only L-car working, it makes sense to give it to you, rather than keep two officers overtime."

Cainen knew it was useless to suggest that an A-car split up and one of the two officers do the school talk. He knew it because of the unpleasant grin on the sergeant's face. As Cainen took the assignment

159

paper from Fritsch's outstretched hand, he noted an additional reason it would have been useless to argue.

The school wasn't even in Cainen's assigned basic car area. As a rule, all school talks were handled by day watch *and* by the basic car of the area. That way, the students got to know the police officer covering their area. But now it was less important to the Department that a rapport be built up than that Cainen be singled out and forced to work overtime.

Cainen lowered his bag into the trunk and shut the lid. Without a second word, he walked in through the rear station door.

Thompson, who had gotten off-duty and was in his jeans and T-shirt walking out to his personal car, passed Cainen in the hallway. He stopped to talk with the grinning sergeant, who was standing in the lot.

"Did you hear the latest Cainen joke?" asked the officer.

"Nope," answered the still-grinning sergeant.

"How many heterosexual San Franciscans does it take to change a lightbulb?"

"I give up. How many?"

"Both of them!" Thompson burst into laughter for the seventh time since he had first heard the joke.

Fritsch joined in his laughter.

"Gotta run."

Fritsch slapped Thompson on the butt in a gesture of camaraderie as the big man walked to his car.

* * *

Despite his five years on The Job, Cainen had never conducted a school talk. He had either been promoting or working the higher crime watches of P.M.'s and A.M.'s most of his career.

Being a resourceful officer, Cainen walked to the CRO of Hollywood Area. They would have the necessary information, since these talks were primarily a CRO function.

"Excuse me."

Cainen found it hard to believe that the extremely overweight Hispanic woman in front of him was really a sworn officer.

Otelia Perez turned around to face whoever it was who was addressing her. She, like everyone in the station, had heard rumors about Cainen. But unlike most officers, Otelia didn't care about anything that didn't directly affect her. She judged everything by how much effort it required her to expend.

160

"What can I help you with?"

Cainen was surprised by the monotone, bored voice projected from the officer wearing a billowy light blue dress. Not in an impolite way, Cainen privately wondered if Tall and Fat stores also carried clothes for short and fat people.

"I'm supposed to do a talk to a group of elementary school students today. Do you have any handouts or guidelines on what I'm supposed to talk about?"

A fair question, thought Otelia. She had never been asked it before. Maybe the rumors were true, because a heterosexual cop would have known to bullshit his way through the class and get the hell out of there as quickly as possible.

"We don't do those talks. We're too busy."

Cainen noted that the desk the female officer was sitting at was empty except for a blank nameplate. The "in" box was also empty.

"Is there any particular topic that's supposed to be addressed?"

Well, he certainly used big words for a gay cop. "No, just tell the kids about the stuff on your Sam Browne belt and tell them to call 911 in emergencies."

Cainen was perplexed. So every cop in the city gave a different talk? What a way to run a Department.

"Okay. Thanks a lot. I've never done a school talk before."

"You won't have any problem. The kids just want to know if you've ever had to use your gun. It's an easy talk. Don't sweat it."

"Hey, thanks for the info." Cainen turned to leave.

"Aren't you on mornings?" called the woman without rising from her seat or changing her monotone.

Cainen turned. "Yes."

"They're supposed to have a day watch unit do the school talks."

"OK. I'll let them know," replied Cainen, being careful to keep the sarcasm out of his voice.

Cainen walked out to his car and drove out of the parking lot heading in the direction of Walker Elementary.

Cainen thought about the woman's suggestions and rejected them almost immediately. Kids, even youngsters, were more sophisticated these days. TV made them that way. They had already seen "Adam 12" reruns. Hell, these kids, growing up in Hollywood, had probably already gotten high or been offered drugs. They had probably seen at least one stabbing or murder. And with gangs running rampant, many were destined to join a gang and develop their hands at graffiti, if they hadn't already done so.

161

A talk about dialing 911 was bullshit. The talk by a police officer had to have some impact. A lot of impact. Enough impact to change their lives, or at least affect some major decisions in their later lives.

The big push of the Department was in Drug Abuse In Schools: DAIS. Cainen had given several DAIS talks on his own time to temple and Boy Scout groups. But never to a gathering so young.

And gangs. The youth of L.A. had to be impressed to stay away from and out of gangs.

But how could a Mr. Goody-Good cop, who had never taken drugs or been in a gang, convince streetwise elementary school kids to refrain from these vices?

Cainen pondered this problem as he passed the park recreation building on Gardner that he had observed the first time he had gone to the Neighborhood Watch meeting at Mr. Miranda's.

True to habit, sitting on the same steps drinking from the 7-Eleven Big Gulp was the leader of the gang. Cainen had finally developed enough information to determine that the twenty-five-year-old fair-skinned boy with the closely cropped hair was the ringleader of the Aztlan gang.

Also true to habit, Riddler was seated on the bottom step, drawing with markers on the cement. *Doesn't that boy ever go to school?* Cainen thought to himself.

Cainen turned the car and slowly drove up the path and across the grass, stopping with his grill facing the two gang members.

The leader stood. "Hey, we didn't do nothin' wrong."

"I didn't say you did," retorted Cainen. "You have a guilty conscience?"

"Hey, I wasn't really writing on the ground," added Riddler, trying to conceal his markings with his shoe.

"Why you always picking on us, Cainen?"

Cainen was surprised that the leader knew his name. But not *too* surprised. Especially since it was the leader who had put a contract out on his life.

"Save the lecture. I need you to do me a favor."

This was enough to shock the leader into silence for a moment.

"Come on down here."

Cainen watched the hands of the two carefully as they walked down the steps toward him. He noted that the leader walked with a limp in his right leg. Cainen let it go as part of the youth's gangster walk.

"What's your name?" Cainen asked the leader.

"Gonzalez. Why? What you want, man?"

"To begin with, I am not 'man.' You can call me 'sir,' 'Officer Cainen,' 'Officer,' or by my first name, which is Steve."

Still keeping his eyes on Riddler and on the leader's hands, Cainen held out his right hand for Gonzalez to shake.

Stunned for the second time in less than a minute, the gang leader stared at Cainen's proffered hand in disbelief.

"You for real? You high or something?"

"No," replied the officer. "And what's *your* first name?"

"Rudy. Rudy Gonzalez." He pronounced it with a long *o*.

"Nice to meet you, Rudy. Now shake my hand." Cainen had to show who was in control right from the start, even if he had to do it in a nice manner.

The gang leader shook Cainen's hand. Cainen knew that he had won the test of wills and would be able to control the situation.

"I need a quick favor from you two. Rudy, I need you to talk to a group of little school kids. And I need you to tell them about the evils of drug use."

"You jokin'?"

"No. Not at all." Cainen stared at Rudy with unblinking eyes. "You see, these kids are pretty sharp. And I've never used drugs and these kids are gonna know it. And they ain't gonna buy any story from me about how bad drugs are for them. But they'll believe you if you tell them."

Rudy's eyes had steadily been growing wider as Cainen talked. He stared at Cainen incredulously. "You're not high. You're crazy!"

Cainen spoke under his breath. "There's a whole bunch of officers back at my station that would agree with you."

"What'd you say?" asked Rudy.

"Never mind." Without turning his back to Rudy, Cainen walked around his patrol car and opened the passenger side door.

"Before you take a ride with me. I'm gonna check you for weapons. I'm not going to look for anything else. Just weapons. Since you're not going to be handcuffed, this is for my safety."

Rudy knew the routine. Walking to the passenger side of the car, he turned around and put his hands on his head and spread his legs. "Man, I knew you was gonna do this."

Keeping his eyes on Riddler and his gun leg back, Cainen moved forward and took Rudy's fingers in his left hand. Cainen patted Rudy down, finding nothing.

"No hand grenades or bazookas, huh?"

"Very funny."

"Go ahead and sit in the front."

"Man," Rudy saw the icy look in Cainen's eyes. "I mean Steve, I can't ride in the front. What if one of my homeboys see me?"

"All the one-man units transport suspects in the front seat. Just put your hands behind your back and pretend that you're handcuffed, if that'll make you feel better."

Rudy, shaking his head in resignation, sat in the front. Cainen shut the car door as Rudy put his hands behind his back.

Cainen walked to Riddler, who defensively took a step backward.

"What you want with me? You already got Rudy."

"I need you because you're special. I need you to talk about something else."

"What's that?"

"I need you to tell these kids how bad and how dangerous it is to be a gang member." Cainen couldn't help himself. He smiled.

Riddler's mouth dropped open in amazement at what he had just heard.

"You serious?"

"Serious as a gang war. I need you to convince them that they should never join a gang." Cainen frisked Riddler. "Get in the back."

"Hey, Cainen. I can't do it."

Cainen stopped and looked at the frightened youth. "What's up?"

Riddler lowered his voice. "I can't go into the class with Rudy and say that it's bad to be in a gang. You know." Riddler's eyes never left the front seat of the patrol car where his leader was seated.

"I know that Rudy's the leader of Aztlan. But you're with the police department today. Not with Aztlan."

"Hey, I just can't."

Cainen saw that Riddler was genuinely frightened. He walked to his driver's door and opened it up. He stood facing Riddler as he talked, holding the door with his left hand.

"Rudy. I need someone to tell these kids how bad it is to be in a gang. About how dangerous it is. Would you mind if Riddler talked about that? I mean, since you're already doing the drug talk, it would be better if someone else talked about gangs."

Cainen leaned over and looked directly at Rudy. Cainen's eyes danced mischievously. "That is, unless you'd rather do the talk about how bad gangs are?"

Cainen could feel Riddler just about faint behind him.

To Cainen's surprise, and the gang leader's credit, Rudy replied, "Hey, fuck it. Riddler can tell them about how bad it is to become involved in a gang. Hey, someone's got to help kids do right things, right?"

Cainen's expression was mildly respectful. He knew why Rudy had become the gang chieftain. "You know, Rudy, you're all right." "You're OK, too, Cainen. But I still think you're three cans short of a six-pack." Rudy pointed to his forehead with his index finger. "But I mean that respectfully, you know."

Riddler got in the back seat, behind his ringleader.

Seated in the front, Cainen started the car. "Rudy? Riddler?"

In unison, they both replied, "Yeah?"

"Put your seat belts on."

Cainen drove to the school.

* * *

When Jeff regained consciousness, he was tied to the van floor facing upward. As soon as he awoke, he began crying.

Despite orders from Charlie and requests from Cameron, Jeff could not control his sobs. All Jeff could think about was the childhood remonstrations of his parents about the dangers of hitchhiking. As any responsible parent would do, they accompanied these advisements with graphic stories of the events that had befallen the unwary ride-taker.

Charlie's kicks did nothing to stifle the sobs.

After several miles of driving with the unrelenting wails, the sound seeped through Lisa's drug-soaked mind. The cries reminded Lisa of her younger brother. Though she had been a child herself, Lisa had often been tasked with the duty of caring for her sibling.

Lisa kneeled beside her wheel hub perch and stroked Jeff's hair, trying to shush him. Her soft touch did little beside rearrange the blood-soaked mat.

"Puh-leese, please can I have my clothes back?" cried Jeff. Though he had promised no torture, Charlie had stripped Jeff before restraining him. The only clothes remaining on him were his white socks and white Jockey shorts.

Jeff's shirt had been used to stop the flow of blood from the head wound, caused when Charlie hit him with the rock.

When they reached Highland and Franklin, Charlie directed Cameron away from the freeway. Charlie had Cameron drive east on Franklin into the parking lot of a small park.

As soon as the van stopped, Cameron came into the rear. Charlie once again kicked the prostrate youth. The effect was to raise the decibels of the boy's cries, rather than diminish them.

"You better stop being a crybaby, you cocksucking faggot!"

165

Amid his crying, Jeff's voice took on the singsong fashion often heard during the tantrums of a punished juvenile.

"But I'm not a faggot. I just want to go home. Please let me go home!" Another wail.

"You ain't got no home, only a homo." Charlie laughed at his crude attempt at humor. "Your piss-poor home is the street."

As only youth can do, Jeff immediately understood Charlie's perception of his kidnapping victim. "I'm not a hustler. I live in Canoga Park. My mom and stepdad are there. Please don't hurt me. I just want to go home."

"You're a fuckin' liar." But even Charlie's voice was unconvincing.

"Maybe he's telling the truth," Cameron cautiously offered. He wanted to avoid Charlie's rage and would have rather stayed in the park than gone out to choose a victim.

"The fuck he is. The faggot just can't act like a man. He can suck them off, but he can't be one!" But Charlie's usual rage lacked conviction.

"Please," pleaded Jeff, "I don't suck anybody off. Can I put my clothes back on?" Amid his crying, Jeff involuntarily tried to lower his manacled hands to cover his privates.

"Fuck you; you're gonna die like every other faggot!" yelled Charlie. "Only you're not gonna die from AIDS."

Terror raced through the boy. "I'm not a faggot. I just want to go home and see my mom."

Jeff's words enacted images in Lisa's confused mind. Surprisingly, along with the images, Lisa felt emotions.

"You deserve to die. Out here every night spreading AIDS. And I'm gonna stop you from spreading your plague."

"You're going to let him go."

Standing to the trapped youth's left, Charlie was stunned to hear Lisa speak. And to challenge him?!

"He's not a prostitute," Lisa said simply.

"I was just hitchhiking home," sniffed in Jeff, grasping for salvation. "I gotta be home by twelve or my mom will kill me."

The irony was lost on all of them.

"Please let me go home."

Charlie ignored the boy, staring intently at Lisa. "What did you say?"

Lisa was unperturbed. She had already experienced Charlie's worst. A few more bruises made little difference.

Besides, there was something about the boy that reminded her of her baby brother, before he had died of an overdose.

"He's not hustling. He was hitchhiking home."

"At Highland and Santa Monica?! Who you kidding?" yelled the leader of the group.

"You gotta let him go," Lisa said again in her matter-of-fact tone of voice. "He doesn't have AIDS."

Lisa hated all the murders. But she would not let this boy die. He had awakened her mother's instinct. And she could use Charlie's own words against him.

"Bullshit! This punk is out there hustlin'. He's probably dyin' of AIDS already. We're just doin' society a favor by offin' him."

Lisa felt that she was winning. Charlie was referring to the boy as "him," instead of as "the faggot." She pushed on.

"If he's not having sex, he doesn't have AIDS. He's just a child. Look at him, Charlie." She was forcing Charlie to further acknowledge the humanity of his intended victim.

"Please, I just want to go home," sniffed Jeff. "I just wanna see my mom. Please. I won't tell anyone."

Charlie grabbed at the excuse. "We can't let him go. He's already seen us."

Lisa responded, "He's only seen us in the dark here. He doesn't know what we look like or our names. Besides, he won't say anything 'cause he knows you'd come back and get him." Lisa looked at the boy.

"I won't say anything," replied the boy. "Please just let me go. My mom'll be worried."

"Where do you live?" asked Charlie.

"I live at 34113 Roscoe Boulevard, in Granada Hills."

Charlie reached behind the boy and pulled the blood-soaked shirt out. He unrolled it and threw it over Jeff's face.

"You ever say shit to anyone, and I mean anyone, you're dead. I'll come out there and kill your fuckin' mother, you son of a bitch. If you go to the doctor, you tell 'im that some hustler smashed your head in. You got that, asshole?"

Jeff's muffled voice responded in the affirmative.

Charlie turned to Cameron. "Drive us behind Arthur J's."

As Cameron moved back to the front, Charlie leaned over to where Lisa was stroking the boy's head. His voice was a mean whisper.

"You ever fuck with me again and it'll be the last time."

Lisa didn't really hear Charlie. As soon as he had leaned over and slowly, but forcefully, turned her head to face him, she had retreated back into the cloudy world that was her mind. She only came out of it when the van had parked behind the coffee shop at Highland and Santa Monica Boulevards.

"You're going to let him go?" challenged Lisa.

"Yeah." Charlie took out a ten from the money he had stolen from the unconscious jogger. "Go get us three hamburgers. And fries."

Lisa took the bill but didn't move. "Not until you untie him."

Charlie fumed. "Untie him," Charlie ordered Cameron, then turned on Lisa in a threatening voice: "Now get me some fuckin' food."

Lisa waited until the boy's hands and feet were undone, and then she climbed out through the front passenger seat of the van.

"Can I have my clothes please?" asked Jeff.

Cameron handed him a jumbo plastic trash bag from the corner of the van. "They're in here."

Jeff set the bag down at his feet and quickly slipped on his trousers. He put his shoes on and then kneeled down to tie the laces.

That was when Charlie kicked him full in the face.

The boy's head flung backward, and his body flew back against the passenger seat. Charlie quickly stepped over to the youth and turned him over.

"You're gonna let him go, aren't you?" asked Cameron in confusion.

"Yeah, right. He's gonna go, all right. But I ain't lettin' anybody identify me." Charlie stared at Cameron in a not-so-lightly veiled threat.

Charlie set his knee in the small of the boy's back. Jeff was struggling to remain conscious. Several of his teeth fell out of his bloody mouth.

"Grab that bag," ordered Charlie, pointing to the now-empty clothes bag.

Cameron picked it up and walked over to his leader.

"Put it over his head."

"What?"

Keeping his right knee on the boy's back, Charlie grabbed Cameron's shirt and pulled him down so that their faces were touching.

"Put the fucking bag over his head and hold it there."

Cameron did as he was told. Charlie latched onto Cameron's hands and forced them over the seventeen-year-old's neck, pressing tightly.

Jeff was being choked and suffocated at the same time.

In his groggy mind, Jeff couldn't comprehend what was happening. His mind kept telling him that the reality wasn't true. He should be walking away from the van. He had heard the man promise to let him go. What went wrong?

Jeff looked to his left, at Cameron and Charlie. He flailed his arms, but Charlie quickly grabbed them and held them down.

168

To the two murderers, the translucent brown plastic made Jeff's face appear like that of a cartoon character trapped in a washing machine.

Charlie felt his erection immediately snap to attention.

Even in his semicomatose state Jeff's natural reflexes fought for life-giving oxygen. Jeff's muffled yells and vain attempts to free himself rocked the van.

Finally, Jeff arched his back. To the shock of Cameron, who thought of Linda Blair in *The Exorcist*, Jeff turned his head to stare at his killers.

Jeff opened his mouth and sucked in the brown plastic. The bag stretched over Jeff's face, in a tight funereal veil.

A sound like a gasp seemed to come from Jeff's chest, as his eyes protruded from his skull. His frame convulsed for several seconds under Charlie's knee.

Jeff's body gave up its valiant fight and lay silently twitching.

Charlie ejaculated in his blue jeans.

* * *

On the second story of the elementary school, Cainen found the room number designated on the assignment sheet. He guided his two charges into the open door.

An older, gray-haired lady who could have been on the recruitment ad for schoolteachers came up to greet him, warily eyeing the two young Hispanic men.

"Hello, I'm Mrs. Farnsworth. We've just got the second class in here."

Cainen looked around and saw three other women, two of whom Cainen assumed were Spanish-speaking teacher's aides. Seated at miniature chairs were about one hundred ten-year-olds. Great.

Cainen noted that Mrs. Farnsworth was still looking concernedly at his two guests.

"These are two of our guest lecturers. This is Rudy, and this is . . ." Cainen realized that he didn't remember Riddler's true name. Thankfully, Riddler picked up the clue and held out his hand to introduce himself.

"Bobby Casitas. Nice to meet you, ma'am."

Mrs. Farnsworth relaxed noticeably. "Oh, how nice. I didn't know that the police department had guest speakers."

Neither did they, thought Cainen.

"Nice to meet you, boys," lulled Mrs. Farnsworth, as she led the little entourage to the front of the room.

169

The antsy children didn't stop moving as their attention was drawn to the front. Cainen noted that several of the students were thin Asian children. He assumed they were Vietnamese.

"Today we have a very special treat, class," chimed Mrs. Farnsworth. Cainen noted that the two teacher's aides were quieting some of the students in Spanish.

"I want you to be on your best behavior today," continued the teacher. "Remember, no talking, and raise your hand if you have a question or if you have to go to the bathroom."

Oh, great, thought Cainen again.

"Our special guest is Officer Cainen from the Los Angeles Police Department. And he has some more guests that he will introduce. So everyone say hello to Officer Cainen."

The entire class said, "Hello, Officer Cainen," enunciating each syllable so slowly that Cainen wondered how long each question would take.

"Good morning, boys and girls." Cainen looked at each of the children. "Does everyone here understand English? *Ustedes comprendes Ingles o solamente Espanol?*"

One of the Latin teacher's aides answered, "They all understand English."

One of the small Asian boys raised his hand.

Cainen pointed to him. "Yes?"

"Ti doesn't speak English." The boy pointed to an even smaller Asian child sitting to his left. "He only speaks Vietnamese."

"Do you speak Vietnamese?" asked the officer.

The boy nodded his head yes. Cainen had thought so.

"Would you translate for me and tell Ti everything I say?"

The boy again nodded affirmatively.

The teachers and aides looked at each other approvingly, mentally commending Cainen for the manner in which he handled the children.

"Thank you for doing that for me," continued Cainen.

Cainen discussed the 911 emergency line, Neighborhood Watch, never riding with strangers even if they say they have your mother's permission, and all the capabilities of his Sam Browne belt. He also answered the question about whether he had shot anyone.

"No, I've never had to shoot anyone. Police officers don't want to hurt people; they want to help them. We only carry guns because some criminals do. Most police officers never ever shoot their gun. Only on TV. That's make-believe. The real world isn't like television. In the real world, the police try to put bad people in jail, not shoot them."

Then Cainen introduced Gonzalez.

Gonzalez started slowly and haltingly and built up momentum.

"And that's why drugs are bad for you. You just don't ever want to get involved with them. You know, if someone says drugs'll make you feel good or something, they're not telling you the whole story. They're not telling you about all the bad effects.

"And if your friends call you chicken 'cause you won't take drugs or take a hit off a joint, then you don't need them, you know. If they try to get you hooked on drugs, then they're not really your friends anyhow.

"You know, you can see that I walk with a limp. Well, I ain't doin' that to be tough, you see. It's 'cause I used to drink and drive. And drinkin's just as bad for you as usin' drugs.

"So one time I was too loaded—you know, high on drugs. And I got into a car accident. And you know they had to take part of my leg, so I got this permanent injury. You don't know what you're missing if you mess with drugs. Like I could never play any of the school sports with any of the other kids 'cause of it. That might not seem like a big deal now; you might even want to miss PE. But it's a big deal when you get into high school.

"And I lost my son because of drugs. He's just about your age. My wife, she was a good woman, but she left me because I couldn't keep a job. I just wanted to get high all the time, you know. And when you get hooked, well, you steal all the time. Even from the ones you love, 'cause you need the money to buy drugs.

"And when you're hurtin', well, you lose your temper a lot. I said things and did things that hurt my wife and my little son. All 'cause of drugs.

"But the bad people who want you to try a joint or coke or something, they don't tell you all this sh—stuff. That's why I'm tellin' you. 'Cause I been there.

"And if you try somethin' small, like a joint, well, then you try somethin' bigger. So you shouldn't try nothin' at all. Like they say: just say no to drugs.

"You gotta believe in yourself. You know what's right and wrong better than anyone else does."

There was silence in the classroom. The students were obviously moved by what they had heard. It had had a profound impact on them.

The entire class had stopped fidgeting. The only sound was the whispering of Vietnamese into Ti's ear.

And the students weren't the only ones who had been affected by the impromptu speech. The teachers stood and watched Rudy in silence also.

171

Rudy turned to look at Cainen, who returned his look with a new-found respect.

When Cainen changed places with Rudy, moving to the center of the room, he shook the younger man's hand and clapped him on the shoulder. "Good job, Rudy. Very nice. Thanks," Cainen said softly.

Rudy nodded. He, too, had been affected. He hadn't known what was built up inside him.

Self-condemnation is a difficult food to digest. But it's very nutritious.

Cainen cleared his throat, and the children who had been watching Rudy turned their eyes to Cainen.

"I'd like to give our first speaker a little round of applause in appreciation for his speaking to you today."

The teachers led the clapping.

"And I would like to introduce our next guest, Mr. Casitas."

Riddler didn't realize that it was him that Cainen was referring to and looked to the doorway to see who was going to enter.

"Bobby?"

"Oh, yeah," responded the little gangster. He took the center of the room, and Cainen faded to the side again.

Riddler was not as eloquent a speaker as his leader.

"OK, like I need to explain to you about being a gang member." He quickly looked apologetically at Cainen. "I mean about how bad it is to be in a gang, OK.

"I know all of you see the writing on the walls. And some of you might think it's real tough to be in a gang, and that you're a bad dude if you're in one, OK. But that's not the case, OK.

"Bein' in a gang is a real bad scene. I mean that all you do in a gang is break the law. You know, commit crimes."

Riddler looked toward Gonzalez, who didn't change expression.

"And you know where that can get you?"

In a moment of silence, a Mexican boy seated in the center raised his hand. Riddler pointed at him.

"Jail?" the child asked.

"That's right."

The other kids murmured among themselves.

"That's right. You might end up in prison. If you get in a gang, you're gonna wind up goin' to jail, or youth camp, which is even worse. You don't get to see your mom or your dad or your sisters and brothers. You have to stay with all these other bad people. And you never get to eat what you want; you gotta—"

Cainen politely cleared his throat, trying to avoid a tangent by the gang member.

"Yeah, OK, well, you know, you can't get caught up in protecting your neighborhood. Your turf. You gotta concentrate on doing good in school and getting a good job. Those are the things that will help you later. If you join a gang, you ain't gonna be prepared for later, OK. You probably won't even live long enough for later.

" 'Cause you never know when a rival gang is gonna try and get you, OK. And once you're in a gang, you can't change your mind and get out, OK. You're in it for good. 'Cause even if you wanted out, you got to stay in for your own protection 'cause the other gangs won't know that you want out.

"And you know what else you get? You get to watch your friends, your own *hermanos* and *hermanas*, die in your arms. 'Cause that's what happens in drive-by shootings. And you always gotta watch your back, 'cause it never stops, you know, the revenge. You never know who's gonna get it, or when."

Riddler lifted the side of his shirt up. A small red scar marked his side.

"This is where I got stabbed last month. I been stabbed three times. *That's* what you get if you join a gang.

"You might think it's tough and macho to be in a gang. But you're wrong. 'Cause the worst part of bein' in a gang is that you can lose your life, OK.

"Even though you're just a kid and your life has just started."

Cainen looked at the rows of mesmerized faces and knew that what he had done was a good thing to do. It was a powerful and overwhelming thing, that was true. But that was what was needed to reach these kids before the gang members and drug dealers outside the classroom reached them.

Cainen silently wondered how many young lives he had just saved by taking a chance in bringing Rudy and Riddler to the school. And he realized that he could never have done what his two gang members had done. They had reached through to these children who were growing up in one of the most violent cities in the world.

The teachers started to come out of their fascination. Cainen walked to the front of the class.

"Do any of you want to be gang members?"

It was a resounding chorus that yelled, "*No!*"

"And what do you tell people who offer you drugs?"

A louder, more emphatic response came from the throats of the future of America. "*No!*"

The yelling helped the students, and the teachers, recover from their astonishment. Mrs. Farnsworth moved to the front of the room. "We don't have time for any more questions. Now everybody thank Officer Cainen and Mr. Gonzalez and Mr. Casitas."

The students answered in a chorus of cacophony: "Thank you."

Mrs. Farnsworth led the three visitors out the door of the classroom.

"Well, that was quite wonderful. It really had an impact on the children." She looked at Cainen. "I'd like to invite Mr. Gonzalez and Mr. Casitas to come back and visit us."

When Mrs. Farnsworth averted her gaze to look at the two gang members, who had their gaze on Cainen, the officer shook his head no.

Mrs. Farnsworth turned back to face Cainen. "We've never had a presentation like this before."

"It's a *very* new program," responded the officer.

"Your department must be proud to have two excellent speakers like these gentlemen in their program. They've really impressed us all, and I think they've had a positive impact on the children. I personally thank you all very much."

"It was our pleasure."

The two gang members also thanked the teacher.

The three guests then walked down the stairs to the police cruiser.

"You guys want a ride back?"

"No thanks," answered the leader. "We don't want to get too bad a rap on us."

Cainen reached into his shirt pocket and took out two LAPD business cards. He drew a big X on the back of each. (That way no one could write on the back. Too many people had written on the backs of business cards given by officers, alleging that they were family members when they were later stopped by other officers. Officers' family members were given special privileges, such as avoidance of traffic citations.)

Cainen handed a card to each of his guest speakers.

"You guys did an excellent job in there. You really helped out those kids. That's my business card with the police station phone number. If I can help you guys out, give me a call."

The three shook hands and the gang members headed toward the school gate. Cainen called Gonzalez back.

"Listen, Rudy. I know a guy from my Neighborhood Watch who has a store near here. He's looking to hire a hard worker. If you're interested in the job, give me a call at the station. I think I can get you in there with a good recommendation."

Gonzalez looked at Cainen. The newfound respect was returned to the officer.

"You know," said the gang leader, "you may be loco, but you're not too bad for a cop. I mean a policeman."

Gonzalez realized that what he had said might not be taken as a compliment by a police officer.

"I mean you're a cool dude, you know. Hey, thanks, man."

Cainen started to open his mouth, but Rudy held up his hand. "I mean thanks, Officer Cainen."

The two shook hands again. Cainen watched Rudy join Riddler and head out the school gate.

Cainen unlocked his car and opened the door. Instead of sitting down, the officer put his left foot on the floorboard. Then he looked up, toward heaven.

Well, Cainen thought, if the LAPD didn't fire him for being gay, then they'd sure fire him for bringing two gang members into an elementary school classroom, despite the immensely positive effect it had on the students.

Cainen sighed. For some unknown, vague, intangible reason, despite all the chaos in his life because of the Department and despite the fact that his fellow officers were trying to either kill him or get him killed, Cainen felt good. His job and his brain had allowed him to do some good on the Earth.

Cainen was reminded of a saying that his sergeant friend, Steve Jinkens, had told him: "When your feet are in the oven and your head is in the freezer, on the average, you are fairly comfortable."

Cainen laughed.

"These are exciting times in law enforcement," Cainen said to himself as he got in the car and prepared to drive back to the station.

* * *

Jeff's muffled yells and his forceful struggling had rocked the van. Elvira, a black transvestite prostitute, had walked past the van, hearing the muffled sounds and seeing the movement.

"Oh, honey, give it to him, baby." Sex in cars parked behind Arthur J's was nothing uncommon. Elvira held the cigarette higher in her fingers and continued out onto the sidewalk to ply her trade.

The rich owner of a bank, who was a pedophile that frequented AJ's in search of young boys, also saw the spasmodic jerking of the darkened van. His only reaction was one of jealousy. Someone else had bought some sex before he was able to. The banker hurried inside to see what boys remained.

When Jeff lay limp, Charlie and Cameron both sat back, catching their breath. The boy had given them quite a struggle.

Charlie ordered Cameron to help him load Jeff's body into the plastic bag. Charlie used the youth's shirt to wipe off the blood from the van floor.

Rushing Cameron, Charlie peeked out the side van door before sliding it open all the way. Seeing no one, he and Cameron hurriedly carried the plastic bag to the large orange trash bin behind the restaurant. Charlie lifted the lid with the edge of his palm, and then they hefted the bag into the dumpster. Charlie closed the lid the same way.

The two hurried back into the rear of the van. Charlie checked the floor and ensured that there was no bloodstain.

"I-I-I thought you weren't gonna k-kill him," squeaked Cameron.

"And let him go to the cops and spill his guts? No fucking way." Charlie leaned into Cameron again. "No one snitches on me."

Cameron had no plans to do anything of the sort. Not now. He had been driving when the boy was picked up. And Charlie had forced *him* to suffocate the youth.

Cameron heard the front passenger side door open and sank back into the shadows in the rear of the van.

Lisa climbed through the area between the seats. She held a greasy white bag.

"Where's the boy?"

"He left," answered Charlie smoothly, looking at Cameron out of the corner of his eye. "What'd you expect him to do, sit here and wait all night for you to come back?"

Lisa was unsure. "You mean you just let him walk out of here?"

"Just because I said I'd let him go doesn't mean I was going to baby-sit the fucker," Charlie answered angrily. "Let him find his own fucking ride home. You got the burgers?"

Lisa handed him the bag, satisfied that the youth had been unharmed. "Yeah, but I got four. I didn't know if the kid was still going to be here."

"That's OK. I'm hungry. I'll eat the extra one." Charlie handed the hamburgers wrapped in white paper to the other two.

Lisa took the burger and carefully wrapped the paper back so that it only covered half the sandwich. She believed that Charlie was telling the truth. She had underestimated his psychopathy.

Lisa didn't know that psychopaths not only could lie convincingly, but the reason they could do so was because they actually believed their own lies.

When they finished the burgers, Charlie drove the van back to the motel.

It never occurred to Lisa that if Charlie had really let Jeff go, he would have hightailed it out of the area as fast as he could drive the van, just in case the kid contacted the cops.

But Lisa was lost in the reverie of her childhood with her younger brother, before the boy died and before her soul had stopped living.

Two hours after the van departed, a homeless man went through the trash looking for something to eat. He pushed the brown trash bag aside and picked up a can of Mountain Dew and drank from it.

Shortly before sunrise, an old Chevy truck pulled up beside the dumpster and another man got out and raised the lid. The man saw the body in the brown plastic bag and carefully lifted the bag out. The man set the bag down on the side of the dumpster that was hidden from the view of cars driving through the gas station on the corner beside Arthur J's.

The man then collected all the bottles and all the cardboard from the dumpster, closing the lid with his ungloved hands when he had finished. He loaded the recyclables into the back of his truck and drove off.

It wasn't until nine in the morning when a restaurant employee went out to wash down the back alley that the grisly bag was reported. And the employee didn't observe the bag until he was almost completely done with his chore. By the time the homicide detectives arrived at eleven, any evidence that might have led to the killers had already been cleaned away or contaminated.

The Assignment

Most people forget that the "news" is a business, a profit-making enterprise, rather than a public service. News does not occur; it is made. That is why newspapers have the tendency to sensationalize a "good story." Tabloids like the *National Enquirer* and the *Star* just take the same postulate to the *n*th degree: that if it's too incredible or too horrible to be believed, people will buy it. The fact that the *Enquirer* is the number-one-selling paper in the country proves this. That the publication is sold primarily at supermarket checkout stands does nothing to detract from its huge sales volume. What other newspaper would be able to have its mainstay being "Elvis Lives" stories?

So the story of the murder of a seventeen-year-old Valley student, and the grisly circumstances surrounding his death, made the front pages of every local paper by the next day. By the end of the week, the national wire services had carried the story to every major paper in the country.

Most of the papers and the accompanying editorials theorized that the youth had been kidnapped in the Valley, probably within walking distance of his home, and that he had been sexually assaulted. In other words, "no one's children were safe." Anywhere.

The story caught like wildfire. The fact that Jeff's mother was the vice-president of the Granada High PTA did nothing to detract from the publicity.

Before the week was over, PTA groups from throughout L.A. County were demanding better protection from their respective police agencies. And those parents that weren't preparing petitions for the mayor of Los Angeles were busy organizing phone trees to overrun the lines of the L.A. police chief.

The *L.A. Times* broke the Metro section story that an anonymous source within the Department had stated that the rumors were that there had been numerous such grisly, as yet unsolved, sex murders.

This did nothing to quiet the local mass hysteria. Neither did the fact that the L.A. police chief had remained unavailable for comment.

The chief had never before passed up an opportunity for free publicity for his future political aspirations. Why now?

Parents had to juggle their work schedules to be present outside their children's schools when the schools let out. In the Valley, mothers had to rearrange doctor and salon appointments in order to pick up their kids.

These parents were as frightened for their children's safety as they were pissed off at the PD for their missed appointments. In the twentieth century, everyone got charged for a missed appointment.

And everyone was angry about the afternoon traffic jams in the residential neighborhoods caused by the swarms of concerned parents. (The jams had always happened before, but no one had anything they could blame them on.)

A reluctant Los Angeles police chief scheduled a meeting with his chief of staff.

"OK, Jim, let me have it."

"Well, sir." The chief of staff cleared his throat. The Job was similar to the Greek battlefields, in that the bearers of bad news were often the ones first punished.

"Sir, the National PTA Congress has issued a statement demanding stepped-up patrols around all school campuses in the L.A. area until the murderer is found. And the city council has called a special session for this Thursday."

"And the mayor?" The chief was concerned about his primary nemesis and major political opponent.

"Surprisingly," the chief of staff grasped at the good news like a small ledge on the face of a steep mountain, "the mayor has refrained from any public comment."

"He's probably just busy preparing some big news conference that will put the full blame on my shoulders."

"Actually, sir, he has requested a closed-door meeting with you to discuss this matter. As soon as you have the time. Maybe he isn't playing this one as a political football."

"Bullpuckey. He doesn't know any other game. He's still bitter that he only made it to sergeant when he was in the Department. He thinks he would have been a better chief."

"We know that isn't true, sir."

This momentarily mollified the chief. He knew that he had to do something fast before his political career washed down the proverbial drain. But what? He needed to keep his main stanchions, the pillars of law-enforcement support, behind him if he ever expected to win the mayor's race. Or the gubernatorial nomination.

The chief smiled at his secret ambition. But he needed the support of the Parent-Teacher Associations.

Well, he was the chief of police. And even if he hadn't worked the streets very long, he had solved a lot tougher situations than this before. A lot tougher nuts to crack. Hadn't he survived the Police Explorer scandal? And wasn't he renowned for his inventive drug abuse program for schoolchildren?

"What about putting some of the vice officers out on the streets as hustlers?" asked the chief. "Like we do with the trick task forces?" In

179

this attack on heterosexual prostitution, women LAPD officers posed as prostitutes and arrested men for solicitation.

"We've already tried that, sir," explained the chief of staff, who had anticipated the question but had let the chief feel as if he had thought of it. "We can't get anyone else to volunteer. When we have done it, the officers have been made right away. The bunboys seem to be able to smell the undercovers."

In actuality, the hustlers made the cops right away because they dressed in baggy pants or shirts, instead of the tight clothes needed to entice a customer, and because they looked so uncomfortable in a homosexual environment.

Those officers that had made it past the cursory scrutiny always failed to pass their first test. The officers were too macho to squeeze the crotch of the hustler who tested them to see if they were a cop.

The chief of staff summed this up in one sentence to his boss. "The undercovers just can't fit into the gay scene."

"Well then, find me a gay officer! Surely we haven't fired all of them?"

The chief of staff immediately thought of the movie comedy *Airplane*. But he kept it to himself. He didn't think the police chief would find it humorous if he answered, "No, we still have some gay officers. And don't call me Shirley."

"I thought you might ask about that, sir. I've taken the liberty of bringing you the list of suspected officers from Internal Affairs."

"We still have that? I thought we stopped keeping a list back in '79."

"No, sir. We just told that to the Police Commission."

"Did I know we were still keeping the list?"

The chief of staff never ceased to be amazed by his boss's ignorance. "Yes, sir. You approved of the retention."

"OK."

The chief held out his hand. The chief of staff got out of his chair and handed the list to his boss. The big chief set it on the pad in the center of his humongous desk to review it. It was two pages long.

The list was made up of male and female LAPD officers, on separate pages, that were suspected of being homosexual. The list included officers that had come to the attention of the Department when they had gotten into fights with their same-sex roommates. It also included the names of those officers tipped off by jilted homosexual lovers, male prostitutes, other departments that had come into contact with the officer in a primarily gay environment, and officers who had been disciplined for their off- or on-duty involvement with transvestites or hustlers. The last category only included the few officers who had been able to overturn their firing by taking the case to an appellate court.

The suspected sexual orientation of most of those named on the list remained unverified. Some of the male prostitutes who had given the names of officers had only done so in exchange for their not being given a criminal charge. To the hustlers, the name of any sworn officer would do.

And, of course, the list included the names of those discovered to possibly be homosexual during their background investigation. It was a requirement that the investigators make the notification to place the suspected name on the list.

"Is anyone on this list not a screwup? I think I recognize almost all of these names from IAD's Reports on Administration of Internal Discipline. Swissgood was accused of molesting his own teenage son! I don't want to put a guy like that on the street with a bunch of juvenile bunboys. The press would have a heyday with that one!"

The chief tossed the list on his desk and sat back.

The staff officer felt appropriately chastised. He had expected such a reaction from a man of as high a moral character as the chief and had prepared for it.

"There's Cainen."

"Cainen . . . Cainen . . ." The big chief put his fingers together like the steeple in the child's nursery rhyme and reviewed the name in his mind. "Didn't they uncover something in his background?"

"Yes, sir. But only that he had gone to a discotheque that was supposedly frequented by homosexual clientele."

"Which one?"

The junior chief looked into his file folder and shuffled some papers before answering.

"The Odyssey."

"That was in Wilshire Area," replied the big boss, having learned all the major gay hangouts from his meetings with the gay community back in 1982, when a furor had arisen over alleged police discrimination.

"And that disco used to attract a lot of male prostitutes, if my memory serves me correctly."

The junior chief felt at a loss for an appropriate response.

"I, uh, wouldn't know, sir. I don't have any personal experience with the place."

The boss smiled. "I certainly would hope not. So what's your suggestion?"

The commander pulled his chair up to the chief's desk.

"Well, sir, Cainen has never been accused of misconduct except for that one thing in his background. And he's a sharp cookie. He was first in his academy class, the class president, and he promoted to FTO right off probation."

"You sure he's gay?" questioned the chief. The chief, like many ignorant, prejudiced people, naturally assumed that gays and lesbians were found among the dregs of society instead of throughout every stratum.

"It would certainly seem so. He's always lived alone, close with his family, never taken a date to his area Christmas parties, and he was once spotted near Drakes on Melrose."

"Drakes may be one of our biggest cruising problems, but Melrose is a major hangout for all kinds of kids."

"Cainen also drives a Suzuki Samurai."

The chief laughed. "Well, I guess that just about clinches it." The Suzuki was known on the Department as the gay version of a Jeep.

"What do you suggest be done?" the chief asked of his junior man a second time.

"I think we have a double-edged sword. We put Cainen out on the street. Being gay, he'll fit right in. We appeal to the overachiever in him. He'll want to do the job right. And he'll probably picture himself being a savior of gay youth. I think he's our best chance to nail whoever's out there."

"And if Cainen refuses?"

"Judging from what Captain Wilson tells me, there are a lot of officers willing to bring complaints against the guy. I'm sure he'd accept the assignment if his choice was to face a trial board on some charge of sexual harassment of a heterosexual officer."

The chief was unshaken by the hint of blackmail brought to his attention. If it came down to anything, the chief could deny knowledge and let his staff officer take the brunt.

"You said Captain Wilson?"

"Yes, sir. Cainen's already assigned to Hollywood Area."

"Does he have any experience working vice?"

"Yes, sir. He's done a loan to the PED team."

"Sounds perfect." The chief sat up straight in his large chair. "Go to it. And I don't want to hear back from you until this thing is over and the psychopath out there is behind bars."

"What about the request from the mayor?"

"I'll meet with him as soon as you bring me the perp's arrest report. Stall the mayor for now."

"Yes, sir."

The chief of staff got up and opened the heavy oak door to let himself out. His boss called to him as he was closing it behind him.

"Jim!"

"Yes, sir?"

"What are you going to do if Cainen gets killed?"

The commander stepped back inside the room and shut the door. He walked over to the chief's desk and lowered his voice. The commander feared that the chief idolized J. Edgar Hoover so much that he might record all his office conversations.

"Look at it this way, sir." The staff officer nodded his head and smirked. "One less homosexual in the Department."

The chief smiled. The junior man exited the office, closing the door behind him.

The head of the Los Angeles Police Department picked up the phone and dialed his wife. He wanted her to know that he'd be home early for dinner.

* * *

William Morris Leaks had been a Los Angeles Police officer for nine years. He had spent six of those years assigned to the 77th Street Area patrol division A.M. watch, before being transferred to Hollywood.

Leaks had finally received one too many complaints about his treatment of blacks. It wasn't the suspects that complained about the treatment; they knew better. A complaint against an officer by a suspect might result in beatings. Not just one beating, but every time the officers caught the suspect in the field. Word traveled fast among the officers.

The complaints against Leaks were from the residents of the area. They complained that he was rude, made racially offensive remarks, and generally made it known that he didn't care to be among "black folk."

Leaks was a different type of cop. For example, since all officers and detectives worked in teams, they used an interrogation scam with their arrestees called "good cop/bad cop." This technique, when acted out properly, usually resulted in a confession.

In the scam, one cop acted as a "bad cop," threatening to beat a confession out of the handcuffed arrestee. His partner, the "good cop," held the officer back, telling the arrestee to confess before the "bad cop" took over the interview. For variety, partners often switched their roles.

Leaks played his own version of the technique, called "schizophrenic cop." In it, Leaks played *both* parts.

Leaks's mother had been an actress back in the forties. She had been one of the first to sign with the William Morris Agency during that period. In remembrance of happier times, before she lost her photogenic youth, she had named her eldest son after her talent agent.

Unfortunately for the officer, his initials made him the literal butt of practical jokes. His name, B. M. Leaks, was known to every parent that had to change diapers. It was also recognized by his fellow officers.

Leaks didn't only dislike blacks. As he told his fellow P-2 patrol officers, he was the most unbiased person he knew. He hated all minorities equally. Blacks, spics, kikes, Chinks . . . any of them. But he especially hated faggots.

His favorite line to a new partner was: "You know why West Hollywood is like cereal? Because it's filled with fruits, nuts, and flakes."

Like the code of silence in the Department dictated, even those that disapproved of the joke kept their mouths shut.

Leaks had transferred into Hollywood after the big shake-up. He hadn't particularly wanted to go there; he just wanted out of the "ghetto."

Leaks was well known by the Hollywood officers before he transferred in. Leaks was not only known because of his unique name; he was the subject of an infamous LAPD legend. (Because of its infamy, it was also one of the most popular LAPD stories.)

After his third year of working from eleven at night until eight in the morning, Leaks found that he couldn't fall asleep on his days off.

Like all morning watch officers, Leaks was prone to "catch a few" at his favorite "hole," during the later hours of his watch.

Since police departments, like Norm's coffee shops, are open twenty-four hours a day, every day of the year, every police agency in the country has officers that use a hole.

Though officers may have to work all hours of the night and day, it is not "normal" for a human to stay awake during the hours of darkness. If you consider police work normal, that is.

A hole, in police lingo, is the place where officers can go for their catnaps when there's nothing happening on the street or on the radio. Usually this is just prior to sunrise, between 4:00 and 6:00 A.M.

As happens with any trade, officers develop the uncanny ability to focus on radio calls that are prefixed with their call sign. The most famous call sign is "One Adam 12."

No matter how loud the officers are talking or how busy the radio traffic is, police officers become instantly alert when they hear their call sign precede the dispatcher's information.

Police officers can even do this in their sleep. Only occasionally do officers forget to turn their volume up or accidentally leave their radio off, requiring supervisors to call out a police helicopter and send out the troops to find the missing and unresponsive unit to ensure that they haven't been ambushed. Usually one of the "good-ol'-boy" supervisors knows the location of each officer's hole.

Holes are areas that are out of sight of both the public and supervisors. They may be closed underground parking lots or even an area in the corner of the police lot. (Supervisors check everywhere except their own backyard.)

More often than not, an officer's hole will be in a large fenced-in business that has a driveway entrance, such as a lumberyard. If the business has been burglarized and the owner has had to respond, the A.M. watch officer may coax a set of keys from the unwary owner, ostensibly to conduct "checks" of the lot for burglars during the nighttime. Of course the only ones who enter the lot after hours are the officers looking for a place to catch some shuteye.

Not that the owner would mind. After all, he or she is getting first-rate guard service for next to nothing. It's not coming out of his own pocket, except, of course, in his taxes.

When Leaks found that he couldn't fall asleep on his nights off, he remembered how easily he slept while at his hole.

Legend had it that Leaks went to the Motor Transport Division of the LAPD and got himself an old cruiser seat (at a police discount, of course, which meant *free*). Leaks then went to Radio Shack and bought himself a cheap police scanner.

Setting the car seat in his living room, he sat back and turned the scanner on. He was asleep within seconds, and slept like a baby.

Leaks never had trouble sleeping on his days off since then.

In Hollywood, however, Leaks chose to work the day watch. Days was the easiest watch to slough off on, having few "red light and siren" calls. Leaks's best buddy, Tommy Champion, worked the morning watch. If Leaks came in early, they could grab a cup together before his buddy went home.

It was with Champion that Leaks had come up with the idea to finally rid the division of its fruit copper.

"You heard the latest Cainen joke?" Leaks asked Champion as they had coffee together behind the doughnut shop on Western.

"Probably," answered the officer who had recommended that Cainen be killed.

"What does AIDS stand for?"

"Fag disease?"

"Nope . . . Anal Injection of Death Serum."

The prejudiced officers guffawed.

Champion was the first to stop laughing. "You know we met on morning watch. We agreed not to back up the fruit."

"Yeah, we agreed to the same thing on day watch," explained Leaks. "But there's no hotshots happening during the daytime."

"We gotta do something else to get this guy off The Job."

"I have an idea that'll work," commented Leaks.

"Whatcha got going?"

"You don't want to know. That way you won't have to deny anything."

"Oh, come on. Give me a hint."

"No way. You'll hear about it when it happens. Everybody will."

"You gotta tell me!" exclaimed Champion, who was also overweight and spent most of his free time eating while at work. "If anybody asks, I'll lie and deny."

"Hey, you lie," added Leaks, "and I'll swear to it."

The officers laughed at the common, and true, phrase often heard among LAPD officers.

It was less than fourteen days later that the complaint was sent to Internal Affairs by Sergeant Fritsch. The complaint was from a twenty-six-year-old transient cocaine addict named Steve Andrews. Andrews alleged that he had been detained by Cainen while he was sleeping in the park at Fountain and Vista. Cainen had told Andrews that he was searching him for cocaine. According to the cocaine addict, who admitted that he had gotten high just prior to Cainen's arrival, Cainen had repeatedly squeezed his groin during the supposed search.

Sergeant Fritsch had been specially assigned to the investigation by Captain Carter. The addict had not come into the station voluntarily to make the complaint but had been brought in by Officer Leaks. Andrews told the investigating sergeant that he had received subliminal messages from Cainen that he was homosexual and wanted to have sex with him. Andrews supposedly stated that he did not respond to Cainen's advances, and so the officer had finally left him alone.

According to the complaint, Cainen had threatened to come back and "get" Andrews if he mentioned the groping to anyone else.

The complaint did not explain how the investigating officer had determined that "subliminal messages" had been sent. It also did not address how Andrews could have been sleeping if he had just gotten high on cocaine, a central nervous system stimulant.

Internal Affairs chose not to handle the complaint but assigned it a number and referred it back to Fritsch for handling.

With no independent witnesses and an unreliable complainant, Captain Carter had recommended that Cainen be suspended for two days. The captain's recommended penalty was for "improperly completing a Department document."

Fritsch could not sustain Andrews's allegations of impropriety. In reviewing Cainen's DFAR, the log showed that Cainen had failed to write in a vehicle stop that he had made between 0235 and 0245. A review of the radio transmissions for Hollywood Division during that period revealed that Cainen had stopped a vehicle driving without its headlights at 0240 hours. After determining that the driver was not drunk, Cainen had let the violator go with just a warning.

Every officer in the Department kept these types of incidents off their logs. Cainen had a habit of logging every activity that he did. But in the same time period, Cainen had been impounding a stolen vehicle from the same location. The car without the headlights had driven by and Cainen initiated the stop, keeping the other recovered vehicle in sight.

Though most LAPD officers were even less conscientious than Cainen in log completion, the Department manual required that officers log "every activity of a law-enforcement nature."

The penalty recommended by Captain Carter would ensure that the entire complaint would be placed in Cainen's personnel package for the duration of his career. Any time Cainen sought promotion or a change of assignment, the supervisor reviewing his package would see that Cainen had been accused of making improper sexual advances. Improper *homosexual* advances.

Though the recommended penalty was only for two days, it would affect Cainen's entire career. In fact, it would just about end it.

Nine days after the closed-door conference between the chief of police and the chief of staff, Cainen was ordered into a meeting by his A.M. watch lieutenant, Jerry Wilder.

In Captain Carter's office, the entire complaint was explained to Cainen. Cainen was offered a choice. He could accept the penalty, thereby effectively ending his career, or he could take a Department trial board, where two police captains and a civilian would review the complaint and listen to testimony before they invariably agreed with the already-completed investigation.

Cainen was given another alternative. PED needed someone to work a special assignment that was dangerous but needed the expertise that Cainen possessed.

Lieutenant Wilder explained that the chief of police, in a magnanimous gesture, had agreed to waive the complaint investigation if Cainen took the assignment. As Wilder explained it: "The chief doesn't want to put anybody without a perfect package into this sensitive of an assignment."

Cainen smelled a setup. But he saw no way out of it. He told his lieutenant that he would need a week to think it over. Wilder gave him three days. It was the longest three days of Cainen's life.

With the three days that he had taken off work, Cainen spent the first day debating whether he should come out of the closet. He could no longer deny who or what he was. Not to the Department and not to the people he needed to see if he was going to try to save his own life. There is nothing more agonizing than making this type of decision and opening up your private life to such scrutiny.

Cainen didn't cry over his predicament. He hadn't cried in ten years. But he agonized, over and over. He couldn't eat or sleep.

Cainen had always been a decisive person. He never hesitated in making a decision. His career had helped him become even more of a decision maker. By the second day, Cainen had reached his decision.

If the people he needed to see had to know he was gay to help him, so be it.

Cainen used his contacts to set up a meeting with the president of the Police Commission, a closeted gay city councilman, and a deputy mayor of the city of Los Angeles.

On the third day, the day before he had to let Lieutenant Wilder know his decision, Cainen met individually with the three members of the city government.

He started at nine in the morning with the president of the Los Angeles Police Commission.

* * *

Cainen was warily nervous as he made his way to the office of the Police Commission. Walking past the security desk at Parker Center, Cainen kept his eyes straight ahead, not even acknowledging the presence of the officers behind the desk. Now that the terrorist threat of the Olympics was over, the officers were back to their lax state.

Taking the stairs instead of waiting for the elevator, Cainen was aware of the stares and subsequent whispers among the couple of officers dressed in suits that he passed. He could imagine more than overhear the context of the advisement shared between the knowing and the unknowing. Cainen was sure it was just a slight deviation from the old advisements that had occurred whenever he was in a police building. He had overheard more of the statements than he cared to remember. Several of the speakers had *wanted* Cainen to overhear them.

"That's that fruit officer from Hollywood" or 77th or Central. Wherever Cainen went, the officers as much as the Department kept tabs on him. The statement would inevitably be accompanied by a nod of the head, and the newly initiated fag-baiter would turn to look at the man being referred to.

Only now the advisement would be different, Cainen was sure. Now it would be something along the lines of: "That's the fruit officer that groped the fifteen-year-old in the park."

In the game of "telephone" that kids play, a story is whispered into one ear and passed throughout the classroom until the last child hears it and says it aloud. Without exception, the spoken story is grossly different from the one that first started the whispers.

The same is true for rumors among the police department officers. The embellishments, making Cainen's action seem so much more atrocious, would just be starting. By week's end, Cainen would undoubtedly have been arrested by the FBI for interstate transporting of transvestites for sexual purposes.

For now, Cainen walked down the stairwell to the basement level, and his appointment with the president of the Police Commission.

Unbeknownst to Cainen, the commission president had already reviewed Cainen's entire Department personnel package. He had also reviewed the personnel complaint initiated against the young officer and the accompanying investigation by Sergeant Fritsch.

The president had been highly impressed by the accomplishments and outstanding package of Cainen. He noted that the young single officer had spent a majority of his days off taking law enforcement classes. Most of the classes were to develop his expertise as a patrol officer in arrest and control tactics.

Cainen had more expertise in the area than any of the officers instructing at the academy. To the president of the commission, tasked with having to review every use of deadly force by officers, this was training that he would have liked to see the police chief institute for all of his men (*and women*, the president chided himself).

In fact, the commission had highly recommended that the chief increase the in-service tactical training in arrest tactics that was currently given to patrol officers. The chief had balked at the idea, as he did at almost every idea the commission suggested.

Following political expediency, since the commission was made up of mayor's appointees, the review board stopped short of making their suggestion into a formal recommendation. The commission was still suffering from the fallout from their recommendation that the Department do away with the bar-arm chokehold. Part of the fallout included increased shootings and baton beatings by officers.

Had Cainen's package only had the tactical classes, the president would have been leary of the type of officer he was going to meet. Very possibly, the young man would be a macho bully, impressed with the book *Survival Tactics*, which was like a survivalist's guide for cops, complete with secret weapons.

But Cainen's package was also filled with dozens of letters of commendation from the public. Compliments for his Drug Abuse In Schools (DAIS) presentations to youth groups, lectures to community organizations, and, most rare, even letters from members of the public to whom Cainen had issued a traffic citation who were impressed with his professionalism.

No, this was a young man who took classes to professionalize himself, to *avoid* hurting people. The amount of money alone that Cainen must have spent to take the classes was enough to impress the leader of the city's civilian review board. (The commission president had no way of knowing that Cainen's survival had depended on taking the classes, since no one would back him up.)

The complaint and investigation disturbed the president, who was a former deputy district attorney. He had been a lawyer in private practice for almost twenty years now, and the complaint contained too many loopholes.

The attorney was serving his third term on the commission, having outlasted any of the other political appointees, who had fallen into disfavor. Having done so, he immediately recognized when the Department was out to get someone. And that was clearly apparent here. But why would they only recommend a two-day suspension? Because they wanted the complaint put in the young officer's package, and two days off was the minimum penalty.

The commission president was also familiar with the chief's opinion of homosexuals. He had been on the commission when the chief had reported that the vast majority of child molestations had been committed by homosexual men. Thank God a renowned doctor, who was also a member of the gay community, had come forward and challenged the chief's statement, which had made its way into the papers.

The president knew of the chief's religious beliefs. Though the top manager wasn't a born-again like his assistant, he was still a fundamentalist. And that had a bearing on his view of sexuality.

The president recalled when, amid cries of brutality and harassment from the Los Angeles gay community, two of the police commissioners had recommended that the chief recruit from the gay community. In a furious response, the police chief had threatened to disband all of his crime prevention task forces if the commission tried to bind him to that recommendation. Behind the scenes, he had also threatened to expose the married member of the commission who had been caught making a solicitation during a trick task force.

Even with the backing of the mayor, there failed to be a majority decision on the matter from the five-member board.

So the commission president thought he was familiar with Cainen's predicament.

There was a light rap on the door to the somber meeting room.

"Come in," said the man who supposedly oversaw the policy making of the police department. (In theory, the commission made the policy and the chief carried it out. But both parties knew that the chief actually did both.)

Clint Preyhorn, the officer assigned to assist the commission (and watchdog it for the chief), opened the door and peeked in.

"Officer Cainen is here to see you, sir."

"Yes. Send him in."

A moment later, the young officer, who appeared too intense for his age, was shown into the room by Preyhorn.

The president stood and offered his hand. The meeting table was clear except for a pipe and tobacco pouch. The commission leader had long since memorized anything significant from Cainen's package and had let Preyhorn return it to the Personnel Division.

Cainen took the proffered hand uncomfortably. The door had been shut behind them by Preyhorn. Cainen had never before admitted his orientation to anyone associated with the Department. In fact, to anyone. And admitting one's sexual preference was difficult to do when you were alone with another man behind closed doors.

Mostly, though, Cainen was shaken because Preyhorn had walked directly up to him in the waiting area. Preyhorn had addressed Cainen by name and told him that the commission president would see him momentarily.

Cainen hadn't given his name; the officer had *known* it. That caused a bad premonition. Cainen wondered whom the officer was notifying at this very moment.

"You have quite an impressive package for a young officer. Anyone would be envious of such a personnel file. You have my compliments and appreciation. You are an exemplary officer."

The president was addressing him. The chart outside the commission office showed pictures of each of the top managers of the Department. Lines connected the chains of command, with the highest ranking officers above their subordinates. At the top of the Department was the chief of police. Above him were photographs of the five commissioners. Over them all was a picture of the man sitting before Cainen.

Cainen had been raised in a chain of command since age fifteen. He had a great deal of respect for this man. He pushed aside his concerns about Preyhorn.

"I don't think everyone on the Department would agree with you, sir."

"How's that?" asked the older man.

"Well, sir," Cainen tried to make sure that his voice sounded deep and masculine, "I'm homosexual."

"I realize that it must be tough out in the field for you if that is your sexual orientation," stated the president sympathetically. "But the city has an ordinance forbidding discrimination. The Department abides by that policy. You can only be judged by the work-related things you do."

Cainen could see that this might be an uphill battle. The commission president knew he had to stick to the party line. But the commissioner was not prepared for the story that followed.

Cainen's package had demonstrated that the young man was a credible officer. His statements were to be taken as truthful. His demeanor and mannerisms supported this belief.

Still, it was hard for the president of the Los Angeles Police Commission to believe what he was hearing, what was being told to him.

The president filled his pipe with tobacco and lit it up. He hoped that the sweet aroma that filled the air would clear away the stench of corruption.

It didn't.

Cainen finished. He had dismissed his fear that the office was bugged. It was too late to matter.

He had summarized everything that had occurred to him in the form of harassment and threats since he had come on The Job. That included what he theorized had happened between Leaks and the cocaine addict that had made a complaint against him.

The summary had taken twenty minutes.

The president cleared his throat. "What you have told me is incredible. Don't get me wrong; I believe you. On the commission, we have heard stories about the treatment of suspected homosexual officers. But no one has ever come forward before now. What is it you want me to do?"

"Sir, I would like to protect my package. I need to have the personnel complaint canceled. Otherwise I will have to accept the assignment that's been offered to me." Cainen paused momentarily to look at the man puffing his pipe. "I will do anything to prevent my package from being ruined. I don't know what the future has in store for me, but I know that my personnel file will need to be spotless."

"The city has very specific guidelines for personnel issues. The Department has specific guidelines for personnel complaints," stated the commission president, avoiding the real issue. "The commission established those guidelines to protect the parties involved and ensure that there was objectivity in the process.

"You will just have to trust the process. If you think that the complaint or the recommended penalty is unfair, you can take it to a trial board."

Cainen held his patience. "Sir, a trial board is made up of two captains who are obviously concerned about promoting in the Department, or they wouldn't have achieved that rank. And the third member is a civilian political appointee. They aren't going to overturn the recommended penalty of the *chief of police*." (The chief has to approve and endorse any penalty recommendation.)

The commission president had more experience in disciplinary matters than the young officer with the unblemished record before him. He latched onto the subject with gusto. That way he could avoid dealing with *other* issues.

"I think you'd be surprised. The boards are a very fair practice. Almost half of the cases presented wind up with a decreased penalty."

"But any penalty would mean that my package would contain a complaint that implied the equivalent of my being a child molester!" Cainen was losing the battle with his patience. He wanted to retain a professional demeanor.

"I think you're exaggerating. A cocaine addict's word is hardly reliable."

"It's career suicide. I won't take a chance of that trumped-up complaint going in my package."

Both Cainen and the commission leader made realizations. Cainen realized that he was willing to risk his life by hitting the streets without a gun and badge, to protect his package. The commission president, seeing Cainen losing his cool, realized that maybe the young man before him wasn't the level-headed officer he had thought. Still . . . the young officer's package was exemplary . . .

The president didn't even realize the irony of his thoughts, that Cainen's point was well taken in that he would be evaluated on his package more than anything else. Even the president was doing it right at that moment!

"Well, it is your choice how you pursue the matter. There is very little I can do at this point," concluded the commission president. "What do you think you will do?"

With his realization, Cainen had lost all his gusto. His face took on a passive, resigned look. This caused the president to wonder further about the mental state of the man before him.

"I'll take the assignment."

"That doesn't sound like such a bad assignment. It sounds to me like you're being entrusted with quite an important task. The Department wouldn't assign you such an important matter if they were really out to get you."

The president stood in a gesture of dismissal, now that the issue was closed in his mind. He would need to set up a meeting with the police chief to discuss the information in a private session.

"Keep me posted on how your career is going. You're a remarkable young man to have gone through everything that you have," said the leader. "I'm sure the Department will back you up. I don't know why you're so hesitant about taking the assignment recommended by your lieutenant."

Cainen shook the hand that was offered him. He had a firm handshake as his eyes looked deep into the older man's.

"Because I don't think I'll live through it," he said before he turned and walked out the door.

* * *

The meeting with the deputy mayor and city councilman went no better. The deputy mayor was extremely sympathetic and supportive. She was so shocked at what she heard that she interrupted the mayor in a meeting and briefed him. She then whisked Cainen into his office.

The mayor was noncommittal, merely promising to contact the president of the Police Commission, who was his appointee. Despite

Cainen's statement that he had already met with the man and that it would do no good, the mayor stood by his only remark. The top political officer in the city made only one other statement to Cainen, and that was to tell the officer that he doubted there was anything he could do.

The deputy mayor, who had been much more supportive, simply looked on without comment. There was little else she *could* do.

The city councilman Cainen met with had been a top contender for the mayor's seat if the current black mayor had vacated. His only true competition would have been the police chief.

The councilman and the chief had been bitter adversaries on many issues before; in fact, they had never seen eye to eye.

Cainen knew this because he had volunteered to work the LAPD Memorial Celebrity Golf Tournament, which was held each year to raise funds for the families of slain officers.

Cainen was assigned to guard the player/celebrity lounge. At the exact moment that the chief walked in wearing his golf outfit, the city councilman, who was also competing, exited the room carrying his clubs.

Cainen saw the two make eye contact. Neither had wavered. The councilman, like any good politician, had finally said a terse, "Good afternoon, Chief," and then offered his hand. It may have been a symbol of a temporary truce, or perhaps it was show for any press that might have been lingering in the area. (If it was for the second reason, it was a useless gesture, since every member of the media was aware of and reported on the ill-developed relationship.)

The chief had shaken the hand. As soon as the councilman exited to go out on the course, the chief had looked at his bodyguard and then down at the hand that had touched his adversary. Cainen had watched the chief rub the hand roughly down the side of his gold slacks in a gesture of aversion.

In Cainen's meeting with the councilman, he was told that there was little that could be done to control the chief or alter the way he ran the Department.

The city councilman did take the time to explain the political realities of the situation to Cainen. Though this wasn't much consolation, it was more than the other two referrals had offered.

The councilman explained that in Los Angeles, unlike most other metropolitan cities, the chief was a civil servant. As such, only a charge of incompetence could be used to remove the man. And since the chief was the same man who had developed the Drug Abuse In Schools (DAIS) program that was the model for the entire country, it was unlikely that such a charge would hold.

Cainen was told that it would be political suicide to try to take on the chief. This was probably why the mayor had not offered any assistance.

The citizens of Los Angeles were so fed up and overrun with crime that they would probably elect the police chief to be the next mayor. No matter what the police chief was like, the councilman explained.

The chief had started a mayoral campaign in the prior election when the mayor had hinted that he was not going to run for reelection. The chief had proved to be a formidable opponent, garnering almost all of the Republican vote immediately. (For the first time in history, the registered voters in Los Angeles almost divided along the lines of their two primary parties.)

But the chief was no match for a minority incumbent. His campaign fizzled when the mayor changed his mind and announced his intentions to seek a second term.

The chief was so angry over the turn of events by his incumbent opponent that he vowed to stay on as the chief of police for as long as his adversary filled the mayoral seat.

Though the chief had over thirty years on the Department and was eligible for retirement, he had vowed to stay on as chief just to be a thorn in the mayor's side.

The councilman had summarized his position by stating that there was little he could do for Cainen except make it known to the Police Department that he was keeping his eye on the officer.

He told Cainen that the chief was uncontrollable and had proven that characteristic repeatedly.

Unlike the other two politicians Cainen had met with, the councilman did present another alternative: resignation. An intelligent young man like Cainen should have no trouble landing a job in the private sector, he said.

If Cainen still wanted to remain in police work, it was likely that the Department would leave his personnel file alone if they attained their goal of his resignation. Then Cainen could join a police agency elsewhere.

Both Cainen and the politician knew this was a fallacy. Even if the Department left his package unblemished, as soon as a background investigator from a prospective agency called LAPD, he would be given the rundown verbally.

And the same situation would reoccur.

Cainen recognized that the city councilman knew how bad the Department was and that he believed what he had been told by Cainen.

With deep emotion, Cainen explained to the councilman that he would not resign, that he would not give up without a fight. He would not put his tail between his legs and leave quietly.

Cainen would not do what every other gay on the Department had done when they were "found out."

Cainen told the city councilman that he had met homosexual officers that had been forced to resign in fear of exposure to their families or on trumped-up charges. And these officers felt belittled by the experience.

These former officers lived with their secret shame for the rest of their lives. It was not the shame of being who or what they are. It was the shame of being a police officer, a symbol of righteousness, and not standing up for what was right. The shame of turning the other cheek before the first slap even landed.

It was a shame that never diminished. They would carry it to their graves. It was a marking on their souls that was as deep as any physical scar.

Cainen would not give up to the man who had forced every other gay to leave the job. A man who believed that gays were naturally submissive, and so they would always leave quietly rather than oppose the wrongful taking of their careers.

Taking away an outstanding officer's career simply because of his sexual orientation was wrong. And it was a wrong that Cainen planned to stand up against.

Lowering his voice, Cainen told the city councilman and his assistant (the councilman had asked permission for her to be present) that he had taken an oath when he became a police officer, and that oath had bound him to uphold the laws of the city, state and the federal government. And within the Declaration of Independence was the belief that all men were created equal and that all people were guaranteed certain inalienable rights; among them were the rights to be free from persecution and to pursue happiness.

Cainen was willing to be the first to stand up to the man who had taken these rights away from homosexual police officers. Even if he got killed in the process.

VII

Mike

Mike was twenty-two years old, standing at an even six feet, weighing 160 pounds. He was also blond with blue eyes.

Mike had only worked the street twice before. The first time was with his gay friends on a dare. While he was standing there, a handsome Italian man drove by in a new Mercedes. Mike's friends said that the man wouldn't come back. But Mike thought that the man had looked at him. Sure enough, the man came back and picked up Mike. The two exchanged numbers and got together at a later date for dinner and hot sex.

Mike was a prostitute. He worked through an ad that he ran in the California *Advocate* gay newspaper.

Young All American Blond in L.A.
22 yr old college football hero for hire
blue eyes, 6', 160 lbs.   Mike (213) 612-6577

When prospective clients called, Mike asked them, "What can you tell me now?" He also asked them what they looked like and if they had dark hair.

Mike often asked the caller his nationality, since he was partial to Jews and Italians, with dark hair and brown eyes. If the callers weren't too old and if they fit the description, Mike lowered his rate. As Mike put it, "It sounds like you look pretty nice, so I'll only charge you fifty dollars. For older guys, I usually charge seventy-five dollars."

If the caller was really good-looking or was eighteen years old, Mike did the client for free.

"Hey, it's not charity if I have a good time."

But his friends, who also hustled, chastised him for giving "freebies." As they put it, "business is business." But Mike wasn't guided by what his friends told him. They had also told him that they would never accept under fifty dollars. So Mike had called them under an assumed name and described himself, and they had said it would cost him "only thirty-five dollars."

Mike always asked the callers, "What are you into?" He didn't get involved with certain sexual scenes. Many of his callers said that they wanted to be spanked, tied up, or urinated on.

Mike knew that he was gay. But he'd also been with women several times.

Like many of the prostitutes that worked out of a newspaper or magazine, Mike lived in a rented house with three other gay young men. Two of the others also placed ads under assumed names. In fact, Mike was surprised to find out that one of his roommates had been hustling even before Mike started.

Also like many of the other hustlers, Mike wanted to become an actor. But unlike his peers, who never took any steps to pursue their goals, Mike was taking acting classes. He was also making connections through his acting teacher.

Mike made money through this association. He was paid over $600 for modeling for the cover of a collegiate clothes magazine. He also received $1,000 for doing a TV commercial.

In Mike's opinion, he had an advantage over many of the other actors who came to Hollywood to be discovered. He was willing to sleep with men to further his career. In his opinion, anyone who wanted to become an actor had to be willing to sleep with guys. He shared this viewpoint with his acting teacher, who confirmed Mike's thoughts. In fact, the acting teacher had sex with Mike instead of taking tuition. The teacher just advised Mike not to sleep with producers and directors indiscriminately, but to target those that would really move him.

In his limited acting assignments, Mike several times saw a "stage mother" bring in her teenage son or daughter and offer him or her to a producer or director to do with as he pleased.

Mike usually worked two days a week, doing two or three clients a day. "This usually gets me a couple hundred bucks," he told anyone who asked. Mike's phone rang about every fifteen minutes if he didn't disconnect it. He only connected it when he felt like working or was waiting for his agent's call.

Originally, Mike bought the phone strictly to give his agent the ability to reach him at all times. Now, due to his expanding, steadfast, but vexing clientele, he used an answering machine with a message asking for a callback number.

This week, Mike's only client had been a well-built eighteen-year-old that made Mike wear a football helmet while he performed oral sex on the hustler. The teenager wanted Mike to ejaculate into a condom so that he could drink from it.

When the teenager first called, Mike could tell that the youth was masturbating while they made arrangements to meet. Not only was the boy breathing heavy, but he asked Mike, "What are you wearing right now?"

It was not uncommon for his clients to ask Mike to wear a rubber while they orally copulated him. More than once, the man crouched between Mike's large thighs had explained, "We need to do it this way. If my wife caught anything, how would I explain it?"

Mike's favorite part of hustling was acting out people's fantasies. Because of Mike's athletic build, he was often asked to participate in sports-related escapades.

His favorite had been with a twenty-one-year-old that later became his friend. The boy was involved in the movie industry, and paid Mike $250 for one night of action.

Mike and the young boy played basketball in the boy's private gym until they were sweaty. After that, they went back into the main house (Mike figured that the house belonged to the boy's parents, who must have been out of town) and laid down a blanket and wrestled. They then ripped off each other's clothes.

The boy made Mike pretend that they were two friends whose wives were out of town together. The boy wanted Mike to act like he didn't want to do what he was doing (having sex with his male friend).

Another of Mike's regular clients was a young man who worked for the record studios. The client's job was to fix up "dates" for well-known actors and singers for their public appearances. The young man told Mike that in the prior week he had set up girls for one box office star and two top singers, one from Australia and one from England.

It had been obvious to Mike why the stars didn't have female companionship of their own to bring along.

Mike's least favorite client was an older man who got off while tickling Mike, who had to lie and say that he was ticklish in areas of his body that he wasn't. As Mike explained it to other hustlers, "Being an actor helps a lot."

Mike got many calls from high-school-age boys who wanted to act out their fantasies. One young stud who lived with three girls called up and told Mike that he was too good-looking to pay for sex. As Mike later told his own roommates, "He was."

Mike tried to limit his clients to the younger guys, only taking the older ones when he was hard up for cash. If he did accept an older client, he stuck to only having the man perform oral copulation on him.

200

With the younger ones, Mike usually preferred to be in the dominant position, though he had been a bottom. In Mike's opinion, if they
were really good-looking and hot, forget the rules. "Anything goes."
Mike had never gotten a sexually transmitted disease and had
never had any run-ins with law enforcement. Mike mistakenly thought
that he would never get busted because he asked every client, "You're
not associated with any law enforcement agency, are you?"
Like many people, Mike thought that cops would hold themselves
to a higher level of integrity than the average person.
Mike's favorite aspect of his current profession was the gifts that
his clients brought. Because of Mike's good looks, many of them bought
him nice gifts. One of his regular clients, who was a commercial airline
pilot, brought Mike airplane tickets. This allowed Mike to visit his
family in Brainerd, Minnesota.
Mike had grown up in Brainerd, where he had lived with his
mother until he was eighteen. His mother had become a judge in Minnesota because it was "fashionable." She charged Mike rent to live at
home, unless he did some of the repairs around the house. Mike's
father had left when he was young and remarried soon after the divorce
was final.
Unlike his counterparts, Mike never used any illicit drugs, including marijuana. Also unlike the other hustlers, Mike believed that most
men were bisexual. To his thinking, most of the people at the gyms in
L.A. were there for homosexual reasons: to impress other men. "After
all," Mike told his tricks, "guys are more selective and choosy than
women."
Similar to his female counterparts on Sunset Boulevard, Mike periodically developed personal friendships with his clients. Many of the
people who use prostitutes want someone to talk with as much as to
engage in sex.
Mike shared the common misconception that comfort, security,
and love were just around the corner . . . arriving, possibly, with the
next trick. Mike didn't acknowledge to himself that one of the reasons
he hustled was the same reason that people frequented singles' bars.
Mike was actually "looking for Mr. Goodbar." The difference, of course,
was that Mike was making money while he was searching.
Many of the street youth's clients were movie stars or involved
with the movie industry in some way. Mike once fell in love with one
of his clients who was a producer. Not only had Mike expected to make
it into a movie, but he had told the man that he was giving up hustling,
because he couldn't sleep with other men while he was in love.

The producer had advised Mike not to "do anything that you'd regret." The relationship had ended two weeks later.

Mike's only lover had been a fellow eighteen-year-old drama student that Mike met while they were in high school.

The way Mike usually worked was to direct the prospective client to a phone booth near Mike's home. He then gave directions, guiding the client to his home. He did this because many of the men who made appointments failed to show up, and he didn't want any flakes having his address.

Maybe because it was close to income tax time, or maybe it was the recession, but whatever the reason, this week the calls hadn't been coming in to Mike like they usually did.

So Mike had fallen back on his best natural resource: his looks. And Mike hit the pavement for a third time.

It was to be his final time.

Sergeant Barkley

Cainen immediately liked Sergeant Barkley. He would have trusted the man, but trust did not come easy to Cainen anymore. He had trusted his fellow officers, and they had burned him. Lost trust is like lost virginity: once it's gone, you can't recover the innocence, even if you do wear a white dress on your wedding day.

Barkley was the assistant Officer In Charge (OIC) of the Prostitution Enforcement Detail, referred to as PED. There was a lieutenant above him, but the lieutenant OIC worked office hours.

Barkley was the acting OIC on Cainen's first night of assignment to the Detail.

Cainen had been introduced to the acting OIC by Lieutenant Wilder. Unlike most kiss-ass supervisors, Barkley chose not to talk to his new officer in front of the higher-ranking man.

Cainen respected Barkley for taking him up to the break room to talk. As soon as they entered the room, Barkley pulled two chairs away from the one card table in the room and plugged two quarters into the coffee machine to get them each a cup of the lukewarm brew. In response to the question from his new supervisor, Cainen asked for his with cream and sugar. (If Cainen had been getting the coffee for himself, he would have held in the EXTRA button for more cream and sugar, but he didn't want to appear like a sissy in front of a supervisor who was probably going to hint at the rumors.)

After checking the poker hand on the side of the cup, Barkley got right down to business. Cainen noted that Barkley knew his way around. If you wanted to talk privately in the police department, you did it in a public place, like a hallway or a break room. While the walls don't have ears, the officers listening on the other side of them do. Any attempt at privacy instantly arouses the suspicion of paranoid officers, and the rumor mill begins grinding.

Cainen's respect grew as the assistant OIC spoke. Unlike other sergeants, Barkley didn't try to ignore the rumors or act as if he hadn't heard them. But when he stated what he had heard, the sergeant didn't ask Cainen to clarify anything. In fact, Barkley instantly denigrated the rumors, referring to the officers who breathed life into them. Barkley referred to them as being "no better than a bunch of old spinsters who have nothing important in their own lives."

Because Barkley didn't solicit information, it was apparent that he didn't care if Cainen was homosexual, heterosexual, bisexual, or even transsexual.

"I don't give a shit what anyone says," explained the sergeant, "unless I hear it right from the person. Hell, if the oral boards would have believed half the shit that was written in my ratings, I never would have made it to sergeant."

Barkley sipped his black coffee. Cainen took the opportunity to try his decaf with cream and sugar. Cainen didn't usually drink coffee, but a refusal would have put up an unnecessary wall. It would have been as impolite as refusing tea from his martial arts instructor.

"We both know that the LAPD's slogan is bullshit," continued the supervisor, voicing what was written on the Department recruitment literature. " 'All our cops come in one color.' My foot! They may wear blue, but they bring all their personal prejudices with them when they put on that uniform.

"Unless you fit in and go with the flow, unless you commune with the LAPD mentality, whatever the hell that is," Barkley added sarcastically, "the officers of this Department can make you feel like a mother-in-law on a honeymoon."

On a small table in the front of the room, a color TV constantly played on at low volume. When an officer came into the break room to buy a candy bar from a machine, Barkley pretended to watch the set until the officer left.

"I ask the same thing of all my officers. You work eight for eight. No fooling around or extra-long breaks. While you're on the clock, the citizens deserve your service. I also ask that you keep me informed of where you are, what you've got going, and what you've learned."

Cainen had the strong impression that Barkley purposely mixed up his grammar and roughened his talk. He had probably done it for so long that he might not even realize that he was doing it.

Cainen understood the probable reason for his supervisor's behavior. It was a lot easier to get officers to do things if they were asked by a supervisor who was "one of the guys." A supervisor that didn't fit in would have to give orders, rather than make requests.

Barkley might not have a college degree, but Cainen knew that he was an extremely intelligent individual who missed very little.

"I heard some rumors," Barkley continued, "and I don't know if they're true or not. It's hard to believe that police officers wouldn't back up another officer just because of . . . who he was.

"But it wouldn't be the first time."

Cainen saw a twinkle in the sergeant's eyes.

"I know of one LAPD sergeant in the south end that had a live chicken and a tarantula put in his locker!"

Cainen wondered if *Barkley* had been that sergeant, but he kept silent.

"Whatever happened before," Barkley said in a serious tone, "isn't the point. While you work for me, every PED officer will back you up. I personally guarantee it."

Cainen wondered if Barkley could really exert that kind of control. He *wanted* to believe it.

"I appreciate that," Cainen said. He meant it.

"I don't know what kinda bug they got up their ass at PAB," Barkley said, referring to the Department brass by the headquarters initials, "but this idea of putting an unarmed undercover officer out on the street as a kidnap decoy sucks the big one. It's about as intelligent as giving condoms to kindergartners and expecting them not to fill them up with water."

Cainen smiled at the mental picture. It was the first time he had heard *that* one.

Cainen still had the unshakable feeling that Barkley was trying to act like a hick. So be it. If Barkley gained security in the role, more power to him.

Cainen pretended to sip his cup of burnt Cremora, which was now cold. The sergeant continued.

"Lieutenant Wilder is loaning a two-man unit to PED. We're maxed out, with the Hollywood Chamber of Commerce ripping the chief a new asshole because of the ladies still on Sunset."

Female prostitutes had worked on Sunset Boulevard for as long as Cainen could remember. They were more a part of Hollywood than Grauman's Chinese Theater (which had been bought by Mann's, anyway) or the stars on the sidewalk. And the women had been working Hollywood longer than either!

In recent years, the corner of Crescent Heights and Sunset had become a haven for underage female prostitutes. But as a child in L.A., Cainen remembered his parents pointing out the "ladies of the evening" between Crescent Heights and Fairfax Avenue. Every time the relatives came in from out of state, a trip was made to point out the attraction.

When business took a turn for the worse in the biggest tourist locale in the world, the Hollywood Chamber of Commerce took action.

Crime had taken over the sidewalks of Hollywood, as cruisers had taken over the streets. Residents of the area were fed up with prostitutes turning tricks in their driveways, oftentimes telling the *residents* to be quiet. They were tired of waking up each morning to find Fido or Muffy chewing on a used condom.

The ensuing letter-writing campaigns meant nothing to the chief of police. The letters were round-filed, piling up in the trash. And the requests of the local city council members meant even less. But when the Chamber held a press conference to blast the chief's inaction and lack of enforcement in the City of the Stars, the Department brass (always responsive instead of proactive) responded immediately. It would not do to have the chief's political ambitions tarnished by such an imbecilic morals issue. So that press conference became the midwife for the Prostitution Enforcement Detail.

Despite the nightly raids by PED, the girls usually returned to the street before the officers finished writing their arrest reports.

The chief complained that this was not the Department's fault. Each girl had several fake Las Vegas IDs and used a different alias upon each arrest. Without benefit of attaching a prior arrest record, the law required the girls to be OR'd (released on their own recognizance).

The Hollywood Chamber of Commerce countered by purchasing a $100,000 computer tracking system and donating it to the Detail. The system enabled officers to identify prostitutes with a large number of false names. After each arrest, a list of priors was attached to the original report, allowing the city attorney to seek a maximum sentence.

Since the implementation of the system, many of the women had returned to Vegas. Others operated out of call-girl services or massage parlors. Some hard-learners, however, remained on the Strip.

PED was currently in the midst of a major enforcement action to clear off Sunset once and for all. At least this is what the Department told the Chamber it was doing in appreciation for the computer.

In actuality, no one on the Department wanted *all* the prostitutes to leave, least of all the officers assigned to PED. If all the prostitutes cleared out, the Department would lose some funding, and those officers assigned to PED would be forced to return to the drab and dreary duties of ordinary patrol.

No officer liked to be tied to a radio. In PED, there was minimal supervision, maximum freedom, and, most importantly, *real* police work (e.g., "observation" arrests, instead of those resulting from a citizen's phone call).

As an LAPD officer had once told an *L.A. Times* reporter, "A high crime rate is our job security."

All of Barkley's PED officers were busy making the "stats" that would in turn make the chief look good when he held his next press conference.

As Barkley explained it, the A.M. watch commander, Lieutenant Wilder, was going to loan two of his officers to PED. The officers would be Cainen's support, in plainclothes and a plain car. They would watch

Cainen from an out-of-view location while Cainen walked the Boulevard.

Without a police radio on his person, these officers would be Cainen's only link to the Department. And to backup.

However, even the best-laid plans of mice and officers can go awry.

Loans in the police department were supposed to be used as awards, to be given to the hardest-working officers. A loan to a specialized assignment gave the officer more diversified experience, which, in theory, made the officer more promotable.

Unfortunately, LAPD supervisors often used loans in a more punitive mode. If a watch or division had a "problem child," that officer often became the problem of another area.

And so it went in this case. Lieutenant Wilder was tired of the repeated complaints from his sergeants about one particular officer who spurned supervision.

Unbeknownst to Cainen or Barkley, Lieutenant Wilder had already chosen who was going to be loaned to PED. He had chosen B. M. Leaks.

As Barkley concluded his introduction to Cainen, he had no idea that the officer who would be guarding Cainen was the very same one who had forced Cainen into the PED loan in the first place.

"So all I ask is that you keep me informed," finished Barkley. "Let me know where you are and what you find out. In return, I'll watch your back from the Department end of it."

Barkley gulped down the last of his coffee and tossed the worthless poker hand into the trash can.

"Thanks," said Cainen. He meant it.

Cainen again pretended to take a sip from his cup.

For some reason, Cainen felt like he was relating to his new sergeant as if the man were a father figure, instead of in a supervisorial role. Maybe this was because Cainen had lacked such a relationship while he had been growing up. He dismissed the thought.

Barkley extended his right hand. Cainen took it in his hand and shook it firmly.

"Change into whatever clothes you're gonna be wearing out there," said Cainen's new boss, "and I'll meet you in the PED office."

Cainen nodded affirmatively.

Barkley started to exit the break room.

Cainen heard the theme song by Mike Post from "Hill Street Blues" coming from the television. For the millionth time, Cainen wondered why real police work couldn't be as simple as it was on TV, where cops never took a shit and always got over their prejudices.

Cainen saw Barkley stop in the doorway and turn back to him. He looked serious.

"I want you to know that you can be honest with me, Steve."

Cainen continued to look at the older man. The informal use of his first name had not been lost on Cainen, particularly because he hadn't heard another cop use it since he had come on The Job.

"And if you don't drink coffee," the acting OIC, added, smiling, "just let me know. I'll buy you a 7-Up, or I'll save the two bits."

Barkley didn't wait for a reply. He winked at Cainen and walked off.

Boy, he's sharp! thought Cainen. *Barkley doesn't miss a thing.*

Cainen was glad that Barkley was on *his* side. He'd make one *hell* of a tough adversary if he weren't!

*　*　*

Before he went into the motel, Charlie walked over to the gutter and grabbed a handful of mud and weeds. He smeared this on the back license plate of the van.

The dirt and plant matter stuck to the plate, all but obscuring the letters and numbers. Since the van had no front plate, Charlie wiped his hands on his pants and didn't bother repeating the procedure.

Charlie walked to the cheap motel room that Lisa had rented. It was the same motel run by the Koreans, but they were in a different room.

Lisa had gotten some Quaaludes from Luther and was well on her way into oblivion when Charlie finished his transaction with the young black.

Charlie used some more of the cash he had robbed from the jogger in the park. Charlie bought a rock of "crystal." The methamphetamine would send him speeding like a rocket, the opposite of the downer Lisa had taken.

That was cool; it was better with her out of it.

Charlie didn't want Lisa messing up any more of his "missionary work," as he now referred to it.

No, the bitch had caused enough trouble. With one hustler shot in the street and another laid out like a peanut-butter-and-jelly sandwich in a Ziploc Baggie, this was not a time to be taking any more chances. No more mess-ups.

Charlie had watched the TV news for over a week now and had seen the big brouhaha that had occurred when the boy in the bag was found.

No, there couldn't be any more mistakes. The cops would probably be out in force now.

That was why Charlie was shooting up the crystal. He needed to clear his head and focus on the night's activity.

Charlie put the tiny rock on the top of the torn Coke can. Standing by the sink in the fetid bathroom, Charlie added a few drops of water on top of the crystal. The mix lay in the concave bottom of the can.

Using a bandanna hankie from his pocket as a tie-off, Charlie held one end in his mouth and tied it above his biceps. Charlie then flexed his hand a few times to make his veins more prominent.

Charlie took a matchbook out of his pocket. Lighting a match, he held up the can and put the match under the center.

As the can top grew hotter, the crystal melted into the water. Charlie quickly set down the can and took a cigarette from the pack rolled into his T-shirt sleeve. He broke the cigarette open and removed the cotton from the filter. Charlie dropped the cotton into the liquid and picked up the syringe he shared with Lisa and Cameron. Sticking the tip into the small circular piece of cotton, Charlie drew the liquid up, hoping the cotton would catch most of the impurities.

Finding the vein in the bend of his arm, Charlie looked for the spot beneath the latest track marks. Finding it toward the start of his forearm, Charlie pierced the skin and lifted up the vein with the needle to be sure it was in.

Seeing the blue line pulled tight against his translucent skin layer, Charlie slowly pushed the plunger down. Real slowly.

As the intravenous drug mixed with his blood and rushed to his unwary heart, Charlie felt a warmth spreading up his stomach and down to his thighs. Charlie was instantly erect.

Knowing that he would soon put the erection to good use, Charlie ignored the appendage and Lisa's form on the bed.

Begrudgingly, Charlie withdrew the empty syringe from his arm. He pulled the bandanna from around his arm and carefully wrapped the syringe in it.

Syringes were hard to come by, and this one would be used many more times before it was thrown away.

Charlie began to feel hot and flushed. The agitation started almost immediately.

Charlie walked quickly out of the room, leaving the door open. He would have to get Cameron out of Luther's room, where they were getting high, and then get Lisa awake enough to make it into the back of the van.

As Charlie's mind sped through his plans for the night, he knew that the crystal had cleared out any unimportant concerns that he had had.

No, all his plans were set. The necessary precautions had been taken. All he needed now was to continue his missionary work. And all he needed for that was to pick out a volunteer from the Boulevard.

Charlie needed the crystal to stay awake. Tonight was going to be a very long night.

A very long night.

Charlie pounded on Luther's door with the baseball bat he was holding in his hands.

* * *

Cainen instantly loved the Boulevard. With every one of his senses alert, his years of martial arts training were put to the test.

Cainen had to constantly watch his back in the ever-dangerous street life. Cainen loved the street for one reason more than any other: for the first time in many years, Cainen *knew* who his enemies were.

At first, Cainen was guarded and watchful. It would not be unlike the LAPD management to have put another undercover on the street to try to catch Cainen in some unsavory act. Because the brass believed that gays had no morals, they may have thought Cainen would have sex with a hustler.

As the hours passed, Cainen dissected the possibilities in his mind. Why would the LAPD try to get him on additional charges when they already had a complaint against him (regardless of how ridiculous it was)?

It didn't make sense, so Cainen relaxed.

Besides, he truly believed that if the LAPD had had any other viable alternative to putting him out on the street, they would have done it. They wouldn't have taken even the slightest chance of a homosexual officer solving the case and getting any publicity. Cainen had seen how they reacted to that scenario with his graffiti paint-over project.

And if the LAPD had stuck an undercover officer out on the street to try to nail him, Cainen would have spotted the guy. So would the other hustlers. Within his first hour of leaning against the white railing of Arthur J's, Cainen had overheard the hustlers talking. One of their stories was of the nervous young cop who had been trying to blend in earlier in the week.

One of the effeminate hustlers had coaxed the undercover cop into the bathroom of AJ's with the promise of information. Once there, the queenie hustler had squeezed the cop's crotch. The cop had turned deathly pale and then hurried out onto the street and down the Boulevard, never to be seen again.

Cainen had also been self-conscious and prudent because he had to learn the rules of the hustling world. You don't jump into the society of a foreign country without first learning what is taboo. And the life on the street was as different from normal U.S. life as if one had been transported to another planet.

The police management had assumed that a gay would fit into the street life. That was because the management assumed that gays and hustlers were tantamount to the same thing.

But homosexual prostitution is as much a counterculture of the gay community as heterosexual prostitution is of the straight lifestyle. Cainen soon learned that the majority of the customers of the hustlers were, in fact, married businessmen who ventured out of their quiet little straight life to get a quick release for their restrained homosexual desires. Cainen also promptly learned that the majority of the hustlers pictured themselves as straight. Their self-images had them thinking that they were heterosexuals who were exploiting the gay community for money. Cainen didn't buy it, of course, instead preferring to believe that the hustlers were closeted homosexuals, who had bought into the negative image of gays sold by society.

The way Cainen figured it, unless they enjoyed the sex, why didn't they stick to other antisocial endeavors to make cash, like drug dealing or robbery?

For their own self-respect, these young men only released their hidden desires in return for money, justifying the act to themselves in a true capitalist fashion.

Yep, though they bragged about being the arch-enemy of society, these young boys had really bought into the American dream!

Unfortunately, many of these assholes didn't limit themselves to prostitution, Cainen learned. Standing on the corner of Formosa and Santa Monica on his second night out, Cainen heard a hustler named Keith describing his secondary enterprise.

Keith told Cainen how he charged fifty dollars a trick. But if the "guy" fit certain characteristics, Keith would "take the guy off."

Keith would take all the guy's money and jewelry and his car keys, threatening to kill the guy if he came after him.

"You don't take off the wimps," Keith explained, " 'cause they're the type that will get you back. You take off the married ones, 'cause they can't go to the cops. The cops will call the guy's wife if he makes a report."

Keith told Cainen that he worked with a pawnshop on Melrose Avenue that bought all of the stolen jewelry at rock-bottom prices but without question.

It was difficult for Cainen to fit into a lifestyle that was so alien to him. Luckily, though, a life of living in the closet had made it easy for Cainen to lie about who and what he was.

Only a couple hustlers asked Cainen anything about himself. Most were content to accept him as he comfortably presented himself.

Cainen spent his nights on the Boulevard talking with hustlers and circumspectly seeking info about the killings.

Cainen enjoyed talking with the hustlers and hearing life stories far more exciting though as devastating as his own. He noted that the hustlers loved to talk about themselves. It appeared that they had no one to talk to, that no one really cared about them. The people in their lives were only interested in exploiting them.

Though the hustlers thought that they were the ones doing the exploiting, like most people committing so-called victimless crimes, they themselves were the victimized and exploited. The tricks only feigned interest to get into the boys' pants. The other hustlers that claimed to be friends just wanted drugs or money. So the hustlers were more than happy to talk with Cainen.

Through talking with them, Cainen learned his first two rules of the street: you never challenge an embellishment, and you can ask about anything *except* what the hustlers did in bed. When Cainen inadvertently violated either of those two rules, the hustler walked to a different corner to work and there was no more conversation.

Just because the hustlers' lives centered around sex with men didn't mean that they actually wanted to admit it. Especially to themselves.

Cainen also learned that a hustler's life, though dangerous, was simple: stay up on drugs all night, bumming cigarettes off other hustlers, then turn a trick for fast food, drugs, and a room for the night (in that order).

There was no planned retirement for this occupation.

On his fourth night on the Boulevard, Cainen got into his first sticky situation.

Many of the youngest girls from Sunset Boulevard had come down to Santa Monica Boulevard to avoid having to have a pimp. The girls had sex with one of the Boulevard hustlers in return for the "boyfriend" guarding her against any poo-butts who wandered down.

On this night, Cainen accidentally got caught in the middle of a dispute between the hustler he was talking with and two enterprising young men who had moved down to the Boulevard to get some fresh meat for their harem.

The fifteen-year-old subject of the argument had exited Shakey's Pizza on the Boulevard when the two guys in the Chevy pulled onto the side street.

The girl apparently knew the two from prior harassment.

"Hey, little momma!" yelled the two as they drove past her a second time before parking. "Why don't you come work for us? We can make you a lot more money than these fag boys can!"

The girl walked over to where Cainen and the hustler were standing. As the two from Sunset Boulevard got out of the car, leaving the windows rolled down, Cainen saw them walking toward his corner.

It was a salt-and-pepper team, one black and one white, both about twenty-three years old. They didn't look like they were interested in inviting the group to play Scrabble.

"Hey, baby," crooned the black one, "come on up to Sunset, where the real men are."

Cainen's only thought was, *Isn't there* anyone *that doesn't gay-bash?*

Cainen noted that the two young men separated, instead of standing together. One stood on each side of the group of hustler, prostitute, and Cainen. Judging their placement, Cainen positioned his feet accordingly. On top of everything, Cainen wanted to avoid a scene. He didn't want his backup to charge over, ruining the entire operation. If Cainen had learned anything, it was that news traveled fast on the street. He would be hard-pressed to bullshit his way out of how two plainclothes cops came to his rescue.

"Come on, baby," said the white poo-butt. "Dump these two queer-baits and come take a ride with us."

Cainen saw the hustler bristle. Like every other hustler, this one had bragged that he had taken karate for six years, while he was living in Wisconsin.

"Go fuck yourself," replied the little lady. She moved closer to her protector.

"Let's get into the car and talk over a business proposition," said the black guy.

"She told you she wasn't interested. So get lost." It was the hustler.

The white man from Sunset was wearing a cut-off T-shirt, blue jeans, and boots. From his back pocket he whipped out a switchblade, with the blade extended. He held it up to the face of the hustler.

"Why don't you let the lady speak for herself, fag boy."

Cainen knew he had to do something. He debated taking the knife out of the man's hand and breaking his wrist. But he didn't want to cause any suspicions due to his karate prowess. Besides, the black one was wearing a green army coat, and his right hand was still in one of the big pockets.

Brains before brawn.

"Why don't you guys just let us walk out of here, huh?" Cainen said in a mild voice.

"So the other faggot speaks, too." The knife changed position to face Cainen. "You wanna be brave, suck-butt?"

Cainen stole a quick glance. His backup wasn't running over.

"No," replied Cainen, "I just want us to walk away from here."

"Well, maybe we aren't finished with you guys yet. Maybe we'll just walk over behind the Shakey's?"

Cainen knew that such a move to a dark location would be lethal. For someone. He had to think quickly.

Cainen very slowly reached out his hand to the hustler. He had removed a quarter from his pocket and handed it to the other man.

"You want him to go call the cops for you, faggot?" asked the man with the knife.

"Nope," replied the undercover officer casually. "I want him to call an ambulance."

This surprised the two from Sunset. Cainen moved his hands into a defensive position before continuing. He glared at the black man, choosing him as the smarter of the two. He watched the knife out of his peripheral vision.

"Because if you don't let us walk away from here, I'm going to take that knife away and ram it so far up your ass that it'll take a brain surgeon to remove it."

The black guy looked into Cainen's eyes while the white one tried to figure out what Cainen had said.

"Let them go," said the black quietly.

"No fucking way. Let's take this bitch up to Corliss and let him talk to her."

Corliss was obviously the pimp these two were poo-butting for.

"Let 'em walk."

The white guy kept his knife out between Cainen and the hustler.

Cainen looked for his backup. They should have come running by now. Of course, he and his adversaries were in a tight half-circle, blocking a view from the street. Maybe his backup was waiting to see what was going on.

Cainen nodded toward the east. The hustler saw the movement and took his girlfriend's arm. The three turned and slowly walked away from the two poo-butts.

"Why'd you let them get away?" asked the white one as he folded up the knife and put it in his rear pocket.

The black guy watched the three hustlers as they walked down the block. The one who had talked had made him nervous. As he had grown up in the ghetto, his gut reactions had kept him alive more than once.

"We know where to find 'em if we want 'em." He fingered the folded switchblade in his army jacket pocket.

The two returned to their car and started up the noisy junker to return to Sunset Boulevard.

Cainen looked back from the direction they had come. He saw another car, a Pinto, pull out from a side street and turn its headlights on. There were two men in the front seat of the Pinto.

Cainen said good-bye and walked on ahead of the male and female prostitute.

He had seen a variation of the stunt he had pulled used in the cop movie *The Blue Knight*. It had worked then, too.

Still, Cainen hated relying on movie tricks for his survival. His backup had been there, but they hadn't left their car. It disturbed Cainen that they hadn't at least driven by to get a closer look at the suspicious encounter.

Maybe they hadn't been able to see what was going on, even with their binoculars, because of the angle at which the five had been standing.

Grasping that plausible explanation, Cainen didn't tell Barkley about the incident.

* * *

Officer William Morris Leaks sat in the Pinto and couldn't believe that he was assigned to protect a faggot police officer. It was all the more ironic because he had done everything he could to get the officer kicked out of patrol. And now here he was, sitting in the hotbed of faggotism amid the hustlers of Santa Monica Boulevard, watching some fruit officer get his jollies.

In his nine years of being on The Job, Leaks had avoided a vice assignment like a plague. There was no way he was going to work an assignment that put his groin within arm's reach of any faggot.

And now this.

215

He debated whether to drive over to the Del Taco farther down on Santa Monica and grab a plate of nachos.

Leaks took another bite out of the Hostess pie he was holding and looked over at the probationary officer in the passenger seat. To make matters worse, he had been assigned a black probationer as his surveillance partner. Shit. If it wasn't fags, it was underqualified blacks.

Maybe this was all because of that fag city councilman that was trying to stay in the closet.

Regardless, Leaks didn't plan on sitting on this stakeout too much longer, anyway. He'd be damned if he was going to miss his lunch break!

"What's he doing, Miller?" asked the senior officer.

"He's talking with the same guy and this girl that just walked over. What's a girl doing out here?" Miller continued to peer through the windshield of the car with the binoculars.

"She's hustlin' just like the guys. It's safer here than on Sunset." Another mouthful of pie. Leaks looked down into the filling. Shit, there was more fruit walkin' the sidewalks than there was in this damn pie.

"Two guys just got out and joined them. I can't see what's going on, but they don't look too friendly." Miller lowered the binoculars and looked at his partner. "We'd better take a drive by and see what they're up to."

Leaks squinted through the windshield. His vision had been getting worse each year, but he was too macho to wear glasses.

"Naw, Cainen will signal us if shit happens. Just keep watching." He rolled down his window and threw the empty wrapper outside. Most cops kept their windows lowered to hear any gunshots or screams that might occur. And to hear if someone tried to sneak up to their car. But Leaks didn't like the cool night air and, like many cops with the John Wayne syndrome, believed that he was invulnerable as long as he had his badge on.

"It looks like they're arguing," said Miller. "The white guy is holding his fist in Cainen's face, like he's threatening him."

Being a new officer, Miller didn't know that you weren't supposed to take your eyes off the subject while you spoke. Anything could happen in the space of a few seconds. But Miller lowered the binoculars and turned to face Leaks, who was stuffing a Ding-Dong in his mouth.

"Don't worry about it," Leaks said between swallows. He didn't bother to look across the corner at Cainen or the others. "We can't just rush over there like the Lone Ranger and blow Cainen's cover, right? He'll signal us if he needs us."

Miller was in his last month of probation. By the rules of the LAPD training officer's manual, Miller was to be treated as if he were a full-fledged officer. But everyone in the Department knew that wasn't the case.

A probationer was a probationer. It had been drummed into their heads throughout a rigorous six-month academy, and it had been rammed further down their throats during their year of field probation. "While you're on probation, you have no rights," they had been told time and time again by training officers and sergeants.

A probationer's only goal was to get off probation. Every one of the 600 probationary officers in the Department could recite the exact number of months, days, and probably minutes left until their year was up. A large party was held at the end of probation, celebrating the return of basic human rights to the classmates that had graduated from the academy the year prior. And they thought they had those rights, until their next working day, when they found out that being the junior police officer-2 also put them in a category somewhere below station janitors. So the new fully sworn officers settled for making life miserable for those still on probation.

Such was the LAPD totem pole. Like they say on The Job, "Waste matter rolls downhill. Don't try to stop it with a strainer."

The code of silence was even stronger for those officers on probation. If they broke the code, they lost more than backup; they forfeited their ability to ever work in law enforcement again.

If a probationer ever failed to support the "lies and denies" of his senior partner or training officer, his next rating would be a fully documented "unsatisfactory." The rating would be rife with examples of the young officer's unsafe tactics.

Once you were terminated from the LAPD, no other department would hire you.

So Miller did what the LAPD had trained him to do. He followed the advice of his training officer and shut up.

While Miller continued to watch the events unfold in front of his eyes, Leaks leaned his head back on the carseat and slumped down behind the wheel. He shut his eyes to grab a quick catnap.

If it was fags that were being killed, who cared anyway? Certainly not the police department nor the public. The only ones who cared were other fags, and maybe that one faggot officer.

* * *

Cainen was most impressed by two things: by how young some of the street hustlers were and by one of the organizations that constantly hit the streets trying to get the hustlers off it.

One of the kids that Cainen met was a twelve-year-old black boy. The boy spent the nights working the street. When he got tired, he would ride the bus downtown and back, sleeping in the safety of the moving vehicle.

The youth kept a twelve-inch butcher knife in his left sock: "In case a trouble, you know." He had been picked up by police officers several times because of his age. Most of the officers were the Municipal Transit Authority police who handled the bus lines when the drivers called in.

The boy bragged that due to his age and innocent appearance, his legs were never checked for weapons. He rode in the backseat with the officers in front of him, with the twelve-inch knife within reach.

Cainen made a mental note.

Cainen was exceptionally impressed with the outreach workers from Children of the Night (CON). The organization sent workers out onto the streets twice a week to offer shelters, jobs, and ID to the hustlers.

Cainen had been confronted by workers from dozens of different groups. The majority of them had been religious zealots, offering food and shelter in return for conversion and constant prayer.

Even these organizations only guaranteed minimal time within a home. At the end of the prayer period, the "reformed" hustler would have to hit the streets again, this time going door-to-door requesting donations for the religious group. Cheap labor was how Cainen saw it.

The other organizations only offered shelters for hustlers under eighteen. No one except the CON people seemed to notice or care that most of the problem youth hitting the Boulevard were already eighteen.

Young women arriving in downtown on the bus lines were greeted by pimps and poo-butts recruiting them for work. The trained eyes of these flesh-dealers could pick out a runaway in a second.

Knowing exactly how to approach the girls, whether to offer them a meal, a place to stay for the night, or a chance at modeling and stardom, these men recruited the girls for Sunset Boulevard work.

Once the girls said yes to anything, they were free game. Many were told that they were loved by the pimp, who bought them daily gifts until they hit the streets.

Others were drugged and held hostage in a room where they were forced to accept the advances of men brought in by the poo-butts. A refusal meant hanger-beating and cigarette burns.

CON spent a good deal of time working with the Administrative Vice Unit of the LAPD, freeing the kidnapped girls when tips were given to them. They also hit Santa Monica Boulevard to help the hustlers.

Male prostitutes were quite different from the females. The boys seldom had to "run" away from anything. They were often asked to leave their run-down homes by their mothers. Where else could they go but the glamorous city that they had seen on television—Hollywood?

Arriving at the Greyhound station in Hollywood, they were often penniless and hungry. Wandering around Hollywood Boulevard, they bumped into other youths who told them of the fortunes to be made from famous producers and movie stars who picked up young boys on Santa Monica Boulevard.

Other boys on the Boulevard were gay high school students from Los Angeles. Without any counseling available about their orientation and with no one to confide in and seek information from, these lonely youths also followed the rumors and wandered onto the Boulevard. On the Boulevard, they were not alone, like they felt when they were in their high schools.

When hunger is gnawing at your stomach like a dormant volcano about to erupt, you quickly sacrifice all the societal standards that never put much on the table anyway.

After a few easy tricks, the boys on the Boulevard had more money in their pockets than they had ever seen in their lives. And the drugs were abundant.

After a few nights, these formerly starving youths laughed at the prospect of leaving the easy cash of the street and taking a fast-food job for $4.50 an hour. And for those boys under sixteen, they wouldn't be hired in the city anyway.

But some of the youth who had just hit the streets, regardless of age, could be salvaged before they became too caught up in the lifestyle. CON concentrated on these youths.

Unlike the religious zealots, CON was founded by a woman who had been working on her doctoral thesis on runaways. The woman became distraught over the large number of young girls on the street involved in prostitution. To her further amazement, there were virtually no resources within the city of Los Angeles for the teens.

There were dozens of referral agencies listed in the city directory. But in tracking down through each phone number, the result was the same: each agency referred you to another. There simply were no shelters for teenage girls.

So the doctoral student began taking the girls into her home. After she received her degree, she founded the CON organization. With funding from several sources, including the Playboy Foundation, the organization sent workers out to the street to assist the "throw-away" youth.

Many of the CON outreach workers were concerned gay and lesbian adults. Most of them remained in the closet for fear that the discovery of their orientation would deny them the ability to work with youths. Many of the other workers were actual reformed hustlers and prostitutes who had been saved from the streets by CON and were now productive working members of their communities. In gratitude, these former prostitutes worked to save other youths like themselves. Their savvy and knowledge of the street were what was most convincing and attractive to the kids they came across.

Unlike every other organization "helping" the kids on the street, the CON workers never pressured the youths. They treated the kids as adults and let them know that the organization was there if they wanted assistance.

The workers from religious organizations passed out miniature Bibles telling the young adults that they were sinners. Outreach counselors from the city's Lesbian and Gay Community Center passed out cards telling the kids their rights when they were stopped by the police. The counselors also told the hustlers that the police had to identify themselves if they were asked.

The CON workers passed out cards that gave a twenty-four-hour hot line number, an office number, and a list of services the organization offered.

That was why CON received over twenty thousand calls a year on their hot lines from kids wanting to get off the street or out of other abusive situations.

Despite everything Cainen was learning about street life and outreach organizations in the city, he was learning little that was helpful to the case.

Cainen kept Sergeant Barkley apprised of anything that he heard on the Boulevard. He had passed on some great tips about drug dealers working out of cars, when and where big deals were going to be transacted, and what local stores were going to be burglarized. It seemed that many of the hustlers supplemented their incomes with drug dealing.

But Cainen came up pitifully short on hard information.

Until he met the Cowboy.

VIII

Cowboy Peter

Peter was twenty-five, thin, and five foot eight, with dark blond hair and blue eyes. He had started hustling when he was fifteen.

Peter was born in New York, but his family later moved to Sacramento, California. His family consisted of his mother and a younger brother.

Peter had received a general discharge from the navy when he was eighteen. As Peter liked to explain it, he was discharged because of his musical talent. Peter played the drums and harmonica, and the ship's band had consented to letting Peter play with them. When the group members suddenly changed their minds, Peter threw the band's equipment overboard. So, in a convoluted sort of way, his discharge was due to his musical abilities.

When Peter had started hustling ten years prior, he had worked on Selma Avenue in Hollywood. During a prior "Clean Up Hollywood" campaign, the LAPD put undercover officers out to harass the hustlers and their customers. The harassment was so bad that even the courts protested the arrests. But, as happens any time a "den of iniquity" is shut down, the demand remains, so there is a reopening at a new location.

Before the police had successfully closed down Selma Avenue, Santa Monica Boulevard had become an even more desirable "meat rack."

"There was nothing to do in Sacramento," Peter told Cainen when they were standing on a corner. "Except maybe stuff like surfing.

"I was too young back when I started hustling at fifteen. But now [at twenty-five], I've seen and done it all.

"In the old days, I couldn't walk fifteen feet without getting picked up. Now you could walk from one end of town to the other and no one stops.

"Maybe it's because I'm too old now."

Unlike the other hustlers, Peter joined the gay subculture as soon as he hit Hollywood. "I kept getting fucked over by these older gay guys," he explained to Cainen. "So I figured why not get paid for it."

When Cainen met Peter, the young man had been living out of his car for four months. It had been the family car, and Peter's brother had fixed it up and given it to him.

"When I need a bath," Peter told the undercover officer in a tutorial tone, "I pay the six dollars a night and go to the Club Bathhouse. I bought a ten-dollar membership, so I get a room with my six bucks in any state I go to."

Peter explained that the Club Bathhouse operated in several states and were basically bathhouses with a television, gym, sauna, private rooms, and an orgy room.

Peter didn't admit to Cainen that he also worked at the baths, charging a small fee in exchange for sex from the older clientele that frequented such establishments. Ten percent of his take went to the manager of each bath.

Peter only worked the Boulevard at night. In the daytime, Peter hit up an employment agency for work.

"But shit, you need twenty years' experience to get any kinda job nowadays."

Peter's past jobs had included ditch digging, dishwashing, and selling Christmas trees. Though Peter made over a hundred dollars a day selling trees, he quit because he didn't like the boss.

"Shit, the navy promised to give me a career. But there isn't that big a call for machine gunners in the real world!"

As Elliott Liebow put it in *Tally's Corner**: "Getting a job, keeping a job, and doing well at it is clearly of low priority . . . At any given moment, a job may occupy a relatively low position on the streetcorner scale of real value." Holding down a job might be secondary to taking drugs or getting laid.

With business being slow, Peter had "trashed" for food, going through the dumpsters behind supermarkets. Behind the Ralph's on Fairfax and Santa Monica, Peter had found two loaves of bread and a head of lettuce.

"I had lettuce sandwiches," Peter explained with his wry sense of humor.

Peter hadn't eaten in two days, and Cainen gave him five dollars to grab something to eat.

---

*Elliott Liebow, *Tally's Corner: A Study of Negro Street Corner Men.* Boston: Little, Brown, 1967.

Peter told Cainen that in his ten years of sporadic hustling, he had never been harassed by the police and had never harmed any of his customers. Cainen assumed that because Peter had a gay identity, he wouldn't hurt his fellows.

When an LAPD patrol car slowly drove down the street toward them, Peter led Cainen to his car parked nearby, and they both huddled down inside.

"Hustling is the way to make bucks," Peter explained to Cainen. "It's nice to make some extra money, and the only way to do that nowadays is to make it all at once.

"Between food and rent, $150 a week doesn't cut it, because the government takes out too much!"

Peter's best friend was Kevin, a twenty-one-year-old from Oregon. Kevin came from a farm and had given Peter a cowboy hat when they first started hanging around together.

Peter had adapted his hustling look to match the younger man's. Peter liked the macho image of being a cowboy, and it seemed to bring in a little more business from men who wanted to act out their fantasy of being "roped in."

Peter and Kevin often hustled together, since Kevin, with his brown hair and mustache, also wore a cowboy hat. Kevin looked the part, complementing his hat with a full Levi's outfit.

Kevin had been married for almost five years and kept his wife in an apartment a block above Sunset. Kevin and Peter often stayed together, since Kevin always argued with his wife and would stay out until she came down to the Boulevard, pushing the stroller with their one-year-old, to get him.

Another reason that Kevin didn't stay at home was the Catch-22 situation the government put him in. As with other government aid situations, he was expected to work to support the family. But because he was unskilled, he could not make enough money to support the household. But in order for his wife to get government assistance, he could not be present in the home. So Kevin was forced to stay away from his wife.

Kevin's wife was pregnant again and expecting soon. Because of this, Kevin was in need of some additional money. Peter laughed as he told Cainen how Kevin had borrowed a knife from one of the other hustlers. Kevin's intention was to rob his next trick.

Peter and Kevin were standing together when Kevin got picked up. Less than a half hour later, Kevin returned to the corner, walking from the west end.

Peter thought it was hysterical that Kevin had been robbed by the purported customer, who not only took all of Kevin's money and his Timex watch, but also the knife.

"I couldn't understand why Kevin got so upset," Peter explained to the undercover policeman. "I mean hè was planning to do the same thing to the other guy."

When Cainen asked Peter why he hustled sporadically, Cainen was impressed with the philosophical insight with which he responded, "I only stay on the street until I get sick—sick of people."

About fifteen minutes into their first conversation, Cainen had realized that Peter's lights were on, but nobody was home. He wasn't all there, mentally.

For example, Cainen had asked Peter why he didn't just drive down to the missions and eat the more nutritious, free food there. Peter had responded that he hadn't really been down and out enough to eat at a mission. Yet he wasn't above "trashing."

Peter had been checking with the unemployment offices in Van Nuys each weekday morning for work. He always arrived by 7:30 A.M. Because veterans received preferential hiring status, Peter had made up some years (1990 and 1991) and told them he had been honorably discharged.

He had yet to get some work.

When they parted ways the first night they met, Peter had shared his philosophy with Cainen.

"I don't care about nothin', really," the young man had explained. "You can make a million different decisions each second. But every decision I make comes out to the same thing—nothin'.

"Sometimes I feel like I want to get a gun and shoot everybody. Sometimes I want to shoot myself.

"I just find it hard to believe that some of these guys are still out here hustling on the street. They've done it for so long, and they know it doesn't get them anywhere."

* * *

Charlie was hyped. He was really flying high.

Lisa was passed out in the back of the van. He had roused Cameron from Luther's and made him wait in the back holding the bat.

Looking in the rearview mirror, Charlie could see that the curtain was closed, hiding the back of the van from view. The big bloodstain that had gotten on the curtain behind the passenger seat had dried and looked like a food stain.

Charlie checked the sideview mirror. There were no cop cars behind him. Looking ahead, Charlie couldn't see any of the distinctive blue and red light bars towering above the car roofs.

The TV and newspapers hadn't said anything about suspects or about the brown van. The police could have been withholding the information, but Charlie didn't think so. He figured they just didn't have any descriptions. Yet.

Some of the TV stations had referred to the suspect as a "kidnapper." So they really hadn't found the bodies. Charlie had known that Lancaster would turn out to be great for dumping the bodies.

And a lot of the TV stations had referred to him as a "suspect." That meant they thought that one guy was doing it! *They don't know about my little family*, thought Charlie, smiling and thinking of his namesake.

Cool.

Charlie intended to make sure the police didn't get any additional leads. If there were no witnesses left alive, Charlie figured it diminished their chances of getting any clues.

Still, Charlie knew that he had to be careful. The PTAs were out in force, and that meant that the police would be out on the Boulevard, making a show for the public.

Charlie had seen more than one teary-eyed mom on the news being all worried about her missing kid.

Fuck 'em.

Charlie looked to the right and felt his penis twitch. Standing on the corner was a big blond guy. He looked like a football player.

"Damn," Charlie whispered under his breath. A shorter, brown-haired hustler had walked out of the shadows and was talking to the big guy.

Charlie drove slowly past the pair, keeping his eyes on his quarry. He made a left on La Brea and drove down to the next street. Making another left, Charlie drove up the side street past the closed businesses. The van came out on the Boulevard directly across from the big blond and his shorter friend.

Charlie watched the pair. The fags were talking like they were friends, yet they were out here working the street, peddling their butts.

Fuckin' faggots. Especially that shorter brown-haired dildo.

Charlie made a right and drove away from the pair, watching them in his sideview mirror. As the two got smaller, Charlie saw a Jaguar pull up. Charlie slowed the van, staying in the right-hand lane.

Damn! The blond guy was talking with the driver, probably setting his prices before getting in. Shit. Charlie *knew* that this was the right guy to take tonight. He could just feel it.

Keeping his eyes on the sideview mirror more than on the windshield, Charlie felt his penis actually jump.

The blond had walked away from the car and was talking to the shorter guy, pointing to the Jaguar.

Charlie hit the turn indicator and pulled into the left lane. This was no time to get stopped for a ticket.

Waiting until the traffic cleared, Charlie made a U-turn. As he drove slowly toward the corner one block east of La Brea, he saw the brown-haired guy hesitantly open the door and get into the Jag.

The Jag pulled away from the curb and drove off down the Boulevard.

No witnesses, thought Charlie.

The blond guy now stood there all alone, looking through the windshields of passing cars, trying to meet the eyes of the lone male drivers. It was the hustler's version of an OPEN FOR BUSINESS sign.

Charlie's penis started to harden as he thought, *It's my lucky day!*

When the brown van slowly pulled to the curb in front of the tall blond, Mike had the same thought.

* * *

The martial arts had taught Cainen to rely on his reflexes but always think out all possible avenues of response. Before standing still, Cainen always went down an unconscious visual checklist in his head. He monitored people, what they were wearing (what it could conceal), where their hands were, the topical landscape (curbs and any obstacles he might trip over), and directions of escape.

Cainen applied this same process to dealing with situations. Prior to ever hitting the Boulevard, Cainen had spent many hours consciously reviewing situations that could occur on the street. Such situations had included his being discovered as a cop, his attempted kidnapping, an approach by an armed suspect or several suspects, and what he would do if he was stopped by LAPD officers. This last one he thought of in various situations, such as if they recognized him or if he was with another hustler when it occurred.

After Cainen became familiar with the Boulevard, he reviewed every option over in his mind and added in the additional knowledge.

He also added in a situation in which he needed backup, but it didn't come.

So much for the cavalry.

But on his second week into the operation, Cainen almost blew his cover. In thinking of predicaments that involved the elements of the assignment, i.e., cops, hustlers, and bad guys, Cainen had missed the most obvious situation: the tricks.

Cainen had just met the tall, handsome blond who was a newcomer to the Boulevard nights. Cainen had been walking down the Boulevard when he saw the striking blond hair under the streetlight.

Cainen couldn't fail to also notice that the young man had obviously been lifting weights for several years.

In a completely professional manner, but in keeping with his undercover role, Cainen had approached the young man as a new source of information. He had gotten no real clue about the murderers so far, and a new face held the hope of new information.

As Cainen talked with the former high school football player, who was exceedingly masculine but comfortable in his gay identity, Cainen found himself being strongly attracted to the man. Cainen admired the youth's comfort with his own identity. Cainen wished that he could have that comfort within himself, that acceptance (and pride?) of who and what he was.

Thoughts flashed through Cainen's mind that he would love to make a date with the football player and pay for his services. Anything just to be near the tall stud, to be held in the well-developed arms that were under the football jersey the man was wearing.

Only twenty-two, the young man had an Aryan bearing. He had a self-confidence that was like a model's yet was not arrogant. And Cainen found that he couldn't keep his eyes off the youth.

Self-consciously, Cainen glanced around for his tail unit. The backup team might notice something odd. Cainen slipped right back into character, though. Business was business, and his was to catch a murderer. Or murderers. He pushed the other thoughts back. They were nothing more than idle reveries.

Cainen knew that he would be the consummate professional, that he would never act on any of these ponderings.

So Cainen nonchalantly pumped the young man for information. But his thoughts were elsewhere, dreaming of having met the man somewhere else. Anywhere else.

Perhaps in high school, on the football team.

And that was when Cainen almost blew his cover.

As Cainen talked with Mike, a metallic brown Jaguar pulled to the curb. Staying clear, so as not to interfere with the hustler's business while gaining information, Cainen moved back to allow Mike to approach the vehicle. Cainen knew that a fancy car meant big money to the hustlers.

The passenger side window soundlessly slid down as the husky blond moved over and leaned beside the car. Cainen assumed they were ambiguously setting a deal for money and acts when he heard the verbal exchange between the driver and the youth.

Cainen was surprised as Mike turned and walked back to where he stood. With disappointment evident in his voice, Mike said, "He wants you."

Cainen was dumbfounded. He had never considered the possibility of a trick stopping for him.

"Me?" was all Cainen could think to say.

"Go for it; he's rich," Mike replied.

Cainen had never looked in at the drivers and, therefore, never gave a visual clue that he was interested in being picked up. *That way they won't think that I'm hustling, and they won't stop,* he had thought.

The undercover officer suddenly noticed that Mike was looking at him curiously. Cainen immediately realized how stupid his thoughts were. A little voice in his mind said, *Why the hell else would you be standing on the corner of Santa Monica Boulevard in Hollywood in the middle of the night if you weren't hustling?*

Cainen saw his position for the first time not as an undercover officer but from the perspective of the people outside the Department.

No wonder the hustlers had talked with him so freely about themselves. It was an automatic given that he was one of them.

Maybe his asking the hustlers to share their lives was unprincipled, Cainen suddenly thought.

The officer again realized that Mike was watching him. The look of curiosity in the football player's eyes (because he was attracted to the man, Cainen thought of him as a football player instead of as a hustler) was slowly changing from curiosity to suspicion. The officer knew instantly what he would have to do. To do anything else would be too suspicious and could jeopardize the entire investigation.

"Of course," slipped out of Cainen's mouth, before he could swallow it. He felt himself blush in embarrassment at his own stupidity. He walked past the young stud without a second look.

They should film this for undercover officers' school, Cainen thought as he walked to the Jag. *Film it as a comedy.*

Cainen opened the door and sat down in the Jag without saying a word. As the car moved away from the curb, Cainen knew that the man couldn't be undercover vice. Not only had all vice operations been canceled during the stakeout, but there was a better reason.

With the way cops drive, no Jaguar dealer would trust loaning them a car.

* * *

"Hello. How are you?"

Cainen looked over at the man for the first time. To Cainen's surprise, he was not an old troll. Since a Jag was an expensive piece of machinery, Cainen had assumed that the driver would be someone who could afford it, someone at least fifty years old. Instead, Cainen was looking at a young man who couldn't have been over thirty.

The driver's hair was cut in what Cainen's high school classmates had called a bowl cut. It looked as if the barber had placed a bowl over the man's head and cut around it. Despite this, the man was attractive, though a little bit too cute and too thin for Cainen's taste.

"I'm fine, thanks," Cainen answered.

"So what do you like to do?"

"Actually, I was just out waiting for a friend." Cainen knew how lame that sounded, especially since he was sitting in the stranger's car.

"You're a handsome man, but I'll bet you hear that a lot?"

"Uh, thanks. Would it be possible for you to let me out here?"

Cainen didn't want to offend the stranger, but the follow-up car was undoubtedly closing in. Cainen let the stranger drive far enough away so that they'd be out of Mike's view when he got out.

Cainen thought to himself how stupid his reaction had been. He could have just gotten into the Jag with the stranger and then made the man drop him off a couple blocks away. He could then have walked back to Mike and alleged that the man was into a scene that was just too weird for his tastes. Cainen had seen this happen several times with other hustlers.

Oh, well, you live and learn.

"Why don't you take it out and show it to me?"

In his reverie, Cainen had forgotten where he was for the moment. What a way to be brought back to reality.

"Uh, that's OK. I just want to get out."

"Right here?"

"Yeah, that's fine. If you'll just pull over to the curb."

"You don't really want to get out, do you? If you take it out and show it to me, I'll give you twenty-five dollars. Just let me see it."

"Can you let me out here, please."

"You're really a good-looking man. I'd love to take you to my house in Beverly Hills, but I have friends from out of town staying with me. But they'll be gone tomorrow. You have a hotel room we can go to?"

"No, sorry, I don't. Uh, can you just turn around and take me back?"

229

They had driven pretty far, and Cainen didn't relish the idea of walking all the way back. He turned around in his seat and looked out the back for his tail car.

"Listen, I'll give you fifty dollars if you'll let me touch it."

"That's a lot of money," Cainen responded, sitting straight again. "You're a good-looking guy. You should just go out to the bars. You wouldn't have any trouble meeting someone."

"I don't want *someone*," cooed the stranger. "I want you."

"I appreciate the compliment, but why don't you spend your money on one of the other guys on the Boulevard? They can use the help."

"I'd rather spend my money on you. You must need the money, too, or you wouldn't have been out there."

Put me in my *place, didn't he*, thought Cainen.

"Listen, can you please just pull over and let me out? I'll grab a cab back," Cainen said sarcastically. They had driven so far that Cainen was worried about being stopped by a sheriff's car. Now *that* would take some explaining . . . about why he was operating outside his jurisdiction.

"I'll give you a hundred dollars just to show it to me," pleaded the cute stranger. "That's all the money I have on me."

Cainen turned to face the man, who was just a few years his senior. A hundred bucks? Was this guy kidding?

Cainen could see by the look in this guy's eyes that he wasn't. Wow, a hundred bucks. Hell, since he didn't have a body mike on, he could get away with it. A quick flash and be $100 richer.

Cainen considered it. But only for a moment, and not very seriously. Still, it made Cainen wonder if he was in the wrong line of work. *A hundred dollars just to show his dick?! That's better pay than he was making as a cop, and he wouldn't even have to get shot at!*

"I really appreciate the compliment," Cainen said. "There's a dozen other guys who could really use the cash and I'm sure would be complimented by the attentions of someone as good-looking as you. But I really was just waiting for a friend. It was really nice to talk with you, and perhaps I'll see you out here on another night. But I've got to get back."

The man looked at Cainen with a longing in his eyes. (Cainen wondered if that's what *he* had looked like to Mike and worried at the thought.)

"You sure?"

"Sorry, not tonight." Cainen laughed inwardly despite his deadpan face. "I have a headache."

"I'll drive you back," the man finally sighed.

As the Jag made a U-turn, Cainen saw his cover car continue straight for one block and then mimic the movement.

When the Jag was three blocks from the corner Cainen had been on, he asked the driver to let him off. The driver made a right and turned onto a side street and pulled over. The driver looked at Cainen with an unsatiated longing in his eyes.

Cainen was glad that the driver had pulled onto the side street. This way the Jag would continue south and wouldn't drive by Mike's location. Less suspicious.

Out of his peripheral vision, Cainen saw a pair of headlights turn the corner behind him and quickly pull to the curb, dousing the lights. It was good that his follow-up car was on his tail.

Cainen patted the young man across from him on the arm in a consoling gesture and opened his car door. He stepped out and bent down to wave and smile at the man.

"You sure you—" started the man, but Cainen cut him off as politely as he could.

"Thanks, but maybe some other time. Take care."

Cainen shut the door and walked back toward the seedy nightlife he had gotten used to. Back toward the Boulevard.

As he passed the cover car, he saw the probationer's curious gaze and the sour glare of Leaks. Cainen nodded his thanks and continued up the street.

Mentally reviewing his actions in verbal reporting format for his later discussion with Sergeant Barkley, Cainen determined to explain the whole affair in a positive light. He would sum it up by stating that he had eliminated a potential suspect in the case.

It had just been a lonely fairy, Cainen thought derisively, before he remembered that he was one, too.

As he walked back to the location where he had last seen the football player, Cainen's ruminations focused on a review of the feeling of being trapped in the Jaguar.

Cainen was a cop. Perhaps he was even more of a cop than he was a gay man, if separation of such an integral part of one's being was possible.

Cainen had been involved in police work for ten years. He had only admitted his sexual orientation (he still had trouble referring to himself as "homosexual," even in his thoughts) for three years.

Like all cops, Cainen preferred to be in control of his environment. That environment could be with other people, a party, a group, one friend, in a movie theater or a restaurant. But cops wanted control over their part in anything.

After years of dangerous assignments, they had seen too many of their fellow officers killed while off-duty because they weren't in control: they had sat with their backs to a door when the robbers came in or they hadn't been prepared when they walked into the bank and the robbers ordered them onto the floor.

So cops controlled everything they could, and what they couldn't control they often rebelled against.

This was one of the main reasons that their divorce rates were so high. Cops, and their associate psychologists, liked to blame the divorce rate on the stressful job or the bizarre hours they worked. It was hard for a policeman's wife to accept that *any* job would force a man to work eighteen hours straight and then attend court for another eight hours. Nope, the shrinks said in their voluminous reports, the wives thought their husbands were cheating.

What actually caused so many divorces was the officer's refusal to allow his wife and children the freedom to express themselves, to make mistakes, or even to be individuals.

It was just one of the hazards of The Job.

Not that the husbands were perfect angels. Every police station had a "Code X" sheet. The officer assigned to the desk manned the clipboard and monitored the officers signed on it.

Whenever a married officer wanted to liaison with his girlfriend, he would sign up on the "Code X" clipboard. If he so desired, he could include his girlfriend's phone number. The officer would then tell his wife that he was required to work a late-night task force. If the wife called in to verify it or speak with her husband, the desk officer checked the assignment board. If the name wasn't there, he checked the "Code X" sheet. With the name signed in on the clipboard, the desk officer confirmed that the husband was working. He then explained to the officer's wife that her husband was in the field and unavailable.

If the officer had left a contact phone number, the desk officer would tell the wife that he would radio her husband and have him call her back.

Many an officer had been called away from "duty" on top of his girlfriend by the expectant ringing of the telephone.

While Cainen had been in the Jaguar, he had been at the mercy of the thin man at the wheel. Not that the officer couldn't have taken the man; he easily could have. But he hadn't had control of the steering wheel, and the man had been very reluctant to stop the car.

To civilians, and to patrol officers, the obvious thing to have done would have been to identify himself as a police officer.

This was also the worst thing to do.

The secret to undercover work was information control. That was why terrorist groups operated in cells and antiterrorist police/army units operated on a "need-to-know" basis.

There was no telling who the driver of the Jag was going to come into contact with in the following days or even minutes. If he picked up another hustler on the way to his home in Beverly Hills and told the hustler of his encounter with an undercover officer, that hustler would undoubtedly share the info on the street. And if a description of Cainen was given with the information, the entire case would be blown.

That was the difference between plainclothes assignments and undercover assignments. The undercover role was similar to the "deep cover" agents used by foreign powers for espionage. The *mission* of the operative is what guides the operative's actions.

A plainclothes cop, like a vice officer, would take action at any violation of the law. If the vice officer was assigned to arrest homosexuals cruising the parks, he would also be expected to act if he witnessed a robbery.

An undercover officer has a specific goal. That goal is to get information necessary for the solution or the prevention of a crime.

The LAPD used to operate a unit known as Police Intelligence and Information Gathering (PIIG). Typical of the chief of police, he assigned undercover officers to any organization existing in the city that was not supportive of the police. There were undercover officers at every meeting from the Lavender Left (a gay group) to the Black Panthers.

The organizations infiltrated by the LAPD included political groups that were unsupportive of the LAPD's intelligence gathering activities, including the American Civil Liberties Union. The police department insisted that they only infiltrated groups that advocated criminal activities, sometimes even including the violent overthrow of the government. But the information gathering by the Department was even found in local political campaigns.

Unfortunately for the police department, these groups were protected by the U.S. Constitution. The chief of police, believing he was omnipotent, had overruled these protections.

The chief's actions cost the taxpayers millions of dollars in settlement costs when the groups aligned and filed suit due to the spying. What was uncovered rocked the very foundations of the police department: thousands of photographs of peaceful and law-abiding gatherings that had been taken surreptitiously . . . from *within* the meetings.

Though the Police Commission disbanded the PIIG unit, the police brass immediately instituted the Domestic Terrorism Strike Force.

Photos were still taken of peaceful protests and gatherings, whether they be the American Communist Party or the Gay Pride Parade.

Cainen's role was that of solving the most heinous crime—homicide. But his position was akin to that of the undercover officers of PIIG.

Cainen could not take any action that would identify him as an officer. He could do whatever he could to stop a crime from taking place, such as he had when the salt-and-pepper team had threatened the female prostitute, but he could not act as a law enforcement officer. At least not yet.

For now, he had to gather as much information as he could about whoever was killing the hustlers, and he had to relay that information to his supervisor for review and action by the Department management.

His job was to stop the fucker who was murdering these street kids.

Cainen intended to be successful in his mission.

As in most undercover assignments, the UC operative was almost never present when the final curtain fell. The UC would find out where the criminal was staying, but it was the detectives that served the warrant and made the arrest. The UC, for his safety, stayed out of sight.

So Cainen did not expect to actually catch the murderer of the hustlers. But he absolutely intended to develop the leads that would enable the detectives to locate and prosecute the asshole.

Cainen also intended to gather as much evidence as possible so that the murderer, when nailed, would be held to answer for his evil deeds.

Despite that, Cainen knew that Barkley was going to yell at him for taking the unnecessary chance and getting into a suspect's car.

Oh, well.

Cainen was one block away from his original corner when he saw that the football player, Mike, was leaning into the open passenger window of a brown van. At first, Cainen thought he recognized the van, but he couldn't recall where he had seen it.

As Cainen watched, Mike opened the door of the van and sat down inside. The passenger door closed, and the van pulled away from the curb and into the left lane.

It was too far away for Cainen to make out the driver. The van was coming toward him, however, and Cainen would catch a glimpse when it passed. He would also memorize the license number.

Later, at the police station, Cainen could run the plate through the LAPD computers and determine the registered owner of the van.

The van was in the left lane when it passed Cainen. Through the dirty windshield, Cainen made out a husky young male Caucasian with long brown hair as the driver.

The van had no front plates. Mike was facing the driver, talking, when the van passed, so he didn't see Cainen turn to watch the rear of the van.

The light over the rear license plate was out. Cainen could see the plate because of the streetlights overhead. But the plate was obscured by dirt, which aroused Cainen's police instincts even more.

Cainen was straining to make out the plate numerals when a shadow to his right moved toward him.

Cainen quickly turned to face the new potential menace.

"Can I bum a cigarette off you?" said a blond hustler with a cowboy hat on. "It's me: Peter," the hustler added, lifting the front of his hat. "You remember . . . the cowboy."

Dismissing the threat, Cainen returned his attention to the street. The van was nowhere in sight.

It was the last time Cainen saw Mike.

* * *

Charlie drove on through the night. The darkness enveloped the van as if Satan had opened the doors of hell.

When the van passed the northern hills of the San Fernando Valley, a thick fog rolled in, blanketing the 405 Freeway in an opaque haze. Even to a person as satanic as Charlie, the fog seemed like a tangible evil shroud.

Charlie was forced to slow the van. There was no roadway in view, only humbled clouds reflecting the van's headlights.

Periodically a California Highway Patrol car passed by at a slightly faster pace. Charlie could see the lone officer looking from right to left for the remains of some hapless accident victim.

It seemed like an eternity before the van approached the Lancaster city limits. The fog had lifted, replaced by a darkness as empty and foreboding as the previous cloud cover.

As the van left the freeway, Cameron's head appeared through the van drapes like an ethereal body. Charlie watched Cameron's pale features gaze through the windshield as if he were trying to locate some unseen landmark. The head then vanished as quickly as it had materialized.

From the vantage of a passing plane, the van would merely have appeared as two disembodied headlights, vainly searching through the desert. Perhaps they were looking for the vehicle they had belonged to; more likely, it was some engineer looking for a repair site.

The van reached the dirt road that led to the mines. The bouncing of the van shook the unconscious body strapped to the floor in the back.

Charlie leaned forward, trying to see the ground to avoid driving over anything that could cause a flat.

The Stygian darkness of the desert night prevented Charlie from seeing anything except directly in front of each light.

The van suddenly reared up like a boat at sea as the front passenger wheel drove over a large rock. The van hit the desert ground with a slam, bottoming out the van's antiquated shock absorbers.

In the back, Mike moaned.

* * *

This second meeting with "Cowboy" turned out to be Cainen's first break in the case. Due to Cowboy's years on the street, he had his ear to the ground and was privy to all the gossip from his fellow entrepreneurs.

Cainen didn't have any cigarettes, but he accompanied Peter to Carl's Coffee Shop, where there was a machine.

Personally, Cainen refused to purchase anything from Carl's, since he had read that the owner funded right-wing antigay candidates and organizations. But he figured that the five quarters he gave to Peter were going to the cigarette vendor instead.

Cainen wasn't any happier when he saw that the Cowboy had purchased Marlboros.

Cainen didn't know it at the time, but the five quarters he gave to the broke hustler were a cheap offering in return for the invaluable information he was going to receive.

The Cowboy looked older than he was, as did most of the "youths" on the street. Because of this, Cainen had negated his sage ethic to never judge a source by face value. Cainen assumed that Peter wouldn't be able to provide any newsbreaking insights, since he wasn't getting any business. (When Cainen was a youngster, his mother had taught him that to *assume* anything was to make an *ass* of *u* and *me*.)

Since Mike had gone off with a trick, Cainen had nothing better to do, so he hung around Peter. Just as when they first met, Peter talked about his life and confabulated street philosophy, this time to a silent companion.

Cainen was still composing his verbal report to Sergeant Barkley in his mind when the Cowboy shocked the young officer by bringing up the subject of the disappearances.

"And you know what?" said the street-savvy young man as Cainen tried not to appear as if he was clinging to each word. "Every one of the kids that disappeared was blond."

Peter unconsciously ran his left fingers through his dark blond hair while he smoked with his right hand. "I won't take rides with any guy I don't know if he's driving a van or a car with tinted windows."

Cainen suspected that Peter got few offers and, in reality, would ride with anyone that offered.

Cainen also thought of Mike, then immediately dismissed the speculation. It was ridiculous for him to be concerned about (or attracted to!) the hustler; the profession had its risks, and Mike was old enough to know that. Besides, every dopehead in high school and every macho guy and gang member drove a car with tinted windows.

Still, how likely was it that these types of guys would be picking up hustlers?

Cainen didn't know, but it was food for consideration. (In spite of himself, Cainen worried for Mike's safety.)

When Cainen parted company with the Cowboy several hours later, he had the report for Sergeant Barkley composed in his head.

He had finally developed a lead. The Cowboy had told Cainen that at least twelve blond hustlers had disappeared in the prior three months.

Even if some of the hustlers had just moved on, this was a much higher number than the LAPD had anticipated. Cainen was proud of his accomplishment in obtaining the information.

Cainen handed Peter ten bucks and told him to get a decent meal. He then gave the signal to his backup car that he was cutting out for the night.

The Pinto didn't waste any time in starting up and heading to the station.

Cainen walked the two blocks to his Samurai parked on Fountain. He drove quickly to the station, anxious to give his report to the supportive supervisor.

Cainen was also anxious to get through with his duties and find an all-night drugstore.

He had formulated a plan and was antsy to get started with it before the morning.

*   *   *

Cainen got more than a few stares when he reported to work the next evening. The officers at Hollywood had always elbowed each other, gawking at Cainen's attire of a white tank top T-shirt and tight blue jeans. But now they made no attempt to hide their leers of contempt and dislike.

After Cainen grabbed a juice from the machine in the break room, he walked into the roll call room for the PED roll call. Cainen used the rear door, but even the sergeant at the front of the room failed to hide his conspicuous gape at Cainen.

The officers in the room turned to look. The excited whispers were followed by mocking laughs amid the officers. Someone whistled the high-low wolf call of attraction usually reserved for members of the opposite sex. Howls of approving laughter followed.

Cainen saw Barkley, standing against the side wall in the front, nod toward the doors of the room. Without taking a seat, Cainen turned and exited from the rear doors he had just come through. He waited in the hallway for Barkley to come through the front doors.

"Let me grab a fresh coffee first," said the sergeant, walking into the adjacent break room.

Cainen noted the use of the word "first" and was disappointed that Barkley wasn't in his usual good mood.

"They should label it 'iced coffee' if they're going to serve it cold," exhorted the usually uncomplaining sergeant from in front of the machine.

Yep, thought Cainen, *this man is definitely not in one of his better moods*.

When they were seated in Barkley's office, with the door closed, Barkley stared at Cainen without speaking.

Cainen shifted in his chair, uncomfortable under the critical gaze of his senior.

Barkley sipped his coffee, grimacing at the sour taste, despite his being accustomed to it. Barkley set the cup down on the desk. The desktop was strewn with watch assignment sheets, where Barkley was obviously laboring with days off for the Detail for the next deployment period. *No wonder he was in as sour a mood as his coffee!*

Cainen admired Barkley. He was one of the only supervisors in the entire Department that took the time to try to give the officers the days off they requested. Most supervisors just went by seniority, assigning junior officers single days off in the middle of the week. It wasn't like the police department could close on weekends and holidays!

Barkley cleared his throat, and Cainen cleared his mind. Cainen looked at the senior officer respectfully.

Cainen was wearing a blue windbreaker over his tank top. He moved one arm to release the vinyl that clung to his sweaty armpit.

"You couldn't find anyone who liked you as a brunette?" It was a humorless joke. Barkley hadn't meant it to be funny.

Cainen was embarrassed and didn't reply.

"What are you up to?"

Cainen's practiced explanations seemed lame, so he discarded them. You don't prevaricate to officers that have integrity. Cainen noticed that the supervisor was staring at the bright blond streaks highlighting Cainen's hair.

"I'm not going to get any info if I don't fit the part," Cainen explained.

"Fit what part? The part of a hustler or the part of a homicide victim?"

Cainen felt put in his place (again!). He remained silent.

"Listen to me, Steve." Some of Barkley's congeniality had returned to his voice. Since Cainen wasn't too much older than Barkley's son, Cainen considered it the sergeant's "fatherly" tone of voice.

"You're a good cop," stated the sergeant. "You don't have to prove yourself to *anyone*. Least of all yourself."

Cainen watched the older man in silence.

"Whatever people's biases are, that's their problem, not yours. You're a good cop and you don't need to pay attention to them.

"Whatever you've got in mind, forget it. A medal of valor doesn't do anybody any good if it's pinned to a coffin."

"I'm just trying to develop enough leads to solve the case," defended Cainen.

Barkley saw through the younger cop. "You are not to get into any more cars. I don't care if your cover gets blown or not. No more rides. Do you understand me?" Barkley evidently sensed the younger man's torment. His voice was empathetic, not harsh. But it was no less demanding. "I want you to agree to that."

Cainen stared at Barkley. "No more rides," he repeated. His voice was firm.

Barkley wasn't satisfied.

"And your backup will know that you're not to get into any cars and they'll be advised to intercede if you attempt it."

"Tim." It was the first time that Cainen had used the sergeant's first name.

"No, Steve. Don't 'Tim' me. You sound like my son. I want you coming out of this alive, and getting into a serial killer's car is an unnecessary risk. The issue is closed."

The two strong-willed men looked at each other. Barkley won. Cainen looked at his shoes.

"Maybe changing your hair color will get you more info," relented the sergeant. "I'll defend your actions against anyone who makes any insinuations. I'll also sell it to the lieutenant. As for the officer who made the cat call—"

"Don't sweat it," interrupted the homosexual officer.

"It's not a question of sweating it; it's a question of improper behavior. When he's back out working a radio car," continued Barkley, "the other officers in PED will think twice before they act out. But you realize that despite your good intentions, there's going to be a lot of talk."

Cainen realized it. It was nothing new. The only aspect that had changed was that an LAPD supervisor was in his corner for the first time.

"Yeah, they're going to ridicule me and say that 'the fag's finally found a job he likes.' They're going to say that 'the fruit's exploring his new homosexual freedom.' Something to the effect that 'he can finally express his true faggot colors.'"

"Probably something to that effect," smirked the supervisor. "Well, I'll cover for you as best I can. Now go to work."

"Thanks."

Cainen walked out the door. Barkley watched him leave, feeling as he did when he was at home and his son was going off to school.

Barkley did defend Cainen to those officers that asked. Most didn't bother.

Three days after his pep talk, Cainen summoned Barkley to the Hollywood station parking lot. Cainen walked the supervisor to the police parking area and stood beside his Suzuki Samurai.

"I figure it must be important, with you walking me out here to talk." Barkley looked at the poker cards on the side of the coffee cup in his hands.

"Actually, I walked you out here to show you something."

The older man immediately looked at the black Samurai. When he noticed nothing out of place, Barkley walked to the rear of the vehicle. Cainen joined the sergeant, who stood staring at the Suzuki's rear license plate.

"I don't suppose you've decided to explore your newfound sexual freedom?" The sergeant's remark was said in a serious, yet sardonic, tone of voice. The remark was reminiscent of Cainen's own words three days prior.

240

"I had nothing to do with it," explained Cainen. "A friend walked by my locker and asked me if I was crazy. He told me that some officers were out at my car, laughing. I decided to check out the joke. I don't know how long it's been like that."

Barkley hadn't looked up from the license plate.

It hit Barkley a lot harder than it had hit Cainen. It was the first time Barkley had witnessed any harassment firsthand.

The importance of the situation wasn't lost on either officer. An officer's personal property, particularly his car, was strictly off-limits. Unlike an officer's locker, an officer's personal vehicle was considered sacrosanct, untouchable. This was an unwritten law of the Department.

And someone had violated that prohibition.

Barkley now believed the rumors that Cainen hadn't received backup on his calls.

"What do you want me to do?"

"Nothing," said Cainen. "Just so you know what's going on."

Barkley was still staring at the plate.

"I'll take it off later," said the officer. "I'm going to go hit the Boulevard." Cainen turned and walked away.

The coffee had cooled in Barkley's hand, even colder than it came from the machine. For that and at least one better reason, Barkley said, "Shit."

After tasting it, Barkley held the cup out to his side. Without looking at it, Barkley tilted the cup, spilling out the watery brew. Even in his reverie, Barkley was conscious to avoid blemishing his shoes.

Barkley stared at the license plate a moment longer. Actually, he just looked at the license plate frame. Then he turned back toward the station. The paper mill of the Department didn't stand still for minor emergencies like earthquakes or the 1984 Olympics. It sure wouldn't pause due to the harassment of one police officer.

The dealer's license plate frame on the Samurai had read: "Van Nuys Suzuki." The frame had been removed from Cainen's car by an officer. In its stead, reattached to the personal vehicle, was a different license plate frame. This one read: "Gay & Proud."

* * *

As the brown van descended southbound into the San Fernando Valley, Cameron sat in the passenger seat with the boom box in his lap. Lisa still lay wasted in the rear.

Charlie, still driving, was not even aware that he was steering with one hand. As the tape neared its end, he had unconsciously begun squeezing his hardening groin through his jeans.

Cameron had noticed, but had wisely continued to stare listlessly through the windshield.

On the tape, Mike the hustler, once a majestic blond model and athlete, was now reduced to a quivering, slobbering baby. As the torture bore maddeningly on, Mike's cries, moans, and pleas reached a crescendo.

Mike's hysterical begging for mercy became a momentary scream. It was his last moment.

As one side of the ninety-minute tape reached its end, so did Mike's life.

The tape player clicked off, startling Cameron.

On the freeway, the van passed above the Sylmar Juvenile Hall, where Los Angeles stored its incorrigible future. As the van passed, Charlie looked over his right arm (his left covered his lap) and glared at the boom box.

Charlie was angry that his pleasure had ended so abruptly. And too soon.

* * *

Sitting back on his raised heels, Mr. Hisky looked over his students. In his peripheral vision, he observed Master Kim doing the same from the vantage point of his office.

Though Master Kim rarely taught any students other than black belts, as a traditional Korean master he oversaw every class, even the little tykes.

Each student wore a white *gi* bearing a small Korean flag over the heart. The class members sat symmetrically, breathing in through their noses and out through their mouths. Some of the newer white belts who found the meditation position too painful sat cross-legged on the mat.

As much as Hapkido was a physical self-defense, it was also a discipline of the mind. Breathing, particularly cleansing breaths before and after each class, helped the students to center themselves.

And, as the third-degree black belt instructor knew, they were *all* students, including himself. Because they were all still learning.

At the start of the class, the breathing helped the student to empty his or her mind of the day's stress, to better concentrate on the night's lesson.

At the end of class, the breathing relaxed the students, reminding them to keep the techniques of pain and destruction inside the studio, unless it was absolutely necessary to use them elsewhere.

Hisky looked at Steve Cainen. Cainen had joined after Master Kim promoted his first group of black belt instructors. The master was now on his third group.

Steve had studied other styles before joining the studio. With almost three years of training, Steve was already good enough to test for his black belt. That was fast, real fast. But Steve was good. One of the studio's best, though he avoided tournament competition.

Yet Steve had delayed his promotional testing. After receiving the first stripe for his brown belt, Steve had not signed up for the promotional tests.

Steve had learned the next belt's techniques, so it wasn't that he was not prepared. Despite the complexity of the test, with its midair spinning kicks, Hisky knew that Steve could pass it blindfolded (and, Hisky smiled, would have to do just that!).

While he was unsure of the reason for the delay, Hisky had noted that lately Stephen was . . . off-center.

The breathing exercises allowed a person to center himself.

Though the others didn't notice it, with Hisky's trained eye he could see that Steve's muscles were tense and his breathing was shallow, not deep. Not deep *and* cleansing.

Seated on his heels, the balls of his feet pressing the mat, Steve's thumb and index finger formed an *O* as his hands rested on his knees. But Hisky noted that the fingers were not touching.

Something was bothering the brown belt.

For Steve's sake, Hisky extended the meditation an extra two minutes.

* * *

The night after Cainen's grand entrance into roll call, Leaks was in the locker room getting on his gear. He was Pissed, with a capital *P*.

On The Job, officers couldn't pierce their ears or wear jewelry, except for a wedding ring. They weren't allowed to have a beard, unless they were undercover. Even their hair had to be neat, and trimmed above their ears. Shit, they weren't allowed to have long sideburns, and even *Elvis* had those!

That was why just about every LAPD officer had a mustache. That was the only freedom of appearance that was permissible in the Department. And even a mustache had to be uniform in appearance, nothing too bushy and it couldn't extend past the corners of the mouth. That was written in the manual!

And now some faggot got to dye his hair.

Leaks remembered that Roger Putvin, his old training officer, used to spray-paint his bald spot brown, claiming that it looked like hair. Maybe from a distance. Like from the North Pole or something. To Leaks, it just looked like brown spray paint. But hell, spray paint wasn't the same as dye. Dye was something for women, or fruits.

This was some fruit officer who was finally getting to hang around with his own kind and was beginning to take on a fruit fly's characteristics.

What next? Lip gloss and fingernail polish?!

Leaks didn't buy the line of horseshit from Sergeant Barkley. How the fuck would Cainen know that only blond hustlers were being killed? It didn't even make sense. If some psycho was gonna do the world a favor and off all the bunboys, why the hell would he only waste blond ones? No way! He'd get ridda all the brown-haired maggots, too. That's just the way things go (at least to Leaks's way of thinking).

That was why Leaks had gotten together with his friend Tommy Champion from A.M.'s. He knew where Tommy would be in the morning and met his old partner at the Shortstop.

When Leaks arrived there, Champion was wearing a button on his shirt. It was the same button that he usually wore on the inside of his police uniform jacket, where the supervisors couldn't see it.

After Champion arrested a belligerent suspect, he would turn out the lapel of his jacket, showing it to the handcuffed suspect.

The button read: SHIT HAPPENS.

Leaks had sat down beside Tommy, ordering a brewski. Beer was cool, but hard liquor in the morning was too strong for Leaks's taste.

Leaks had talked to Champion about Cainen. If Cainen was so fired up about his newfound heritage that he was starting to display his true colors (or *untrue* colors, if you asked Clairol), then he should declare his preference to the world. And since Champion worked the least supervised shift, he had the best access to the station parking lot.

Leaks and Champion had joked that Cainen should get a personalized license plate for his Suzuki that read "6UL DV8." They had cracked up on that one.

Leaks himself had a personalized plate. It read: "P2 4EVR," which Leaks felt summed up his career goals in the Department.

They had come up with a plan, and Champion had smirked, telling Leaks that they would soon see how proud the little faggot was of his newfound freedom of expression.

"Hey, I'm not putting the guy down," stated Champion in mock seriousness as he chugged another Scotch. "Everyone has a right to live their own life."

"You're a bleedin'-heart liberal," chimed in Leaks, nursing his Bud. "I bet you even got an ACLU membership card in your wallet."

"I'm so liberal, I don't believe in deadly force." Champion's speech slurred as the alcohol took effect. "I only shoot cans."

"Yeah," clarified his former partner, "Mexi-cans, Puerto Ri-cans, and Afri-cans."

They had laughed so hard that Leaks had to run to the john or he would have wet his pants.

Smiling at his reverie, Leaks finished strapping on his gun and ammo pouch and went out to guard the same officer he was harassing.

* * *

Talk on the street was better than a newspaper or a telephone. Within minutes on the street, Cainen learned who had drugs, when vice was working, what vice raids had gone down, and when major fights or crimes were going to occur.

At Orange Avenue, by the Shakey's pizza parlor, Cainen passed by two youths with Bibles attempting to recruit a disheveled hustler. As he went around them, Cainen heard the hustler retort, "Hell, it was because of people like you that I got kicked out of my house in the *first* place!"

Cainen continued west until he reached La Brea. He didn't cross the main street. He was looking for Mike, and Mike had said that he stayed on LAPD's side of the Boulevard, since the LAPD patrol cars didn't bother with enforcement like the sheriff's cars did.

Cainen noted that few of the boys were working, perhaps because it was still early.

Cainen checked for his backup car, noticed it across the street, and turned around. He felt sorry for them that he wasn't standing still, which made their job much easier and much less conspicuous, but it was worthless for him to stand alone in the hope that some hustler would come up to him to divulge information.

When Cainen reached Mansfield Avenue, he observed cars with male drivers slowing down. *Must be slim pickin's on the street tonight,* he thought to himself.

Cainen ignored the drivers' attempts to get his attention, even when they circled five or six times. That was Sergeant Barkley's orders.

Cainen walked back to Sycamore. That was the Cowboy's usual hangout.

As Cainen stood in the shadows on the northwest corner of Sycamore and Santa Monica Boulevard, a brown van slowly prowled by in the slow lane.

A shiver traversed the lengths of Cainen's spine. He remembered that the last time he had seen Mike on the Boulevard was when the young athlete had gotten into a brown van.

Cainen thought he recognized the van driver as the same one who had picked up Mike three nights ago.

As Cainen remained on his corner, the van circled a second time and pulled to the curb beside the undercover officer.

* * *

"Fuck this!" yelled Leaks, hitting his fist against the dashboard. "That fucking asshole won't stand still! What am I supposed to do? Drive up and down making U-turns every three blocks for the whole friggin' night?"

Miller just sat mutely beside the training officer. He guessed that Leaks was really angry because he was hungry and couldn't get into his sack of Hostess goodies while he had to steer the car.

When they had first come on, Leaks had told the probationary officer that he hadn't had a chance to eat dinner and was starving. At their first opportunity Leaks said that they would swing by Del Taco and grab something nutritious to eat.

"Well, fuck it. I'm fucking hungry. If this guy is just gonna walk up and down the street, nothing's gonna happen to him anyway. And the sarge forbid him to get into any cars. So why are we out here anyway? Nothing's gonna happen to the guy with all these drivers watchin'," said Leaks, justifying his next action.

"Let's go grab something at Del Taco and bring it back here to eat." His decision reached, Leaks turned on the engine and lights and pulled the Pinto up to the Boulevard.

"Shouldn't we advise Cainen that we're going?" asked the probationer.

"And how the fuck would you like to do that without blowing his cover? Drive up and say, 'Excuse me, Officer, but us undercover cops are hungry'?"

Miller felt chastised. He had forgotten his place as a probationer. Even in situations where he knew right from wrong, his status as a junior officer meant that he had to accept the imperfect judgment of his training officer.

Miller kept his mouth shut. He had been cautioned to follow that course of conduct in the academy, and he had heard the horror stories from his classmates of those probationers who had forgotten their servile status.

Like all police officers who choose a wrongful course of action, Leaks had second thoughts about leaving the scene of his surveillance. And like all officers who want to err, Leaks tried to justify his action.

"We'll be back in a minute. And we're supposed to get a break anyway."

With that, Leaks made a right and headed east for three blocks to the fast-food drive-through.

Cainen didn't see the car pull out. His view was blocked by the brown van.

* * *

Three days after the murder of Mike, Charlie's bloodlust was no less diminished. As so often happens with serial killers, the time periods between the killings was diminishing gradually.

During the three-day interim, Charlie watched the television news. The topic of the "male-prostitute killings" was relegated to the end of the programs and focused primarily on the efforts of the local Parent-Teacher Associations to lobby for increased school security.

Mike's disappearance was not mentioned.

Cameron had spent the days sleeping at the motel and the nighttimes at Doggies or with the other street kids on Hollywood Boulevard. Lisa, on the other hand, stayed within the motel. When she wasn't playing with the motel owner's children, she was in Luther's room exchanging sex for drugs. Usually Quaaludes.

Lisa was only too willing to accept Luther's painful tenderness rather than being the object of Charlie's brutal, sadistic lovemaking.

If you could call it lovemaking.

By the third night of stalling, Charlie could no longer harness his lethal potential. The mental confines were too restrictive, and he commandeered Lisa from the owner's front office.

While Charlie smeared fresh mud over the rear license plate of the van, Lisa quickly sneaked away to Luther's room and got wasted on Ludes. Entering the passenger side of the revving van, Lisa climbed into her spot behind Charlie's seat and fantasized about being back in the owner's office. As the Ludes took effect, and the tingling spread to her fingertips, Lisa left her physical surroundings and ventured away from the unpleasant eventuality.

Charlie had gone on a shoplifting spree the day before to obtain any additional tools he required. During the previous night, he had used Lisa as a lookout while he siphoned gas from the minicam vans in the KTLA Channel 5 lot on Sunset Boulevard. Tonight Charlie stopped only once to snatch Cameron out of Doggies. He had Cameron sit behind the passenger seat.

With the baseball bat.

Charlie was all prepped to go. He had given the blanket-wrapped shotgun to Cameron and put the .25-caliber in Lisa's pocket. With an increased police presence in the area, they might get stopped by the cops. If they did, Lisa and Cameron would be the ones to go to jail. The most they could do to him was give him a speeding ticket!

However, Charlie's initial excitement decreased as he drove down the Boulevard.

The hustlers were sparse tonight. Though it was just past seven, there should have been more kids out working the street. There appeared to be more social workers and Bible-thumpers than there were hustlers!

This was the earliest that Charlie had ever operated. It was safer and more prudent to work during the early-morning hours when the traffic was lighter.

In Charlie's mad desire for human destruction, he had thrown caution to the wind. He needed to hurt someone.

Though there were several male black hustlers and some Caucasian brunettes, Charlie subconsciously ignored them. To his eyes, they didn't exist. They might just as well have been lampposts.

Charlie's attraction was to blonds. Part of his sadistic inclinations included a sexual characteristic. This characteristic was a homosexual attraction to blonds.

This peculiarity probably stemmed from Charlie's mother being a bleached blonde, as many of the hustlers were.

Though Charlie's mother was a single parent, she had played a dominant and domineering role in Charlie's adolescent life.

His mother had also been an incredibly abusive parent during Charlie's developmental years, a time when Charlie had been defenseless against her vicious onslaughts.

It was very possible that in Charlie's sick mind, every time he raped and murdered a hustler, he was merely acting out his aggression toward his mother. At least that was how a psychiatrist for the defense would explain such behavior at a trial.

It was just as likely that Charlie held disdain for every human being and he unconsciously chose to target those individuals he was attracted to sexually.

In either case, Charlie had almost given up when he spotted a hustler standing on the northwest corner of Sycamore.

Though the hustler only had blond highlights, on a night as sparse as tonight was, and with Charlie's desperate desire for someone to harm, this young man would do.

When Charlie passed the hustler the first time, he thought he recognized the face. Though the face looked familiar, there was something different that prevented Charlie from recalling where he had seen the man before.

Charlie couldn't place the hustler as the same young man who had angered him three nights prior. With Cainen's highlighted hair, he looked different from when he had momentarily interrupted Charlie's pickup of Mike.

There was something about this hustler that made Charlie pass him the first time—something about the way he stood or how he carried himself.

To Charlie's keen streetwise eye, there was a physical bearing about this hustler that didn't match the assailability of the other hustlers.

But Charlie was anxious. His desires needed fulfilling, and he had put them off for three days. Hell, he had been ready to waste another one while he was still driving back from assassinating Mike!

On his second pass, Charlie steered the van over to the curb by the hustler with the blond highlights.

* * *

As soon as the van pulled over, Cainen's mind went into overdrive. Sergeant Barkley's words kept repeating themselves over and over again in his mind: *"You are not to get into any more cars. . . . No more rides."*

Cainen's feet were working without his having given them an instruction. As he walked toward the passenger door of the van, he recognized it as the same one that Mike had gotten into.

Cainen looked for his backup, but he was now too close to the van to see the other side of the street. Backing up now, to take a look across, would be too suspicious.

His backup had been there a second ago, Cainen reassured himself.

Instinctively, Cainen checked out the van. He saw a sliding door on the passenger side. No windows there.

Cainen hadn't noticed if the license plates were still obscured by dirt.

249

As he stood with his hand on the windowsill of the lowered passenger window, Cainen surreptitiously glanced inside. His view of the rear of the van was impeded by a cloth curtain—a bad sign.

As Cainen spoke, he assessed the young male driver.

"What's happening?"

"Just out for a ride. Thought you looked like you needed a lift."

The young man talked easily enough. He didn't seem nervous. He had long brown hair and a stocky build. Cainen couldn't see any weapons readily accessible, but he knew that didn't mean that one wasn't within easy reach.

Cainen figured that even if the driver did pull a weapon, with one hand occupied with the steering wheel he could be disarmed easily.

All the same . . .

"Whatcha got in the back?"

"Just a mattress." The driver winked at Cainen. "And I got a six-pack back there, too. You lookin' to party?"

"Well, actually, I'm working."

"Hey, I can relate," answered the long-haired driver. Typical of martial artists, Cainen thought how that long hair could be used to the driver's disadvantage.

"If you want to make some dough, I'm willing to pay for some company. Hop in."

The driver set the van in gear. The van engine was still going.

Cainen knew he couldn't hesitate long.

Charlie also knew it.

Cainen only debated for a moment before he made a decision and opened the door to step up into the van.

After all, Cainen figured, he had his backup.

Cainen doubted that Leaks would follow Barkley's directions and intercede. Leaks wasn't nearly that motivated.

Instead, Cainen figured that Leaks and his probationer would follow from a discreet distance to see what occurred. If anything went wrong, Cainen could just jump out and signal the backup car to continue following the van.

In this manner, Cainen could solve the dilemma of what had happened to Mike. And if the van turned out to be a dead end, Cainen could say it was a friend or an informant. If it was the killer, then the glory of nailing the suspect would override Barkley's worst ridicule.

Regardless, he hadn't become a police officer just to wimp out of any dangerous assignments. If he chickened out, then he was validating all the preconceptions that LAPD officers had of gays.

As Cainen pulled the passenger door closed, he saw the Cowboy in the sideview mirror. The hustler was about twenty feet away, walking westbound toward the corner. The Cowboy's eyes were on the van.

As the van pulled away from the curb, Cainen realized that in any case, he was disobeying the direct order of not only his superior, but someone whose judgment he trusted.

The young man driving was saying something. But Cainen ignored him because there was a movement behind the curtain.

Instinctively Cainen tried to duck. However, he was prevented from completely avoiding the blow by the protrusion of the dashboard—that, and because Charlie's hand had seized his throat.

IX

The Kidnapping

Steve Cainen had always pictured himself as a superspy. He had read all of Ian Fleming's James Bond novels during his early teens. And he had reread them each year until he was twenty-one.

Steve didn't know if reincarnation was true, but if he had had a prior life, Steve *knew* that he must have been a Samurai warrior. He would have preferred to have been a *ninja,* a master assassin. The ninjas were expert fighters, in all forms of combat. But Steve believed in karma. After all, he hypothesized, there was little choice in this regard for those who believed in it.

Steve attributed his supreme regard for duty, honor, and righteousness to his prior life. He felt that he could not escape his obligation to these principles. *Shigata ga nai.* It was Steve's lot in life.

In keeping with his superspy self-image, Steve had figured that he could get himself out of any dangerous endeavor.

But he could not come up with a plan at the moment.

His head was throbbing from where he had been hit. When he had regained consciousness, he had kept his eyes closed and had listened. But his ruse had gained no additional insight into his plight.

Cainen could feel that he was naked. He slowly tested each muscle and joint, but only his head appeared to be injured.

He knew that he was still in the van. He could feel metal on his wrists, probably handcuffs from the feel of it.

These handcuffs held his arms spread out to his sides and above his head. It felt like rope was tied to his ankles, keeping his legs apart and secured to the floor.

Cainen deduced that he was in the rear of the van. He was face up on the floorboard, spread-eagled.

But why was he naked?

Cainen never let fear consume him, even slightly. He acknowledged fear as a necessary emotion for survival.

Despite his conviction, Cainen registered a slight adrenaline increase.

Like any spy worth his salt, Cainen peered through tightly lidded eyes in an attempt to determine in which direction the van was headed.

It was pitch-black in the back of the van. There were no uncovered windows to give Cainen a clue.

Similar to the feeling one gets after falling into a catnap at work, Cainen assumed he had been unconscious for a long time. In his morbid thoughts, Cainen pictured the van passing out of the city limits . . . passing the "Now Exiting City of Los Angeles—Pop. 3,684,392." While growing up in L.A., Steve had wondered which number was his. Not that it would matter now. In his mind he pictured a workman in white overalls coming to the sign the next morning. When the man finished his job, it would read: "3,684,391."

Unless he could think of something. Quick!

Cainen shivered.

"I think he's waking up."

It was a young male voice. To his left. Above him.

The voice didn't sound threatening.

"We're almost fucking there. The hustler isn't going anywhere."

From the driver's seat. It must be the long-haired guy. The one who picked him up. *That* voice sounded menacing.

Cainen had to determine how many opponents (not *enemies*, when you thought like a samurai) he would have to take out before he could develop a plan.

He kept his eyes closed.

"I just want to get this over with. The cops are all over the place in L.A."

If you only knew how close they are! Cainen thought as the young one spoke. His words meant they were out of Los Angeles. How far out? And why?

Cainen felt a cool rush of adrenaline as an answer.

Or was it fear?

"Shut the fuck up," said Charlie. "You agreed to get rid of these AIDS-infected faggots. How'd you expect to do it? By writing a fuckin' engraved invitation for them to commit suicide?"

The van turned off the highway.

Boy, is it dark! thought Cainen. *Well, at least their intentions are clear. They're going to kill me.*

Cainen tried each of his restraints. The cuffs were so tight that his circulation was being cut off. Slowly, so as not to make a sound, he firmly tested the chains.

They were solid. The ropes around his ankles were equally firm.

The van steered onto a dirt road. It drove slowly for the remainder of the ride.

It stopped.

As the driver crawled into the back, Cainen opened his eyes fully. The first thing he saw was the driver lifting up a shotgun with his right hand.

"How you doin', you fuckin' faggot?"

Cainen didn't reply. His thoughts were flying by at 100 miles an hour. And none of them had the courtesy to land.

To identify himself as a cop would mean instant death. They would be afraid of his training, and they wouldn't want to leave any witnesses. After their dozen murders (that Cainen knew of), they wouldn't hesitate to add one more.

Working undercover, Cainen never carried anything that identified him as an officer. This was because of just such a situation.

No, they could have killed him at any time. They were keeping him alive for a reason. And as much as Cainen didn't want to contemplate it, there was only one purpose for tying him down in such a way.

To torture him.

As if in reply, Charlie kicked Cainen in the ribs.

"I'm talking to you, faggot."

Cainen replied by exhaling a long breath between clenched teeth. He hoped his rib wasn't broken.

Charlie pushed the shotgun against Cainen's throat.

"Let me introduce myself. My name's Charlie. Perhaps you know my dad, Charlie Manson. I was named after him. And I'm right proud to be his namesake."

Charlie laughed.

Cainen couldn't remember having heard that Manson had a kid. Besides, this guy was too old to be Manson's kid. Though, on reflection, this psycho could be progeny of *that* psycho. Boy, what an egomaniac! Talk about delusions of grandeur.

Charlie scraped the gun down Cainen's body until it rested on Cainen's penis.

"Maybe I should just blow your fucking cock off, so you can't go spreading AIDS? Of course then you'd just bleed to death." The menacing laugh followed.

"Why are you doing this?" Cainen regretted saying it even before he finished. This guy didn't have answers to his ravings.

Charlie pushed the shotgun barrel down harder.

"Why am I fucking doing this? Why am *I* fucking doing this?! Why are *you* going around fucking monkeys? Why are *you* spreading AIDS, you fucking disease?!"

Charlie leaned down beside Cainen's face, as if to confide in him. "Someone's got to do God's work. And the police haven't got the balls. They've sold out to all the liberals and minorities. They've even got a fuckin' suck-ass, do-nothing black for a mayor in Los Angeles!"

Well, at least I share one of his opinions, Cainen thought wryly. Cainen speculated that Charlie had heard one too many KKK speeches.

Cainen leaned his head back to look at the other young man, who was seated behind the passenger seat.

Charlie noticed. "That's my bro', Cameron."

"Why you tellin' him our names for?" whined Cameron.

"What's the big deal? It's not like he's ever gonna tell anyone." Another mocking laugh. The laugh was as evil as Charlie. "So here's what we're gonna do. We're going to have some fun."

Cainen didn't think that the "we" really included him. But he kept the rumination to himself.

Cainen had never understood why his sense of humor seemed greater when he was under the most stress. (Right now he could have done a stand-up routine!) His cousin Perry, the sociology professor, would have said that it was a defense mechanism, that it helped him cope in times of great pressure. Cainen had copied his sense of humor from Perry. Perry had copied it from Groucho Marx, Woody Allen, Lenny Bruce, Loudon Wainwright III, and Perry's father.

While Charlie went for something in the glove box, Cainen started mentally preparing himself. His years of martial arts training had taught him much about mental preparation, as had the police academy.

Cainen had little doubt about what was coming, but he would not lose himself in the anxiety of waiting.

Cainen began with *Pranayama*, starting with deep, cleansing yogic breaths. Breathing in through the nose and pulling the breath down to his stomach, Cainen filled his chest cavity last. Holding it for several moments, he then let it out in a long, slow breath from his mouth. He cleared out the last bit of air by putting his tongue between his teeth and pushing inward with his stomach.

Cainen began to focus. Meditation might lessen the upcoming pain.

In *The Man with a Golden Gun*, James Bond was strapped naked to a chair with a hole torn in the seat. The villain had placed a rattan rake under the chair, attached to a pedal. Whenever Bond refused to answer a question, the villain would stomp on the pedal and the rake would slash Bond's privates. (Cainen had no idea how close fiction and reality had become.)

As a Jewish youth, Steve had imagined himself being tortured by Nazis. Steve believed that he could withstand any agony to avoid being a traitor to his country. Steve felt that no matter how painful the torture, it was better to suffer than to give up the ideals of America. As Joan Rivers had joked, "I'll tell you nothing, you Nazi pig!"

Cainen had focused on a spot on the van ceiling. He was getting closer to the spot, emptying his thoughts and concentrating on his breathing. Then Charlie returned with a lighter in his left hand.

Charlie walked down to Cainen's feet. Cainen strove to get closer to the spot on the ceiling, as if he could find protection for his physical being within the spot.

Despite his attempt to focus, Cainen heard the lighter wheel being flicked. It sounded 100 times louder than his own ragged breathing.

Charlie began talking softly, as if he were involved in a religious ritual . . . or a sexual experience.

Charlie kneeled down between Cainen's legs. As he extended the lighter down toward Cainen's testicles, he felt his penis beginning to become erect.

"You're gonna like this. Yeah, you're *really* gonna like this. I'm gonna help you *burn* all those impurities out of your body."

Charlie's voice was low and raspy. Then Charlie began screaming. He was screaming in agony.

Cainen felt someone loosening his handcuffs. But they weren't any looser, just wet. Something was dripping from his wrists. It took Cainen several seconds to realize that it was blood dripping from the handcuffs, and that it was *he* who was screaming.

Cainen's entire body had lifted off the van floor when the flame touched his testicles. The handcuffs on his wrists had torn away the skin.

Cainen retained the presence of mind to order himself to avoid pulling his entire body weight against the metal binds on his wrists. If he was ever to get out of this (*I will get out of it!* he told himself), he could not fight if his wrists were broken.

Cainen had vowed not to scream. He had vowed to himself that he would remain quiet and hang tough no matter what they did to him.

Because his entire self-image depended upon it, it had taken Cainen several moments to realize that indeed it had been he who was screaming.

The self-reliant, shatter-proof, impenetrable self-image that Cainen had held since his early youth began shattering.

In that moment, Cainen realized that he would not only have given the Nazis his troop's position, but each member's name, religion, home address, and whether they were circumcised or not!

Cainen commanded himself to focus. Sweat streamed off his rigid body. Every muscle of his karate- and weight lifting–toned body felt as if it was flexed.

Cainen willed himself to relax. Realizing that he was holding his breath, he again began deep-breathing.

Charlie held up the lighter. Pleasure, or sexual desire, registered on his face. His voice was thick.

"Turn it on."

Cainen willed himself not to move his head, not to look at this new torture. He closed his eyes. But his heart beat faster and his head involuntarily rotated toward Cameron.

Cameron looked pale. He leaned over and depressed two buttons on a boom box by his side. When the music didn't come, Cainen realized with increasing horror (and disgust) that they were recording his murder!

A voice, far back in Cainen's police mind, told him that if *his* torture was being recorded, then so must have the other torture-murders. Evidence.

Cainen heard the screaming again. And this time he immediately knew it was his voice.

Cainen had many bones broken and had been injured many times in karate matches. He had also been kicked in the crotch. But there was no agony like this. His whole world was on fire.

Cainen arched his back, the only unrestrained part of his body. The rope burned the skin off his ankles. The cuffs dug deeper into his wrists, peeling the skin down to the bone. Blood poured from his wrists.

Cainen's head banged against the floorboard, opening the wound where Cameron had first hit him. Blood seeped under his head and back.

After several seconds, or an eternity, the flame stopped. Several seconds later, Cainen stopped screaming. He smelled burning flesh and felt nauseous and light-headed. He was breathing hard and fast. The respiration sounded ragged. Cainen realized that he was hyperventilating.

He had to focus. To concentrate. To reach his center.

In karate and in Kung Fu, all inner energy comes from a point between the navel and the groin. This point has different names, depending on the country originating the martial art. Cainen knew the area as the *t'an t'ien* from Kung Fu.

The martial arts teach that the inner energy, or *ki* (pronounced "key"), that emanates from this point is the central life force of a person and of the universe.

Cainen tried to concentrate on this point. Instead, he vomited.

Cainen turned his head to avoid choking. Because he hadn't eaten that day, all that came out was saliva. The saliva mixed with the blood from his head wound and with the sweat that was dribbling off his body.

Charlie held up the lighter again. Cainen looked down the length of his body at Charlie's sweat-misted face and realized that Charlie was a sadist as well as a murderer. He was getting off on this! He was enjoying the power and control as much as Cainen's agony. Despite all the rape investigations Cainen had completed, it was only now that he fully realized what it must be like for a woman to be victimized in such a manner.

Cainen knew that there would be no hesitation in his killing Charlie, if ever the opportunity presented itself. But he didn't see much likelihood of such an opportunity arising in the immediate future.

Cainen believed in God. Or at least in *a* God.

So Cainen started to pray. Silently, so that Charlie wouldn't be given any satisfaction in his power trip.

Cainen fought to remain conscious as Charlie put the flame under his testicles a third time.

Charlie held the lighter under Cainen's scrotum for several seconds. Steve's scream mixed with Charlie's moan as Charlie ejaculated inside his blue jeans.

Cainen continued screaming. And Charlie felt himself immediately becoming erect again.

Cainen felt the pain coming from further away. Distant. Small grey dustclouds filled his vision. The nausea was ending. Only the smell of burnt skin remained.

* * *

When Leaks and Miller returned with their nachos, Cainen was nowhere to be found. Though he didn't give a shit about the undercover officer, Leaks was worried about his own malfeasance.

Tossing the half-eaten nachos into the backseat to gorge on later, Leaks raced the Pinto up and down the Boulevard and the neighboring blocks. He even checked the sheriff's side beyond La Brea, where he was stopped by an LASD patrol unit for going through a stop sign. Impatiently badging his way out of the stop by holding his open wallet out the window, Leaks resumed his unsuccessful search.

Leaks was hesitant to contact the sarge. As much as Barkley was one of the boys because he spent his career in the streets, he was also a principled motherfucker.

He wouldn't be happy with them losing Cainen, particularly not if he knew it had been in exchange for an unauthorized nachos break.

As it grew later, Miller grew anxious.

"Shouldn't we notify Sergeant Barkley that we lost him?"

"Yeah, we'll notify the sarge," countered the senior officer. "Let's just check a couple a more places. He probably just went to take a leak." *Or to get a blowjob, more likely. And because of that faggot, now my tit's in a wringer!* thought Leaks.

"Yeah, we'll notify Sergeant Barkley." *But first I have to teach this snot-nosed probationer the "birds and bees" of police work,* thought Leaks. *Covering for your partner means more than watching his back at a burglary call.*

When I lie, kid, you better swear to it.

* * *

Maybe I'm dying.

No, I'm losing consciousness. I'm . . .

Cainen's head rolled to the side. His eyes closed. His body lowered, almost gently, to the van floor. Blood dripped from his head and from the bindings on his wrists and ankles.

Cameron thought Cainen had died. He looked at Lisa. She was still spacin'.

"Is he dead?"

"No," Charlie's voice rasped, "the faggot just passed out."

"You gonna waste him?"

"No, I'm gonna take him out dancing! Of course we're gonna waste the pervert. But not yet. Help me turn the faggot over. I want to have some fun first."

To Charlie, his victims were subhuman. He almost never referred to them as "him" or "the person." Instead, since they were chattel under his control, Charlie used derogatory pronouns to refer to the objects of his aggression.

Cainen's ten years of training had reached further into his psyche than only his conscious being. His subconscious had become the hardened core of the samurai that he imagined he had once been.

Perhaps, if souls really do return to Earth in some universal plan, Cainen's inner psyche truly was that of a former warrior.

All people have inner strength that is concealed beneath the surface. Everyone is aware of this power, and even hardened criminals avoid attacking children in the accompaniment of their mothers in respect of this awareness.

Therapists, citing primal scream therapy, suggest that this strength stems from our ancestors. Not from mothers and fathers, nor even grandparents, but from the first slime that had the tenacity to crawl from the ocean onto the solitude of land.

Few people have conscious contact with this untapped reserve of determination. Army Delta Force, Navy SEALS, and martial artists have learned to control, or at least communicate with, this powerful reserve. This *ki*.

Cainen's *ki* called to him. It ordered his physical body to respond. No one can tell what chemical reactions spewed between the neuron synapses, but something overrode Cainen's pain and exhaustion. Something brought Cainen closer to wakefulness.

Something internal advised Cainen that his opportunity was near.

"Cover him with the shotgun while I turn him over."

Charlie handed the shotgun to Cameron, who put it under his arm. Cameron aimed the gun at Cainen but kept his finger off the trigger. He didn't want to accidentally shoot Charlie.

"What you doing?"

"I'm going to turn him over." Charlie undid the rope around Cainen's bloody ankles.

Cainen felt his legs being lifted and his body turned. He remained limp but peered through his almost-touching eyelids. He heard the young voice to his left.

"Man, this guy's out cold."

Charlie reached into his pocket and took out the handcuff key. He handed it to Cameron.

"Just unlock the one wrist near you. Leave the other one cuffed in case the fag wakes up."

"Why we turning him over, Charlie?"

" 'Cause I'm gonna fuck this faggot up his asshole!"

Cainen heard that. He remained limp, but the anger welled inside him.

This piece of a shit didn't care about AIDS. He wasn't on any mission to stop the spread of a disease. You could be sure he wasn't going to use a rubber during anal intercourse!

The anger grew all-encompassing and powerful. The duplicity of the situation infuriated Cainen.

This scum didn't give a fuck about AIDS or anything else. He was just senselessly victimizing homosexual young men for his own sadistic pleasure. He was killing for killing's sake and trying to use a deadly disease as an excuse.

Just as suddenly, the target of Cainen's anger abruptly changed. Simultaneously, the anger grew geometrically.

The anger was no longer directed at Charlie. Cainen realized that he had been set up. For five years, Los Angeles Police officers had tried to set Cainen up; they had tried to get him killed. And for five years, Cainen had outsmarted them by staying one step ahead. He always carried his gun, anticipated their next move, and watched his back. No matter how hard the LAPD tried, Cainen had remained a professional.

Then the chief had appealed to Cainen's sense of law-enforcement duty, to his dedication to his profession. And Cainen had hit the street without a weapon, without real backup, and without anyone with integrity knowing where he was.

The chief could probably claim that I had initiated the entire investigation on my own. Or that I was out hustling, Cainen thought.

In either case, the LAPD would be free from blame for my death. And, in either case, the Department could finally discredit my integrity.

"See," the chief would say, "homosexuals really *can't* be cops . . ."

It was an all-win situation for the LAPD management and a no-win situation for Cainen.

* * *

Sergeant Barkley had had the two officers report back to the station immediately. Even though Leaks had the discretion to avoid the radio and use a landline, Barkley didn't want to hear it over the phone. He wanted to *see* the two when they told him what had happened.

He wanted to know what caused *this* royal fuck-up.

The story didn't fly by Barkley. Leaks told the whole story with Miller, the probationer, looking as if he had lost a contact lens. The youth never took his eyes off the floor.

It could have been that the probationer was embarrassed about the accidental loss of their officer. But Barkley had been on the street too long to buy that. And Cainen was too good of an officer to have messed up, unless something had gone down without Cainen's voluntary involvement.

"So you're telling me that Cainen signaled you that he was done for the night?" questioned the sergeant.

"Yes, sir," answered Leaks.

Miller was silent.

"And why didn't you watch him until he got safely to his car?"

"We had never done that before. Cainen always parked near the Boulevard, and it would have been suspicious for us to follow him up the street. We always just headed back to the station at the same time."

"And there was no way you could have misunderstood Cainen's signal?"

"No, sir."

"Miller?"

The young man stayed silent at first. Then he looked at Leaks, then down at the floor again before answering. Barkley missed none of it.

"No, sir."

"And what was the signal?"

"He would take out a comb and comb his hair. Then he would hit the brush against something before putting it back in his pocket." Leaks again.

"No chance he was just combing his hair?"

"No, it was definitely the signal."

"Miller?"

"No, sir." Still trying to find that contact lens.

"So maybe something happened to him while he was walking back to his car."

"You know how Cainen is, Sarge, getting into strangers' cars and all."

Barkley fixed Leaks with a cold stare that left no doubt about his knowing how Cainen was. *Yeah, I know how he is, Leaks, and I'd take one of him over ten of you,* Barkley thought.

"You'd better go and look around the area that he was parked," was all the sergeant said. After a moment, Barkley added, "I'll get the rest of the PED officers to look around the area with you."

"Yes, sir." Leaks again; Miller was looking at the door as if he had finally remembered where he had left his contact lenses. Outside this room, that was for sure.

Both officers exited.

There was no use in further questioning these two, thought Barkley. *Miller had just gotten his first real indoctrination to police work. With that obsequious behavior of his, he's chosen his side and will have to live forever with his decision. We've all had to make that same decision, and once you do, there's no going back. The cover-ups just become bigger each time.*

But there was no doubt that there was some "lyin' and denyin' " going on here, surmised Barkley.

Leaks had *never* called him "sir" before.

262

* * *

Cainen's anger had become a separate entity, a glowing, ethereal body distinct from his own. But Cainen didn't move or open his eyes.

"Just flip the fag on his side," ordered Charlie, taking the handcuff key back from Cameron.

Cainen felt Charlie roughly pulling his left leg over his right, tugging on his right shin in an effort to roll him onto his stomach.

Cameron pushed on Cainen's left shoulder, rolling him onto his side.

Cainen's left wrist and both legs were free.

And that was when Cainen moved.

With all his anger focused, Cainen pulled his knees up into his chest, at the same time sliding down. The chain on his right wrist pulled taut.

As Charlie tried to straighten up, Cainen kicked his left foot out as hard as he could. The kick caught Charlie square in the chest.

The force of the kick propelled Charlie backward toward the rear of the van. Charlie hit the back doors. The power behind the kick caused the rear doors (which Cainen didn't know were there) to fly open. Charlie soared backward out the rear of the van.

The movement sent excruciating agony and nausea throughout Cainen's entire body, all emanating from his groin.

Cainen blocked all sensation out of his mind. He knew that he only had precious seconds.

With his eyes now adjusted to the dark, Cainen spun his body toward the front of the van. He saw Cameron raising the shotgun.

Using the side of his right foot to increase the width, Cainen kicked upward as Cameron took aim. Cainen's foot struck the shotgun barrel, sending it speeding upward. At the moment that it struck the ceiling of the van, it discharged.

The blockage of the barrel caused by the roof caused a small explosion, blowing a fist-size hole in the ceiling and simultaneously bending the shotgun barrel.

Cainen hadn't stopped to watch. In Kung Fu, any technique, no matter how disabling, is considered ineffectual without follow-up. This had been drilled into Cainen for years by his teacher (prior to taking Hapkido), until no technique had fewer than five moves.

In order to spin his body around, Cainen had lifted up his extremities and then dropped them at once on the van floor. The move had sent waves of semiconsciousness through him. His damaged groin throbbed in agony, as the pain fought for dominance in his mind.

263

In a haze, Cainen's next move was a common karate technique. Placing his lower left foot behind Cameron's front leg, Cainen turned it so that the top of the foot hooked Cameron behind the Achilles tendon.

As hard as he could, Cainen lashed out with his right foot, hitting Cameron in the thigh. With Cameron's lower leg being held in place by Cainen's hooked foot, Cameron's knee became a fulcrum, snapping, sending him backward and down.

Cameron's back and head struck the rear of the passenger's seat before slamming down onto the floorboard. Taking time to aim, Cainen raised his right foot high above Cameron's head. Still lying on his side, Cainen paused only for a moment before his heel sped downward, crashing into Cameron's throat.

Cainen could feel the van floor under his heel as it crushed Cameron's larynx.

Cainen's labored breathing mixed with the gurgling from Cameron's open mouth. Cameron's eyes glazed over as he drowned in his own blood.

* * *

It had been over an hour since the officers had last seen Cainen. That was too long, thought Sergeant Barkley. He called the vice lieutenant at home to make the notification.

"Where do you think he is?" asked the lieutenant.

"I don't know, Marc, but he always came directly to the station after he finished a shift." Barkley paused before continuing. The pause was out of concern, not for dramatic effect. "I think he's in trouble."

"You think he got picked up by the murderer?"

It always amazed Barkley, who had spent his entire fifteen years out in the field instead of in an office job, that even experienced cops assumed that the most heinous crimes were committed by one culprit instead of several. It was almost as if they wanted to limit the extent of evil by supposing that one person was an exception, rather than the rule.

"I'm not assuming anything other than that he's a good cop and good cops stick to a routine. Something's caused Cainen to deviate."

"And?" A one-word question.

"And I think we shouldn't take any chances. The rumors are that this person or people have killed more than once. Maybe as many as a dozen times. They won't hesitate to do it again."

"What should we do?" The lieutenant was panicking. Lieutenant Bonderville had eleven years on The Job. Except for his first two years after the academy and his first year as a sergeant, all his time had been in administrative assignments. Manuals and Orders, Records and Identification, and as an assistant or adjutant to the brass.

Like most of these "golden boys" who held the rank, they didn't know shit from shinola. They just didn't have the experience. Decisions were made by field supervisors. Regardless of whether the decisions were good or bad, the Department judged them by the end result. If the end result was positive, the golden boys grabbed the credit. If the feces hit the fan, the field supervisor's uniform caught the crap. This shielded the golden boys from too much damage to their illustrious careers.

"I think we'd better CYA," said Barkley. This was *always* the name of the game. "I'll have the PED units look around Santa Monica Boulevard for any sign of Cainen. You'd better notify Captain Carter, so he can call Captain Wilson at home. Wilson will probably notify DHD or the chief of staff."

DHD, Detective Headquarters Division, handled all the major notifications. If anything happened to anyone and it might affect something to do with someone, you notified DHD.

"OK, I'll call Carter," replied the lieutenant.

Of course you will, to appear competent and in charge, thought Barkley. *And you'll want me in a position to handle all the decision making. Major scapegoat time. I might as well volunteer; I'm gonna be drafted anyway . . . and it isn't the first time.*

"I'll handle things here in the field."

"Good," sighed the higher-ranking officer. "I'll get back to you if Carter has any additional instructions."

Or any words of wisdom, thought Barkley. He was about to say good-bye and get to work.

"Oh," interrupted the lieutenant's voice, "do you happen to have Captain Carter's home number?"

* * *

The reserves of his training tantalized Cainen. He was instantly alert for a counterattack from Charlie. None came.

Cainen realized that he would need to free himself immediately in order to offer a defense.

Immediately.

There was no time to crawl around trying to locate a key that could have dropped anywhere inside the van.

Studies completed at the University of California in Los Angeles in the 1970s demonstrated that people with training in concentration,

265

such as yogis and martial artists, could extend the electrical fields that emanated from around their bodies. Those involved in the study were able to increase their auras at will. The electrical fields were photographed with special cameras.

The martial artists explained that the energy was *ki* and that the power could be directed toward another person. It could also be directed against an object, such as a board, thereby breaking the board before a hand went through it. They explained that this protected the hand against injury.

Of course, callouses also protected the hand.

Whether the phenomenon was true or not, Cainen knew that concentration could direct *ki*. This was especially true when the body was used as a fulcrum.

Ignoring the pain in his groin, Cainen kneeled on his left knee. He put his right foot flat and braced his right elbow with the manacled wrist atop the knee.

The fingers of Cainen's right hand splayed open and shook, first slowly and then violently.

Cainen concentrated, willing the energy to his right hand. He visualized the energy as a glowing red ball, picturing it emanating from his *t'an t'ien* and rising up his center and down his arm to the trapped wrist.

His concentration only wavered for a moment, when his humor reminded him how smart criminals were. They often hid handcuff keys inside their belts as part of the buckle.

How much easier *that* would have been!

Concentrate.

The mind cannot wander if you don't let it.

Focus.

Cainen visualized what he wanted to happen. The energy reached his wrist and his splayed fingers. He pictured the handcuff snapping from his wrist.

Using his elbow and knee as a fulcrum, Cainen pulled up with all his considerable strength. His right hand shuddered convulsively.

Cainen's anticipation and hurried breathing sent a rush of adrenaline through his body. Adrenaline, which is a prehistoric "fight-or-flight" reaction, is also a natural anesthetic. The anesthetic effect numbed Cainen's mind to the pain of bone against metal.

Cainen willed the cuff to snap. But that didn't happen.

The weakest point in a handcuff is not with the cuff itself. The cuff is solid steel with steel ratchets. The weak point of the cuff design is in the soldered chain links.

Many PCPers, high on PCP and immune to pain from the analgesic, have snapped the links in handcuffs. Special double-connected cuffs were designed specifically because of this.

Neither of the two handcuffs, one grasping the bolt in the van floor and one on Cainen's wrist, detached.

But the solder separated.

Using a "Kiai" yell, which gives 10 percent more power, Cainen pulled up and outward.

And the chain link snapped.

A second later, Cainen crawled up front and exited out the driver door of the van.

The police academy teaches that you never pursue a criminal directly in his line of travel. When the suspect jumps over a wall, the officer should go farther down the wall. If the suspect is waiting to ambush the officer, the ambush is avoided by this tactic. Many an officer has given a surprise by going over a wall and landing behind a suspect, who was waiting with a two-by-four in his hands.

Cainen flattened himself against the van. He crouched down and looked under the van. He could see no movement and no standing feet.

Cainen looked up. As he had expected, the moon was full. (*Shit like tonight could only happen under a full moon.*)

Clouds periodically eclipsed the moon, throwing the desert (Cainen saw that it was desert) into a darkened nocturnal landscape.

Crouching low to make himself less of a target, Cainen glided soundlessly to the end of the van. There, Cainen paused and looked around behind the van.

Charlie was gone.

Charlie couldn't have reentered the van, or Cainen would have heard sounds and felt the van shift under Charlie's weight.

So Charlie was out there, possibly armed.

Cainen looked around him. Only blackness.

Cainen debated whether to try to start the van and locate the police or pursue Charlie. The debate was short.

Charlie was evil. Evil as pure as Charlie could not be allowed to remain on this Earth—remain and continue to harm innocents. How many more would be harmed by Charlie if he got free?

How many more victims?

Would Charlie be given the death penalty? Cainen asked himself. *Would a technicality free him? Would he be paroled in five years like many of the murderers in California? Maybe in three years if it was a manslaughter conviction? Or maybe put in some insecure facility if it was determined he was crazy?*

How long would I have to watch my back until Charlie tried for vengeance? Cainen wondered.

No. One way or the other, it would end tonight. There would be one more death in this desert.

* * *

Before Barkley could raise the PED units on the radio to transfer them from Sunset to Santa Monica Boulevard, the strange stuff started to happen. It started with Lieutenant Bonderville's return call.

Less than ten minutes after hanging up the phone, Barkley was back in his office talking with the lieutenant again.

"Tim?"

"Yes," answered Sergeant Barkley.

"Listen; Carter doesn't want PED concentrating on Santa Monica Boulevard. Without any prearranged task force, he could get in trouble."

"What the hell are you talking about, trouble?! Don't you think Cainen's in *trouble?*" Barkley accented the second "trouble" with a dash of sarcasm. *What the hell was going on here?* he thought. *An officer might need assistance.* Barkley didn't give a shit if the officer was gay, bisexual, or a hermaphrodite. The LAPD affirmative action slogan said: "Our cops come in only one color—blue."

"Now, Tim, don't get bent out of shape."

At thirty-eight, Barkley hated a condescending tone of voice—especially from a golden boy.

"Tim," whined the lieutenant, "we don't *know* that Cainen's in trouble. Cainen knew the risks when he accepted the assignment. So let's just wait a bit while Carter runs it up the fagpole." Barkley heard the lieutenant blush. "I mean *flagpole.*"

A Freudian slip if Barkley had ever heard one. He knew what was really going on in the lieutenant's mind. Or in Captain Carter's, since the lieutenant was just following orders.

Barkley also knew that it was useless to try to change any LAPD manager's mind. It was like trying to buy a different color of toilet bowl cleaner. You had two choices: blue or bluer. It was just their mind-set.

Barkley was silent.

"Uh, Tim?"

Silence.

"Listen; I'll get back to you as soon as Carter talks with Wilson."

268

And Wilson talks to Bureau, Bureau talks to Office of Operations, OO talks to chief of staff, and the chief of staff tries to track down the chief at some political dinner.

That could take the rest of my life, thought Barkley. *More likely, it could take the rest of Cainen's.*

"All right, Marc. You know where to reach me," said the sergeant.

The buoyancy came back into Bonderville's voice. He had gotten Barkley to give in, without having to resort to pulling rank.

"Great, Tim. I'm glad you'll go along with the program. I'll get back to you as soon as I hear something."

"OK, Marc." Before the phone was hung up, Barkley was up and moving. Grabbing his Sam Browne off his desk, Barkley snapped the fasteners to hold it to his thinner inner belt. At his age, he was too old to support the twenty pounds of the belt while he was in the station. Why ruin the back? Besides, it was too uncomfortable to wear while sitting.

Barkley didn't like to admit that he really took the belt off as a silent protest to being trapped behind a desk. He hated being out of the field. If he ever made it to lieutenant *(which wasn't likely without a single stupid, useless college class),* it would only be because he was tired of doing the work for all these university-educated, indecisive bureaucrats like Bonderville.

His belt attached, Barkley virtually ran out to his patrol car. Bonderville had said that PED couldn't besiege Santa Monica Boulevard; he hadn't said that Barkley couldn't.

Making sure his second radio in the Convertacom was on, Barkley drove to the Boulevard. Barkley circled the area repeatedly, from Western to La Brea and on into sheriff's territory. He ignored the friendly waves of the passing deputies in their patrol cars. No time for anything but finding Cainen, he thought.

Thirty minutes later, Barkley began checking the main hustler bars. He started at Numbers in West Hollywood, a chic restaurant-bar at Sunset and Crescent Heights. Here the older clientele paired off with the young boys in the booths, while the available meat stood against one wall.

With negative results and an increasing frustration, Barkley checked the Spotlight and every other bar with male prostitutes. At each bar it was the same. The bartenders stopped serving and watched; then the patrons began whispering among themselves.

Though uniformed cops often did "bar checks" inside the straight bars, to cruise the women, they never entered the gay bars except to raid them.

One might think that the bars would appreciate a uniformed presence due to the increase in gay-bashings. Instead, they feared harassment, unjustified arrests, and their lives and careers being ruined.

Being a sympathetic and intelligent man, Barkley understood the feelings of the bar occupants. Everyone in the bar stared at him as he looked around for Cainen.

At another time, Barkley might apologize or explain his encroachment. Not tonight. They would just have to forgive his lack of etiquette this once. There was just no time.

Barkley hurriedly exited each bar, as the customers turned to look at the bartenders for some clue to the intrusion.

Barkley had discussed Cainen many times with his wife. He had told her of Cainen's bravery in the face of such adversity and of his own wonder at how someone as intelligent as Cainen could possibly think that he (one man!) could challenge the system.

And he told his wife of Cainen's unwavering integrity.

Together, Barkley and his wife had developed a mutual respect for Cainen (and an unspoken wish that he *could* best the system).

Barkley and his wife could also relate to Cainen's fight. Barkley had come from a strict Scottish Protestant family. His wife, with the maiden name Manriquez, was from an even stricter Mexican Catholic household.

It was Barkley's second marriage. His first had ended when he entered the police academy. No respectable Scottish wife would stand by while her husband entered a field historically reserved for Irishmen! He married Maria less than a year later.

Neither of the families forgave Barkley's prior divorce. Their respective religions would not allow it. And neither accepted the current marriage for the same reason. It infuriated them more that Barkley's marriage to Maria was even more enduring and peaceful than their own.

Barkley cherished his wife. And she worshipped him. And except for one night every 730 days ("Whether I need it or not," Barkley was prone to boast during poker games at LAPD divisional steak fry gatherings), he was completely faithful to Maria.

He knew that he could not face his wife until he had located Cainen.

At 2100 hours, 9:00 P.M., Barkley returned to Hollywood Station for another call from Lieutenant Bonderville. No news yet; the lieutenant was just checking in. By 2110, Barkley was back in the field.

Feeling useless, Barkley started checking the gay bars and dance clubs in the area.

Cainen had to be somewhere!

* * *

Steve Cainen was thirteen when he switched from Edgar Rice Burroughs to Ian Fleming. He had skipped Burroughs's science fiction novels, instead concentrating on the Tarzan books. Steve idolized the ability of one man to beat the elements through his highly honed skills. *That* he could relate to.

Steve read all of the Bond books each year for much the same literary reason. He was as much fascinated by Fleming's cosmopolitan prose as by Bond's ingenuity.

Steve retained his collection of Bond and Tarzan books. He had continued reading the Bond series when John Gardner took over, but it was only when his brother handed him the paperback. And Steve always returned it when he was done.

It wasn't the same.

Gardner provided an outstanding protagonist, but his writing couldn't match the worldliness of Fleming. It was like reading a movie screenplay.

In Fleming's *Doctor No*, Steve had read that people had difficulty fighting in the nude. In one chapter, Bond was successful in his attempt to outfight the bad guy. Though Bond had been rousted from his bed (Bond always slept naked; the essence of any heterosexual superspy, sleeping beside the beautiful blond female double agent), his training had allowed him to overcome his inhibitions and provided him with the requisite skills.

As always, Fleming's writings caused Steve to think long after he had put the book down (which he found difficult to do). Steve filed away each bit of information in the expectation of later need.

As soon as Cainen had gotten his own apartment, he had practiced fighting techniques in the raw before going to bed each night.

So there was no hesitation before Cainen retraced his steps around to the front of the van as he cautiously searched for Charlie. Only one of them would leave the desert this night.

Though the Lancaster wilderness was primarily a flatland, out-croppings of rock could be seen in the moonlight. Hills of dirt, from the long-ago mineshaft excavations, provided additional areas for a person to hide.

The bottoms of Cainen's feet were calloused from karate and bare-foot jogs. Cainen still walked slowly and carefully, with bent knees, avoiding any sound while listening for any crack of brush. He knew that even with a full moon, it was his ears that would provide him with any warning as to the location of his quarry.

Cainen also walked slowly due to the constantly increasing pain that rose like a monolith from his groin.

Cainen cautiously passed by one of the dirt mounds. Perhaps his senses were dulled due to the pain he was experiencing, or perhaps his adversary was more skilled than he in stalking. In either case, it was too late when Cainen heard the swinging of a two-by-four board behind his head.

* * *

The chief had finished his evening jog near his home in Sherman Oaks. He remained a fit runner, jogging away the tensions and turmoil of his position. Periodically he joined SWAT or Metro in their runs. It wasn't that he particularly liked anyone in those units; it was just that the men in these units were typically as conservative as he was. They did police work the good old way: kick ass and take names. They hated politicians and public opinion as much as he did. And they were all men (No women yet, thank God!) and mostly white, except for their new captain, who was a sharp manager, despite being black. Besides, the chief's presence among the backbone of the Department was good for morale. And Metro was as close to the patrol backbone as he was willing to get without wanting to perform a major chiropractic job.

This evening, the chief was joined by his Chicano bodyguard. It took some getting used to, having a young Chicano with him, since he had become used to the older white marksman he used to travel with.

This Chicano boy was the toughest member of the elite Metro unit. He looked like all he did was work out. *And with the majority of mental asylum rejects living in L.A., I can use the extra protection*, thought the chief.

Besides, the boy was church-going, even if it wasn't the *right* church.

Using the towel on his porch, the chief paced, cooling off. Five miles at night and three in the morning. *Whew! Show me another chief in California who can keep up with that regimen. Or in the whole United States for that matter.*

The Chicano boy was coming up his driveway. Usually the boy went home directly after the run . . . probably to work out some more. *I can use the panic button direct to Van Nuys Division if I have a problem*, thought the Chief. *Something else must be up.*

At the top of the drive, the bodyguard stopped respectfully.

"Problems?" questioned the chief of his loyal aide.

"Sir, your chief of staff just paged me. He wants you to call him at home right away."

"OK, thanks. I'll take it inside. See you tomorrow morning at 6:30 sharp."

"Good night, sir."

The chief waved a hand and went inside his front door. *The wife must be cooking*, the chief thought as he sniffed the air. He hoped that whatever the problem was, he wouldn't have to leave his house. The chief of the Los Angeles Police Department only had one thought as he made his way toward his den: *All I want now is a nice, cool shower before dinner.*

* * *

With only enough time to duck in order to protect his head, Cainen was struck fully on the shoulder blades. Instinctively, Cainen locked out his legs and turned his head sideways after the blow. His open palms and forearms absorbed most of the fall. But the pain in his upper back was nothing compared to the torrent flaming from his testicles, which were jarred by the strike.

Cainen felt the wetness as all of his wounds bled afresh. His mind did an immediate evaluation of his ability to defend himself. His shoulders were only bruised, but the waves of nausea caused by his groin injury were hindering his ability to counter.

Cainen's years of training made his responses automatic. As he immediately rolled *into* his opponent, instead of away, the second strike of the board hit the ground instead of his head.

Charlie had armed himself with a weapon, probably one of the rotted mine shaft coverings. Cainen preferred to leave both his hands unencumbered, thus free for any eventuality. That way, he could do twice as much as an opponent with one weapon.

When Cainen rolled into Charlie's shins, he was facing up. Turning to his side, parallel with Charlie, Cainen spread his legs wide. Placing his lower left leg behind Charlie's calves and his right leg in front of Charlie's knees, Cainen closed the scissor, knocking Charlie backward.

Cainen rolled away quickly, pausing to catch his breath and swallow the bile in his throat.

The secret to a successful defense against an impact weapon, such as a board, was the same as that against a sword. In Hapkido, Cainen had trained unarmed against a sword. The secret was to stay in close.

An impact weapon is used in swinging and slashing motions, which can't be accomplished in close quarters. Very few people were skilled in close-quarters fighting.

But Cainen needed time to clear his head. He needed to regain his breath. He needed to *focus*.

And he needed to control and direct his *ki*.

Instead of closing in on his downed opponent, Cainen stayed out of striking range and stood up. Taking a defensive stance, he turned to face the outline of his opponent.

Charlie was also standing.

*　*　*

Inside his den, the chief flipped on his antique gold desk lamp with the cashier's green shade. Sitting behind the mahogany desk, he lifted the receiver and pulled his head back to look at the automatic dialer from farther away. He hated getting old, and he'd be damned if he was going to wear glasses.

Squinting, the chief pushed the correct button. The automatic dialer was his only concession to the modern era of office appliances.

The chief of staff answered after the first ring. That was a bad sign.

"You wanted me to call you, Jim?"

"Yes, Chief. We have a slight problem. Cainen is missing."

"Who?"

"Cainen, the gay officer we put undercover on the hustler murders?"

"OK, right. He's missing from the street?"

"Yes, sir. He was out on Santa Monica Boulevard, undercover. He signaled to his backup to call it quits for the night and then disappeared. Captain Wilson wants to know what you want him to do."

"How do you know that Cainen didn't go home?"

"They've called his home. No answer. The PED sergeant is taking a ride by there now."

"Well, maybe he's out playing around."

"He always checked out with the PED sergeant, making his report for the night. He never ended this early before, and he always went directly to the station after his tour."

"Well, don't notify his family. That's all I need is for one of them to contact the media."

"Do you want Vice and PED to hit Santa Monica Boulevard and see what they can turn up?"

"No. That might generate publicity. Let's just lay low for awhile. For all we know, Cainen might be out having sex with some man he met. Let's just take it easy until we hear something."

There was a long pause, as if the chief of staff had something else he was debating saying.

"Anything else, Jim?" queried the chief of the most powerful police force in the United States. "If not, just brief me tomorrow morning on any of the developments."

The chief of staff had just been subtly informed that this matter was not important enough for the chief to be disturbed at home.

The staff officer felt that the media implications of this circumstance were as urgent as the danger to Cainen's life. He wanted the Department to be a step ahead of the press. That would give all the brass time to put on a united front.

But the chief was the chief. And he'd been caught with his pants down before—like when he told the press that he agreed with his predecessor, former Chief Daryl Gates, that "casual drug users ought to be taken out and shot."

But the chief always made it through the media scrapes. And the city council always backed him.

Still . . .

"Uh, sir?"

"What is it, Jim?" The chief was getting annoyed. It wasn't like a staff officer to question him. He demanded absolute loyalty, and he had established a chain of command that surrounded him with yes-men.

"The mayor's office called about this."

"Damn the mayor! This is a police department matter. We'll handle it in the morning. Good night." The chief hung up.

Both officers stared at their phones as if they were living beings, rather than inanimate objects of communication.

The staff officer was staring at the receiver in his hand until he realized how foolish he must look. He hung up.

He had been chastised. A religious man like the chief only used swearwords when he was really riled. And riling the chief of police was a bad career move. It had cost more than one staff officer to be moved to a closet as an office, in charge of broom issuance, with no secretary or assistant. Five years prior, one of the captains did a study on Department morale in which anonymous line and staff officers said that the cause of poor morale was the chief.

Boy! The chief hadn't liked that one. The chief had wanted the name of every officer that had been interviewed. Rather than reveal the names of those whom he had promised anonymity, the captain had destroyed his records.

Though the captain came out number one on every promotional exam since, he had never been promoted.

Nope. Cainen would have to fend for himself. Gays never should have tried to come on The Job.

The chief of staff rubbed his temples, in an effort to assuage his conscience. It wasn't the first time.

The LAPD wasn't a good place for people with a conscience.

The staff officer thought of his retirement again. Three years, six months, and thirty-six days to go.

But who's counting?

The chief of police was also counting. When he got to ten, he took a deep breath and relaxed.

Damn politicians! Damn gays! Everyone telling *him* how *he* should do *his* job. What did they know about law enforcement? Did they have thirty years in the profession?

Maybe I'll run for mayor this next term. Really shake things up. Show them how the citizens support law and order.

The chief took his eyes off the phone. He took another deep breath. He leaned his head back and sniffed the air.

Putting the towel around his neck, the chief stood and headed for the kitchen. *Time to see what Mother is cooking up*, he thought.

* * *

Cainen was bent at the waist, his hands at his thighs, forcing away the waves of nausea. Facing his standing opponent, Cainen debated whether to use his voice to psychologically disadvantage his opponent. He needed some way to gain the advantage over Charlie's better physical condition. Instead, Cainen chose to save his energy and do cleansing breaths.

He saw the outline of the board rise above his opponent's head. The silhouette spoke. The voice was low and menacing.

"You're dead, faggot. I'm gonna crush your faggot head. You're gonna die like every other homo. Only you ain't gonna have time to die of AIDS, you piece of shit."

Cainen remained silent. Let his enemy use up energy verbalizing. It gave Cainen time to recuperate. He wasn't as strong as his opponent in his weakened state. And he had wounds he had to protect. Though he could block out much of the pain, the nausea made it nearly impossible to concentrate.

The outline took a step toward Cainen. He was stalking Cainen like a tiger stalks its prey. Too cautious and too much in control. Cainen's mind automatically digested the weaknesses in his opponent's movements.

"You know, faggot, all those other gay boys I killed, they deserved to die. All I was doing was keeping us good people alive by clearing out you AIDS-spreaders. Those other faggots deserved to die."

Like a fuckin' TV evangelist, Cainen thought. *I feel like I'm in the Twilight Zone and I got stuck on a fundamentalist religious channel.*

Cainen noted that Charlie's movements didn't match his words of hatred. Charlie maneuvered forward without crossing his legs over each other. He could keep good leverage that way. It was obvious he was a street fighter, dangerous when in control and if given the opportunity.

Cainen had no intention of giving him such an opportunity. He knew he had to gain the upper hand if he intended to survive. He had to not only anticipate Charlie's actions; he had to *cause* them.

Causing opponents to act was one of the skills that *karatekas* learn prior to getting their black belts. Verbal Aikido. Even many police departments taught a course in what they called "verbal judo."

"Did you butt-fuck them before you killed them, Charlie?" Called him by name. Guaranteed to get his attention. The questions would be off-the-wall enough to break his concentration.

After a moment's hesitation, Charlie replied. "Yeah, I fucked 'em. They had a real man once in their miserable lives before they died." Charlie laughed.

Still in a low, menacing voice, Cainen thought. *Still too much in control.*

"If you fucked them, Charlie, then you probably caught AIDS." Silence.

That would get to him. I have to get him angry.

"You liked fucking them, didn't you, Charlie?"

More silence. More.

"You liked it a lot. Felt good to you, didn't it, Charlie?" Cainen put a taunting inflection on the use of his opponent's name.

No response, but Cainen could hear the tempo of Charlie's breathing increase.

It was working.

"Have trouble getting it up with girls, Charlie?" Cainen made sure that his voice was strong. He waited. It shouldn't take long.

"Fuck you, faggot! I fuck lots of girls!" But Charlie's mind fixed on when he went soft on Lisa in the motel room several weeks prior. *But that was because she was having her period*, he thought to himself unconvincingly, breathing hard.

Cainen had noted that Charlie had yelled his response. Yelled loud in anger and defensiveness.

Charlie had finally lost his cool—and his concentration.

"You know why you liked it, Charlie?" Cainen's voice was calm, speaking matter-of-factly as if he were talking about the weather, or something that was common knowledge.

"I'll tell you why, Charlie. Because you're a closet case, Charlie. You're a latent homosexual." Cainen raised his voice. "You liked butt-fucking them because you're a fag."

"Diiiiie, motherfuckerrrrr!" The silhouette raced toward him, board in both hands above his head.

Cainen had his left foot forward and his right leg back, shoulder-width apart. He was standing straight, now, with both his knees bent. His hands were open, his left slightly higher than his right.

In defenses against weapons, timing is everything. It must be perfect.

Tomoenage, like every judo technique, requires balance and a low center. As Charlie rapidly closed the distance, the board started downward toward Cainen's head.

Instead of attempting to evade the blow, Cainen moved in toward his opponent. While Charlie's arms were still above his head, Cainen met the downward slash by forming a *V* between his own raised and crossed wrists.

Rather than meet force with force, Cainen continued moving his arms downward. His left hand grabbed Charlie's right wrist. His right hand moved down to Charlie's left shoulder, grabbing the shirt tightly.

Due to the momentum, the board continued downward.

Cainen leaned back, offering no resistance to Charlie's forward progression. Then Cainen bent all the way back, laying his back on the ground. With his head raised, Cainen pulled Charlie forward, propelling him on top of Cainen's prostrate form.

It was too late for Charlie to stop the momentum.

Cainen's left foot was flat on the ground, but his right foot went up, catching Charlie on the left side of his groin.

Charlie's mouth was already open in surprise; a rush of air escaped as Cainen's right foot made contact.

Cainen pushed with his right foot. Charlie was airborne, directly above the individual he had tried to strike with the board. The board flew, abandoned, to Cainen's left. Charlie's arms flailed in an attempt to break his fall.

Cainen's hands still pulled Charlie. Charlie's lower body moved faster due to Cainen's kick, somersaulting him in midair. Before Charlie crashed to the ground, Cainen released his grip.

Cainen immediately stood and turned to face his opponent in a crouched position of advantage. And that was when he heard the sound of splintering wood.

It was followed by an echoed bloodcurdling scream.

* * *

Barkley had checked everywhere without locating Cainen. With no relief call from Bonderville, Barkley called upon his resources as a street cop.

Hitting Santa Monica Boulevard on foot, Barkley sought information. And its source—informants.

Starting at Arthur J's restaurant and moving north on Highland, then west on Santa Monica, Barkley stopped each of the street people he came across. Young, old, male, and female, Barkley described Cainen and asked if they had seen him. The sergeant remembered the tight jeans and tank top that Cainen had been wearing when he reported for work that night.

Sifting through false leads and misinformation, Barkley further interrogated the male prostitutes. First, he promised them that he wasn't looking to make an arrest. He only wanted to locate a young man who needed medication. If that didn't yield results, Barkley threatened to hold the hustler in jail until he located the person he was looking for.

The second scenario usually yielded better results. Still, no one had seen Cainen get into any cars or leave the Boulevard in the company of another hustler.

At Santa Monica and Sycamore, Barkley ran into the Cowboy.

The Cowboy denied any knowledge of a young man in tight jeans and a white tank top. When he further denied any knowledge of *anyone* on the street, claiming that he had just started working, Barkley became skeptical. Real skeptical.

The Cowboy looked as if he *lived* on the street.

Barkley was tired of the interrogation game. He handcuffed the Cowboy right away.

"You know," explained the sergeant, "I hate liars. Almost as much as I hate murderers. And since you're concealing information, you're an accessory to murder."

This panicked the Cowboy enough for him to make a speedy admission that he had seen the young man Barkley described. As Barkley's pulse quickened, the Cowboy, who said his real name was Peter Quinn, admitted working the same corner as the young man Barkley was looking for.

It wasn't until Barkley had led his handcuffed prisoner two blocks back toward his police car that the worst of his fears were confirmed.

Admitting that his real name was Peter Bishop, the Cowboy pleaded not to be taken to jail. There was a no-bail warrant for him for a robbery in El Paso.

The Cowboy told the unrelenting sergeant that the hustler he had described had gotten into a brown van driven by a long-haired youth. The Cowboy was just playing by a rule of the street: sell anyone down the river for self-preservation.

The Cowboy told the now-subdued sergeant that the word on the street was to avoid brown vans. Those hustlers who had accepted rides in brown vans had never been heard from again.

A frantic Barkley pushed the hustler down to a seated position on the curb. Using the radio on his belt, Barkley called for a PED unit to pick up the unlikely duo.

The sergeant had the PED unit drop him off at his patrol car so that he could bring it back to the station. He had the PED unit officers book the Cowboy into a holding cell while he dialed the lieutenant's home.

*　*　*

Cautiously, with the moonlight shrouded by a cloud, Cainen inched forward. He remained in his stance, with hands up and ready, moving on the balls of his feet. He shuffle-stepped across the dirt. With the ball of his right foot (his toes were pulled back), Cainen struck a hard object and stopped.

When the moon freed itself from the passing cloud cover, Cainen saw broken boards. He also saw a gaping hole in the middle of the wooden mine shaft cover.

The tormented souls of those Charlie had killed could finally rest in peace; their murderer had joined them.

And if Charlie had a soul, it would forever be in anguish, haunted and outnumbered by his innocent victims.

Cainen limped back to the van.

*　*　*

Back at Hollywood Station, Barkley's nerves were frayed. He had hung up with the lieutenant over thirty minutes ago. The lieutenant

280

had told him that someone had notified the mayor's office and that the chief of staff wanted the head of whoever had done it.

What the lieutenant had failed to confide in Barkley was that *he* had made that notification. Like every "golden boy," the lieutenant had his own ambitions of chiefdom. In anticipation of this ascendency, Bonderville had made liaisons of his own within the city administration. Working in Hollywood, the most press-conscious area of the city, this deed was simple.

The lieutenant had told Barkley to stay put until he got back to him.

Barkley paced in front of his office door. The Detective Division of Hollywood Area was large, divided by four-foot-high partitions separating almost two dozen wooden desks. The desks sat side by side in three rows. Each desk hosted a city-issued phone. The room was empty except for Barkley.

Every two or three minutes, Barkley slammed the side of his fist onto a desk, saying, "Damn."

Barkley hated inaction.

Again Barkley looked at the clock on the wall and then at his wristwatch. Forty-five minutes! What the fuck was taking the lieutenant so long?

An eternity later, the phone in the PED office rang. Barkley picked it up immediately.

"Barkley here."

"It's Marc, Tim."

"What's up?" He had already relayed all the information he had gathered from the Cowboy to the lieutenant during the previous call.

"I spoke to Captain Wilson directly."

"And?" Barkley demanded impatiently.

"Hold on for a minute, Tim."

Barkley bit his lower lip.

"He woke up the chief of staff," answered the lieutenant, too calmly and stoically for Barkley's liking. "The chief of staff had already spoken to the chief. The chief doesn't want to deal with this matter until the morning."

Barkley could barely restrain himself; he found it difficult to talk. His face had taken on a beet-red color as he spoke through clenched teeth. He could restrain himself no longer.

"Whatthefuckareyoutalkingabout?!" yelled Barkley, "Didn't you hear a single thing I told you about what the Cowboy said?"

The voice that responded was firm. It was a strong voice of confident authority due to the lieutenant's higher rank. Because of the chain of command, the Department would back any decision the lieutenant made. Yet it was obvious to Barkley that the voice coming over the phone was simply repeating what the lieutenant had been told.

"Tim, take the rest of the night off. Go home now. Have one of the PED units book the Cowboy for the warrant or for any charges you have. I'll be in first thing in the morning and *personally* interview that bunboy. We can take additional action after I talk to him."

Oh, that makes me feel much *better,* thought Barkley. *I'm much more confident now that* you've *taken control.*

Barkley felt anything *except* reassurance. It was a sell-out. Barkley felt betrayed. All the brass was acting hinky, and whatever bug had crawled up their collective bureaucratic assholes had crawled in too far and got stuck.

Barkley had an idea what that bug was.

Cainen was homosexual.

"Tim, did you hear me?"

Yeah, I heard you, you needle-dick, pinprick, motherfucking, no-balled, brown-nosing, piece-of-shit Benedict Arnold.

"Yeah, I heard you. Good night."

Satisfied, the lieutenant gave in a little.

"I'll call you at home tomorrow after I find something out."

Like I could almost go home and face my wife, Barkley reflected. In silence, the sergeant hung up. He looked at the clock. It was after midnight. It had been five hours since Cainen was last seen.

The clock blurred in his mind as he pictured his career going down the drain. Fifteen years and a pension could be blown by one indiscretion.

Long ago, Barkley had realized that cops would act like cops, and dirt-bags usually got what they deserved. Like his counterparts throughout the nation, Barkley knew that the court system was ineffectual in punishing offenders or deterring recidivist criminals.

Thus, Barkley kept his mouth shut when cops beat their arrestees (if they deserved it), made them swallow their own dope, or picked them up and put them upside down into trashcans (as Barkley's first partner had a habit of doing).

At what price is integrity? Where do you draw the line? thought Barkley. Every police officer had to answer this question in his career, as Miller, Leaks's probationer, had done. But what started out as small exceptions, such as gratuities, easily blossomed into excessive force and perjury.

It was the accepted way. The status quo.

But when it came to their own, cops hung tough. Sure, some racist officers still wouldn't back up black officers, and periodically a watch of officers tried to teach a new female officer a lesson by being slow to respond to her request for an additional unit. But when an officer needs help, even God puts on a gun. Everyone responds. Fast.

So where had the exception come with Cainen? Just because he was gay? (Without realizing his reaction, Barkley shook his head from side to side.)

Of all the levels in the Department, the top brass were known as the worst decision-makers. They operated on the principle that field officers should be treated like mushrooms: feed them shit and keep them in the dark.

But would they knowingly let an officer get killed just because they didn't approve of whom he slept with?!

The Department had always held officers to a higher "moral" standard than any other civil service branch, or any private business, for that matter. Management's view of public morality was consistently out of sync. Until 1980, the Department not only fired homosexual officers; they also fired heterosexual officers discovered "cohabitating" with women. Luckily, mused Barkley, married couples were allowed to sleep together!

Subconsciously, Barkley came to a decision. His thought process raced to catch up.

Killed.

Killing.

If I don't do something, deliberated the sergeant, *that would make me an accessory to* murder.

His thought process had caught up. One of the benefits of having fifteen years in field assignments is the many and varied contacts one makes within and outside the Department.

Being a pleasant, outgoing, easily trusted person, Barkley had many friends. One of his friends was Danella Wilder.

Danella was a highly intelligent, gregarious, slightly overweight reporter for Associated Press International. API was one of the two primary news networks operating out of Los Angeles on a national wire service. API articles were teletyped throughout the world. Any news that might appeal to a readership was pulled off the service and presented in local papers throughout the United States, from the *Gainesville Times* to the *New Orleans Herald*.

Danella had been one of Barkley's "once-every-730-days" indiscretions. Danella had liked Barkley almost immediately. When she brought up her weight problem, he told her that she "provided warmth in the winter and shade in the summer." Since both were mature adults (though Danella was single), they knew beforehand that their solitary liaison would not extend any further. Nonetheless, Danella's passion and loneliness, and their combined intelligence in the singularly unenlightened world of police work, caused the two to remain in contact as friends.

The relationship was based on mutual respect, as well as an understanding of what it was like to demur to superiors less competent and less intelligent than they.

Since Danella had served in the Army Press Corps, Barkley often jibed her about an oxymoron like *military intelligence*. Invariably Danella responded with a quip about "law-enforcement ethics," and they would both laugh.

Danella had passed up many assignments (though not a single offer of promotion) to keep the police beat. The press room was located on the bottom floor of Parker Center. She worked the nine-to-five shift, from 9:00 P.M. to 5:00 A.M. Though it took more than one pot of coffee, this was the time when the big police stories broke.

As she was at headquarters and had her informal sources, this shift had given Danella more than her share of front-pagers.

Though a reporter from UPI, her competitor, was supposed to be in the office, Danella usually found herself working alone.

Danella was alone that morning at 1:00 A.M. when Barkley phoned.

Barkley's usual cheerful banter was missing from his greeting. Recognizing the tone of voice, Danella refrained from making any jokes and reached for her notepad.

Danella's many lines of notes made no reference whatsoever to the identity of the caller.

Just in case.

And when her story was finished, she would shred her notes to prevent later discovery by search warrant or subpoena.

* * *

Trekking back through the utter blackness of the desert night, Cainen's body started going into shock. Cainen felt his injuries as dull throbs increasing in intensity as his dragging steps were jolted by a rock or some debris.

A devastating exhaustion crept over Cainen, urging him to lie down and sleep. But Cainen knew he needed medical attention to prevent serious infection. Such an infection in his groin could become more perilous than his current injuries.

Cainen's bruised back caused him to walk hunched over. It took all of his remaining willpower to get back to the van. His condition was aggravated by his agonizingly slow, dragging step due to his injuries.

Miraculously, Cainen located the van. The rear doors were still open. The passenger door was still ajar, as he had left it.

Cainen leaned against the rear side panel, gulping air. His dulled mind told him that he had to get some clothes on and drive the van. He had seen that the handcuff key handed to Cameron was attached by a string to the van key. So they had not been lost with Charlie.

Holding his breath against the pain, Cainen used his arm muscles to support himself on the back doors as he pulled himself up and into the van.

It was darker inside than out.

Keeping his feet flat, Cainen moved slowly toward the front as his eyes adjusted to the darker interior. Cainen heard his own breath rasping from his parched throat.

As his eyes adjusted, Cainen realized that he was looking down the barrel of a gun. A small but deadly .25-caliber automatic.

He hadn't noticed the woman.

Tied down as he was and focusing his attention on the two males that had walked around him, Cainen hadn't thought that there was a third suspect.

A fatal mistake.

Still perched behind the driver's seat, Lisa held the gun from her pocket out toward Cainen with both hands. Her right index finger rested on the trigger.

Lisa knew she would probably go to jail if the man facing her got to civilization. She also had no idea what was going to happen to her.

Since leaving home, she had just followed Charlie around. Despite the abuse, Charlie's orders had given her life direction.

Even in Lisa's drug-hazed mind, she realized that if Cainen was back, that meant Charlie was gone.

Maybe dead, maybe gone.

In Lisa's drugged mind, there was little difference.

With Charlie and Cameron gone, Lisa had no direction. She had never functioned for herself.

Maybe she could go back home, she thought for a moment. As she faced Cainen, she envisioned her mother and abusive, incestuous stepfather . . . of the beatings and forced submission. Lisa thought of what her life had been like and how little it would change in the future.

And all because of this man, the one she was pointing the gun at. If she let him take her back, she would go to jail. More pain and suffering in her already pain-filled life. That would be intolerable.

On the other side of the muzzle, Cainen's mind was alert again. His life, and his preparation, demanded it.

Cainen saw that the girl held the gun out with extended arms, as amateurs do. Easier to take the gun away in that position.

Pro's hold the gun close to their side, able to fend off an attack with their free hand and still get a shot off.

But sometimes amateurs were more dangerous than professionals. They were more skittish and unpredictable—easily frightened and more likely to have an accidental discharge.

Cainen had immediately noted that the girl's finger was on the trigger.

But the girl was also out of arm's reach. And Cainen could not kick, particularly a spin kick, with any speed or accuracy due to his injuries.

Cainen always watched an opponent's eyes, because they often forecast intentions or movement. Cainen was frightened by what he saw in this young woman's eyes. Even in the darkness, Cainen could see that these were the eyes of someone much older. In them, Cainen saw unendurable anguish and despair. The eyes were devoid of any spark of life. Of any hope.

That, more than anything else, scared Cainen enough that he remained immobile.

Cainen had no hesitation about striking a woman. He had gotten over that false chivalry some time ago. In karate, particularly during sparring, it was a conscious decision to scale that mental block. He had been kicked in the balls more than once in a moment's hesitation to hit a female.

His knowledge that a woman was as dangerous as a man was reinforced as a police officer. Not only were some of the greatest terrorists in the world women, but once during the handcuffing of a female shoplifter, she had pulled a fingernail scissors out of her change purse and tried to stick Cainen in the face. Only his adroit reaction saved him from permanent scarring or blindness. He still wound up with a hole in his arm out of the deal.

It had taken three stitches and a commitment to never again underestimate the threat posed by a woman. Cainen knew that the longer he procrastinated, the more dangerous the situation could become.

But the eyes!

Cainen slowly bent his rear leg at the knee. If he sprang, jumping high to protect his head and turning sideways to lessen the target, he might be able to cover the distance and grab the weapon.

If he could jump.

Cainen slowly bent his front knee.

Lisa's mind worked faster than it had in a long time. All her pent-up emotions at the unfair victimization of her life by others were released in the assumption of Charlie's death. The Quaaludes in her system amplified the sensation.

All of the beatings and all of the rapes flashed through her mind. Yet her face never changed expression. No tear slipped from her eyes.

Though Lisa did not have the education to view events in a philosophical mode, she knew there was little hope for a world that would allow a child to be accosted as she had been.

Unbeknownst to either of them, Lisa and Steve had very similar childhoods, and victims of abuse later make cognizant decisions about the directions of their lives. Some internalize the abuse, continuing to punish themselves; some internalize the guilt, incorrectly feeling that they were somehow responsible for or deserving of others' improper advances; and still others vow to end the pattern of victimization.

There was no communication between Lisa and Cainen. Perhaps they both knew it was too late for that—that pleas or requests were useless. Or perhaps they didn't want the humans inside to contact one another, complicating the necessity of one having to kill the other.

With an uncertain future, and no supports to rely on, Lisa made a decision similar to the one Steve had made years earlier.

To end the abuse.

Steve had garnered strength in his ability to cut off all emotions and survive as an individual with no concern for the rebuke of others. Lisa, on the other hand, could see nothing but a void. She knew of nothing better, and therefore could not visualize a better future.

It was this void, this utter emptiness, that Cainen saw in the young woman's eyes.

Had it not been for his concern for self-preservation, Steve would have seen the depth of the little girl's torment. In empathy, he may have tried to comfort her.

Instead, Cainen crouched and prepared to leap.

Lisa's arms shook. The muzzle, pointing at Cainen, rocked.

She had made her decision. No more pain and no more suffering.

Because of the unfairness and selfishness of others, Lisa made her decision to take a human life.

As the muzzle shook, Cainen, still watching the girl's eyes, saw that a decision had been reached. Simultaneously Cainen saw a look that confused him. A look that communicated a desire to end . . . pain?

He had to act now.

Before Cainen could leap, Lisa turned the gun around and put it in her mouth.

287

The policeman in Cainen took over. He yelled, "No!" and leapt, forgetting that armed suicide victims were as dangerous to others as to themselves.

At the sound of the gunshot, Cainen instinctively flung himself to the floor, covering his head and neck with his arms. His injuries prevented a judo roll.

Most of the impact was absorbed by Cainen's elbows and the balls of his feet. Still, the pain sliced through him like a lance. He screamed once when it felt like his testicles were exploding.

Then he lost consciousness.

*　*　*

The phone rang twice.

It was an angry police chief who picked up the telephone on the nightstand. Five years as chief of police brought him instantly awake without the need to clear his throat. Nonetheless, the chief paused to look across the nightstand at the matching twin bed to see if the disturbance had awakened his wife.

Though Mother didn't move, it was his gut feeling that she had been conditioned by the middle-of-the-night calls much the same as he had. On those occasions when he had called her from his office after midnight, the phone was always picked up before the second ring.

The chief spoke into the phone in a harsh whisper. It was a harried chief of staff who responded.

"The press has the story on Cainen."

The chief's silence worried the promotion-minded commander even more.

"Who leaked?" asked the chief.

There was hesitation in the chief of staff's voice. It was well known that the chief did not tolerate "I don't know" as a response, any more than he accepted excuses.

"We don't know yet, sir. I have Captain Wilson working on it." The staff officer hoped that his use of the plural would avoid any direct antagonism from The Boss. As every manager in the Department does, the staff officer attempted to lay the blame on the next level down in the chain of command.

The chief of staff released an audible sigh of relief when The Boss ignored his lack of information.

"I want his balls. Or her balls. No one goes outside of this Department without my permission."

The change from the usually pious man to the hard-nosed cop again scared the commander.

"Of course. I'll have the name first thing in the morning," stammered the subordinate to his master. "What do you want done now?"

"Are you in your office?" asked the chief.

"I'm still at home. I just got the wake-up call from DHD."

"Well get to the office. Why do you think we issue you a take-home car?"

"Yes, sir. I'm on my way."

"And get my driver here. Fast."

"Yes, sir."

"Get IHD to make all the notifications and get the bulletins out." Though the Department had switched from *Investigative Headquarters Division* to *Detective Headquarters Division* almost ten years prior, the chief insisted on using the antiquated acronym.

"I'll get right on it. Where will you be, sir?"

"Where the hell else would I be?!" roared the chief, temporarily forgetting the woman in the bed across from him who had been his companion for thirty-seven years. The chief sat up and looked guiltily over to ensure that she hadn't stirred. "I'll be in my office, where I'm usually at when the damn press starts looking to lay the blame."

In a brutal whisper, the chief added, "I want his balls when this is over."

On the other end, the staff officer knew that his boss was referring to the officer who had dropped the bone to the press.

The staff officer was about to guarantee that the chief would get the anatomical part in question served to him on a silver platter when he realized that the top cop had already hung up on him.

The chief of staff knew that he would have to find out who had talked to API, or the silver platter might very well wind up between his own legs!

"Damn Cainen!" quipped the invertebrate staff officer as he hung up the phone. Reaching into the closet, he grabbed a hanger with a suit, shirt, and tie already accessorized on it.

As the chief of staff exited the bedroom, he didn't bother to look over his shoulder at his wife lying in their nice, warm, queen-size bed to see if his antics had waken her.

* * *

When Cainen awoke, he was lying on his side, dry-heaving, his hands between his legs in a rocking fetal position.

Cainen's mind sought the center of his being and couldn't locate it. His body was just a mass of profuse pain.

Willing himself to move, Cainen pushed up to a lying position. Looking in front of him, Cainen saw two bodies sprawled behind the driver's compartment.

Cameron's body lay on its back behind the passenger seat. His eyes were open and lifeless.

The girl's body was flung over a hump behind the driver's seat, on her back. Her right hand was against the side of the van. Her left arm hung limply in the center area, lit by the moonlight that streamed between the seats.

Thankfully, the girl's head hung on the opposite side of the hump.

Cainen didn't need to see in the dark to know that the side of the van and the back of the driver's seat were spattered with blood and brain matter.

Cainen dragged his lower body over by Cameron and felt around for the key. His hand bumped a string, and the keys jingled down the step on the side of the van.

Not wanting to lose the keys, Cainen was careful to put his hand downward and not side to side. He picked up the keys and realized that he had no pocket to put them in. He was still naked!

Closing the side door with as little movement as possible (every movement sent shards of agony through his body), he half-crawled and half-dragged himself to the rear corner of the van.

By lying flat on his back, Cainen was able to pull on his blue jeans, but he couldn't button the fly or waist.

Putting the keys in his right pants pocket so he wouldn't lose them, Cainen did five minutes of yogic breathing to steel himself for the pain of his upcoming ordeal.

Slowly standing up, with a great deal of shaking and weakness, Cainen walked over and picked up the .25-caliber. Unloading the round in the chamber and removing the clip, Cainen put them in his rear pocket and let the gun drop to the floor.

It didn't matter that his fingerprints were on the gun. If anyone questioned his version of the events that evening, the lab report would show the powder residue on the girl's hand, which would prove that she had fired the weapon.

In an agonizing hobble, trepidation in each step, Cainen inched himself out the back of the van and secured the doors.

Shuffling at a snail's pace, Cainen walked stiff-legged to the driver's side and opened the door.

Suddenly, Cainen was overcome.

The emotional wall that Steve had erected since he was twelve years old, and which had stopped him from feeling the consequences of the years of LAPD harassment, and the recent taking of two lives, came shattering down.

Where Cainen's physical body endured, his emotional being succumbed.

Cainen plummeted to his knees, surprised by his own actions. The mental wall that still remained stopped Cainen's conscious mind from relating to the effects of his feelings. But his overwhelmed emotions demanded release.

For the first time since childhood, Cainen's emotions took control, demanding relief from the unbearable pressure.

With a look of astonishment on his face, Cainen sat back on his haunches. His left hand was still holding the side of the open van door when his head slumped downward.

Triumphant in their strain, feeling the taste of victory that had been put off far too long, Cainen's emotions shot out like a bucking bronco confined too long in a pen.

As he sat in the desert moonlight, an unwitting sob escaped from this man of steel.

And then Cainen did something he hadn't done in a long time. A *very* long time.

He cried. Long and hard.

* * *

Barkley had been pulled in for a debriefing. The detectives now assigned to the case by the chief of staff, via DHD, interrogated him in his own office. The PED lieutenant sat in, in the event that he might gain some information that he would need later to protect his own butt.

As soon as the detectives finished with him (for the first round), Barkley called Maria to let her know he would be late. How late he couldn't say. But she might consider forwarding his mail to Hollywood Station.

The detectives next targeted the Cowboy. While the hustler was interrogated in the jail interrogation room, which allowed the interview to be surreptitiously recorded, Barkley was instructed by Bonderville to advise the PED teams that they would be working OT.

Barkley was anxious to get started on the written report that the detectives would inevitably request. The sooner he completed it, the sooner he'd get out of there.

Both Captain Wilson and Captain Carter were due in any minute. As Barkley saw it, the proverbial shit was about to hit the fan. And *everyone* was looking for cover. Undoubtedly, if this situation was no different, they wanted someone of slightly lesser rank and more culpability to act as their human shield from the flying dung.

Barkley just hoped that Danella was able to hold out. Undoubtedly there was another set of detectives, probably from Internal Affairs, in her office at this very moment.

In any case, thought the sergeant, rumor had it that Robbery-Homicide, the big boys, as well as a platoon of Metro, was being called in to coordinate the search effort. Supposedly bulletins with all the available suspect info had already been teletyped to all the jurisdictions in Southern California.

If Cainen could be located (alive, God willing), he would be found within the next twenty-four hours. Everything and everyone had been activated.

Turning away to hide his smile of satisfaction, Barkley reflected that *this* was what should have been done in the first place. Hours ago.

The smirk quickly faded from Barkley's face when he saw the Supreme Being walk into the Hollywood Detective area.

The chief looked like he wanted blood.

Barkley silently hoped he had enough in reserve with the Red Cross.

* * *

When Cainen sufficiently recovered, he got in the van and drove until he reached the Foothill Freeway.

Semiconscious and in shock, he made it to the far side of the San Fernando Valley before his weaving caused him to bump into the barrier in the center of the freeway.

Stopped in the emergency lane, Cainen reached down to turn off the ignition. As he did so, he passed out into a coma.

Slumped over the steering wheel of the van, Cainen stayed there for two hours, until 4:30 A.M., when a passing Highway Patrol car pulled up beside the van to check it before calling a tow truck.

Seeing the driver slumped over the steering wheel without a shirt on, the CHP officer assumed he had another drunk driver that had passed out on his way home.

It wasn't until the CHP officer had opened the driver's door and shined his flashlight past the driver into the rear of the van that he knew there was nothing routine about this stop.

Pulling out his gun as he ran back to his patrol car, the state traffic officer used his other hand to get the radio out of his belt. He yelled into his radio about needing backup.

It wasn't until he had gotten back behind the security of his police car's door that the young officer remembered to advise the dispatch center about the two bodies and the blood.

* * *

Within the main CHP dispatch center, the watch sergeant was standing behind the dispatcher when the second frantic call from the young patrol officer came in.

The sergeant had been sitting at his desk reading an article in *People* about the SPCA's campaign against a certain male movie star's attachment to gerbils when the Valley Area operator had waved her arm to get his attention.

Walking back to his desk, the seasoned supervisor pulled an alert out of his notification box. It was the watch commander's duty to review all incoming teletypes to determine which were pertinent.

Confirming his suspicions, the Highway Patrol supervisor dialed the LAPD phone number typed at the bottom of the page.

"LAPD, Detective Headquarters Division."

"Yeah, this is Sergeant Soulliere of the CHP Communications Center."

"What can I do for you, Sergeant?" asked the LAPD detective assigned to the desk because of a back injury he had received in a car accident during a pursuit nine years earlier.

"Yeah, you guys sent out a bulletin about an hour ago looking for a brown van. You might want to send a Devonshire unit over to the 405 southbound just past the Foothill Freeway. I think we've found your vehicle. And it's a mess."

* * *

Sergeant Barkley's phone call had initiated a series of newspaper articles that had given Cainen a folk hero status throughout Los Angeles, especially within the gay community. The news had hit all the national papers, including a small article on the front page of *USA Today*.

The following week's issue of *People* had decidedly dismissed the subject of animal cruelty in favor of discussing the "Mini–Manson Family." It was the horrid photo of the cadaver of seventeen-year-old Jeff on the cover of *People* that caused the big media storm. Cainen's academy photo took up the entire page across from the story.

Someone had leaked Cainen's home address and phone number. All the television talk shows that called requesting Cainen's appearance received the same recording: "The number you have reached is no longer in service and there is no new number." The post office had been given his mother's home as a forwarding address.

The mayor and the City Council of Los Angeles publicly lauded their common hero. The police chief refused comment. The police chief's only friend on the Department, the commanding officer of Press Relations, refrained from commenting on the incident except to begrudgingly admit that Officer Cainen had done an excellent job of police work.

Behind the scenes, the city fathers waited for any backlash. The police management made use of their many and varied media contacts to ensure that the public knew that Cainen had been properly covered the entire time and that any danger he had exposed himself to was strictly due to his own malfeasance.

Sergeant Barkley was disciplined for his role in the breaking of the story. There are no secrets and no secret sources from an organization that can devote over eight thousand officers and teams of top-notch investigators to uncovering that secret.

With Cainen being the biggest name in the news, the mayor's and city council's stance on the issue, and the Department's fear of their own omission coming to light, Barkley's only discipline was an admonishment that his primary loyalty was to the Department.

Nothing was put in writing, of course.

Cainen's family was tight-lipped. No one from the media got a single comment. And the LAPD's investigators got less.

No one heard from the face in the newspapers and magazines and on virtually every channel on TV.

Cainen had disappeared.

X

Up North [Epilogue]

Between the California Gold Rush of 1849 and 1915, 48,000 Victorian-style houses were built in San Francisco. These houses were originally built to copy the villas of Northern Italy, so the dwellings were referred to as Italianate.

Following this period, the Stick-Eastlake style, referred to as "Stick," became recognizable by its ornate millwork apparent on the facades.

Prior to 1880, the Queen Anne style, designed by architect Richard Norman Shaw, was the fad, with round turrets and bay windows.

The tendency of the Americanization of the English language is to simplify words to their most expedient form. This proclivity is most apparent in American names: James becomes Jim, Theodore is called Ted, and William answers to Bill or even B.

The same idiosyncrasy occurred with San Francisco architecture. By the 1880s, the Stick and Queen Anne styles were combined by San Francisco nouveau architects. This design then took on a generic nomenclature, being referred to as "the San Francisco style."

Just as the Central states have their tornadoes and the South has its hurricanes, so California is blessed with earthquakes. Additionally, in most California cities, smog makes the air a visible commodity; what is left of nature is camouflaged by noise, traffic, and trash. Several times a year, Nature reasserts her dominion, perhaps to remind those on the West Coast that she is angry with the abuse. "Heaven hath no fury like a woman's scorn." And Nature was never angrier or more disastrous than in 1906. The San Francisco earthquake and its fiery denouement destroyed all but 16,000 of the Victorian homes.

In recent years, proud San Franciscans (the same ones who cringe if you refer to their city as *Frisco*) have taken to refinishing the detailing on their Victorian homes by painting the ornate structures in high-toned, if not gaudy, colors.

Few San Francisco Victorians bear less than three colors: one for the siding, one for the woodwork, and a bright shade for the doors and window frames.

To the uninitiated Southerner (a person from Southern California, not *the* South), crass as *they* are, the architecture is less romantic than it is reminiscent of Main Street, USA, in Disneyland.

But to those who have come to love and cherish this large Northern California community, it is simply "home."

To these loyal fans, the residents' fellowship, in perhaps the most ethnically diverse metropolis in the world, is the single most important reason for remaining in San Francisco. These faithful occupants view San Francisco as a residential neighborhood with all the amenities of a large cosmopolitan city.

In Los Angeles, for example, a resident wanting service from the gas or phone company is asked to remain home for an entire weekday. The resident is told that service will be provided sometime between 9:00 A.M. and 5:00 P.M. More often than not, that same resident receives a 4:45 P.M. phone call asking if he can also remain available on the following day.

In San Francisco, on the other hand, a resident is told that "Jim" or "Marge" will be there within the next hour to assist them. If additional parts are needed for the involved personal appliance, the repairperson directs the resident to the local hardware store and volunteers to wait to install the aforementioned part ("to save you the expense of calling an electrician").

As long as a person can develop an appreciation for extremely cool and breezy weather, San Francisco offers a city in which the residents have consciously agreed on the uniform goal of sustaining the community.

Despite a surprising frequency of gay-bashing, San Francisco hosts the most liberal and tolerant community in the United States. (Timothy Leary is considered to the right of the average SF resident!) Viewed as a modern-day Sodom and Gomorrah by many citizens of the Bible Belt, SF is nonetheless the most popular vacation site of numerous cosmopolitans. Many of the rich fly to San Francisco for the evening just to enjoy the sumptuous dining offered in the City by the Bay.

These travelers share the view that the abundant, effervescent, and unconstrained San Francisco nightlife makes up for the twenty-hour-a-day fog that permeates the environment.

The abundant tanning centers, located on virtually every major street, provide a popular pastime for San Franciscans. Whereas Los Angelenos make a day of it by heading to the beach, San Franciscans achieve the same results during their lunch breaks. And without the sand. Unlike most of their countrymen, who have heeded the surgeon general's warning about the dangers of ultraviolet rays, Californians have upgraded skin cancer to an art form.

On those rare days of sunshine, the neighborhood parks of SF become transformed into towel-strewn havens where residents can lie out and soak up the few hours of sunlight while rubbing on dark brown tanning butter. The most popular places of refuge are Buena Vista Park and Delores Park (referred to as "Delores Beach" on sunny days). Both these parks are located in the area of the City known as the Castro. Just as Los Angeles has West Hollywood's Santa Monica Boulevard (at San Vicente), and New York has Christopher Street, so San Francisco has the Castro as its communal and unofficial gathering spot for gays and lesbians.

San Francisco and Los Angeles are as similar in their gay communities as they are poignantly different.

San Francisco divides its gay nightlife into three main areas. "SOMA" refers to the area south of Market Street, which encompasses an array of leather and Levi's bars. This includes bars where men do country and western dancing, two-stepping, twirling, and generally do-si-doing each other.

The leather bars accomodate large numbers of leather-clad men in black motorcycle outfits, most of whom arrive by taxi. Hundreds of dollars are spent on these outfits, pieces of which may later be worn during sex with other "leather men."

Interspersed with the leather crowd are uniformed men in marine, army, navy, and police outfits. While none of these "few good men" have been police officers, some of the military outfits are genuine, issued to the wearers during their enlistments. Many of the medals of valor worn by these men were earned at high costs.

Some of the men wear police uniform accessories, while others sport the full regalia. In Southern California, these men would be detained or arrested by the police (or *fired*); in San Francisco, it is the quintessential macho image they seek.

Amazingly, the week before Halloween, these same individuals spend *hours* at Macy's, Emporium, and Nordstrom's, picking out the gowns, high heels, earrings, and wigs they will wear.

The area south of Market also hosts several enclosed alleyways used for cruising when the bars close at 2:00 A.M. Prior to AIDS, hundreds of men would gather in the darkness in hopes of meeting their lifetime companion. Or at least an anonymous quickie.

Polk Street also contains a multitude of gay bars. Some of these are neighborhood piano bars, while others host transvestite drag shows. Hustlers line the sidewalks of Polk, periodically visiting the adult arcade to make an expedient twenty bucks inside a video booth.

Despite the steady stream of humanity within these other areas, the Castro remains the most renowned. This neighborhood houses the most concentrated number of gay residents.

Within a two-block area, the Castro hosts over a dozen bars frequented almost exclusively by gays or lesbians. On weekend mornings, gay and lesbian political groups cover the intersection sidewalks with tables, hawking for petition signatures for everything from legalization of homosexual marriages to preserving the California mountain lion. (In Los Angeles, these activists would have been immediately arrested for "blocking the sidewalk.")

Additionally, because of the unlimited compassion within this community, SPCA volunteers bring cages of doomed cats and kittens onto the streets, knowing they will be adopted before nightfall. For similar motives, these felines are only outnumbered by the vast amount of beggars harbored within this small strip of concrete.

On Sundays, the sidewalks swarm with androgynous men and women in leather, tank tops, cowboy boots, and Spandex, all of whom are supposedly destined for "brunch." Rather, the populace is enjoying the camaraderie of being among their own, of being surrounded by people supportive of their lifestyle and orientation. It is here, more than anywhere else, that the sense of community is most vibrant.

With the exception of the frequent carloads of teens driving through the Castro yelling antigay epithets, the occupants of the Castro feel safe in their boundless numbers. In fact, when the bashings increase in the area, the community provides their own roving patrols for protection.

Perhaps Castro's greatest claim to fame is its twenty-four-hour Walgreen's drugstore. Just as Arizona has Circle K and Los Angeles abounds with 7-Eleven, San Francisco lodges Walgreen's.

The Walgreen's at 18th Street and Castro is unique; it stocks the largest selection of personal lubricants and rubbers in San Francisco and possibly the world. As it is an all-night convenience store, this merchandise makes up a mainstay of the business. With the amount of lubricant in this one store, San Francisco could outlast the United Arab Emirates in the event of another oil embargo.

The Castro area is often referred to as the "gay ghetto." This is somewhat of a misnomer, since gays can be found in large numbers in every bastion of the city.

Unlike most cities, in San Francisco gays are not relegated to one area. They can be found in business attire in the financial district as easily as in Macy's. Wells Fargo, PG&E, and the Morrison and Forrester law firm all employ large numbers of gays and lesbians.

Homosexuals move into the Castro to be free from the persecution and self-guarding that they experienced throughout most of their lives. In this area, they are free from judgment, except for the occasional tourist videotaper on a field trip into the "sexually perverse."

Within their area, gays and lesbians can do those things most heterosexuals have taken for granted since childhood, such as holding hands. Such a simple, loving gesture outside of a gay ghetto could result in death at the hands of others bent on protecting "society's morals."

Gay ghettos serve the purpose of reassuring the newly initiated that, unlike in high school, they can belong. That they are not alone. That they are not bad. Eventually, when their self-esteem is high enough, these fledglings outgrow the invisible barriers of the ghetto.

Until the AIDS crisis, the Castro was a gay male bastion. But just as the south of Market gay dance clubs were bought out by the ever-increasing straight cruise bars, so have lesbians moved in where gay men have died.

The gays don't seem to mind, though, since the lack of parking spaces tends to lessen when lesbians move in . . . and the sidewalks become increasingly blocked by motorcycles. (The lovers of these motorcyclists are invariably the most beautiful women in the city.)

It is the gay money that vastly improved the Castro. Gay money built West Hollywood into a rich residential and entertainment zone. The Castro was rebuilt in the same manner.

Despite the crush of humanity, the Castro, like most of San Francisco, is spotless in contrast to comparable areas. On every commercial street, a trash can sits on the corner. The cans are enclosed by decorative rock patterns, for aesthetic value, with attached metal hoods to help prevent overflow.

When prejudiced politicians ply their biased trade each year by attempting antigay legislation, a sign posted in the Castro during the afternoon will gather several hundred demonstrators by nightfall.

The Castro serves as the origination of most homophile protests, followed by a march down Market Street to the government offices downtown.

Most cities assign police officers to demonstrations with the intent of controlling them. In typical atypical fashion, the San Francisco Police Department successfully approaches the endeavor from the opposite perspective. The SFPD delegates officers to assist and protect the demonstrators. SFPD police cars cover the front and rear of the throng, clearing a pathway and ensuring the safety of the participants.

The Castro itself is patrolled by gay and lesbian San Francisco Police officers. These officers are able to discern the problems of the community they serve, easily solving lover disputes and alleviating the embarrassment gay crime victims experience when describing particular crimes.

The city of San Francisco has over one hundred openly gay and lesbian police officers, and the county hosts the first sheriff to unabashedly recruit from the gay community. Unlike in Los Angeles, the SF officers do not spend their patrol time writing jaywalking tickets or canvassing adult video stores. They are too busy enforcing those laws that have victims. In San Francisco, the officers would rather spend their time arresting gay-bashers than arresting gays.

And this was the reason Stephen Cainen moved to San Francisco. And to the Castro.

Additionally, the tentacles of the LAPD reach throughout every law enforcement agency in Southern California, including those that receive the calls from the LAPD brass requesting surveillance of suspected gay LAPD officers vacationing in their area.

Since the 1970s, the San Francisco Police Department has not been on such reciprocal terms with the LAPD.

In the late 1970s, the first Gay Pride Parade was held in San Francisco. The intelligence reports compiled by the LAPD were many times larger than those prepared by the host department. Several years later, this surveillance came to the attention of the San Francisco police chief. The SFPD chief casually informed his LAPD counterpart that the cameo appearances by LAPD undercover officers were no longer welcome in the City by the Bay.

That was also why Steve moved there.

On a bright, sunny, cool morning, Steve walked up from his apartment on 18th Street. The post office he was venturing to was located on the opposite side of Castro Street.

As he walked, Steve once again marveled at the Disneyland-esque architecture, so different from the prefab housing of L.A.

For the first time, Steve noticed that the tops of the houses on the north side of the street between Noe and Hartford formed a perfect U. The highest points were at each corner and the lowest was the center dwelling.

Steve had moved up from Los Angeles two weeks after the "incident," as he came to think of it. He had spent those two weeks in the hospital. The involved investigation relative to Steve's kidnapping and the resulting three deaths necessitated detectives constantly interviewing Steve in his hospital bed. Though the doctor had recommended that Steve stay for an additional week, as much for psychological healing as physical, he left the hospital. Within three days, he had moved up to San Francisco. On his second day in SF, he located and rented an apartment with the money he got from his pension—which was returned to him when he resigned from the Department.

Steve was still having problems dealing with the psychological repercussions of his having taken two lives.

It wasn't that Steve thought he had done anything wrong; he hadn't had a choice. Even if he had had a choice, Steve realized that he probably would have killed the two. He would not have wanted the courts to unleash such evil, nor would he have wanted to wait for these two to wreak some illogical vengeance plan. He had debated the point before he went after Charlie, a few weeks and an eternity ago. And while he had confidence that he could defend himself, he also knew that he could do little about a drive-by shooting.

So he had made his decision and ended it that night. The night of "the incident."

Believing that he might possibly be the reincarnation of a Samurai warrior, Steve had thought he would be able to deal with taking a life. Or lives.

As a hardened street cop, Steve had thought that one more death would mean nothing to him, even if it was at his own hands.

Steve had thought wrong.

Or perhaps it was the look in the eyes of the three who had died. None had had the same look.

Few people had the experience of looking into someone's eyes before he or she died. Though Steve had seen dozens of dead bodies as an LAPD officer, he had never actually *seen* someone die. He had never looked into their eyes before life deserted them.

Until "the incident."

The girl had taken her own life. Her eyes had said that she wanted an end to the pain and suffering.

No more torment.

There was also the young man Steve had had to kill before he went after the leader. That one had been surprised to die then. Despite that, his eyes had looked sort of . . . lifeless. As if he had already lived longer than he expected to.

And the leader's eyes. Charlie. These were the ones that haunted Steve most through his often-sleepless nights.

Charlie's eyes had shown evil—a malignant evil. And a hatred of mankind.

Could life be so unfair to people so young? Steve wondered. *Could there be that many youth in America who would choose death over living, because living was so painful?*

Steve knew the answer. Knew it because he himself had experienced such an emotion.

His childhood. His adulthood. His treatment by the LAPD.

Steve had wanted to die.

Instead, he had killed. *Uchiai no ri no koto.* Kill or be killed.

Still, thought Steve, *if it hadn't been for those three people, I might very well have continued down a path of my own demise.*

Those three had freed Steve. Freed him from his own constraints as much as from the binds that tied him to the suffering at the hands of the LAPD.

Those three had opened up a door for Steve that allowed him, for the first time, to judge his *own* self-worth, instead of judging himself by how others viewed him because of his badge and gun.

Steve owed them. And that was why he had trouble sleeping. That was also why, when it was finally over, Steve had done something he hadn't done in over ten years.

He had cried.

The human condition. Why would a world allow eleven American teenage youths to commit suicide each day just because of their sexual orientation? Why would a world not provide them with public schools that provided education and counseling about their sexuality?

Why would a world not try to save them?

Why would a world not care?

The human condition.

Steve had always wondered if there was a single *cause* of homosexuality. And after all he had been through, Steve thought he had finally discovered the cause: being honest with oneself.

Steve had not cried since "the incident." He could only remember crying twice in his life since he was eight.

He had cried once when he begged his mother for mercy as she slapped and kicked him. Though Steve was twelve at the time, he had crawled on the floor to avoid her blows, pulling the mattress off his bed in a vain attempt to shield himself.

And he had cried once when he was sixteen. He had learned that a classmate was dying of cancer. Hodgkin's disease.

Steve had taken the only book he had found on the subject from the library. He had paid for the book, telling the librarian he had lost it. He had read the book at night in bed. The book had said that in its late stages there was no cure for the disease.

He had not cried because he was losing a friend. And he didn't cry because someone was dying. Steve had cried at the unfairness of the loss. If God was truly merciful, why would he let a fifteen-year-old die, a boy who had never harmed anyone?

Even as a youth, Steve could easily accept harsh realities, such as death. What he could not accept then, as now, was anything that was unjust or unfair.

It was a concept that may have come from his previous life and certainly predestined his future career.

As he made his way to the post office, Steve walked with a distinct limp. The doctor had said that there would be no permanent injury to his testicles, except scar tissue. But it would take a while to heal, and the pain was part of the healing process.

Steve wasn't worried about the physical damage; he really wasn't expecting to have children.

He was more concerned about the emotional healing process.

At Castro Street, Steve waited at the sidewalk for the light to change before continuing up 18th. San Franciscans passed him by, crossing against the red light.

Steve realized that old habits died hard. (*Just like some people!* Steve thought ruefully of Charlie's death.)

At the green light, Steve crossed, passing the Walgreen's on his right.

Steve walked up to the post office on Eureka. He waved to the overweight clerk who sat behind the counter. As always, she waved back, shouting a cheery, "Hello!" (*People are so nice here*, Steve thought, his mind unconsciously comparing S.F. with L.A.)

At PO Box 14504, Steve dialed in his combination and pulled out the rubber-banded stack of mail that had been forwarded via his mother in Los Angeles.

Having once taken the private investigator's test, Steve knew that anyone could get someone's forwarding address from the local post office for one dollar. (*The good old Freedom of Information Act*, Steve thought sarcastically.) So Steve had had his mail forwarded to his mother, who mailed it to his PO box. This provided two barriers against his being located by any LAPD officers.

Though he hadn't left a forwarding phone number, with gas and phone records being accessible through personal contacts, Steve didn't think this would keep any ambitious LAPD detective away for long. But at least it would slow them down and give him a chance to recover.

Maybe by the time they do find me, he thought, *I will have found a good Kung Fu studio up here to begin practicing again.*

As Steve limped painfully back down 18th Street, he went through his mail. Another get-well card from his mother, who had remained his staunchest supporter. Another TV talkshow request. Another newspaper article about him clipped by a friend of his in L.A. And a letter with a city seal. *The City of Los Angeles.*

Surprised, Steve looked at the postmark.

Three days old.

But how . . . ?

Steve looked at the mailing address. It hadn't taken them as long as he had thought it would. The letter had been mailed directly to his post office box.

As Steve crossed Hartford, he opened the letter. The letterhead was emblazoned with the gold-and-silver city seal. Underneath, the letter displayed that it had come from the office of the mayor. Steve immediately disliked the letter when he saw it was directed to "Sergeant Cainen."

He skimmed the letter:

You have distinguished yourself as one of L.A.'s finest . . . exemplified the values and traditions of the Los Angeles Police Department . . . As the mayor of the city you served so well, I would like to honor your self-sacrifice and distinction in the apprehension of these heinous criminals . . . This plaque will be presented to you at a dinner in your honor at the Los Angeles Police Academy on . . . attended by your fellow officers and members of the press . . . The police chief and I welcome your presence at this event in a tribute to your accomplishment.

Steve didn't look at the date of the event. He skipped down to the signature block and saw that it was signed by the mayor.

As Steve reached the corner at Noe Street, he stopped at one of the stone trash receptacles. Without a second look, Steve tossed the envelope and letter with the city seal into the trash.

As Steve limped down 18th Street to his apartment, he slowly shook his head from side to side in consternation. Then Steve did something he hadn't done in a long time.

He laughed.